Chasing a Dream

Alison J Barley

FIRST EDITION

Published in 2025 by
GREEN CAT BOOKS
19 St Christopher's Way
Pride Park
Derby
DE24 8JY

www.greencatbooks.com

Copyright © 2025 Alison J Barley
ISBN: 978-1-918028-03-4

Disclaimer:
Although this novel references Kilburn Pit and Kilburn
Station as active locations in 1950, it should be noted that
Kilburn Pit was not operational at that time, and Kilburn
Station ceased passenger services in 1930. Any portrayals
of these sites as functioning or any events depicted as
occurring there are entirely fictional and originate from the
author's imagination. This story is a work of fiction; any
resemblance to actual persons, living or deceased, is purely
coincidental.

DEDICATION

To Mum and Dad,

For your unwavering support, endless encouragement, and quiet strength.

You taught me to persevere, and to believe in myself. Everything I have achieved has its roots in the foundations you set for me. Thank you for your constant love and support.

This book is for you.

CONTENTS

Acknowledgements	iv
One	1
Two	11
Three	19
Four	29
Five	39
Six	45
Seven	54
Eight	61
Nine	70
Ten	78
Eleven	85
Twelve	92
Thirteen	102
Fourteen	111
Fifteen	120
Sixteen	125
Seventeen	131

Eighteen	137
Nineteen	143
Twenty	150
Twenty-One	161
Twenty-Two	167
Twenty-Three	176
Twenty-Four	186
Twenty-Five	193
Twenty-Six	201
Twenty-Seven	210
Twenty-Eight	218
Twenty-Nine	226
Thirty	233
Thirty-One	241
Thirty-Two	250
Thirty-Three	258
Thirty-Four	267
Thirty-Five	276
Thirty-Six	284
Thirty-Seven	293

Thirty-Eight   301

Thirty-Nine   309

Forty   317

Forty-One   325

Forty-Two   335

Forty-Three   344

Forty-Four   353

Forty-Five   362

Forty-Six   371

Forty-Seven   381

Forty-Eight   391

Forty-Nine   400

Fifty   409

Epilogue   419

ACKNOWLEDGEMENTS

This book would not exist without the unwavering support of many people, but most of all, my wonderful husband Chris who has lived with the creative moods and subjected himself to multiple read-throughs and first stage editing. Your belief in me on the good writing days and the difficult ones has carried me further than you know. Thank you for your patience and for reminding me to keep going when the words refused to come. This story is as much yours as it is mine.

My sincere thanks go, not only to Chris and my parents, Bryan and Joy, but to my sister Angela, brother-in-law Craig and my children Megan and Nathan, you have all spurred me on in your own ways to help this novel reach all the way to the end.

To my early readers, Barbara and especially Margaret whose encouragement and infectious enthusiasm has helped me to shape this novel into what it is today.

A heartfelt thank you to Eileen, for the endless tales of life as it was in Kilburn in the 1950s – your stories sparked more than one chapter, that no amount of research could replicate.

Thanks also to Mrs Pat Brown for the use of the Brown name, and to the late Alan Brown for his insights into 1950s burial practices.

To all the team at Green Cat Books, especially Lisa for guiding me through the whole publishing process and patiently answering my endless questions.

I would like to pay tribute to the memory of the 80 men who lost their lives in the Creswell Colliery Mining Disaster on 26th September 1950. This year marks the 75th anniversary of that tragic day - a somber milestone that calls us to remember not only the lives lost, but the families, friends, and communities changed by the events underground. Their courage, sacrifice, and the deep bonds of the mining community remain an enduring legacy. Though this story is a work of fiction, it is written with heartfelt respect for those who worked in the coalfields and the generations who lived in their shadow.

And finally, to every reader who picks up this book: thank you. Stories live when they are read!

ONE

Kilburn, Derbyshire.
Thursday 10th August 1950

Stella Felton sobbed as she sat on her grandma's stairs. The deathly sound of her grandfather's chronic cough was a gruesome noise that she had become accustomed to. But this time it sounded different... worse than usual. It was obvious that something was wrong, why else would her mother have taken a bucket, towels, water, and the whiskey bottle in for him? She listened as the relentless sound of her grandfather's echoing hack was disturbed periodically by a sharp intake of breath. Other than that, the house was quiet... That was until Stella heard her aunt welcoming someone in. She peered through the banister and listened.

"This way please, Doctor Keys," Sheila Marks directed as she scurried through the kitchen towards the sitting room.

That was where her grandfather slept now, in a makeshift bedroom. The doctor, a tall, slender man with stiff brush-like hair and a pencil moustache followed briskly before shutting the door behind him.

Stella sighed and tried to take her mind off it by reading her latest Enid Blyton book, 'Five Fall into Adventure'. Stella had been given a Famous Five storybook from her grandfather almost every year since the first publication eight years ago. She had already read the first four chapters, but as she turned the pages and tried to concentrate on the words, her

1

mind kept drifting to her grandfather. They had always spent so much time together, either reading or creating their own stories and poems. She loved him dearly and could not bear the thought of him being unwell.

Suddenly, the sitting room door opened again, and the doctor reappeared, closely followed by her grandmother. Stella watched as he placed a hand on her grandmother's shoulder.

"I am sorry, Mrs Downing. He is in God's hands now," the doctor said before seeing himself out.

Stella could not stand it anymore and decided she must find out what was happening. She tucked her book under her arm and made her way quietly downstairs, into the kitchen where her grandmother was staring out of the window.

"Grandma," she whispered softly, "what's wrong?"

Elsie turned sharply, unaware that her granddaughter was even in the house, let alone behind her. "Crikey, Stella, you made me jump. I thought you were at home."

Stella's head dropped to her chin. "Dad told me to get off out of his way, so I thought I'd come here and see Grandpa."

"Grandpa's sleeping. I think it's best if you come back later, Stella love," Elsie sighed, opening the back door. "You go on home now… just for a while." Stella hated it when everybody kept things from her, but she reluctantly did as she was asked and walked the short distance back home… three doors away from her grandparents.

Knowing it would not be wise to risk bumping into her father again, Stella decided to go to her den, a place she had created for herself some years before. Her den was a bush on the recreation ground at the back of her house, but she could access it from a small hole she had created in the hedge at the bottom of her garden. She opened the gate and tiptoed quietly down the entry, to the bottom of the garden, knelt and pushed herself through the hole.

The bush itself was quite extensive, with dark greenish-brown branches and broad oval leaves. In the summer, tiny white flowers grew in flat clusters, followed by small black berries in the autumn. The bushes grew in numbers around the perimeter of the recreation ground itself, but this one took up a large space in the corner and stood much higher than the others.

Over the years that she had been using the bush as a den, she had gathered a few things that made the place feel a little more cheerful; a cushion her mother had thrown out, a small wooden stool her grandfather had made, and a blanket crocheted by her grandmother. She knew she was too old to be hiding away in a den, but it still served as a sanctuary away from her father. She would stay there for a while now and read, before going back as her grandmother had suggested.

****

Jeanie Felton wrung out a cold flannel and placed it over her father's forehead. He had been slipping in and out of consciousness all day, but just at that moment, he was awake enough to ask after his granddaughter. Jeanie reassured her father that Stella would be coming to see him soon.

He tried determinedly to raise an arm and point towards something on the other side of the room, but with his weakness forbidding him, his arm began to shake violently. He managed to find the strength to mouth the words, "Top drawer… right side."

Jeanie glanced around the room and spied the drawer her father was trying desperately to indicate to. "What's in there, Dad?"

Fred tried to speak again, but the words would not form. He sighed heavily and shook his head.

"Whatever it is, I'm sure we can sort it out later, you must try and rest," Jeanie advised.

He shook his head again and managed to find enough energy to move his hand towards his daughter.

Jeanie took hold of her father's hand and realised he was trying to give her something… a key.

Jeanie got up and walked over to the drawer and unlocked it. Inside was a brown envelope marked, 'Miss S Felton, Chapel Street, Kilburn, Derbyshire'.

"What's this about, Dad?"

"Look after it… give it to her when she's —" but his words were cruelly halted by a horrendous coughing bout.

Eventually, the coughing ceased and as the tormenting rise and fall of his chest seemed to labour, he once again slipped into unconsciousness.

Jeanie sat at her father's bedside and looked down at the envelope in her lap. She felt at the contents, wondering what they could be. She was tempted to open it and see… but then, it wasn't addressed to her. But these were different circumstances, her father was dying, and Stella had not been told yet.

It had been two years since Fred had been diagnosed with black lung disease, a consequence of working 54 years down the pits breathing in coal dust. It was a cruel, relentless disease, which in the last few months had worsened and Jeanie was dreading telling Stella it was terminal.

Jeanie's thoughts were disturbed by her sister's sudden entrance into the room, and she gingerly concealed the envelope in her handbag. There were no envelopes for Sheila's sons, but then everyone knew how much Stella meant to Fred.

"He's close, I think," Jeanie whispered to her sister.

"Go and fetch Mam, he needs us all to be around him now." Sheila's exit from the room was as swift as her entrance as she hurried off, returning moments later with their mother.

The women sat at Fred's bedside in an almost deafening silence, awaiting the conclusion they all knew to be inevitable. The only thing they didn't know was how much longer he would have to suffer, how much longer *they* would have to suffer, watching him as he struggled to find each breath. Elsie had felt his pain for the last couple of years; it had been distressing watching his health decline. The transition from the muscular, energetic man she fell in love with all those years ago, to him becoming the infirm old man she saw before her today was pure torment. There was nothing she could do but watch as he grew weaker with each passing hour, fighting to take each breath.

Elsie started to feel wistful, sitting in the dimly lit room. She closed her eyes and gradually, her mind wandered. She could see herself as a young girl of 15, dressed to go out for an evening stroll with her best friend, Norah. They would often take a walk along Bywell Lane, the main road out of the village. It was a popular area for young people to walk, in the hopes that along the way they may find themselves a sweetheart. Elsie and Norah had hoped that, someday, they might each meet eligible young men. And on a warm summer evening in June 1900, Elsie did just that.

It was purely by chance that the two girls started their evening by leaving the village and walking along Bywell Lane. The lane led to a crossroads with the main Derby to Ripley Turnpike Road. As the girls approached the crossroads, Norah noticed a stray dog and Elsie called to it. It seemed playful at first, but then the dog became over-excited and sank its teeth into Elsie's skirt, tugging at it viciously. Suddenly the delicate material ripped, and the dog ran away with a piece of her skirt in its mouth. Elsie was horrified when she looked down and saw a huge tear in her beautiful skirt. How would she explain that to her mother? They decided to head home, and all Elsie could do was cry. The commotion, however, had alerted a young man walking in the opposite direction - a tall, broad-shouldered chap, with the tightest curly brown hair. He stopped to enquire about the girls' well-being. Elsie had never seen him before but even through her tears, she could see what a handsome young man he was.

****

After reading a further six chapters, Stella closed her book. She crawled through the hole in the hedge, back into the garden and crept back up the path, but as she turned to walk down the entry, she bumped into her father.

"I thought I'd told you to clear off out of my sight," Derek Felton snapped.

Stella didn't reply and tried to push past her father, but he grabbed hold of her arm and dragged her back. Instinctively, she tried to talk her way out of it.

"I came back for my book, that's all," she said, in desperation.

"Don't lie to me," he raged, slapping her around the back of her head. "Now bugger off, I don't want to see your face around here till your mam gets home."

He shoved her back out of his way, and she landed with a thud against the entry gate. Stella fought back the tears.

"Mam won't be home for ages yet," she sobbed. "Grandpa isn't well."

"Go tell someone who cares," Derek gibed, as he sauntered back into the house and slammed the back door.

Derek never hid the fact that he could not care less about his father-in-law, they never had got along. Fred had never accepted Derek into the family, he thought

7

his daughter could do better. Fred was certain that Derek was violent towards Jeanie, but if he tried to intervene, Derek would just tell him to mind his own business.

Stella could hear her father laughing away to himself as he walked through the house. She picked herself up and rubbed the back of her head. Soon enough, the concern for her grandfather made her forget her pain, and she wasted no more time getting back to her grandma's house.

****

Elsie felt happy reliving the memories, and they continued to come back to her as she stroked her husband's hand. She stared at him, and no longer saw a gravely ill, aged man, but the stocky young man she had fallen in love with all those years ago. She reminisced as more thoughts of the day they met came flooding back.

The young man, who introduced himself as Fred Downing, noticed that she was upset after the dog had ripped her skirt and offered to walk her back home and explain to her mother what had happened. Fortunately for Elsie, her mother quite happily believed Fred's story and was impressed as to how kind and responsible he was. Elsie was pleased because the two of them were instantly attracted to each other and they began a courtship which eventually blossomed into a wonderful marriage.

Suddenly, Elsie's thoughts were abruptly halted as Fred gasped, his breath leaving his body with a strange rattling sound. Elsie, overcome with emotion, cried out his name in a desperate attempt to somehow rouse him, but it was hopeless. She stared at his body for what seemed like hours, before eventually realising that her husband had passed away.

"Oh, Fred... what will I do without you?" Elsie wailed, leaning forward to rest her head against her husband's motionless chest.

The women sat quietly now, until suddenly their grief was interrupted by the sound of someone entering through the back door.

"Oh, good heavens, Jeanie, that will be Stella," Elsie said in a panic. "Quickly, stop her from coming in." But it was too late, she was already entering the room.

At first, Stella just stared at her grandfather's lifeless body and then at her mother, grandmother, and aunt in turn. The women stared back, none of them knowing what to say.

Stella turned and ran out of the house before anyone could stop her.

"Good Lord, Jeanie, run after her," Sheila roared.

Jeanie jumped out of her seat, grabbed her handbag and chased after her daughter.

Elsie put her hands over her mouth, tears filled her eyes, spilling out onto her cheeks. "Oh, Sheila, I never gave a thought as to how she might react. All I could think about was your dad. I should have let her stay."

"Mam, it's not your fault, you only did what you thought was right. Jeanie will find her. She will sort it out," Sheila stated. "Come on now, getting upset is not going to help matters. Let's go through to the kitchen and I will make us a brew."

Sheila placed a cup of tea down on the kitchen table in front of her mother. Her father's illness had certainly taken its toll on her. Sheila noticed the dark circles around her mother's eyes, which together with her furrowed brow, made her look haggard. Sheila crouched down by her mother's side and grasped her hand.

"Mam, why don't you have a lie down, and I will go across and inform Doctor Keys. He will send Nurse Johnson over to attend to Dad. I'll sort it all, you go and rest, eh?" Sheila said, squeezing her mother's hand gently.

Elsie sighed. "Yes, I suppose." She struggled to her feet and made her way steadily upstairs.

She climbed on top of the bed and glanced over at a photograph on the bedside table. "Oh, Fred, what an eventful life we've had, eh?" She shook her head and smiled. "We were blessed to have had such a wonderful marriage, our daughters, and grandchildren. We always said marriage is like rowing a boat... you must row together. We always rowed together, didn't we?" Elsie mused, before closing her eyes and drifting off to sleep.

TWO

Stella wasn't thinking when she ran back down the garden path. She was far too upset to be concerned as to what her father would do if he thought she was disobeying him again.

She just needed to get to the privacy of her den. She crawled through the privet hedge into the opening in the bush and grabbed hold of one of her cushions. The tears streamed down her face, stinging her eyes. She closed them, trying to make sense of what she had seen, but all she could picture was her grandfather's motionless form.

She had been hugging her cushion for what seemed like ages, trying to absorb everything, when suddenly a ball found its way into her den. Some local lads were playing football on the recreation ground when their ball hurtled its way into the bush that formed Stella's den. The lads often played football on the recreation ground, or 'the rec' as everyone called it. But a ball finding its way into her den was a problem that had never occurred before… until now.

Stella watched as one of the lads headed in the direction of her den. Realising she was out of time, she made the rash decision to throw the ball back out onto the rec, in the hopes that he would not notice. However, the lad, who was intrigued as to how a ball could come bouncing out of a bush all on its own, was now making his way over. Stella watched as he walked to where the ball had rolled to, picked it up and kicked it back towards his friends, but then kept walking towards the bush. Stella braced herself for the certain encounter, and at once two hands appeared, parting a gap in the bush.

"Aye up, what are you doing in there?" the lad laughed.

Stella didn't answer, she was hoping the lad would just see that she was minding her own business and go away. But he parted an even bigger gap in the bush and stuck his head inside. Stella instinctively darted back.

"I won't hurt you," he said. "Are you okay? You look as though you've been crying."

"I'm fine, please go away. I just want to be on my own," Stella finally answered.

"You don't look okay. What is your name?" the lad asked.

"You don't need to know my name. Just go away…please."

But the lad persisted. "I'm William, but everyone calls me Will. Come on… what's your name?"

Stella sighed. "My name is Stella. Now will you go away?"

"That's a pretty name, what are you doing in here, Stella?"

"Nothing," she replied harshly.

"There must be some reason you're hiding in here," Will reckoned.

Stella sighed again. "This is… *was…* my secret den until you and your football found it."

"Sorry. I won't tell anyone your secret, I promise. I've not seen you around before. Do you live here?" Will asked curiously.

"Of course I don't live here. What do you think I am… some sort of beggar?"

"I don't mean inside this bush, silly. I mean, do you live locally? Will laughed.

"Oh. Yes. In one of the cottages behind this hedge," Stella said. "And it isn't a bush, it's my den!" she added sternly.

"It's still a bush though," Will replied jokingly. "I have to go, but perhaps I could come here and see you again tomorrow?" he said, beaming a huge smile that Stella found charming.

"I suppose so. I can hear the others shouting you, so go before they come meddling," she urged, looking sharp-eyed at him.

"See you tomorrow," Will said, before dashing back to his friends.

Stella parted a small gap in the bush and watched as Will joined in with the game again. She noted how quickly he sped around the pitch, tackling one of the other lads to gain control of the ball. She thought how skilful he was as he managed to get past the others and score a goal.

Shortly after, the lads collected their belongings and headed off. As he was leaving, Stella noticed Will look back at her den, as though she were still on his mind. A warm tingle filled her tummy… a feeling that she had never felt before. But that feeling soon turned to one of desperation in the pit of her stomach, serving as a reminder that her grandfather had gone.

****

Jeanie reached the top of the entry and out onto the

street. She looked up and down but couldn't see Stella in either direction. She arrived home and walked up the entry just as her husband, Derek, was on his way out to the pub.

"Is Stella home?" she asked, stopping him in his tracks.

"No," Derek replied harshly.

"Are you sure she's not gone straight up to her room, only she —"

"I've just said no, woman, are you deaf?" Derek yelled, pushing his way past his wife.

"Derek, please, wait. Dad has passed away."

Derek stopped but never turned to face Jeanie, he just stood, waiting for her to continue.

"It was about half an hour ago. Stella didn't realise until she came in to visit him." Jeanie waited for a response, but Derek just walked away without saying a word.

"Derek!" Jeanie shouted after him. But it was no use, he had already reached the top of the entry and was out of sight.

Jeanie's head dropped to her chest. Even before the war, Derek had never been the most loving husband; with his narrow-minded opinions and short fuse. But those defects in his personality had worsened since he came back from being held prisoner of war in Japan. His moods would swing from being silent and detached to being brash and aggressive, and anything in between. Some days he could barely function at all, and on those days, he would be heavily dependent on alcohol. Jeanie clung to the hope that given time, things might improve. But the truth was, that in the two years he had been home, things were getting worse instead of better.

Jeanie made her way into the kitchen and filled the kettle. She suddenly remembered the envelope her father had given her and took it out of her handbag. If she had not heard the entry gate open at that moment, she would have opened the envelope for sure. Instead, she quickly shoved it back into her handbag. Recognising the footsteps, she turned to see Stella charge through the back door.

"Stella!" Jeannie cried, rushing over to hug her daughter. "I'm so sorry, I should have told you."

"Why didn't you tell me?" Stella roared. "I never said goodbye. I wanted to say goodbye."

"We did not want to upset you, sweetheart. Death is a distressing—"

"I know," Stella cut in sharply. "But now I can never say goodbye. I'll never see him again.

It's not fair." Stella ran past her mother and up into her bedroom, slamming the door shut.

****

Elsie woke up with a start, got to her feet and steadily made her way downstairs to find Sheila and Jeanie in the kitchen making tea and sandwiches.

"Jeanie, is Stella alright?" Elsie asked as she hobbled through into the kitchen.

"She's okay, Mam, terribly upset, but she's at home now in her room."

"Thank goodness for that. Sheila, did you get over to see Doctor Keys?"

"Yes, Mam. It's all been taken care of. Come sit down and have a bite to eat, eh?"

Elsie shuffled over to the table and sat down heavily. "Has Bessie Johnson been over, then? How is she these days? I haven't seen her for months."

Sheila sat down at the table next to her mother and took a sip of tea. "Well actually, it was not Nurse Johnson. She's gone over to the coast to look after her gravely ill sister. So, Doctor Keys sent Norah Shaw instead and she very kindly —"

"Norah Shaw?" Elsie cut in. "The midwife? But she left the village years ago." Her face paled.

"Yes, well she's just retired from midwifery, and she is moving back into the village soon. She helps Doctor Keys out from time to time with all sorts of things, if she's needed," Sheila said.

"I did hear that she might be moving back," Elsie remarked. "But I've never seen her, and I certainly never expected that Doctor Keys would send her over."

"Why, Mam? She is more than capable of laying a body out. A lot of midwives do that sort of thing," Sheila said, rolling her eyes.

"Yes, I know that. I just assumed Bessie would have done it, that's all."

"But I've just said that Bessie is away at —"

Jeanie cut into the conversation. "For goodness' sake. Surely it doesn't matter who came to lay Dad out. Just that the job has been done!"

Elsie sighed. "Yes of course. It's just been a long time since I've seen her. I suppose I never thought I would again… it was a bit of a surprise. It is all so overwhelming." Elsie placed a hand across her mouth and began to sob.

"Oh, come on now, Mam," Sheila reassured softly, rubbing her mother's back. "Jeanie is right, it doesn't matter, it's all sorted now."

"Aye, well I think I'll take myself back upstairs and have an early night, it's been a very long day."

Elsie struggled to her feet and Sheila quickly took hold of her mother's arm in a bid to steady her, but Elsie waved a dismissive hand, and without so much as a farewell, hobbled off out of the room, leaving both daughters in an awkward silence. Jeanie eased the lull by suggesting she wash the tea pots.

Half an hour had passed before both women realised that they had sat in silence.

Sheila yawned and Jeanie followed suit. "Well… it's been an awful day, Jeanie. I think I'd better get off home."

"Aye, I need to be going now too, I want to check on Stella."

Sheila got up from her seat at the table. "I'll go up and look in on Mam, let her know we're going. I say, Jeanie, don't you think that was a bit strange earlier when I said that it was Norah Shaw who had been to lay Dad out and not Nurse Johnson? I mean, her reaction was a bit… odd, don't you think?"

"Well, I suppose grief can make you that way. I don't recall the woman myself," Jeanie said. "I thought it was quite right that it should be her. Makes it that bit more personal, I think. I mean, she knows

Mam well enough. She brought me into the world," Sheila laughed.

"Really? I didn't know that."

Sheila nodded. "Yes. Then Mam said she moved away shortly after."

"She must have brought a fair number of babies into the world then, if she was Mam's midwife at your birth. I mean, you're going back a fair number of years there!"

"You're a cheeky madam," Sheila laughed.

"I wonder why she moved away?"

"Something to do with her husband's job, I think. Anyway…" Sheila yawned again.

"Yes…time to go," Jeanie said, as she too stifled another yawn.

THREE

Friday 11th August 1950

Stella got up early and decided to leave the house before her parents woke. Her grandmother had been on her mind throughout the night, and she wanted to check on her. As she reached the bottom of the stairs, she noticed the door to the sitting room was open and her father was asleep on the couch. He would often fall asleep sprawled out across the settee fully dressed, usually with a whiskey bottle by his side. Knowing full well that waking him would have disastrous consequences, Stella pulled the sitting room door shut and quietly left the house.

As she made her way to her grandmother's house, Stella realised that this would be the first visit since her grandfather had passed. A mix of emotions made it all too much and she decided to turn back and head to her den.

It had rained heavily overnight, and the den felt damp, but soon the strength of the sun began to filter through and eventually everywhere began to dry out. Before long, rumbles in Stella's stomach kept letting her know she had missed breakfast again, leading to thoughts of her grandmother's fry-ups. Her thoughts were disturbed by laughter and voices. Peering out of the bush, she noticed the same group of boys from the day before, but Will wasn't with them. Stella watched them play football for a while, waiting patiently to see if Will would join them. But as time passed, her hunger got the better of her, and she decided to see her grandma.

Stella gingerly opened the back door and entered hesitantly; the house bore an eerie silence that she had never noticed before and suddenly she felt awkward.

"Grandma?" Stella called, but there was no reply. She walked through the kitchen to the bottom of the stairs and called again. "Grandma, are you upstairs?"

Elsie's voice echoed from above. "Yes, sweetheart, come on up."

Stella made her way upstairs to the front bedroom where her grandmother was putting the finishing touches to her hair.

"Are you alright, Grandma?"

"I'm fine, love. Now you come here and let me give you a big hug, eh?"

Stella rushed over to her grandmother and flung her arms around her.

"I'm so sorry I made you go yesterday, Stella. It was wrong of me, it was just that… everything seemed to be so… jumbled, you know?"

"It's alright, Grandma, I understand," Stella replied unconvincingly.

Elsie, realising that her account was not enough, continued to try and explain. "Death can be a very difficult thing to understand, and grief… well it kind of meddles with your head."

Stella's chin dropped to her chest. "I would have liked a chance to say goodbye to him, that was all."

"I know, and for taking that chance away from you, I'm truly sorry," Elsie said, pulling her granddaughter close. "Now, shall we go and make a cup of tea?"

Elsie put her hands on the dressing table and used it to push herself up. Her knees had been arthritic for years; some days were worse than others and today they were particularly bad.

"Oh, by heck, my knees aren't half giving me some gyp today —"

"Grandma..." Stella cut in unintentionally. "Is Grandpa still here... I mean is his body still here?"

"Of course, where else do you think he would be?" Elsie noticed that Stella seemed perturbed. "Come on now, you need not worry. The dead won't hurt you, it's the living you must be fearful of... but I think you already know that. Now, I bet you've not had any breakfast. I've got a couple of rashers of bacon, how about I cook you some and an egg too?" Stella's face brightened.

Soon, the enticing aroma of frying bacon filled Elsie's kitchen and before long, she had set the plate of bacon and eggs down in front of Stella.

"There you go, get that down you. Put hairs on your chest, that will!"

Stella giggled. "I hope not, Grandma."

Elsie sat down beside Stella. "I tell you what, how about we catch the mid-morning bus into Derby, and I'll treat you to something nice?"

"If you are sure you feel up to it, that would be wonderful."

"You finish your breakfast up then. I'll finish my cuppa, and we'll get going." Elsie beamed a big smile and set one elbow on the table. She rested her head against her clenched hand and soon, thoughts of Fred filled her mind, taking her back to a time before they were married and a silly argument they'd had over a broken vase.

The vase in question belonged to her parents, given to them as a wedding present by a family friend, Thomas, who was a ceramic glazer at the nearby Denby Pottery factory. Everyone thought it must have cost an awful lot of money and so it took pride of place in their hallway. One day, Fred was messing about with the vase, showing off to Elsie, boasting that he could throw it up in the air and catch it again. Of course, the inevitable happened and Fred dropped it on the floor. Elsie was horrified - her parent's beautiful vase smashed into goodness knows how many pieces. Elsie's father was most disappointed.

"I expected you to be considerably more respectful than that, young man," Elsie's father had said.

Elsie was an only child, whose upbringing had always been extremely strict. She would always strive to do the right thing and was very mindful not to do anything that would bring disgrace to herself or her parents. Fred's foolishness and the embarrassment it had caused did not go down well with Elsie and after a huge row, she decided to end their relationship.

It was not until a month or so later that the family friend, Thomas, who had bought the vase, paid a visit to Elsie's parents. They of course told him what had happened, and Thomas had to admit that the vase was a mock-up.

"How else did you expect me to afford such a thing," he had said to them.

Elsie and her parents were so relieved when they found out, that they all managed to laugh about it. But then she thought of Fred and the argument they had. She had missed him so much, that she at once went to his house to explain. She was so happy to see that he had missed her too, and from that day on, the two of them made a promise to each other that nothing would come between them again. However, a couple of months later, that promise was put to the test when another challenge presented itself...

"Grandma... are you okay?" Stella asked, nudging her grandma's arm.

Elsie's thoughts halted abruptly. "Oh, I am sorry. I was deep in thought."

"We'd better get a move on if we're going to catch that bus," Stella urged, taking her empty plate to the sink.

"You nip up and get my handbag, Stella love, and we'll make tracks."

****

Later that afternoon, Elsie and Stella caught the 4.40 p.m. bus from Derby bus station and were home by 5.20 p.m.

"Let us get the kettle on... I'm parched. Do you want a brew?"

Stella was busy trying on her new shoes. "These are lovely, Grandma, wait till Mam sees them."

"You won't have to wait long, she's here now," Elsie said, as Jeanie came through the door. "Jeanie, love, are you alright... you look ever so pale?"

"I'm fine, Mam," Jeanie said, trying to stifle a yawn.

"What have you got there then?

Blimey, those shoes look almost new."

"Smart, aren't they? We got them from a new shop that has opened in Derby. It is a charity shop… Oxham they call it, or something like that."

"Oxfam, Grandma. It's called Oxfam," Stella laughed.

"Aye, well, whatever they call it… you can't half grab some decent second-hand stuff in there. You have to be blooming quick, mind you, like bees round a honey pot, they were. I almost had to fight someone else to get them."

Jeanie and Stella both giggled. "Grandma has bought some wool too. She is going to knit me a jumper, look… here is the pattern." Stella thrust the knitting pattern into her mother's hand and headed for the door. "Thanks again, Grandma. I have enjoyed our day; I will see you later."

Elsie handed Jeanie a cup of tea. "Stella doesn't seem too bad today. Mind you, she got upset earlier when we went to record your dad's death."

"You have been there already? That was quick," Jeanie said.

"There's no use putting off the inevitable, love, these things have got to be done sooner or later." Elsie yawned and sat herself down at the kitchen table. She looked pale, which made the dark circles around her eyes look black.

"Are you alright, Mam, you look awfully tired?"

"Aye, I'm okay, love. I'm just a bit worn out… my knees are playing me up something chronic today."

"You shouldn't have walked around Derby on them knees of yours. You ought to have waited till Albert could take you."

"Well, I can't walk around Derby on anyone else's knees, now can I?" Elsie laughed.

"I would just as soon get things sorted, Jeanie; I can rest better in my mind. And in any case, Stella needs new shoes, if she is still going with Albert and Sheila to the miners' camp?"

"Aye, she's still going. It will do her good," Jeanie assured.

"Has Derek thought about another job yet, he can't be earning much selling a few bits at the market?"

"He's trying, Mam, but it's not that easy for him, you know?"

Elsie did not respond, she just looked at Jeanie and let out a big sigh.

****

Stella walked along the road, stopped, and looked down at her new shoes. They were so shiny she could almost see her face in them. She had never owned shoes this new before, especially ones that fit comfortably like these did. Usually, she had to wait until one of the older girls in the village had outgrown theirs and then it was first come, first served as to who was lucky enough to be the next owner. She made her way down the garden path and squeezed through the hedge into her den. She took the crocheted blanket out of her bag and laid it out against the hard ground. She positioned herself comfortably against the cushion and took her notebook and pencils out of her bag.

Opening her notebook to a fresh page, she chewed on her pencil and stared into thin air looking for inspiration, but nothing would come to mind. Eventually, she listed a few random words, words that reminded her of her grandfather.

Grandpa

Miners, Miner's Lamp, Dirty Faces.

~~*Hat*~~ *Cap, Braces, New Boots.*

Fishing, Betting on the Horses, Trip to the Seaside, Trip to the Zoo.

"Hello again," Will said, sticking his head through the bush.

"Oh… by crikey. You scared the Dickens out of me," Stella cried, putting a hand to her chest."

Will laughed, "Sorry. I thought you might have been here earlier when I came by."

"I've been into Derby with my grandma. Look… I've got new shoes." Stella lifted one leg to show Will.

"Proper smart." Will's friendly smile beamed across his face. "What are you writing about in that book?"

"Nothing really… well, I'm trying to write a poem, it's going to be about my grandpa." Stella's head dropped. "He passed away yesterday."

"I am sorry. That explains why you seemed so upset when we met yesterday then."

Stella nodded. "He was the best grandpa ever." Stella's eyes welled.

Will did his best to distract her. "You're writing a poem about him, you say?"

Stella brushed a tear away. "Yes… well, trying to,

but the words will not come to me.

Probably because there is no purpose to it all anymore."

"There's always a purpose. You must find it again, that's all," Will smiled.

"My grandpa was the only one interested enough to listen to anything I'd written. He was going to help me become a proper writer. Nobody else is going to do that now," Stella sobbed.

"I tell you what… you keep trying to find some words for your poem and when you have finished it, I'll listen. I mean… if you want me to."

Stella's face lit up. "Really? You would listen?"

"Yes, of course. So, we have a deal then?"

"Yes, we have a deal," Stella said with a smile. "Do you live around here? And how old are you?"

Will laughed. "I live in the next village, in Denby. We have only been there a few months. I've just turned 16. What about you? I mean, I already know you don't live in this bush, but how old are you?"

"I told you before… it's a den!" Stella laughed. "And I'll be 16 in a couple of months."

"What about your dad, what does he do?" Will asked.

Stella sighed. "My dad hasn't done much since he came back from the war. He sells a few bits at the market, that's all really. Did your father fight in the war?"

"Thankfully not, he's a precision engineer at Rolls-Royce, so his occupation was reserved."

"That sounds like an important job," Stella said,

raising her eyebrows.

Will nodded and looked at his watch. "I must go now. Will you be here tomorrow?"

Stella shrugged her shoulders. "I should think so... maybe."

"Good, I'll meet you here in the morning then, about half ten? I'm going to bring something for you," Will said, backing out of the den.

"Really? What are you going to bring?" Stella asked with interest.

"You'll see." Will's voice echoed as he dashed off.

FOUR

Jeanie stood in the pantry doorway, hoping for inspiration. It was always an arduous task trying to cook a meal with a few ingredients, and tonight was no exception. There were a few vegetables left from Derek's allotment but that was all, and with no money to buy anything, Jeanie knew there would be trouble when Derek came home. She felt in the pocket of her apron for a cigarette she had taken out of Derek's pack earlier, and was about to put it to her lips as Stella walked in.

"Oh, by crikey, Stella, I thought it was your father," Jeanie gasped, managing to quickly conceal the cigarette in her apron pocket. "Pop round to Grandma's and ask her if she's got any meat to spare, will you? Hurry though, your father will be back soon enough, and you know he doesn't like to be kept waiting for his tea." Jeanie ushered Stella out of the back door before she had a chance to object.

Jeanie stood at the back door, took the cigarette out and lit it. Nobody knew she smoked. It was only the odd one now and again, but Derek would go mad if he knew. She took a dozen or so deep draws on the cigarette before flicking the butt onto the outhouse roof, then hurried back inside to finish putting dinner together.

Stella arrived back with a small piece of boiled ham. "Grandma said she's sorry but that is all she has left. I'm going to go up to my room till dinner is ready."

"Stella, set the table for me, would you? And have a look if there is enough milk to make up some white

29

sauce?" Jeanie requested as she darted around the kitchen without purpose. "Come on, love, don't just stand there. He'll be home any time now."

Usually, Stella tried to avoid being around when she knew her father was due home, but she did as her mother asked and took what milk was left from the fridge. Just then, the entry gate banged shut and Jeanie froze.

"Bloody hell... he's home. You go up to your room and I'll shout to you when it's ready."

Stella moved quickly towards the stairs, pausing briefly to look back at her mother. She hated leaving her to face the wrath, but she knew her presence would make things worse.

"Go on then, love," Jeanie nodded, and Stella ran off up the stairs. The back door rattled, and Jeanie calmly turned back and checked the potatoes with a knife.

Derek's routine hardly ever differed. His entrance would rarely involve a greeting of any kind. He would simply exchange his shoes for his slippers and his cap for his cigarettes. Then he would either pour himself a whiskey, or a beer, then sit at the table and read the evening paper.

But from there on in, he was like a time bomb ticking away. His patience would wear thinner each time he glanced over his paper, wondering if dinner would be ready any time soon.

"I have some boiled ham for dinner, with some broad beans and new potatoes from your allotment. I've made some white sauce to go with it too," Jeanie tried to sound convincing and hoped that by some miracle the dinner would suffice.

"For Christ's sake, woman, let's see it on the bloody table then."

Jeanie quickly dished out the paltry offerings onto cold plates and walked over with Derek's, placing it on the table in front of him. With trepidation, she walked back to the counter for the other two plates and was about to shout Stella when the time bomb exploded.

"What in Heaven's name do you call this?" Derek griped.

Jeanie turned to face Derek and watched as he lifted one side of his plate and then let it drop in disgust. "What is the matter with you? I give you money to buy food."

"Yes, Derek, but not enough. Everything is so expensive and what with rationing and all, it's really — "

"Pathetic excuses, all the time." Derek shook his head.

"Look, please have mine as well, I'm not particularly hungry honestly. I — "

"For Christ's sake." Derek stood up with such force that his chair fell backwards behind him. He picked up his plate and threw it in Jeanie's direction. It hit the wall behind her, smashing to pieces and dropping with an almighty clatter to the floor, leaving bits of food splattered against the wallpaper.

Suddenly, Stella appeared in the kitchen and tried to defend her mother. "Dad, please... Mam is trying her best."

Derek frowned in disbelief at his daughter's brazenness. His face red with fury, he marched over to Stella, who was now picking up the pieces of broken plate off the floor. He grabbed hold of the collar on her dress and dragged her backwards.

"And just who do you think you're speaking to? You insolent madam."

"Derek, please," Jeanie shouted. "Just leave her be."

But it was too late. Derek violently launched Stella across the kitchen floor as though she were a sack of rubbish. Her head bashed against the back door, bringing her to an abrupt stop.

"That will teach you to interfere!" Derek roared. He then picked up his coat, slipped on his shoes, grabbed his cap, and walked silently out of the back door.

Jeanie rushed over to where Stella lay. "Stella, love, are you alright?"

Stella sat up gently and rubbed her head. "I'm sorry for interfering, Mam, but he shouldn't be treating you that way."

"It's okay, love," Jeanie said, checking Stella's head. "It's me who should be sorry, if I had made more of an effort with dinner, none of this would have happened. Come on, let's get you upstairs, eh?" Jeanie reassured, helping Stella to her feet.

****

Stella woke suddenly and sat up in bed. She rubbed at a large egg-sized lump on the top of her head, which gave a painful reminder of the spectacle her father had created the night before. She checked her clock… it was only twenty past two and she was wide awake. Immediately, thoughts of her grandfather came flooding into her mind, quickly followed by an overwhelming urge to cry, which Stella gave way to.

Eventually, after the tears had passed, she reached for her notebook and pencil. She continued to list random words and make notes of memories and things that reminded her of times spent with her grandfather. Some of the things she wrote brought tears again, but others just made her laugh. Stella put her book down, shuffled her pillow and snuggled back under the covers, eventually managing to find sleep.

A few hours later, creaking floorboards and the sound of doors opening and shutting, slowly stirred Stella to wake. Suddenly she remembered her arrangement with Will and began to wonder what it was he might have for her. Her clock read a quarter past nine, later than she would normally be up, but then she had been awake for two hours in the night. Stella opened her bedroom door and listened… the house was silent. She nipped across to the bathroom and spent as little time as possible in there. She rushed back to get dressed and brush her hair. She stuffed her notebook and pencils in her bag and grabbed her cardigan. She crept downstairs slowly and peered into the kitchen. With no sign of anyone in there either, she rushed in and made a quick search of the refrigerator and cupboards for something to eat but left hungry as usual.

Stella squeezed through the gap in the hedge and into her den. She peered out across the rec. Will was already making his way over and the same warm tingle as before, fluttered in her tummy. He crouched down and made a small gap in the bush.

"Hello again, may I come in?"

"Of course. I wasn't sure you'd come."

"I said I would. I have something for you, remember?" Will produced a book from inside his jacket. "It's a dictionary. I thought it might help you with your writing."

Stella didn't know what to say, she was so taken aback. "Blimey, where did you get that from?"

"My dad let me have it. Mum bought him the latest version for his birthday, so he said I could have this one. Will it help you?"

"It's great, thanks, Will. It's kind of you to think of me."

"So… have you written any more on the poem for your grandpa?"

Stella sighed. "Kind of, but the words won't seem to come to me like they did before."

"Why?" Will frowned.

"It's just not the same now that my grandpa has gone, and nobody else is interested. Mam is too busy, my grandma is too upset and my dad, well… he just thinks books are a waste of time… for girls anyway. I don't see any point in continuing."

"There is every point. I've already said I will listen to your poems. And I think books should be for everyone to enjoy. I have lots at home."

"You're lucky. My grandpa was the only person who ever bought me any books."

"I'll bring you some of mine to read then."

The two of them spent the rest of the morning together. Will even persuaded Stella to venture out on the rec so he could show her his football skills.

"So where do you get your ideas from to write these poems then?" Will asked, as he demonstrated his skill in rallying the ball from one foot to the other.

"Dunno really. Ideas just jump into my head. My grandpa was the same. He's written lots of poems and short stories. When he knew that I liked writing too, he offered to help me. He said I had the makings of a good writer. But that was then..." Stella's head dropped to her chest again.

"Well, I think it's wonderful that you write. My dad likes writing too. He makes up short adventure stories, he's written loads of them. I think you should carry on, I bet it's what your grandpa would want."

Stella nodded, "You're right."

"Good." Will looked at his watch. "I must head home now. Why don't you come with me and have a look through my books? You can borrow as many as you like."

"Oh, I don't know about that. I've never been to anyone's house before."

"It'll be alright, honest. My mum doesn't mind me bringing friends to the house."

"If you're sure it will be alright then." Stella collected her belongings from the den and the two of them made their way to Will's house.

Will's family home was much larger than the small, terraced cottage Stella lived in. There was also a brand-new Ford Anglia parked on the drive. The paintwork was so glossy, that Stella could see her face in it. Will led Stella around the back of the house. The garden was huge, with a range of neatly trimmed bushes and colourful plants. It looked immaculate.

"Blimey, you could fit our garden into one corner of yours," Stella laughed.

"My parents love it. They spend ages out here." Will took off his boots and entered the house, shouting to his mum.

A tall, thin woman appeared from another room. "Mum, this is Stella, the girl I was telling you about."

"Pleased to meet you," Will's mum beamed a smile.

Stella thought Will's mother seemed a bit older than hers; an attractive woman, with a pleasant smile and eyes that seemed to light up her face.

"Would you like some lunch? There is more than enough to go around. I've prepared a ham salad."

Stella suddenly felt a little out of her depth, but she was starving and didn't want to appear rude by declining. "If you're sure, that would be wonderful."

The three of them sat at the table and Stella ate like she had not eaten for weeks, savouring every mouthful, and finishing way before Will and his mother.

"My, you were hungry, Stella, can I get you another helping?"

"No, thank you very much, Mrs. Turner, I'm rather full now."

Will's mother laughed, "You've certainly got a good appetite."

After they had all finished eating, Will told his mother about how Stella was drafting a poem for her recently deceased grandfather. "And Stella is hoping to become an author someday," he boasted.

"I am sorry for your loss, Stella. Has Will told you that his father also likes to write? He is hoping to get some of his work published. The two of you could have a chat sometime?"

"I'd like that," Stella smiled.

"I said Stella could borrow a few of my books. Is that okay?" Will asked.

"Of course. You take Stella up to your room and I'll wash up," Will's mum said, collecting the lunch pots together.

Stella sat on the floor in Will's room. She was amazed at the number of books he had. They were all neatly stacked in proper bookcases.

"Your collection is massive compared to mine. You almost have your own library," Stella joked, choosing four story books. "I suppose I ought to be going now, my mam might wonder where I am."

"I'll walk you back to the rec then," Will said, collecting the books. "You'll need some help carrying these."

Eventually, they arrived back at the rec and Stella took the books from Will. "Thank you for everything. If you're around tomorrow, I'll be at the den after I've been to church."

"I'll look out for you then," Will said with a smile.

There was an awkward moment between the two of them, softened by Will's impulsive decision to plant a quick kiss on Stella's cheek. Stella was taken aback, but before she had the chance to say anything, Will had spun around and was already heading off.

"I'll see you tomorrow, Stella, and I'll expect a completed poem too," he shouted back.

But before she had a chance to reply, he was already out of earshot. She watched him until he was out of sight and smiled to herself as the warm tingle swept through her tummy again.

FIVE

Whilst everything was quiet in the Felton house, Jeanie was up in her bedroom with Stella's envelope, trying to find a more suitable hiding place for it. She felt at the contents again, wondering what could be inside. She was so tempted to open it up but just couldn't bring herself to do it. It had Stella's name on the front and that was that. Jeanie turned the envelope over and noticed something had been written on the back. It read:

'Not to be opened until 25th October 1950.'

"Twenty-fifth of October 1950," Jeanie frowned. "That's Stella's 16th birthday."

Just then, she heard the back door open, followed by Stella shouting up to her. Jeanie just stood there with the envelope in her hand, desperately searching for somewhere to swiftly hide it before Stella came upstairs.

"I'm upstairs, love, I'll be down in a minute, and I'll see if I can find you something to eat."

"It's alright, Mam, I'm off round to see Grandma for a while. I've already eaten, anyway," Stella shouted back.

"Already eaten? Eaten what, and where?" Jeanie bellowed. But Stella had already left, slamming the door shut behind her, which sent a loud thud echoing through the walls.

"For goodness' sake, Stella, must you slam the door?" Jeanie groaned to herself. She wandered around the bedroom, trying to decide whether to open the envelope, when her thoughts were disturbed by a squeaking noise coming from one of the floorboards she had stepped on in the far corner of the room. Looking down, she could see a rise in the carpet above it. Jeanie knelt and pulled the carpet back, revealing a piece of loose floorboard. She moved the floorboard to one side and peered in.

"Perfect," she mumbled to herself. Then, without faculty of reason, Jeanie slid a finger under the seal of the envelope.

Inside, were two more envelopes. One had Stella's name written on the front and the other was unmarked. Jeanie held the unmarked envelope up to the light; she could see through the envelope well enough to know that it held money, and the thickness of the envelope suggested that there were quite a few pound notes in there.

"Good lord," Jeanie burst out. "There must be at least 50 pounds in here."

Jeanie pulled the notes out of the envelope and began counting, laying them neatly on the floor. "Eighty-eight, eighty-nine, ninety. Oh, for heavens…" She continued counting. "A hundred and forty-nine… surely not, a hundred and fifty pounds. But how, why…?"

Jeanie's eyebrows contracted into a crumpled frown. She looked around the room as if searching her mind for a reason. Of course, as nothing in the room was going to give away any answers, she arranged the stack of notes into a pile, grabbed the envelope and tucked the bundle back in. She then turned her attention to the other envelope that had Stella's name on the front.

Jeanie slid a finger under the seal and pulled out the letter. It was backdated to the beginning of January and read:

Sunday, 8th January 1950

My Darling Stella,

If things have turned out the way I planned, you will be reading this letter on your 16th birthday. At that thought, I wipe away a tear, for I know that I shall not be there to see the beautiful young woman I am certain you will grow up to be.

I have much faith that you have continued with your writing, and that you may already be well on your way to becoming the famous author we both dreamed you would become. I do hope so my darling girl, for I am certain you have what it takes.

You will no doubt be wondering about the reason for the vast sum of money I have left for you. To this, my answer is simple. For you to have any hope of success in getting away from the man who dares call himself a father, you will need every penny of it.

If I thought your mother had nerve enough to leave him, I would have left the money to her instead, but I know in my heart that she does not have that strength.

Please, Stella, use this money and do whatever it takes to ensure you do not have to stay a moment longer under his control than necessary. Do your best to take care of your mother too, as I am certain there will be many times she will need to draw on your strength.

Take care of yourself my darling girl and seize whatever opportunity you can to follow your dreams.

Much Love, Grandpa.

Jeanie wiped away the tears that fell relentlessly onto her cheeks, for she knew the painful truth behind the words her father had written. She put the letter and the money back in the brown envelope and sealed it back up. She then concealed the envelope inside a pillowcase and positioned it under the floorboard, taking care to straighten the carpet back down as it was. "Dad, I can promise that's where it will stay until Stella is 16. Just as you have expressed," Jeanie said to herself.

****

"Hello, Grandma," Stella said cheerfully, as she entered the house.

Elsie put a finger up to her mouth. "Sshh, love, not so loud. Mr Brown is in the sitting room with Grandpa."

"Who? What…what for?"

"It's alright. Mr Brown is the undertaker. He and his attendants are here to settle your grandpa in his coffin. Don't look so worried, love, no harm will be done to him."

Stella's cheerfulness ended abruptly. The last memory of her grandfather was distressing enough, but she had not given much thought as to what happened after that. She knew what a funeral was, of course, but she had not given any thought as to what procedures had to be followed leading up to one. Least of all her grandfather's.

Stella's mouth felt dry. She licked her lips to successfully part with her words. "I…see, well I think

I'll go outside a while."

She was about to leave when the door to the sitting room opened and a small, broad-shouldered man appeared. Mr Brown, Stella presumed. The man never said a word, he just nodded at Elsie and smiled at Stella, exposing an uneven row of yellowish-brown teeth.

"Thank you, Mr Brown." Elsie nodded back to the man as he and his attendants left.

"Now that's sorted, won't you stay a while and we'll have a brew, eh?"

Stella noticed that tears had welled in her grandmother's eyes. The thought of leaving her now seemed cruel.

"Yes please, that would be nice," Stella said, sitting down at the kitchen table. Then without really thinking, she decided to tell her grandmother about her writing.

"Grandma, would you like to hear a poem?"

A poem... written by whom?"

"Me. Well... it's not quite finished yet, but when it is, would you like to hear it?"

Elsie smiled. "Yes... what's it about?"

"My memories of Grandpa," Stella said tentatively.

Elsie's eyes welled up again. She lit a gas ring and placed the kettle over it, then sat down at the table beside Stella.

"About your grandpa, you say?" Elsie looked up at the ceiling as if to recall something. "You know your grandpa was pretty good at stringing a few lines together."

"I know, Grandma, he used to help me with my writing all the time."

"Really? Well, he was good with words, he loved poetry and often said he wished he could have been an author."

Stella looked down towards the floor. "I miss him."

"Me too, love," Elsie pulled her granddaughter close.

Stella began to sob, and the tears streamed down her face. Elsie reached into the pocket of her apron and pulled out a handkerchief. "I tell you what... you finish this poem, then how about we ask Uncle Albert to read it out after Grandpa's funeral?" she said, wiping away her granddaughter's sorrow.

Stella pulled away from Elsie's embrace. "Really? I think Grandpa would have liked that idea very much."

"Me too. Now... let me finish making this brew and then maybe we could set to and make a cake. Look what I've got."

Elsie held up a bar of chocolate. "Uncle Albert brought this round earlier... rare as chicken's teeth these days."

Stella laughed and moved away from the table to grab a mixing bowl.

"Wait up, Stella, I've just had a thought. What's the point of wasting such a delicious bar of chocolate on a boring old cake? How about we just scoff the lot between us, right now?"

Stella sat back down at the table. "That's the second-best idea you've had today."

"Aye... and what was the first?"

"Having Uncle Albert read my poem out... of course!"

Later that afternoon, Stella sat on a bench on the rec. It had been a beautiful day, and the sun was still considerably warm. She took out her notepad and read the list of words she'd previously written. She chewed on her pencil and stared out across the rec. The sky was aglow with blended shades of orange, red and navy. She felt so captivated by its beauty, that somehow it inspired her. She began to connect a few words and then a sentence, and eventually, she composed a verse. A tranquil aura seemed to have cloaked itself around her, and the words just kept flowing, line after line, verse after verse, until eventually Stella had a complete poem with which she felt happy.

SIX

Sunday 13th August 1950

Whilst some of the congregation of St Clement's Church knelt upon hassocks, others preferred to sit and bow their heads whilst the vicar, Reverend Bickerstaff gave the final prayer of the Sunday morning service.

"The grace of our Lord Jesus Christ, and the love of God, and the fellowship of the Holy Spirit, be with us all evermore. Amen."

"Amen," the congregation repeated.

After a brief pause, people began to make their way out of the church. Some had preferred to stay a while longer to say their own prayers, just as Elsie was doing.

Jeanie whispered to her mother. "We'll wait outside for you."

Elsie nodded her head in agreement, closed her eyes and began to speak softly.

"Dear Lord in Heaven, please take care of my Fred. He has been a loyal husband, loving father, and grandfather. He is in your hands now, keep him safe in your heavenly kingdom and let him rest in eternal peace until it is time for us to be together once more. Amen."

Elsie opened her eyes and took a deep breath. She stood up slowly, giving her knees a moment to adjust and was about to make her way out of church when a voice spoke from behind.

"Hello, Elsie."

Elsie turned to look behind her. "Norah!"

Norah stood up to speak to Elsie. "How are you? I was hoping I would have a chance to speak with you at some point. You have probably heard by now that I'm coming back to live in Kilburn?"

"Yes, I did hear," Elsie said brusquely.

"I'm glad you were resting yesterday when Doctor Keys sent me over. I would not have wanted my presence to have upset you. I am sorry for your loss."

"That's most kind, but I'd better be going now, my family will be waiting outside."

"Of course. Elsie, can we speak some time? I need—"

"I don't think so, Norah, no. I do have to be going now." Elsie turned, and as quickly as her knees would allow, made her way out of the church.

There were quite a few parishioners still chatting outside, and as she walked through the churchyard, Elsie scoured the crowd in a desperate bid to find her family. Eventually, she noticed Sheila waving and hastily made her way over.

"Is everyone ready to go then?" Elsie said anxiously.

"Yes, Mother, we've all been waiting for you. Are you alright, you look very pale?"

"Yes, I'm fine, Sheila, I'm just ready for a brew," she replied, trying to force a smile.

"Well, why don't we go back inside and have a cup of tea here then?" Jeanie suggested.

"No!" Elsie replied sharply. "Sorry… I just need to be getting back if we're going to be having our dinner on time. That's all."

"You don't have to be cooking us all dinner, you know. You should be resting," Sheila said sharply.

"I'm fine, Sheila, honestly. I want us all to eat Sunday dinner together, but I need to be getting home if it's going to be this Sunday," Elsie said, sarcastically, setting off ahead of the others. "So come on, let's get a wriggle on, eh," she shouted back to everyone.

"Crikey, where's that bee come from that's suddenly buzzing around *her* bonnet?" Sheila said wryly.

Jeanie, Stella, and Albert all chuckled as they set off to catch up with Elsie.

****

Stella scraped the skin off some new potatoes from her father's allotment, whilst her mother prepared a cabbage. Sheila was in charge of carrots, whilst Elsie checked on the joint of beef roasting in the oven.

"That smells delicious, Grandma, I can't wait to tuck into it," Stella said, rubbing her stomach.

Elsie smiled. "I'm doing Yorkshire puddings too."

"Wonderful, I'm starving," she replied.

"Jeanie, will Derek be joining us today?" Elsie asked.

"Yes, he'll be here soon, Mam."

"Hmmm… walk in, eat, and walk out again then?" Elsie gave a look of disapproval to which Jeanie gave no response.

After Derek's conveniently timed arrival, it wasn't long before the family were tucking into a roast beef dinner. All except Jeanie, who was deep in thought, shuffling the food around on her plate.

"Are you all right, Jeanie love?" her mother asked.

Jeanie's attention returned to her plate. "Sorry, Mam, I was miles away."

"Tuck in then, eh?" Elsie replied.

"This beef is cooked to perfection, Elsie," Albert said, demolishing his last few mouthfuls. "And the vegetables... well, very tasty indeed, Derek. You've had a good crop again this year."

Derek's response came in the form of a nod in Albert's direction.

"I'm quite full," Jeanie said, placing her knife and fork on her plate. "I think I'll go and make a start on the washing up." Jeanie picked up her plate. "It was delicious though, Mam."

"Well, if you're not going to eat the rest of that..."

Derek grabbed Jeanie's plate out of her hand, scraped the leftovers onto his own and shoved the plate back in her hand, in such a way that everyone paused for a moment and looked at each other in disbelief.

Jeanie sighed and took her plate off to the kitchen, set it down and began filling the sink with hot, soapy water. She looked out of the kitchen window and noticed the neighbour's cat tormenting birds in the garden. It was relentless in its pursuit of them, hounding them mercilessly. *Why don't they just fly away?* she thought to herself. *Maybe they're just too scared...*

"Jeanie, love, we're going to be swimming in here in a minute," Elsie said, quickly turning off the tap.

"Sorry, Mam, I was miles away."

"What's wrong, love?"

Jeanie looked to the floor. "I just could not eat my meal, knowing that Dad... well, that he's lying in the back room like that. It's—"

"Jeanie, love," Elsie cut in. "Now listen to me, your dad would want the family to be together, especially on a Sunday. He would also want to keep things as normal as possible.

You know his motto... Life—"

"Life goes on... yes, yes I know," Jeanie remarked with a sigh. "Mam, can I ask you something."

"Of course, love... what is it?"

Jeanie moved in closer to her mother's ear and whispered. "Did Dad leave you comfortable, money-wise I mean?"

"Yes, love. Your dad was an exceptionally good manager of his finances. He was always putting money away to save for a rainy day. Why do you ask?"

"Oh, no reason, I just wanted to make sure you'll be alright." "I'll be fine, Jeanie. You must not worry."

****

After the hearty dinner her grandmother had cooked, Stella made her way to the rec, to find that Will was already there, playing football with his friends. She felt a tiny pang of shyness and decided that rather than approach him in front of all his friends, she would sit on the bench and watch from a distance. He noticed her at once though, and waved, and Stella felt the familiar warmth pass through her. The other boys were looking over too, which made her cheeks blush, and she quickly forced a yawn to pass off her clear embarrassment.

After a few more minutes of play, Will had forsaken the game and was on his way over to her. Suddenly she felt a little nervous and fidgeted in her seat. She heard one of the other boys shouting to Will to come back and continue with the game, but Will just carried on walking towards her, waving a dismissive hand to them as he shouted back that he would see them all tomorrow.

Stella relished the feeling of being favoured over Will's friends, it made her feel special.

Looking past Will, she could see the other boys pack up and leave unenthusiastically.

"You're not going to be very popular," Stella teased.

"Never mind, they'll get over it," Will replied. "So how are you today?"

"Ahh, I'm doing alright, I think."

"Shall we go for a walk?" Will asked.

"Sure."

The pair made their way off the rec and down the lane, neither of them said a great deal for a while which made Stella feel a little awkward, and then Will suddenly spoke.

"Did you mind that I kissed you yesterday?"

Stella felt her cheeks blush again. "Erm... no. I suppose I was just a bit shocked, that's all."

"What would you say If I asked you to be my girlfriend?"

Stella's cheeks could not have turned any redder,

which oddly affected her ability to form any sort of reply.

"You don't have to answer straight away, of course. I know you're still really upset about your grandpa. It's just… well… I like you."

Stella smiled quite reservedly, and still not able to form any type of response, she just kept walking. Eventually, the pair ended up back on the rec and took a seat on the bench. The sun was radiant, and the birds sang a late afternoon song that echoed across the sky. Stella closed her eyes and turned her face to the sun, soaking up its rays.

"So anyway, please tell me that you've finished your poem and it's all thanks to the dictionary I gave you," Will chuckled.

"Well actually, I have finished it."

Will turned to look at Stella. "Really? Well, I would love to hear it, if you feel you can read it to me, that is?"

Stella didn't reply straight away, leaving Will thinking he had gone one step too far, he quickly added. "I mean one day, of course, when you feel able to. I don't mean right this very — "

"Right now is perfect," Stella said, before Will had a chance to finish his sentence.

She held her gaze and took a deep breath before speaking in a soft tone.

"Miner's lamp and sooty face, tales from down the pit,
How you insisted wearing that cap that did not fit.
Trouser braces, shoelaces, shiny boots as good as new,

These are the things that remind me of you.
Brylcreem and tobacco, bad knees, and silver hair,
The smell of Grandma's baking as it floated through the air.
Sunday dinners, race winners, a glass of beer or two,
These are the things that remind me of you.
Storybooks and cuddles, day trips by the sea,
Saturdays spent fishing, then your house for our tea.
Scoring goals, playing bowls, card games made for two.
These are the things that remind me of you.
Feeling sad and lonely, now you're no longer here,
Thought of you again today and cried another tear.
Deep despair, hard to bear, what am I to do?
Just remember all the things that remind me of you."

After a second or two had passed, Stella finally broke her fixed stare and looked to Will for his response. She noticed his eyes had welled up with tears.

"Well, what do you think?"

Will sniffed a couple of times and brushed a tear from his eye. He reached out to hold Stella's hand. "That is beautiful, Stella, beautiful. Your grandma will be proud."

Stella smiled. "If you did ask me to be your girlfriend, the answer would be yes."

Will gave Stella's hand an endearing squeeze. The two of them never said spoke another word, they both just sat quietly and enjoyed the rest of the early evening sun.

SEVEN

There had been various visitors to the Downing household in the five days since Fred had passed, with people coming and going to pay their last respects to him. But this day was bustling with family and Stella felt lost in the middle of them all. Standing in the kitchen, she watched as each person went into the sitting room, then re-emerged moments later either distressed or upset. This made her undecided as to whether she should go in or not. Eventually, it dawned on her that her name was being called.

"Stella. Stella! Good heavens, have you lost your ears?" It was Elsie standing behind her.

"I'm sorry, Grandma, I was deep in thought."

"You certainly were," she said softly, managing a smile. "Go on in if you want to, love." Elsie gestured with her head in the direction of the sitting room. "It's alright... go on in and say a final goodbye to your grandpa."

A pale line of tension appeared upon Stella's face. The fact that she didn't reply, and remained glued to the spot, was indication enough that she was unsure of what to do.

Elsie grabbed a kitchen chair and sat down. "Sweetheart," she said. "You have nothing to be afraid of. Your grandpa loved you with all his heart. He would never have done anything to hurt you when he was alive, and he certainly can't now he has passed. You know... you don't have to go in... but, Stella, you must understand that this is the only chance you're going to get."

A solitary tear ran down Stella's cheek, which she quickly brushed away.

"It has to be your choice. I don't want you to have any regrets."

Stella stepped forward and kissed her grandmother's cheek, then without saying a word she turned and walked slowly toward the sitting room. She reached for the door handle and felt her stomach quiver a little. She paused momentarily, taking a final moment to prepare herself, before pushing open the door and peering around it. Not knowing what to expect, Stella felt quite satisfied, that indeed, as her grandmother had reassured, there was absolutely nothing to be afraid of. She gathered herself and continued to enter the room fully.

At first sight, the coffin gave an instant sacred impression, it had been set upon two wooden trestles and appeared to absorb the whole room. The shimmer of the polished oak gave radiance to the dim light and the brass handles dazzled hypnotically. A small altar had been erected at the foot of the coffin and two white candles burned steadily against the oppressive air. As her mind adjusted, she took notice of the sweet-smelling flowers placed tactfully around the room.

Stella approached the coffin and cautiously peered inside. Immediately her eyes met with her grandpa's face, and she felt a little perturbed by his semblance. He appeared younger than she had known, his skin was unwrinkled and except for a bluish tinge evident around his nose and lips, it was practically deficient of colour... porcelain in effect.

His gaunt body, enshrouded in a white gown, filled the coffin, with his arms placed restfully across his chest. The skin on his hands had drooped, leaving his fingers tapered and knotty. A white ring, visible around one finger... was suggestive of where his wedding band had once been.

Stella felt an overwhelming urge to cry but managed to suppress her emotions as she recalled the pain he had suffered for years, compared to the peace he so deserved. She felt assured he had found that peace and with a sense of contentment, she leaned over the coffin and placed a kiss gently upon his forehead. His pallid skin felt like cold marble against her lips and again she felt a pang of perplexity as she wrestled with the emotions associated with the new and poignant experience.

Apart from paying her last respects, Stella had another purpose for visiting her grandpa, one of a more personal nature. She reached into her pocket and pulled out a folded piece of paper... it was her poem. She looked around the room, making sure nobody else had entered, before speaking quietly.

"Grandpa, I don't know if it's possible...but... I'd like to think you can hear me. I wanted to read to you one more time before you must go. It is a poem you see... one I have written especially for you. And although Grandma says she is going to ask Uncle Albert to read it out to everyone later, I want to read it to you first... myself."

Tears welled up in Stella's eyes and spilt onto her cheeks. She brushed them away and began to read each line she had so lovingly composed. It was ironic, how she had read the poem over and over to herself and she had managed to read it to Will without crying and yet now, when she felt it mattered most, the tears streamed relentlessly down her face.

After she had finished reading, she folded the paper neatly into a small square and placed it under the hand closest to his heart. "I'm going to miss you so much, Grandpa."

Stella backed slowly out of the room and bumped straight into her grandma. "Goodness, are you alright? I was just coming to see if you had nodded off to sleep in here."

"I just wanted to read my poem to him." Stella passed her grandma a piece of paper - a copy of her poem.

"You got it finished then?" Elsie put an arm around Stella's shoulder. "In that case, let's give it to Uncle Albert. He will read it out later when we are all back here together. Now it's time for Grandpa to make his final journey. Mr Brown will be here soon to escort him.

You go on with the others, just give me a few more minutes."

Stella complied and made her way back into the kitchen. By now, a lot more people had gathered. She searched for a familiar face and spotted her mother standing in the corner of the kitchen. Surprisingly her father was there too. She hadn't thought whether or not he would bother to attend. Just then, there was a knock at the door, and Mr Brown, the undertaker, walked in. He looked impeccable, dressed in a smart black suit and tie, with brightly polished shoes and a black, short-brim top hat. A captivating sight she had never seen before. He had a confident yet affable manner about him that held everyone composed. He and three other men, two of whom Stella recognised as being Mr Brown's attendants, were also dressed in suits and top hats. Each one nodded an expression of greeting as they made their way quietly into the sitting room. At that point, everyone regarded that as a cue for complete silence.

****

St Clement's church was full of mourners. Elsie sat in the front row alongside Sheila, Albert, Jeanie, and Derek. Stella was on the row behind, with her cousins James and Robert, along with a few other close relatives. The Reverend Bickerstaff spoke of Fred's life and the love he had for his family. Stella listened intently and watched through her tears as her grandmother, mother and aunt were also sobbing.

Eventually, as everyone joined in with the Lord's Prayer, the service ended. The Reverend Bickerstaff had chosen some befitting words of comfort to the family and congregation. He completed the service by requesting everyone's presence in the churchyard for the interment of one 'Frederick Charles Downing'.

There had been a rain shower whilst the funeral service had taken place, but by the time everyone had assembled in the churchyard, the sun was shining brightly and everywhere looked fresh and clean. The rain had left a wetness upon the headstones, which made them gleam against the bright sun.

The church bell tolled in single strokes, slowly and regularly as the cortège neared its destination... the specially marked place where Fred was finally to be laid to rest. Stella listened closely to the reverend as he gave his final sermon and watched as Mr Brown, and his attendants, gradually lowered her grandpa's coffin into the ground. Except for the harsh grating cry of a murder of crows cawing in the nearby trees, Stella felt chilled by the eerie silence. She looked up at her grandmother and thought how pale her face looked. It very much reminded her of how her grandfather had looked earlier, as he lay in his coffin.

"Grandma, are you okay?" Stella whispered.

Elsie didn't answer, she merely took Stella's hand and gave it an endearing squeeze. After what seemed like a lifetime of silence, everyone took turns to throw a handful of soil down onto the grave and Stella instinctively followed suit. She looked down at the coffin, now that it had found its final resting place. She thought how small it looked, compared to how large it seemed earlier when it had rested on the trestles. The Reverend Bickerstaff requested the company of those who could attend a small gathering at the Downing house for a ham tea. But as the mourners were about to make their way out of the churchyard, Albert had something to say.

"Ladies... gentlemen, if you don't mind... a moment of your time please."

Everyone paused, some with puzzled faces, wondering what it was he felt the need to say.

"I was asked if... once we are back at Mrs. Downing's house, I would read a poem. But to be perfectly honest, having already read it, I can think of no better time than the present to share it with you all."

The mourners gradually reassembled, and Albert continued. "It has been composed by Stella Felton, my niece, and granddaughter of Mr Downing." Everyone huddled closer together, all except Derek who, Albert had noticed, had already taken himself off for a cigarette. "It is simply entitled, 'My Grandpa,' and well... I think it's rather good." Albert unfolded a piece of paper, cleared his throat, and began to read out Stella's poem.

EIGHT

Once everyone had arrived at the Downing house, Elsie busied herself making sandwiches and tea with Stella's help. They both listened as Albert was about to give the guests an account of a summer holiday in 1939 at the newly opened Skegness Miners' Holiday Camp. He was about to begin his tale of how Fred had inadvertently swapped a prize from the bran tub, leaving the children wondering what they had found, when he was distracted by Elsie walking in carrying two plates of sandwiches. She handed one to Stella.

"Pass this round everyone, please," Elsie instructed.

"Now then, everyone, ham sandwiches are at the ready, and there's plenty to go around," she said, before apologising to Albert for interrupting his tale. "I'll bring in some cups of tea momentarily," she added, disappearing off into the kitchen.

The Reverend Bickerstaff tucked into his sandwich and asked Albert to elaborate on his story.

"Well, Reverend," Albert began. "Our youngest son, Robert, who I think was about three years old then... wasn't he, Sheila?" Albert said to his wife, and her nod of agreement followed at once.

"Aye, three years old," he continued, "and our eldest son, James, who would have been almost five, were both old enough to enjoy a ride on the donkeys. Grandpa Fred said he would take them, and off he went with the kids. He began to lead our Robert around on this fat donkey, when halfway around the track the donkey decided to 'do his business', right in the middle of the path. Well, the donkey owner gets Fred's attention and points to a dustpan and a huge barrel of sawdust in which to throw the donkey droppings... right?" Albert said, looking around the room to make sure everyone understood the story so far.

"So anyway, later in the week, when the kids ask for another ride on the donkeys, and one of the donkeys does his business, Fred thinks he knows exactly what needs to be done... he thinks to himself... 'I'll pick this up before the owner asks me to'. But when he goes to hurl the droppings in the barrel, he notices there's a kid's toy racing car poking out of the sawdust. Of course, he wonders why someone would want to throw a perfectly good toy away and decides to take it back for James and Robert to play with." Albert started to laugh before completing his story.

"Little did Fred know that he'd got the wrong barrel! He'd only gone and thrown a heap of donkey droppings into the kiddie's lucky dip barrel!"

Everyone, including Elsie and Stella, laughed. Albert, however, was roaring, tears of laughter spilt out onto his cheeks, and he only just managed to continue.

"Imagine the look on those poor little kid's faces, when they pulled out a donkey dropping as first prize!"

"Good Lord above," the Reverend laughed, trying to keep hold of his plate. "That's certainly not my idea of a lucky dip."

Stella finished handing the sandwiches around and

took the empty plate into the kitchen. She noticed that her grandmother had gone out in the backyard and was sitting on a bench. Stella decided to join her.

"Grandma, are you alright?"

"Yes, sweetheart, I thought I'd just come and get a breath of fresh air for a while," she said, putting an arm around Stella's shoulder.

"Grandma. Do all married couples fall out with each other?"

"What has made you ask that question?" Elsie asked with a frown.

"It's Mam and Dad. I just wonder why they never have a good relationship with each other."

Elsie sighed and pulled Stella closer to her. "I know things aren't right between your mam and dad, but I'm sure they still care for each other deep down."

Stella wanted to tell her grandmother just how awful her father could be but was too afraid of any repercussions. Instead, she just smiled blandly.

"Anyway... what about this poem of yours, eh? It was certainly well received by everyone, and I thought it was a perfect time for it to be read."

Stella smiled. "I'm glad everyone liked it. I just wish Grandpa could have heard it."

Elsie kissed the top of Stella's head. "Come on... let's go and dish out these cups of tea.

Albert was still telling tales of Fred and how he won the knobbly knees competition three years on the trot at the miners' holiday camp.

Elsie laughed as she listened to him recall the story of how he managed to be entered into the competition in the first place, and then corrected Albert when he made a mistake over a minor detail.

"No, Albert," Elsie shook her head. "I was the one fetching the ice creams. You were making a sandcastle with James and Robert, remember?"

Albert paused and scratched his head, as if to query the error of this minor detail. "I tell you what, Elsie, why don't you take the weight off your feet, and tell us all your version of the story, eh?" Albert said, patting the empty chair in between himself and Sheila.

Elsie hobbled over to the chair and sat down. Everyone waited for her to begin.

"Well…" she began. "It was 1946, the first year the camp had re-opened after the war. I was on my way back from fetching us all an ice cream, when I saw one of the Green Coat girls talking to Fred. I could see Fred shaking his head and quickly rolling his trousers down, covering his knees. When I finally got over to them, the Green Coat girl said she was looking for men to enter the knobbly knees competition. I said that I thought Fred would make an ideal contender, and that was it, she had his name on the list before he could say anything."

"And Fred didn't want to take part?" the Reverend Bickerstaff asked.

"Well not at first, Reverend, no, but of course we managed to persuade him. Anyway, out of 22 men, Fred won. He won it for the next two years on the trot!" Elsie laughed, throwing her hands up into the air and landing them down on her thighs with a slap. "Two years," she repeated. "They even gave him a nickname… The Kilburn Knobbler. Of course, he entered again in 1949 and lost to a younger miner, Jimmy Parkin from Creswell Colliery wasn't it, Albert?"

"Aye, that was the fella," replied Albert. "And by 'eck, he didn't half take umbrage to that, I can tell you. Knocked his duck right off, did that. Afterwards, he took the hump and vowed never to enter again."

Everyone laughed, everyone except Derek, who sat in the corner of the room reading a newspaper, looking as miserable as sin.

"And I assume this Jimmy Parkin fellow will be defending his title again this year?" the reverend asked.

"I should think so," Albert reckoned. "We'll find out soon enough. We'll be going there shortly, and we always share the same week as Creswell Colliery."

"Well, I should be curious to find out," the reverend chuckled. "And will the whole family be attending the camp?" he asked.

"We'll just be taking Stella with us this year, give her a taste of the salty seaside air."

"Splendid. Well, I'm sure you will all have a wonderful time. Just be careful what you pick out of that lucky dip barrel though, won't you," the reverend chuckled.

Derek folded the newspaper up and tossed it to one side. "Well, I think I've heard enough depressing stories for one day, I'm off to the pub." And without so much as a goodbye, he got up and left.

"Yes, I think it's time I went too," the Reverend

Bickerstaff said. "Home that is, of course, not the pub," he quickly added, coughing nervously, before making his way over to Elsie to shake her hand. "Mrs Downing, many thanks for your hospitality and may the Good Lord bless and keep you."

The reverend then shook hands with Albert, Sheila, and Jeanie before turning to Stella. "God bless you too, Stella, and may I just say what a wonderful poem you wrote. You have the makings of a good writer, I think."

"Thank you, Reverend," Stella said, trying to speak over a mouthful of sandwich.

Jeanie saw the reverend out and then filled the sink with hot, soapy water. "Stella, love, bring me those plates over, would you, and grab a tea towel. I don't want to leave all this for your grandma to do."

Stella did as she was asked, and collected in the teacups, saucers and plates from various places and stacked them up neatly, ready for washing. She picked up a tea towel and began drying the dishes as Jeanie washed them.

"I didn't know you could write poems, Stella," Jeanie said, rinsing soap suds off a plate.

Stella's head dropped, "I've written lots of poems. Grandpa always liked to listen to the things I'd written."

"I would listen too, if I were given the opportunity," Jeanie replied sharply.

"I would have asked, but you're always busy and often upset when Dad —"

Jeanie cut in. "Well let's not bring that up now,

eh? Look, you go and listen to Uncle Albert's tales, and I'll dry the pots."

"Okay, Mam," Stella said, laying the tea towel down on the worktop before heading over to where Albert was standing.

He was looking up at an old photograph above the fireplace. It was of Fred standing with four other men, each dressed in their sooty work clothes, pit boots and knee pads still fastened to their legs. Each held a smile upon their dirty faces.

"When was that taken, Uncle Albert?" Stella asked.

"October 1933, a year before you were born, lass. Your grandpa would have been…" Albert looked up to the ceiling as if to search his mind for the correct information. "Aye, he would have been 53 then."

"Who are the other men?" Stella asked curiously.

"Well, that's Ernie and his brother, Stephen, that's Billy, and that chap next to your grandpa is my father. Gilbert, his name was, or Gill as they called him. Unfortunately, they've all passed now."

"Even your father?"

"Aye, lass, he was killed about four months after this picture was taken. He was working at South Normanton Colliery at the time, a few men from these parts worked there back then. Anyhow, there was an explosion, and my father and Stephen were two out of the eight men who were killed. There were two or three injured too, as I recall."

"How terrible," Stella sympathised, "I'm sorry your father died, Uncle Albert."

"That's why I took the position at Ilkeston Mines

Rescue. I like to think that although

I couldn't help my father, maybe I can help someone else's."

"That's kind, Uncle Albert."

"Thanks, lass," Albert said. "Oh, don't forget your poem, Stella," Albert handed her a piece of folded-up paper.

"It's alright, Uncle Albert, you can keep it," Stella smiled.

"He'd have been right proud of this poem, I think, and proud of you for writing it so beautifully," Albert said, as he tucked the paper back into his pocket.

Jeanie entered the room and walked over to where Stella and Albert were.

"Come on then, Stella, let's go home," Jeanie said, rolling her sleeves down. "Mam, I'll be round in the morning to help you sort out the sitting room. And if you'll take my advice, you'll get yourself off to bed soon, an early night will do you no harm."

"Alright, love, there's no rush," Elsie said nonchalantly. No need to fuss, eh?"

Jeanie just smiled and kissed her mother's cheek before gathering up her things and heading for the door.

****

Later that evening, Stella was in bed reading one of the books she had borrowed from Will, when there was a knock on her door. Her mother walked in and sat on the side of the bed. "I'm always here for you, Stella. I know your dad can be difficult but… well, whatever happened at that prison camp in Japan is responsible for the change in him. Of that, I am sure."

"Why doesn't he talk to you about it then?"

"He just says he doesn't want to talk about it. He gets his temper up if I try, so I don't push it."

"Nothing will ever change then," Stella turned over, away from her mother. Jeanie could only sigh in response and left the room.

NINE

Stella sat in her den. It was pouring with rain, but the expanse of foliage that formed the shrub sheltered her well enough. She was busy reading, periodically glancing up from her book, hoping that Will might make an appearance soon. She didn't have to wait long before he appeared, dripping wet, holding a small paper bag in his hand, and a book under his arm.

He quickly forced his way through, inside the shelter of the shrub. "By heck, it's raining cats and dogs out there, I'm wet through," he said, dripping water everywhere.

Stella laughed. "Yes, so I can see. What have you got there?"

"They're for you, I've just been to buy them from the shop."

Will knelt and handed Stella a bag of pick-and-mix sweets. "Sorry, the bag is a bit wet, and I've eaten maybe two or three already."

Stella giggled. "I meant the book, actually, but thank you anyway."

"Oh, yes, the book. That has got a bit wet too, I'm afraid. It's one of Enid Blyton's.

Have you read it?" Will asked, handing the damp book to Stella.

"Five Go Off to Camp! Brilliant. It is the only one of which Grandpa could not get me a copy."

"Well, it's yours," Will said with a smile.

"Thanks, Will," Stella marvelled, and without thought, she planted a kiss on Will's cheek.

"Are you okay after yesterday? I thought about

you. It cannot have been easy."

Stella nodded. "It was the worst day, I shall never forget it, Will, not as long as I live."

Will put his arm around Stella. "And your poem, did you read it to your grandma?"

"Better than that, my Uncle Albert read it out in front of everyone, after Grandpa's service."

"That's wonderful, Stella, you must have felt very proud."

Stella nodded. "Even the reverend commented on it. He said I had the makings of a good writer!"

Will smiled. "That is great, well done. I hope you are going to keep writing now?"

Stella sighed. "Maybe, if the inspiration finds me again," she said, running her hand across the book. "Five Go Off to Camp… I can't wait to read it. I'm going off to camp soon, I can take it with me and read it whilst I'm there."

"You're going to camp? Which camp?"

"Skegness Miners' Camp, I'm going with my Aunty Sheila and Uncle Albert next Saturday."

"I can't believe it. I'm going next Saturday too," Will said excitedly.

"Really, how come? I mean, your dad isn't a miner so what is the connection?"

"My Uncle Jed is though, well actually he is my dad's uncle, but I call him Uncle Jed.

He's a deputy at Creswell Colliery and he is taking me with him."

"I remember Uncle Albert saying that Kilburn and Creswell share the same week at the miners' camp. Oh,

Will, it's going to be great. Have you been before?"

"No, this will be my first time. Uncle Jed says I'll have a blast though."

"Oh, for sure, I've been for the last two years with my grandparents and my two cousins, James and Robert. They're older now, though, and they're both out at work, so my aunt and uncle said they would take me instead. You'll love it, Will, it is great fun."

"Fantastic," Will beamed.

"It won't feel quite the same without Grandpa though," Stella added ruefully.

"You'll have me though," Will said, nudging Stella's arm playfully.

Stella nodded and beamed a big smile. "Will you be catching the train from Kilburn Station on Saturday?"

"Uncle Jed and I will be going from Creswell Station. I'm off to stay at his house for a couple of days first though," Will said, munching on a handful of Dolly Mixtures.

Stella placed a bookmark in her book. "What for?"

"Uncle Jed is retiring soon, and he and my great aunt are moving house. Dad has promised extra pocket money if I help pack up the last of their belongings. Uncle Jed says there are all sorts of competitions to enter at the miners' camp. It sounds like great fun."

"It certainly is. I can't wait, especially now I know you're going too!" Stella said.

****

Friday 25th August 1950

Stella neatly folded the new jumper her grandma

had knitted and placed it on her bed next to a small pile of other items... a dress, underwear, socks, a comb, a toothbrush, a bathing suit, and a towel.

"Here, let me help you to pack," Jeanie said, holding a nightdress, a pair of shorts and a bar of soap. "Have you got everything?"

"I think so, yes. I just need to remember my book and I think I'm about ready."

"I doubt you'll have time to read, you'll be too busy with all the camp capers," Jeanie laughed. "And with that in mind, you'd better be getting an early night. Mr Jackson will be outside with his horse and cart, waiting for everyone's luggage bright and early as always."

"It won't be the same without Grandma and Grandpa this year," Stella said solemnly.

"And James and Robert will be missing too."

"I'm sure you'll soon make plenty of friends," Jeanie rearranged the clothing Stella had put in her case.

Stella at once cast her mind to thoughts of Will. "I'm sure I will too."

Jeanie smiled and kissed her daughter's forehead. "Bright and early then. Night, love." Jeanie was about to walk out of the room when Stella called her back.

"Mam... you will be alright while I'm away, you know... with Dad, I mean?"

"You do not need to be fretting about that. Things will go on just as they would if you were here," Jeanie said, closing the bedroom door as she left.

"That's exactly what I'm afraid of," Stella whispered under her breath before settling down under the covers.

****

The next morning, Stella woke to the sound of voices outside on the street. She pulled back the curtains and noticed that people had already started to gather outside. She glanced at her clock - ten to seven. Knowing that would leave just under an hour before she needed to be ready with her suitcase, she dashed off to the bathroom. She scooped water from the sink into her cupped hands and shivered as she splashed the pool of ice-cold liquid onto her face. As she grabbed for her towel, she heard her mother shout up to her from downstairs.

"You're up then? I'll make some tea and there's bread and jam for breakfast."

"Great, thanks, Mam," Stella shouted back and hurried back to her room to get dressed.

Stella carried her case downstairs and placed it next to the back door. Her mother was pouring tea from the pot and there was warm toast and a pot of grandma's homemade jam ready on the table. Stella sat down.

"That bread smells wonderful, I'm starving."

"I've made you some lunch for the journey too." Jeanie held up a sandwich wrapped neatly in brown paper. "And also, I know it's not much, but it might buy you an ice cream or two," she said, sliding three pennies across the table to Stella.

Stella looked across to her mother. "Mam, really you should keep this, I —"

Jeanie interrupted. "No, I insist, love, please put it away and let us say no more about it."

Stella beamed a huge smile and without further delay, tucked into her toast. After she had finished breakfast, she picked up her case and made for the door.

"Here, don't forget your coat, love, there's a rough easterly wind that comes off that coast at times, even in summer," Jeanie handed Stella her coat. "Right, if you're all set, grab your case and let's get round to Grandma's. Sheila and Albert will be there by now, I should think."

"Oh, that reminds me..." Stella grabbed the crocheted blanket she had brought from her den. "Now I'm ready."

Out on the street, more people had gathered. Not all would be going to the camp, many just liked to follow the cart down to the station, stand on the platform and wave the holidaymakers off on a safe journey. It had always been a ritual of sorts, those going to camp would assemble at the Travellers Rest Public House, where Mrs Hunt would be busy providing everyone with refreshments. Tom Jackson would load his cart with everybody's luggage ready to take it to Kilburn Station, all in time to catch the nine o'clock train.

As Stella and Jeanie walked up the entry to Elsie's house, the delightful smell of baking filled the passageway. Jeanie opened the back door to find Sheila busy loading freshly baked scones into a Tupperware box.

"Morning all, what a wonderful smell to be greeted with," Jeanie said, peering into the plastic container.

"There's a couple here for you, Jeanie," Sheila said, passing her sister a brown paper bag.

"Oh, thank you… still warm too… lovely. Where's Mam?"

"She will be down in a minute. I think she's feeling a bit sad. She has been reminiscing to me and Albert about the camp from years gone by, and I think it's upset her a bit."

"It's a shame she wouldn't go with you; I think it would have done her the world of good to get some sea air into her lungs. Perhaps she feels it is a bit too soon though."

"Yes, I think you're right, Jeanie," Sheila agreed. "Stella, love, nip up to your grandma, will you, tell her we will have to be going. And where's Albert? Albert!" Sheila screeched at the top of her voice. "Oh, there you are. Take those cases over to Mr Jackson will you, before—"

"I'm already *on* the case, my dear," Albert interrupted his wife jokingly, whilst trying to manoeuvre himself through the kitchen with three lots of luggage.

Stella peered around her grandma's bedroom door to find her sitting at her dressing table.

"Grandma… are you alright? Aunty Sheila says it's time for us to leave."

"Yes, love. Come on in a minute, I have something for you."

Elsie held out her hand to reveal some pennies. "Try your luck in the penny arcade, eh?"

"Thanks, Grandma," Stella kissed her grandma's cheek. "What have you got there?" she asked, picking up a souvenir postcard that read 'Skegness Miners' Camp' on the front.

"Oh, it has you and Grandpa in it. How was this taken?"

"Well, when we went last year, the photographers at the camp had built a huge wooden postcard with a circle cut out of the centre for people to stand behind and pose for a picture. It's in the foyer as you go in, I'm surprised you haven't noticed it yourself?"

"That's clever, I'll have my picture taken and bring you one back as a souvenir."

"Great idea. You'd better get going then, if you're going to be on that train!" Elsie laughed.

TEN

Tom Jackson found a space for Albert's cases. With that being the last of the luggage to be loaded on board, both horse and cart were ready for the off.

"Well, the weather looks to stay fine, for today at least," Tom Jackson joked with Albert.

"Aye, I'm hoping it stays fine all week on the coast too. Mind you, owt's better than being down the pit. What do you say, Amos?" Albert laughed, rubbing the nose of Tom's horse.

Tom looked at his pocket watch. "Well, folks, if that's it for luggage, we'd better be making tracks, the train leaves in 35 minutes."

Tom seized his horse's reins. "Giddy-up, Amos," he said, making a clicking sound with his tongue to gee his horse along. Everyone cheered and followed on at a steady pace behind the cart.

Knowing it was much too far to walk with everyone else down to the station, Elsie stood at her gate and waved as everyone walked past. Stella waved back and blew her grandma a kiss.

"See you next week, Grandma!" Stella bellowed.

Elsie waved until her family were out of sight. She looked across to the pub and noticed Derek hastily shovelling a pile of horse droppings into a bucket.

She shook her head. "By the heck... and a pile of hos' muck means more than waving your daughter off," Elsie tutted to herself.

As she turned to go in, a voice, that seemed to come from nowhere, spoke with humour.

"That'll make his roses grow!" someone said,

laughing.

Elsie turned sharply to see who had spoken and her heart sank. "Norah!"

"There will be fun and laughter awaiting everyone in Skegness by the afternoon, I shouldn't wonder," Norah said playfully.

"Aye, that there will," Elsie said, turning as quickly as she could to make a hasty retreat, but Norah was quite persistent. "I'm sad to be missing camp this year," she added. "But I'm just too busy with the move. We are moving into my parent's old place, you remember where they lived, in that cottage by the toll bar?"

Elsie stopped to listen but remained facing away from Norah. "Aye, I remember it," she said.

"Why don't you pop in for a cuppa one day next week and we can catch up?"

"I can't, Norah, I'm too busy with the jam-making now. I'm in the middle of a batch as we speak, so I must get on." Elsie walked away before Norah made any more suggestions.

"Another time then, maybe?" Norah's voice echoed as Elsie walked up the entry path.

Once inside, Elsie, quite overcome with emotion, pulled a chair out and sat at the table. With her head in her hands, she began to sob.

"Why… why now after all these years must she turn up and want to befriend me again? I've had enough upset without her raking up the past," Elsie mumbled to herself, reaching into her apron pocket for a handkerchief, dabbing tears from her eyes.

****

Jeanie kissed her daughter, and the pair hugged one another. "You have the best time and take good care," Jeanie said.

"I will, Mam," Stella smiled, "I'll see you next week."

"She'll be fine, Jeanie," Sheila interjected, brushing past her sister. "Come on, Stella, let us find some seats."

Sheila and Stella waved goodbye to Jeanie and made their way past the men folk who had formed a chain and were busy passing cases along from off Tom's cart.

"Let's see if we can find ourselves a window seat," Sheila said loudly, trying to speak above the constant hissing of steam coming from the train. She grabbed Stella's hand to hurry her along.

After the last of the cases had been loaded, Albert made his way through the train carriages to find his wife and niece.

"Ahh, there you both are. I knew you would find a window seat, you will certainly get a pleasant view from there," Albert took out his pocket watch. "Two minutes to nine. Well, if the train is on time, I would say we should be sipping afternoon tea by three o'clock," he said with a smile.

At exactly nine o'clock, the guard blew his whistle, clearing the driver to leave the platform. Steam began to hiss and puff and got louder as the train's engine started to clunk and screech into motion. After the driver gave a brief toot from the steam whistle to announce their departure, the engine shifted the train slowly along its track.

"Look, Stella, wave to your mother, she's on the platform," Albert said, trying to point Jeanie out, and although Stella waved, she could not see her mother through the crowd. A few people ran alongside the train, desperate to catch a last glimpse of their loved one before the train rolled past the end of the platform and out of sight, leaving a steamy mist that swirled gently across the now-empty track.

Jeanie left the station and headed back towards the village, calling in at Slater's general store along the way. The bell above the shop doorway announced her arrival, alerting the shopkeeper who was busy arranging tins of fruit salad in a pyramid display.

"Ahh… morning, Mrs Felton. I assume you've been to see them all off on their travels?"

"Yes, I have. Good morning, Mrs Slater," Jeanie smiled. "Please may I have four ounces of ham, two ounces of butter and a pint of milk?" Jeanie passed her ration book over the counter.

Mrs Slater, the shopkeeper, picked up a joint of ham and placed it onto the meat slicer. "It'll be quiet around here for the next week. It's almost like the whole village just up-sticks and moves to Skegness for a week," Mrs Slater laughed.

The shop bell rang again, and another customer walked in.

"Hello, madam, how nice to see you again. How is the unpacking going?" Mrs Slater said to the other customer, as she wrapped Jeanie's ham in brown paper.

"I'm getting there slowly," the woman replied.

"Jeanie, do you remember Mrs Shaw? Although… I guess she will have been away from the village for longer than you would remember. Isn't that right, Mrs Shaw?"

"Call me Norah, please," the woman said, extending her hand out to Jeanie, "I do know your mother, though."

"Ahh… yes. We haven't been acquainted yet, but my sister, Sheila, has mentioned you," Jeanie shook Norah's hand.

Mrs Slater placed Jeanie's goods on the counter. "If that's everything then, that'll be one shilling and tuppence please, love."

Jeanie rummaged through her purse, scraping about enough coins together, and placing them on the counter. "Thank you, Mrs. Slater," Jeanie said, putting the shopping into her bag. "Nice to have met you, Norah," Jeanie said, leaving the shop.

Arriving at her mother's, Jeanie entered through the back door and was greeted with the sweet smell of jam, as her mother busily spooned a fresh batch into various-sized jars.

"That smells delicious, Mam." Jeanie dipped her finger into one of the jars left open to cool and tasted the fruity mixture. "Tastes delicious too."

"Good job it hasn't burned your finger, dipping it into warm jam like that!" Elsie scowled at her daughter.

Jeanie just laughed and kissed her mother's cheek.

"Here, Jeanie, I meant to give you these meat coupons earlier, they are Sheila's. She won't be needing them this week, so you may as well make use of them. Take them to Mrs Bell at the Co-op, or Slater's store, she won't mind you using them either."

"Wonderful, thanks, Mam." Jeanie popped the coupons into her bag. "I have just been into Slater's store. Guess who was in there?"

"There can't be that many folks left in the village today. They are all on the way to the coast, aren't they?" Elsie chuckled.

"It was Norah Shaw. You know the lady who—"

"I know who Norah Shaw is," Elsie interrupted, abruptly. "And? What did she have to say?"

Jeanie frowned. "Nothing… she introduced herself and that was it."

Elsie continued to spoon jam into jars. "Anyway, I assume everyone had a good send-off today? I bet Stella will have a wonderful time."

"She was certainly very excited," Jeanie said, filling the kettle with water. "So, this woman… Norah Shaw, everyone seems to know her, what's her story?"

Elsie briefly closed her eyes and sighed. She wiped her hands on a tea cloth and took a seat at the table.

"There is a story, Jeanie. We were best friends at school, but I suppose we just lost touch. I know she became a midwife because she delivered Sheila. She moved away shortly after that and I've not heard of her since, until now that is. That's about all I can tell you really," Elsie said quite matter-of-factly, hoping her answer would satisfy her daughter, for now at least.

"You were best friends at school? Well now she's moving back to the village, you should both get reacquainted. It would do you—"

"No!" Elsie cut in sharply and Jeanie was quite surprised by her tone.

"Why not, Mam?"

Elsie sighed again. "You know I'm not much for tea and chit-chat, Jeanie, I'd rather keep myself to myself."

"I just thought it would be nice for you to have a friend that you can spend some time with."

"I've got all the friends I want within my family, that's all I need." Elsie got up from the table and felt each jar of jam. "I think these have cooled sufficiently now."

Jeanie looked hard at her mother and frowned. She wondered if there *was* something in Sheila's earlier comment about their mother acting odd at the mention of Norah Shaw.

ELEVEN

By the time the bus had transported the campers from Skegness Railway Station to the miners' holiday camp, everyone was certainly in very jolly spirits. Stella, however, thought that she could happily do without hearing 'Roll out the Barrel' being sung for the eighth time since getting on the bus.

The Green Coats entertainment staff had all lined up outside the holiday camp, smiles on their faces in readiness to greet a fresh week's worth of holidaymakers. As people started to make their way off the bus, through the camp entrance and into the foyer, the Green Coats were handing out entertainment programmes printed in the shape of a suitcase.

Stella recognised a few familiar faces from the previous year, including the camp comic, Slapstick Rick. They all greeted people with merriment and repeated the same ditty over and over as guests walked on through the foyer.

"Ladies, gentlemen, girls, and boys, don't be shy, come make some noise. Let fun and laughter fill the air, enjoy your time without a care."

Sheila rifled through some paperwork as she caught up with Albert and Stella. "Now then," she said in her usual assertive tone. "Here are our keys, Albert, we are in the married couple's chalets, number 212. And, Stella, the single adults' and teenagers' cabins are just at the back of us, you are in number 112. There you go." Sheila handed Stella a key.

"You'll be sharing with a…" Sheila looked at her

paperwork again. "Carole Spencer, do you know of her?"

"Erm, yeah, she's just left school this year, I think."

"And you both get along, do you? I mean you'll both be alright sharing for a week?"

"Oh yes, she's a nice girl. I'm sure we'll be fine, Aunty Sheila."

"Jolly good. Well, shall we all get ourselves settled in then?" Sheila looked at her wristwatch. "Albert, I think you may have been spot on in your estimation for the time of afternoon tea."

Albert smiled. "Did I say tea, dear? I meant a pint of beer." Albert winked at Stella.

"There's plenty of time for a beer or two later on," Sheila said quite strictly.

"Now, Stella, you remember your way around well enough, don't you?"

"Yes, Aunty Sheila, very well."

"Brilliant, then what say we meet you in the dining hall in an hour, and we can gather ourselves over a pot of tea."

****

Stella pushed her key into the lock and turned it. It was her first year staying in a teenagers' cabin and it made her feel very grown up. Previous years had been spent in the children's dormitory with all the other kids, which meant hardly any sleep for the first few nights, and certainly not much chance to read in peace. Stella pushed the door open.

Carole Spencer had already claimed the bed by the window and was busy plaiting her hair.

"Hi, Stella, isn't it?" Carole said, tying a red bow at the base of one plait. "I've left you some space in the cupboard to hang your clothes and there's room in that bottom drawer too."

"Thanks. I've not got that much to put away really," Stella uttered shyly.

"Oh right," Carole looked Stella up and down. "Anyway, you probably won't be seeing me that much, I'll be spending most of my time with my boyfriend, Tommy," Carole said brazenly. "So, you'll probably have the place to yourself…" A smug smile appeared on Carole's face that Stella found quite intimidating.

Hmm…Tommy, most people steered away from him at school. Why would a nice girl like Carole want to get herself involved with him? Stella thought.

"…Anyway, I'll catch you later… or not." Carole winked at Stella before taking a last look at herself in the mirror and heading for the door. "Oh, and do me a favour, if my parents come asking where I am, tell them I'm with Lynne."

"Oh, okay… who is Lynne?" Stella asked, confused.

"Well, I don't know, do I," Carole chuckled to herself as she left, leaving the door to their cabin wide open.

Stella tutted, shut the door, and began taking her things out of her case. Her thoughts turned to Will; she assumed that he and his uncle would be staying in the male quarters of the same type of cabins she and Carole were in. If so, they were on the other side of the married couples' chalets, but she had no idea which one they would be in.

Hoping her path would cross with Will's soon, Stella placed her case under the bed and made her way over to the dining hall to meet her aunt and uncle.

Arriving just in time to see her uncle carry a tea tray over to an empty table, she quickly scanned the dining hall for Will, but there was no sign of him.

"Have you settled in alright, lass?" Albert asked, dropping a sugar lump into his cup.

"Yes, thanks, Uncle Albert, where's Aunty Sheila?"

"She's gone over to the entertainment stand to enter herself in for the 'Ideal Holiday Girl Competition'," he said with a chuckle. He leant nearer to Stella, and whispered, "I think she's a bit old for that really, but don't tell her I said that. Oh, here she comes now!"

Sheila entered the dining hall with a huge smile on her face as she spied the table at which her husband and niece were seated. As she made her way over, her smile turned into a huge grin. She sat down, and Albert poured her some tea.

"So, my dear, have you put your name down then?" Albert asked.

"Don't be silly, Albert, I'm far too old for that. No…I've entered you for the knobbly knees competition."

A stream of tea squirted its way out of Albert's mouth. "What?" he snorted, quickly dabbing his mouth with his handkerchief. "Knobbly knees competition. I could not possibly… and besides, my knees aren't in the slightest bit knobbly. Not enough to win a damn competition anyway!"

Stella giggled. "Sorry, Uncle Albert, but the look on your face just then was hilarious."

"Someone has to take the title from Jimmy Parkin," Sheila laughed, stirring her tea. "And for the sake of Dad's memory, that someone has to be you, my dear."

Stella giggled again, and Albert sighed. "Well, I guess if you put it like that, then I suppose I have no choice."

"Of course you don't," Sheila laughed. "Now then, Stella, I assume you've settled yourself into your cabin alright?"

"Yes, perfectly, thanks, Aunty."

"Good, do you have your entertainment programme to hand?" Sheila asked, selecting a custard cream biscuit from the plate.

Stella waved her programme and smiled. "Right here, Aunty."

"Excellent. So, your uncle and I have been discussing things, and we have a suggestion of sorts."

Stella frowned. "What's that then, Aunty?"

"Well, we didn't think you would want to be following us around all week, so… we thought if you want to spend time with friends, we will allow you to."

Stella wasn't one for friends, except Will, of course. There wasn't anyone else she was too bothered about spending time with.

"Of course, you will still be meeting us for your meals and if you want to join us at any time then… look, I have marked a star on the entertainment programme against the things we are likely to be doing during the week. So, you can easily find us if you want to."

Sheila exchanged programmes with Stella. "It's up to you, we want you to enjoy your time, not be dragged around with us."

Stella nodded, she had never really been given options before and quite liked the feeling of being given a choice. "Thank you, Aunty Sheila."

Sheila grabbed another biscuit. "Well, I speak on behalf of Albert and myself when I say it is about trust. We think you can be trusted, Stella, and that's what growing up is about."

Stella smiled. "Thank you, Aunty Sheila."

"Right, that's settled then," Sheila said, dunking the last bit of biscuit in her tea.

"Anyway, there's plenty of activities taking place this afternoon, including the first match of the ladies' tug-of-war, so I am off to prepare myself for that," Sheila said, as she drained the contents of her teacup. "And, Albert, the match starts in half an hour, I'll expect to see you on the sidelines cheering me on."

As always, Sheila's exit was as rapid as her entrance, which left Albert and Stella gazing at one another in disbelief.

"Well, I'd better get myself over there, because this, I've got to see," Albert laughed.

After finishing the last of his tea, Albert followed his wife.

Stella giggled to herself, then suddenly, as she realised she was left sitting on her own, a wave of loneliness rose inside her. She searched the hall for Will, but there was hardly anyone else left, as most people had either gone off to join in with the contests or cheer their folks on. With her aunty Sheila in mind, Stella decided that watching her tug on a rope would surely provide a certain level of fun not to be missed. She was about to leave the dining hall when a familiar voice called her name. It was Will. Stella's heart fluttered a little and the wave of loneliness instantly disappeared.

TWELVE

Will handed Stella an ice cream. "You'll have to be quick with it, the sun is melting it away already!" Will said, looking down at the little droplets of ice cream that had dripped onto his shorts.

Stella took the ice cream from Will and passed him a handkerchief. "Here, use this."

"Thank you," Will blotted the smatterings of ice cream from his shorts. "Shall we take a walk along the beach?"

The sea air smelled salty and fresh, and there was a gentle breeze coming off the water. Will and Stella trudged hand in hand along the expanse of soft, golden sand. They had walked for quite a distance before Will stopped suddenly.

"Let's go for a paddle," he said excitedly, awaiting Stella's reaction.

Stella sat down on the sand and removed her shoes and socks before quickly jumping to her feet. "Come on then, I bet I'm in the sea before you."

"You're on," Will rushed to take his shoes off. He tried to remove his socks whilst still standing, but he could not balance on the delicate sand and ended up in a heap.

Meanwhile, Stella was already on her way. Will had about caught up with her as she entered the sea.

"Oh, my goodness, it's freezing," Stella yelled, running back away from the water.

Will grabbed a hold of Stella's hand. "You're not getting out of it that easily, a bet is a bet," he laughed, gently towing her back in.

Together, they held hands and jumped the waves as each one came crashing before them, sending a salty spray into the air. Eventually, they both tired and gave in to their merriment. Still, hand in hand, they walked back along the sand to where they had left their belongings. The grains beneath their feet still held a certain warmth from the day, and before them the sun began to set, its burnt orange and gold seemed to stretch everywhere across the sky.

They picked up their shoes and socks and steadily made their way back along the promenade to the miners' camp. They passed a small, grassed area that had been made into a decorative feature with a huge pit wheel in the centre, flanked on either side with an array of seasonal flowers. A wooden bench had been placed in front of the wheel and the pair sat down on it.

Stella noticed a small brass plaque fastened to the backrest and read out what it said.

"Fondest memories of Jack and Hilda, who spent many a happy time here at the Derbyshire Miners' Holiday Centre." Stella gazed into the distance. "What a lovely thing to do."

"We should make this our place to meet up with each other. Look, there's a clock tower over there too," Will pointed to a small tower-like, stone structure with a clock face on the front, and again, a decorative feature abundant with colourful flowers.

"Good idea," Stella said with a smile.

The two of them spent the rest of the early evening watching as other campers busily made their way around camp. Eventually, as the hot afternoon sun disappeared, a cool breeze began to wrap itself around Stella, making her shiver a little. Will instinctively put his arm around her, drawing her nearer to him. An elderly couple passed by hand in hand and smiled warmly at the two of them, as if they had recognised themselves in the youngsters they saw before them.

****

The following morning, Sheila, Albert, and Stella sat at the breakfast table. Two things filled the dining hall, the smell of bacon frying and the low-level hum of everyone's chatter. Albert poured milk from a jug into teacups whilst Sheila followed suit by pouring tea.

"How was your first night, Stella, did you sleep alright?"

"Yes, thank you, Aunty, perfectly."

"Jolly good, and you're getting along okay with Carole?"

"Yes… fine," Stella tried to answer over a mouthful of bacon.

She omitted, however, to tell her aunty that she was certain she had been alone though, since Carole's bed had not been slept in.

"Good. Well, Albert and I are going on a coach trip today around Lincoln, but first, we'll be going to the Sunday church service over in the theatre. You're welcome to join us on the trip, I believe there's still room on the coach?"

"Erm… I think I'll stay here, Aunty. The teens' competitions begin today so—"

"Oh, what fun," Sheila cut in. "What do you have your name down for?"

"Nothing," Stella giggled. "I'm just planning on watching them, that's all."

"Oh, come now, Stella, I can see you winning the egg and spoon race quite easily," Albert joked.

Stella laughed. "I don't think so, Uncle, not unless the winner is the one who drops the egg the most."

After breakfast, Stella sat on the bench by the pit wheel, with her notebook and pencil in hand, working on a sea-themed poem. She looked up at the clock tower, twenty past ten. She and Will had arranged to meet at ten o'clock and she had already been there since half past nine. Jotting random words down in her notebook, Stella had already formed sentences that she could then arrange into verses. She found it easy to lose herself in her writing, just as she could read an enjoyable book. So much so, she hadn't noticed Will standing in front of her.

"I'm sorry I'm late, Stella, I've hardly slept," Will yawned.

"Goodness, why?"

"Well, it would appear that Uncle Jed snores. The man sounds like a darn steam train!"

"Oh dear," Stella giggled. "Have you managed to get some breakfast? The bacon was delicious."

"No, I didn't want you to wonder where I was, so I came straight here."

"You can't miss the opportunity of sampling that bacon, Will. I tell you what, I'll hang on here whilst you go and eat."

"But you've been waiting long enough already."

"It's fine, honestly. I've been working on a poem," Stella wafted her notebook and smiled proudly.

"Well, I am rather hungry," Will rubbed his stomach.

"Off you go then, before they stop serving. I'll be here when you've finished."

Will gave Stella a peck on the cheek and scooted off but in the wrong direction.

Stella shouted after him. "Will! You're going the wrong way," she said, pointing in the direction of the dining hall. "It's that way. You only need to follow your nose."

Will rolled his eyes. "This place is like a rabbit warren."

Helping himself to the last three rashers of bacon, Will slid his tray along the counter and added a fried egg and tomato along with two slices of toast, butter, and a pot of tea.

"You're cutting it fine this morning, young man," one of the catering women said, as she collected pots and wiped the tables.

Will just smiled at the woman and found himself a seat by the window. He swiftly tucked into his breakfast and looked through the window, as people were happily strolling about their business. Suddenly, he noticed his Uncle Jed rush by and enter the dining hall. He turned to see the catering woman shaking her head and his uncle looking up to the ceiling in dismay. It would seem he *was* too late for breakfast.

"Uncle Jed!" Will shouted, beckoning his uncle

over.

"I see you were late too, lad," Jed said, taking a seat at the table. "Although, not quite as late as me, it would appear."

Jed rubbed the stubble that had formed on his chin as he contemplated the bacon on Will's plate.

"Is that nice? Because it looks wonderful."

Will smiled wryly. "It's delicious… looks like you might be in luck, though," Will said, nodding in the direction of the kitchen. The catering lady was making her way over with a tray of tea and toast and placed it down in front of Jed.

"Ahh, you're an absolute diamond, missus, thank you so very much."

"Aye… well don't make a habit of it," she replied, with a coy smile.

Jed poured himself a cup of tea and buttered his toast. "It's not like me to get up late like that, I think I must have slept a bit *too* well."

An incredulous look appeared on Will's face, which he quickly covered with his teacup.

"So… lad. It's the knobbly knees competition this afternoon and my mate, Jimmy, will be doing his best to keep his title," Jed's laugh echoed around the now-empty dining hall. "Are you coming along to watch, unless, of course, you think your knees would make good contenders?"

"Erm… I don't think so, Uncle Jed, no… on both counts, that is."

"Ahh well, if you change your mind, lad, half past seven this evening in the entertainment lounge. Now then… how's about letting your poor old, starving uncle have a piece of that there bacon to put between these here slices of toast?"

****

Stella put her notebook and pencil away in her bag. As she looked up, she noticed her aunt and uncle making their way across the forecourt, to get on the coach bound for a trip around the Lincolnshire countryside. As the coach left, Stella waved them off. Sheila must have noticed Stella at the last minute because she waved back just in time before disappearing out of Stella's view.

As the coach had left, Stella also noticed Carole sitting on a wall with her boyfriend, Tommy. She wondered where Carole had spent the night, then quickly figured out that she would not have to think too much about what the answer to that would be.

Before long, Will arrived back at the pit wheel where Stella was patiently waiting, and the two of them decided that as it was such a beautifully sunny day, they would spend it on the beach.

The stretch of golden sand behind the miners' camp was scattered with row upon row of deck chairs, as it would seem everyone had the same idea.

"What about there?" Will pointed to an area of sand without a deck chair. Stella nodded in agreement. She took her crocheted blanket out of her bag and laid it on the sand.

"Ahh, that's the blanket from your den, isn't it?"

Stella laughed. "You are very observant, aren't you? I often take it places with me. It comes in handy."

Once they had settled themselves comfortably on the sand, Stella noticed a family close by. She smiled as the father spent a good few minutes wrestling with his deck chair, eventually managing to get it assembled and settled down into it. With beads of sweat forming on his head, his wife took a handkerchief out of her bag and knotted each corner, placing the hankie on her husband's balding head to protect it from the sun. Meanwhile, he took off his shoes and socks and rolled his trousers up to just below his knees and his shirt sleeves up to just above his elbows. Stella saw a broad smile appear as he turned his face toward the sun, relishing the opportunity to catch a few rays. His tranquillity, however, was short-lived, as his young daughter had other ideas in mind, in the form of sandcastle building. Although it was clear that he was quite happy to be resting, it pleased Stella no end to see that he was just as happy to get down in the sand and join his daughter in creating the perfect sandcastle.

It made her think of times gone by, spent with her grandpa, and the many sandcastles they had made over the years, but it also made her think of the relationship she had with her father, and how that kind of connection never had, and never would, happen.

"Stella, are you okay, you seem in the middle of a daydream," Will asked, squinting his eyes from the sun.

"Sorry, yes, I'm fine. I was just watching the little girl building a sandcastle with her dad over there. It reminded me of my grandpa and me when we won the sandcastle building contest one year."

Will patted Stella's arm warmly. "It's good that you have so many lovely memories of him. Tell me about the contest."

Stella smiled as she recalled the thought. "We made this big donkey," Stella raised her hand to show how tall it was. "Grandpa kept tipping sandcastles out of buckets, and everyone wondered what he was doing. But then he started sculpting the wet sand to form the shape of a donkey," Stella laughed. "It had very short legs, but it was brilliant fun, and you could tell it was supposed to be a donkey."

Will laughed, "I would have loved to have seen that."

"All the other kids and their dads had made these huge castles with moats around and paper windmills. And there we were with this donkey. He even sat my doll on top of its back."

"It certainly sounds like your grandpa was a lot of fun to be around," Will said softly.

"He won the knobbly knees competition for three years on the trot too," Stella chuckled. "It's funny, he only entered in the first place because my grandma encouraged it, and then because he kept winning, he thought he was invincible, until last year when someone else knocked him off the top spot."

"Jimmy Parkin?" Will exclaimed.

"That's him, how did you know that?"

"He's my uncle's mate from Creswell Colliery and according to the conversation on the train over here, he fully intends on defending his title again," Will chuckled.

"In that case, we shall have to go and watch it later. My Aunty Sheila has signed my uncle up for it. He wasn't best pleased, but I don't think he's got any choice but to go along with it!" Stella laughed.

"Stella, I hope you don't mind me asking, but you never really speak about your dad very much. Did he not come with the family to the miners' camp?"

Stella sighed and looked out towards the horizon, as though she was hoping the sky would answer for her. She wasn't sure how to tell Will about the relationship she had with her father. What she did know, however, was that if she and Will were going to continue seeing one another, she would have to tell him what kind of person her father was. And she didn't want to spoil their time together by going into detail about him.

"It is quite a long story, Will, and I shall tell you about him, just not today. Now then, I believe it's my turn for the ice cream!"

THIRTEEN

The entertainment lounge was packed with holidaymakers watching the various competitions that family and friends had entered. The atmosphere was bubbling over, and the alcohol was certainly flowing. Will and Stella arrived at the lounge to everyone cheering for a gentleman who was on stage, bending an iron bar with his bare hands. Will took hold of Stella's hand and guided her through the bustling lounge, over towards a table where his uncle was sitting with some other people.

Jed beckoned to his nephew. "Will, lad, come and join us," he said, looking beyond his nephew at Stella.

"Uncle Jed, this is my friend, Stella."

"Pleased to meet you, missy. Here, take a seat." Jed pulled out a chair and gestured for Stella to sit down.

"What's going on here then, Uncle?" Will asked.

"This fella is the world champion strong man. He's just bent that beggar with his bare hands," Jed chortled, pointing to the now bent iron bar lying on the floor.

"And now he's trying to smash his record for breaking six-inch nails in less than five seconds. The man's a marvel."

"World champion? So, he travels the world doing this then?" Will asked with great interest.

"Nahh, lad, he's just a ruddy miner from Ripley pit," Jed roared with laughter.

With all haste, the compère ran onto the stage. "Ladies and gentlemen, boys and girls, please put your hands together for the world's number one strong man."

The audience cheered again, and the gentleman gathered up the broken nails and iron bar he had bent into the shape of the letter U. He bowed courteously and celebrated his triumph by fist-pumping as he left the stage.

"Now then, ladies and gentlemen, the moment you have all been waiting for. Please welcome on stage this year's knobbly knees contenders."

The audience was in raptures as a dozen or so men made their way up onto the stage. They stood in a line facing the audience with their trousers rolled up high enough to expose their knees. The compère walked along the line of men, accompanied by an attractive young lady whom he announced as Rita. He asked each man to introduce themselves, whilst Rita made a performance of inspecting each pair of knees.

Stella recognised Jed's mate, Jimmy Parkin in the line-up, the man who took the title from her grandfather the year before. Then she spotted her uncle, Albert, who she thought seemed awkward standing there with stage lights blaring into his face. She scanned the lounge for her aunty and eventually noticed her sitting on the other side of the room with a few other women, each of them cheering their menfolk on.

The compère engaged with the audience, encouraging them to shout out for their favourite pair of knobbly knees. Rita selected a contender, pecked him on the cheek and gestured for him to leave the stage. She did the same with each one in turn until eventually only three men were left: Albert, Jimmy, and another man.

"Ladies and gentlemen, we have our three finalists, but who will win this week's contest? The decision is yours… so come on… let's hear a huge cheer for your favourite."

The compère motivated the audience to cheer loudly as he raised each man's arm. "Will it be Albert Marks from Kilburn Colliery, or will it be Bryan Peters from Denby Colliery, or, folks, will it be our current champion Jimmy Parkin from Creswell Colliery."

Rita and the compère spoke into each other's ears, clearly deciding between them, as to who had received the loudest cheer.

"Ladies and gentlemen, I think we have our winner," the compére said with a smile.

The room fell silent, as everyone waited with great anticipation to hear the outcome. "The winner of the knobbly knees contest for this week is… Jimmy Parkin!"

Everyone in the room cheered and applauded. Rita gave Albert and Bryan a consolation prize in the form of a kiss on the cheek and once again gestured for them to leave the stage. Stella noticed a look of relief on Albert's face as he made his way back to his table, where Sheila greeted him with a hug. Meanwhile, Rita draped a sash around Jimmy with the words 'knobbly knees champ' blazoned across the front. Of course, he also received a peck on the cheek from Rita and the contest was over.

Jimmy, however, thought it would be a clever idea

to scoop Rita up in his arms and kiss her on the cheek, which by the obvious look of distaste on Rita's face, was not particularly well received. After he had finished making a fool of himself, Jimmy made his way over to the table, grabbed his pint of beer and knocked the whole lot back in one go, before sitting down with a thud on the chair opposite Stella.

"There you go, what did I tell you, eh? Easy as pie. It was simple last year taking the title from that daft old fool, but this year, well there was some tough competition I think." Jimmy howled with laughter along with one or two others at the table following suit. Stella, however, was less than impressed and Will could see it in her face. She never said a word though, she just scowled icily at Jimmy.

"Well, I think it's your round, Jimmy," Jed winked, wafting his empty glass under Jimmy's nose.

After taking everyone's drinks order and appointing Will's help, Jimmy scuttled off to the bar. Stella felt a little awkward and tried to relieve her shyness by casually scanning the room and biting at her bottom lip. Jed noticed her apprehension and tried to put her at ease.

"So, missy, how are you enjoying the miners' camp?"

"It's great fun, sir, thank you."

"You haven't come along with us Creswell lot though, have you?"

"No sir, my uncle works at Kilburn Pit."

"Ah, I see. Well listen, dunna mind Jimmy, he's had one too many and he's all mouth and trousers," Jed laughed, just as Jimmy arrived back with a tray full of beer.

"Who's all mouth and trousers?" Jimmy asked, slopping a pint glass down in front of Jed, and dousing him with ale.

"Ahh… you are! Look at what you've done now, yer mucky beggar!" Jed snarled, grabbing for his handkerchief to mop up the spillage, whilst Jimmy's infectious belly laugh enticed everyone else at the table into fits of laughter. "Sit down will you, you daft ha'porth," Jed continued, using his handkerchief to mop the spillage up, whilst all Jimmy could do was roar with laughter.

"Take no notice of Jed, he's a miserable old bugger when he wants to be. Anyway lass, what's yer name?" Jimmy asked, turning his attention to Stella.

Stella, who was not particularly enthusiastic about being drawn into conversation with Jimmy but deciding it best to remain courteous, answered briefly.

"Stella Felton."

"Well, Fella Stelton… what brings thee… to be here… with Will?" Jimmy asked, slurring his words.

Stella did not know how to answer. Thankfully, Will stepped in.

"Stella is my girlfriend—"

"Girlfriend?" Jimmy teased. "Blimey, girlfriend, eh? Does that mean we'll be hearing bedding wells soon… I mean wedding bells?" Jimmy slurred his words again. "Has she got a rich father? I hope she has, Will lad."

Stella was beginning to feel less than comfortable

with Jimmy's behaviour, but as Will seemed to be handling the situation, she remained quiet.

"Stella is hoping to be an author," Will announced proudly.

Jimmy almost choked on his drink, spewing a spray of beer from his mouth in spiteful laughter.

"Author? What need do we have for women to be writing owt? Will lad, you seriously need to have a quiet word with this one."

Everyone at the table fell silent as Jimmy continued jibing Stella. "You see, lass, women… need only be in two places…" Jimmy held up two fingers. "The kitchen and the bedroom," he tipped his head back and roared with laughter. Stella was so infuriated, she stood up and slammed her hands down on the table.

"You, sir, are the most ignorant, pig-headed halfwit I have ever had the misfortune of meeting," Stella fumed, rolling her hands into fists to stop them from shaking.

"Oh, and whilst we're having a less than pleasant conversation, the daft old fool from whom you took the knobbly knees title was my grandpa, and he passed away not even three weeks since. So now who is the daft old fool?"

Stella took off out of the lounge, leaving everyone in shock. Will jumped up out of his seat and scowled at Jimmy before rushing off to catch up with Stella.

Jed, being less than impressed, scuffed Jimmy around the back of his head, sending his flat cap flying. "You stupid bloody oaf. What did you say that to her for?"

"What? I was only jesting," Jimmy bent forward to pick up his cap and almost fell forward off his chair.

Jed grabbed his collar and pulled him back. "All that coming from a bloke whose missus brings home more dough than he does!" Jed shook his head in disbelief.

Will stood outside the entertainment lounge trying to decide which out of the three possible paths Stella could have taken. It was beginning to get dark, but lampposts lit up each path. Will scratched at his head as he looked from one path to another in wonder.

"Place is like a darn maze," he muttered to himself and took the middle path. Before long, he realised that the path led to their meeting place by the pit wheel and was relieved to see Stella sitting on the bench.

"There you are," Will sat down beside her and put his arm around her. "I'm sorry you had to hear all that. The man's a complete idiot."

"You do not need to apologise, Will. The words came out of his mouth, not yours." Stella wiped away her tears.

Will bowed his head and then looked up at the starry sky. "Let's not allow him to spoil things."

He got up off the bench and walked across the green. He turned towards Stella and outstretched his arms.

"It's a beautiful evening. Shall we take a walk along the promenade?" Stella nodded and Will began to walk off, but in the wrong direction.

"Will… it's that way," Stella laughed, pointing to the opposite path.

"I knew that… honestly," he joked.

Stella jumped up off the bench and caught up with Will, and they strolled off together hand in hand.

As they walked, the sound of voices and laughter from the miners' camp slowly muffled and it became clear that nobody else had the foresight to enjoy a stroll along the promenade. After the bustle of daytime activity on the beach, all that could be heard was the sound of the waves crashing against the shoreline close to the promenade.

"It's so peaceful," Stella said, nestling in against Will's shoulder. "I don't think I've ever listened to the sound of the waves crashing before."

"There is certainly something very relaxing about it. Are you okay now?"

"Yes," Stella nodded.

"You certainly gave him what for. I thought you were amazing."

Stella hung her head. "He's right though, isn't he."

"Whatever do you mean?"

"When he said, 'What need is there for women to write', he's right. I mean what chance do I stand… really? It's difficult enough if you know how to get ahead, and I don't, so, I may as well not bother."

"Stella, you must not think like that. You stand as much chance as anyone else."

"Anyone else that isn't female."

"No, anyone else, *regardless*."

"Okay, you name four female authors, and I'll wager, that for each one you name, I can name four male ones."

"Crikey… okay, so… Enid—"

"Other than her," Stella cut in, rolling her eyes.

Will bit the side of his cheek trying to think.

"See, you can't think of—"

"Jane Austen!" Will said suddenly.

"I did mean female authors who are still alive, Will."

"Oh. Alright then… Agatha Christie," Will added confidently. "Look, Stella, please don't put yourself through this." Will turned to face Stella and put his hands on her shoulders.

"You are the most determined, confident and fearless person I have ever come across," he said, as he placed his finger under Stella's chin, bringing her face up towards his.

His voice was now at a whisper. "I think you could achieve anything you set your heart on. And if I believe it, and your grandpa believed it, then maybe you should too?"

A single tear rolled down Stella's cheek, as Will gently pressed his face into hers. Stella happily allowed her lips to find his and softly they experienced their very first kiss.

FOURTEEN

Stella finished reading to the end of a chapter in the Enid Blyton book Will had given her. She snuggled down under the covers and smiled as she thought about Will. It had been the first time she had been kissed that way and was surprised at how natural it had felt. A warm, cosy feeling passed through her body as she closed her eyes to find sleep. She was about to nod off when a very loud knock at her cabin door made her jump. Being cautious, Stella shouted to ask who it was.

"It's Mr Spencer, Carole's father. Is Carole in there?" There was a cross tone to his voice.

Stella looked over at Carole's empty bed and wondered what she was going to say to him. Remembering what Carole had told her to say if her parents came looking for her, Stella answered hastily.

"I think she's still out with her friend."

"What friend?"

"Erm… Lynne?" Stella said dubiously.

"You two better not have any young men in there with you!" he shouted, knocking on the door again.

Stella began to feel unsettled with the situation she suddenly found herself in and didn't know what to say.

"Open this door please," Mr Spencer demanded, banging his fist against the cabin door.

Stella jumped up out of bed, grabbed her cardigan and wrapped it around her shoulders.

"Coming, Mr Spencer," Stella gingerly opened the door and Carole's father charged through. He gave

Stella a menacing look, that reminded her of her father, as he quickly scanned the room, even checking underneath the beds. Upon realising that there was only one way in and out of the cabin, Mr Spencer eventually began to calm himself.

"Have you seen my daughter this evening?"

"No, sir, I haven't."

"I noticed you earlier, with that young man. You were sitting on a bench by the pit wheel."

"I wasn't doing anything wrong, sir," Stella said meekly.

Mr Spencer looked at his watch, "I told her to be back in her cabin by half past ten. It then comes to my attention that she was seen on the beach with some youth. The beach, at this hour of the night!"

"I don't know anything about that, sir... honestly."

Mr Spencer stared hard at Stella. "Who is your father? I wonder if he knows his daughter is hanging around in dark places with young men?"

"I'm not here with my parents, sir, I'm with my aunt and uncle and I arrived back here at half past ten, as I promised them I would."

A look of disdain appeared on Mr Spencer's face, and he turned up his nose. "Hmm...well, even so, what is their chalet number?"

Stella sighed, wondering what trouble this would put her in. "212," she answered reluctantly.

Without another word, Mr Spencer left, leaving Stella feeling most displeased with the situation in which she felt Carole had placed her.

The following morning, Stella woke with a start

upon hearing a key turning in the lock of the cabin door. Carole walked in with a face like thunder and Stella could tell she had been crying.

"Carole, are you okay?" Stella asked, sitting up in bed.

"Thanks to you, no I'm not." Carole dragged her case out from under the bed and began to randomly shove clothes into it.

"What do you mean, thanks to me?" Stella asked quite sharply.

"I told you to tell my parents I was with Lynne. Now I have to go home early."

"I did say that, but your father demanded I open the door. He would have had the whole camp awake if I hadn't. He said someone had seen you on the beach with Tommy."

Carole sat down on Stella's bed. "I'm sorry, I know it's not your fault. Thank you for trying to cover for me and I'm sorry if I've got you into any trouble."

Stella was unsure what to say and just patted Carole's arm affectionately. Carole smiled halfheartedly. She stood up and grabbed some clothes out of the wardrobe. She threw a pair of trousers and a top onto the bed and began to change out of the clothes she had been wearing all night.

As Carole unzipped her dress, Stella noticed two striped, red marks across the lower half of her back and instinctively knew all too well what would have caused them. Stella closed her eyes in despair, climbed out of bed, and gently tapped Carole on her shoulder.

"Carole," Stella whispered softly.

As Carole turned round, Stella threw her arms around her and whispered, "If you need to talk…"

Carole pulled from Stella's embrace and stared hard at her. "What do you mean?"

"The marks on your back. He beats you, doesn't he?" Stella said gently.

Carole nodded, and tears began to stream down her face. "I hate him, Stella. I can't wait to get away from him," Carole cried, burying her face into Stella's shoulder as she sobbed.

Stella held Carole close and gave her the time she needed to let out her emotions, then eventually, once Carole's tears began to subside, Stella withdrew and guided Carole to sit on the bed with her. "You see, I know because my father does the same to me."

Carole was quite taken aback. "I really can't imagine that you would ever do anything to deserve a beating Stella, surely?"

Stella hung her head. "Probably not, no. Sometimes all I have to do is be in the house when he is in one of his moods, and that's enough to bring his blood up."

"Good lord, that's awful," Carole said, putting her hand to her mouth. "If I think about it, I suppose I've deserved every beating I've had."

Stella shook her head. "No Carole, nobody deserves to be beaten. Nobody."

Carole hugged Stella. "Thanks for everything, Stella. I must go, my parents will be waiting for me. Looks like you really have got the place to yourself now," she said, as she opened the door. "Take care of yourself, eh, and maybe I'll see you around."

Stella nodded and smiled warmly, before merely opening and closing her hand in a simple farewell. *Time to face the music,* Stella thought, as she grabbed her clothes and got herself dressed.

****

The dining hall was busy with people enjoying a cooked breakfast, and Stella noticed Sheila and Albert were already sitting by the window tucking into theirs. Although she knew in her heart she had done nothing wrong, she was dreading what they would say. What had Mr Spencer said to them? Would they make her go home too? Butterflies tickled her stomach as she walked over to where they were seated. Sheila was the first to notice Stella's arrival.

"Morning, Stella love, how are you?"

"I'm good thanks, Aunty," Stella replied quite dubiously, wondering when the bombshell would hit.

"Are you not having any breakfast this morning, lass?" Albert asked.

"Oh, erm... yes. I just thought I'd come over and see how you both are first."

Sheila looked a little stern, "Well, I suppose you could say I'm disappointed with how things turned out last night," she said, looking at Albert over her teacup.

"Well, I was going to speak with you about that—"

Albert cut in, "Actually, Stella, we're *both* extremely disappointed."

"I'm sorry, but whatever you've been told—"

Albert cut in again, "I think I deserved to win that knobbly knees competition," he laughed.

"There's always next year, Albert. Now then, Stella, you were saying?"

"Pardon?" Stella said, feeling relieved.

"You started to say… 'whatever you've been told'. Told what?"

"Oh that, I was going to say, whatever you've been told, I thought you had the best knobbly knees, and you should have most definitely won!"

"Oh, you watched the contest then? We never saw you. Mind you, it was so busy in there last night, wasn't it? Who were you with?"

"Oh, just some friends," Stella said quickly. "Well, I think I will get myself some breakfast, Aunty. I'm starving."

Stella jumped up out of her seat and raced across to the breakfast counter before she could say anything else to incriminate herself.

Stella arrived at the end of the food counter, breakfast tray in hand, when she noticed the Spencers in the foyer, with their luggage. They were sitting waiting for a bus to arrive to take them to the station. Stella assumed that since Mr Spencer hadn't been to see her aunt and uncle, Carole must have explained to her father that there was no wrongdoing on Stella's part, and for that, she was most grateful. Feeling relieved, she took her tray back over to sit with her aunt and uncle, painfully aware, that at some point, she would have to find the best way to explain why Carole and her family had left, and that she would now be alone in her cabin.

"So, what are your plans for the day, Aunty?" Stella

asked, tucking into her breakfast.

"Well, this morning I have the second round of the women's tug-of-war contest and then I think we're going to spend a lazy afternoon on the beach. How about you?"

"Oh, I'm entering the balloon competition," Stella said jovially. "And then I think I'm going to try my luck in the penny arcade."

"Ah yes, the balloon competition, I remember. Don't you put your name on a gas-filled balloon and send it off?"

"Yes, and if yours travels furthest, you win! Last year, somebody's balloon got as far as Holland, and he won 10 pounds. Can you imagine that?"

"Well, that all sounds like a lot of fun, Stella, and, if it isn't, you can always come and join us."

"Thank you, Aunty."

Albert rummaged through his pocket and slid three pennies in Stella's direction. "Here, perhaps if you win big in the arcade, we can all stay another week!" he laughed.

****

Stella's heart missed a beat when she saw that Will was already waiting for her on the bench. He looked up, waved, and smiled. There was something about his smile that melted her very being.

"Hello," he said, jumping up off the bench.

He went straight to her, put his hand against the small of her back and drew her close. Their eyes locked in a moment and then he kissed her. Stella felt a spark run through her whole body. A group of young lads walked by and one of them gave a wolf whistle that made Stella pull away from Will's embrace.

"Ignore them, they're probably jealous," Will smiled. "Shall we go and see about this balloon competition?"

Will and Stella wrote their names on a brown luggage label and attached it to a balloon. They were about to let it go when the lady in charge of the competition suddenly stopped them.

"Hang on, you two, you'd better put an address on there, because if you win, we won't know who you are," she said, handing Stella a pen.

Stella handed the pen to Will and suggested that he put his address on the label and then together they released their balloon into the sky. The wind at once took it off in an easterly direction and they stood and watched it until it was out of sight.

"I wonder how far it will get," Stella said excitedly.

"It might get as far as America!"

Stella shook her head playfully. "You aren't very good with directions, are you?"

"What do you mean?" Will said, a look of bewilderment on his face.

"Well, going off in that direction, I should certainly think not. America is west of here."

Will looked up toward the sky and frowned before suddenly realising what he'd said. "I knew that really!" he said mischievously.

"Hmm…course you did," Stella mumbled, rolling her eyes with a certain scepticism.

The pair made their way through the holiday camp

and as they entered the reception area,

Stella noticed there was some activity surrounding a huge display in the corner of the foyer. She realised it was the big wooden postcard where her grandma and grandpa had been photographed the year before. The camp photographers were organising people to go over and have their pictures taken.

"Look, Will," Stella pointed at the display. "We must go and get ours taken."

There seemed to be a lot of interest in the display and quite a queue had formed. Eventually though, it was their turn.

"You go first," Stella said, prodding Will in the ribs.

"Why don't we go together?" Will asked with a smile.

"Excellent idea, young man," the photographer said, beckoning them both over excitedly. "Now, all you need do is stand behind the postcard and look happy. Easy as pie," the photographer chuckled.

Once they had positioned themselves, the photographer took a few snapshots.

"All done, pop back in a couple of days and they'll be ready for you."

The pair smiled at one another and headed off to try their luck at the penny arcades.

FIFTEEN

"Eight shillings and sixpence, wow! I think we should quit whilst we're ahead," Will said with excitement."

"Good idea. Shall we get a bus into Skegness for the rest of the day?"

Will nodded, grabbed Stella's hand, and led her out of the arcade. They did not have to wait long for the bus and were soon on their way to the town.

In all the years that Stella had been holidaying at the miners' camp, she had never *actually* been into Skegness itself. The town was bustling with locals, going about their daily business, and holidaymakers enjoying the various attractions on offer. Will and Stella stood on the pier looking down at the long stretch of golden sand. The beach was packed with families enjoying the continuing spell of pleasant weather.

"I don't think there's a spot of sand free down there," Stella remarked.

"Then let's go and check the fairground out," Will pointed over in the direction of an enormous wooden construction - the Big Dipper!

As they neared the structure, they watched as people in assorted coloured metal cars giggled hysterically as they zipped around a rail track with great speed.

"Wow, I'm impressed, that looks great fun," Will said with a childish grin. "Well, shall we?"

Stella however seemed less than enthusiastic, "I've never been on anything like that before, it goes so fast and climbs up so high. I'm not sure."

"You'll be fine… c'mon, you'll enjoy it!" Will grabbed Stella's hand and hauled her over to the entrance of the ride.

Stella didn't have much chance to put any more thought into it, as they were soon seated along with three other riders in a blue car with the number five painted on the side. The car jolted along the track and steadily began to make its ascent to the top. Before long, it had reached its peak, giving everyone a fantastic aerial view over Skegness.

"Goodness. Will, look down there, everything looks so small from up here," Stella said.

She had hardly got the words out of her mouth before the car suddenly jolted forward again, this time to begin its hair-raising descent, which left her with a strange sensation that hit the pit of her stomach so that she felt it had been left behind. Just as she began to fear that her breakfast might reappear, the ride was over. The car ground to a halt, just at the place where they had boarded it, and where another group of people waited excitedly for their turn.

With a spring in her step, Stella exited first. Following on with a little less enthusiasm, however, were her fellow riders, each of whom stepped off in turn with very pale looks on their faces, including Will, who was cupping his stomach as though it was going to suddenly leave his body.

"I take it you're not quite so impressed after all?" Stella said, trying to suppress a giggle.

Will put his hand over his mouth, "I think I'm

going to be sick."

The ride operator threw back his head and laughed, revealing several missing teeth.

"Nonsense," he chortled. "All you need is a doughnut and you'll be right as rain in no time." The man nodded in the direction of a little wooden hut selling a whole manner of all things sweet.

"Shall we?" Stella said quite flippantly.

"I'm not sure," Will shook his head.

"You'll be fine… c'mon, you'll enjoy it!" Stella said sarcastically, grabbing Will's hand with the same purposefulness that Will had enforced moments earlier.

As they waited their turn in the queue, Will's colour began to return. A huge grin appeared on Stella's face, and she couldn't help but giggle.

"What?" Will asked suspiciously.

Stella took Will's hands in hers, rose on her toes and gently pushed her face into his, kissing him warmly.

"All right, you two, that's enough, you'll turn my doughnut batter sour," the woman behind the counter said, folding her arms and rolling her eyes.

Stella and Will giggled before kissing each other again, unaware of the audience of people that had formed in the queue behind them.

"Come on then, what will it be? You're keeping people waiting!" the woman snarled, shaking her head impatiently.

"Sorry," Will said. "We'll have a bag of your finest doughnuts please, Mrs," he added quite cheekily, and Stella laughed at his impertinence.

The woman scowled at Will before placing four doughnuts in a bag and slapping them down on the counter. "Tuppence," she said sternly, holding her hand out expectantly.

Will rifled through his pocket and placed two pennies in her hand. "Keep the change," he said sarcastically, which annoyed the woman even further.

"Cheeky young devil!" the woman said, shaking her fist, and the pair scarpered off giggling.

They walked back towards the pier and sat down on a bench. As Will opened the bag of doughnuts, the rancid smell of burnt oil escaped.

Stella held her nose. "Thank goodness they don't taste like they smell."

"It's a shame there's not much sugar on them," Will said, offering the bag to Stella.

Stella quickly took a doughnut out of the bag, passing it between fingers to avoid the heat until eventually it had cooled enough to try a bite.

"I suppose... that... was a bit rude of me... really," Will garbled over a mouthful of hot doughnut.

"What was?"

"The way I... crikey, these are hot," Will said sucking in air to cool his mouth. "The way I spoke to that woman behind the counter."

Stella laughed, "It was only a bit of fun, no harm done. I'm sure she's used to handling a bit of lip now and again."

"Well, even so, I feel a bit bad about it."

Stella admired his sensitivity, and after popping the last bit of doughnut in her mouth, kissed him on his cheek. "Eat up, we'd better be making tracks, the bus leaves in 45 minutes."

"Don't you want another doughnut?"

"I think I'll save mine for later," Stella stood up to brush her hands free of sugar.

"Good idea, one is probably enough." Will wrapped the bag up and passed it to Stella before getting his handkerchief out of his pocket to wipe his hands on.

"How much money do we have left?" Stella asked.

"I'm not sure, why?" Will shook his hanky free of sugar, returned it to his pocket and fetched the rest of their earlier winnings out to show Stella.

"I think we have enough for a quick ride on the Waltzer before we go!" Stella said, dragging Will by the hand in the direction of the ride.

"What? After eating a sickly doughnut?" Will's face twisted at the thought.

"Of course, it's all part of the fun!"

"I'm not sure that throwing up on a fairground ride would be classed as fun."

Stella laughed. "Oh… c'mon. You'll be fine."

SIXTEEN

Sheila and Albert slipped off their shoes, tipped them up and watched as tiny grains of sand cascaded out of them like a waterfall. Sheila clattered hers against the wooden balustrade for good measure.

"It's amazing how much sand gets in them, isn't it," Albert said.

"I know, I'll be finding it everywhere for weeks," Sheila replied, checking the inside of her shoe.

They were about to enter their chalet when a voice called out.

"Mr and Mrs Marks, might I have a word?" Sheila and Albert turned to see the camp manager standing in nervous anticipation.

"Of course, Mr Andrews. Please do come on in," Albert gestured with his hand, allowing the man to follow on into the chalet behind Sheila.

"Please, take a seat," Sheila offered, moving some items of clothing from the chair.

"It's fine, honestly, I shan't take up much of your time."

"What can we do for you, Mr Andrews?" Albert asked, looking slightly confused.

"There's been a development that I'm afraid you ought to be aware of."

"Oh? And what might that be?" Albert asked.

Mr Andrews appeared slightly awkward, clearing his throat as if trying to find the best way to explain.

"It's not that bad. It's just...well—"

Sheila began to get impatient. "Why don't you just tell us what it is, Mr Andrews, and we can decide whether it's bad?"

"Of course, of course," Mr Andrews grinned nervously. "You see, it's your niece, well not exactly your niece, but rather the young lady she was sharing her cabin with." Mr Andrews paused and rubbed his hands together anxiously.

"*Was*? Mr Andrews," Sheila retorted.

"What?" Mr Andrews said in a puzzled tone.

Sheila let out a deep sigh. "You said 'the young lady she *was* sharing a cabin with'. What do you mean...*was*?"

"Ah, yes, sorry. Well, the young lady..." Andrews checked his paperwork. "Erm... Spencer, yes, Miss Carole Spencer. It would seem Miss Spencer has gone."

"Gone? Gone where?" Albert asked, snappily.

"Home," Mr Andrews said.

Sheila and Albert looked at one another. "Well, is she unwell?" Sheila asked.

"No, she's quite well," Mr Andrews replied hastily.

"Then why the early departure?" Sheila asked, looking puzzled.

Mr Andrews sighed. "According to her father, Miss Spencer was seen in a rather compromising position with a young man."

"What? You mean in her cabin?" Sheila was horrified.

"No, no, no. On the beach," Mr Andrews quickly added.

Sheila and Albert looked at one another again.

"You see, the witness to the erm... event, told Mr

Spencer. He at once went to the beach, but the couple had indeed gone by then, so he naturally went to her cabin to look for her."

"And?" Albert said sternly.

"And she wasn't there either. It was quite late by this point, and I believe he disturbed and startled your niece."

"Startled her how?" Albert asked.

"I think he assumed that both girls may have been up to no good."

"And were they?" Albert said hesitantly.

"Mr Spencer is inclined to believe not, although when he came to see me this morning, he did mention that he had recognised your niece earlier that evening and that she was sitting on a bench with a young man."

"I see, and what exactly was she up to with this young man?" Albert asked abruptly.

"Nothing, nothing at all, he said they were just chatting."

"Right, and that was all he said?" Albert asked, scratching his head.

"Well, yes. Apart from that he and his family would be checking out early. Miss Spencer was with him too, and she assured me that your niece played no part in any of the... the—"

Sheila cut in, "Shenanigans?" Mr Andrews nodded.

"Well, that is a relief for us then. Mr Andrews, many thanks for taking the time to come and explain," Albert said, moving towards the door.

"There is one more thing," Mr Andrews added

hesitantly. "It is camp policy that no occupant under the age of 18 may stay alone in the cabins. So, I could have your niece transferred across the children's dormitory, unless Mrs Marks prefers to move to the cabin herself?"

"I'll move across," Sheila said with a certain reluctance.

"Very good, I shall see to it that fresh linen and towels are replaced. Oh, and here is the key to the cabin."

"Thank you, Mr Andrews," Sheila took the key.

"No, no. Thank you for your understanding. Enjoy the rest of your stay."

Sheila and Albert watched as Mr Andrews made his way out. Sheila walked across the room and sat down heavily in the chair.

"Why do you suppose she never told us about this over breakfast this morning? I mean, if the Spencers insist that Stella wasn't involved in any way, why didn't she just tell us of the incident herself?"

Albert closed the chalet door and sat on the edge of the bed opposite his wife.

"I don't know, Sheila. It's all rather distressing, if you ask me. What if she has been hanging around with Carole these last few days? What if Mr Spencer's first assumptions are correct? And just who is this young man? Have we given her a little too much freedom?"

"I'll pack my things… I think it's time I had a chat with our niece."

As the Skegness bus pulled into the miners' camp, Stella and Will made their way downstairs, along with one or two others who had also made the journey. They thanked the driver and headed out towards the camp foyer. Once inside, Stella checked out the notice board for competition results.

"Look, Kilburn and Denby ladies are doing well in the tug-of-war," Stella pointed at the results sheet. "Looks like they've won the second round this morning and if they get through this next round, they'll be in the final."

Stella checked the clock on the wall. "Round three starts in a couple of hours. I really ought to be there to cheer my aunty on."

Meanwhile, Will was reading a different notice. "Stella, the teens' dance is this evening, it starts at eight 'o'clock. Will you come along to it with me?"

Stella smiled. "That would be great. I'll meet you at the usual place at half past seven."

"I'll be there," Will said, leaning toward Stella, and kissing her softly. "I've had a brilliant time today. It's been great fun."

"Me too," Stella smiled warmly and headed off out of the foyer, to make her way back to her cabin.

As she approached the cabins, thoughts of Carole's untimely departure returned, prompting an uneasy reminder that she really ought to go and speak with her aunt and uncle about the fact that she would now be alone in the cabin. She decided that telling them both over dinner would be best. Stella pushed the key into the lock of her cabin door and tried to turn it, but it was already unlocked. She pulled the handle down and gingerly pushed open the door. To her surprise, her aunt was busy unpacking her case and turned sharply to face Stella.

"I think you had better come back to my cabin with me, your uncle Albert and I have a few things to discuss with you."

Stella's stomach churned; this could only mean one thing… Mr Spencer must have been to see them.

SEVENTEEN

Will checked the time on the clock tower again for what must have been the tenth time in a minute. *four minutes to eight.* With the teens' dance starting in less than five minutes, Will searched his mind for every probable reason for Stella's absence. *Usual place, half past seven,* he was sure of the arrangement they had made. Maybe she'd changed her mind, perhaps he was pushing his luck. Glancing up at the clock again, he felt a sinking feeling rush through the pit of his stomach. Something was wrong, but what could he do?

He could check the restaurant, maybe the tug-of-war went on longer than expected, which made them all late for dinner, or he could go to the entertainment lounge. If he was wrong with the arrangements, perhaps she was already there waiting for him. Or, he could simply go and knock on her cabin door, except, of course, he had no idea which cabin she was in. But, doing any of these things would mean leaving their meeting place, and since he was quite certain of the arrangement they had made, she could turn up at any moment and wonder where he was. Eventually, he decided it was best to just keep waiting, there would be a perfectly good reason for her failure to appear.

After another five minutes had passed, Will got up from the bench, took a few paces to the edge of the green and stopped. He looked along the path to his left and then to his right, over and over, searching beyond each person in the hopes that she may suddenly appear from behind someone. As time went on, the passers-by became less and less, as by then most people had already made their way to a show, or some other form of entertainment they had decided on for that evening.

Will walked back to the bench and sat down heavily before taking another look at the clock. *Twenty past eight.* Well, that meant that she wasn't coming.

Just then, Will spotted his Uncle Jed and Jimmy Parkin making their way along the path towards him, and he felt slightly relieved. At the very least, this meant he could get his uncle to wait at the bench whilst he made a quick dash to the entertainment lounge. He caught his uncle's eye and beckoned him over. Thankfully, Jed made his way over alone, as Jimmy Parkin shouted something about getting the beers in.

"Will, lad, what are you doing sitting there? I thought you were going to the dance?"

"Uncle Jed, can you do me a favour? Could you please just wait here for two minutes?"

"For what?"

"For Stella. I'll explain later," Will's voice echoed as he sprinted off in the direction of the entertainment lounge.

****

Sheila leaned forward in her chair and rubbed at her ankle, allowing Stella to peer past her aunt and check the time on the alarm clock sitting on Albert's bedside table. *Half past eight.*

"What is wrong with your ankle, my dear?" Albert asked. "Do you think you'll be able to make the final round tomorrow?"

"I think I must have put a little too much effort into the tug of war. I'm sure it will be fine, just something and nothing, I guess... I would be better off wearing something different on my feet though, I don't think these shoes have helped any." Sheila bent forward again, giving Stella another opportunity to look at the clock.

"Do you have somewhere to be, Stella?" Albert asked suspiciously.

"Well actually, I had arranged to meet a friend this evening," Stella said cagily.

"By that, I assume you mean the young man you have met?" Albert asked.

Stella slouched in her seat and fiddled awkwardly with her hair, twisting it around her fingers, then releasing it when it would not tighten any further. She let out a heavy sigh.

"Yes, his name is Will."

"Stella, you must see this from our point of view. What would your father say if he knew we had allowed you to run wildly whilst you were in our charge?"

"I doubt my father would care at all actually."

"Alright then, your mother. She would certainly be none too pleased if she thought we were turning a blind eye."

"Turning a blind eye to what, Uncle? I haven't done anything wrong."

"To the fact you've been hanging around with someone you've just met, and that we have done nothing to stop it. He could be any sort of reprobate for all we know." Stella livened, jumping up out of her seat.

"But that's just it, Uncle, I already knew him before we came to camp."

Sheila sat bolt upright in her chair. "What? I don't understand, how come?"

"I wanted to explain earlier, but there wasn't time before the tug-of-war match started."

"Well, there's time now," Sheila said.

Stella took a deep breath. "Will lives in Denby, he and his family have recently moved there from Creswell Village. His uncle, Jed, well his great-uncle, is a miner at Creswell Colliery and he's brought Will along with him here for the week." Sheila and Albert looked at one another.

"I met Will on the Kilburn recreation ground almost three weeks ago now. We've been friendly ever since."

"So, it's just him and his uncle here then?" Sheila asked.

"Yes, his great-aunt is busy packing up their belongings. They're moving house soon."

Sheila looked to Albert, who was trying to make sense of it all. "Do you know this Jed fellow, Albert?"

"No. The only Creswell chap I know is Jimmy Parkin, you know, 'Mr Champion Knobbly Knees'," Albert rolled his eyes.

Stella knelt in between her aunt and uncle's chairs and looked up at them both.

"When we first arrived here, you were happy to instil your trust in me. I would never do anything to misplace that. Will makes me feel happy, and I'm sure that something has changed in me in these last few weeks."

"In what way?" Sheila asked.

Stella drooped her head. "Losing Grandpa has been the most difficult thing I have ever had to deal with."

Sheila gently patted Stella's head. "I know, sweetheart, it has been for us all."

Stella looked up at her aunt. "But meeting Will has somehow helped me to cope with it. It's strange, but it's as though I have grown up suddenly." Stella knelt up, to look directly at her aunt and uncle. "There is something about him, something… sincere. He is kind and gentle, just like Grandpa was. Will reminds me of him in a funny sort of way. In a way that… I don't know, I just can't put my finger on it."

The room fell silent, whilst Sheila and Albert considered what Stella had told them.

Stella only just realised the extent of what she'd said herself. Eventually, Sheila stood and picked up the entertainment programme. "Well, the teens' dance is almost over, but we could make our way across to the lounge and see if tonight's comedy act can provide some laughter?"

Stella's face brightened suddenly. "May I go over now and see if Will is still there?" Sheila looked to Albert, who merely nodded his approval.

"We should like to meet this young man, though," Sheila said.

"Of course, Aunty," Stella yelled, making haste out of the door.

Sheila took a lipstick out of her handbag and stood in front of the mirror. She applied an even smear of bright pink colour around her lips and gently pressed them together. She picked up a comb and tidied her hair, then, sighing heavily, she turned to face Albert. "Do you think we've done the right thing, letting her go?"

Albert rubbed at his chin. "I think we can trust her. There was something very genuine in the way she spoke."

Sheila nodded. "We will keep a close eye on her in any case. Right, well I think I'll just change my shoes, and we will make our way over there. We will feel happier about it all once we've met Will and his uncle."

EIGHTEEN

Stella was close to tripping over her own feet in a rush to get to the entertainment lounge. She pulled open the door, almost bumping into a young family coming away from the dance. The lounge was full of people coming and going, some had been chaperoning their teenage children to the dance, whilst others were finding a seat in preparation for the evening entertainment, in the form of the camp comedian, 'Slapstick Rick'.

Stella stood by the door and scanned the room looking for Will. When she couldn't spot him, she moved speedily around the lounge searching, but he was nowhere to be seen. Wondering if he might still be waiting at their meeting place, Stella decided to hurry there and get back before her aunt and uncle arrived. Them finding she wasn't here would not do anything to help her cause.

Just as she was about to leave, she noticed Jimmy Parkin walking away from the bar with a pint of beer in his hand. He was making his way towards a small round table in the far corner of the room. Stella looked around, but there was no sign of him being with Jed or Will. He would know where they were, though, but that would mean having to go over and speak to him, a thought she did not relish after the crass way he spoke to her last time.

Stella decided to go to the clock tower and look for Will. She turned hastily, but in doing so, collided with a man carrying a full pint of beer, that she now found herself wearing.

"Woah, steady on, missy," the man said, gazing at his now half-empty beer glass.

Stella inspected herself and felt the cold liquid begin to soak through her clothing. "I am sorry, sir," she said, wiping at her wet dress with her hands.

"You're in quite a hurry, lass… Oh, Stella, I didn't realise it was you!"

Stella looked up at the person who had spoken her name… it was Will's uncle. "Oh, my goodness!" Stella sang out in relief. "I'm sorry, I was late, and I came here, and I couldn't find Will, and I…"

"Calm down, lass," Jed laughed. "I've just left Will. He has been desperately searching for you too!"

Stella felt relieved. "Where is he now?" she asked.

"He's gone back to our cabin, said he was going to have an early night, but he was just upset because you hadn't turned up to meet him. He is keen on you."

Stella wanted to beam a big smile at that thought, but she was too upset that she had missed Will and the dance.

"Don't worry, missy, I'll tell him that I've seen you."

"Oh, please, if you would. Tell him I'm sorry and that I will explain tomorrow. Could you ask him to meet me by the clock tower after breakfast?"

"Aye lass, will do," Jed nodded, beaming a big smile.

Stella thanked Will's uncle and bid him good night. She desperately wanted to get back and out of her wet clothes, but she needed to find her aunt and uncle first.

Missing her opportunity to be with Will, and

having been dowsed in beer, made her feel miserable, but then, at least now Jed could explain her absence to Will. And of course, the fact that her aunt and uncle knew she hadn't been involved in Carole's wrongdoing, made her grateful for small mercies. Stella heard someone calling her name and looked over to see her aunt and uncle waving frantically as though their lives depended on it. She walked over to where they were sitting, hopeful that a simple explanation for her wet dress would suffice and she could be on her way.

"Good heavens, what has happened to you?" Sheila asked.

After Stella gave a brief account of what had happened, Sheila decided that the best way to break the ice with Will's uncle would be for Albert to go over and offer to buy the man a drink.

"Me? But why do I have to go?" Albert grumbled.

"Well, it was Stella's albeit minor infraction, that has led to the poor man losing the best part of his pint," Sheila snapped. "And anyway, you surely don't expect that I should go?"

"I'm not so sure either of you would want to go over," Stella remarked. "Will's uncle is sitting with Jimmy Parkin, and he can be quite uncouth, to say the least."

"Well, if that's anything to go by, what is Will's uncle like, I wonder?"

"Oh, Sheila, that's unfair. You can't tar the man with the same brush," Albert said, raising his eyebrows.

Stella rolled her eyes. "Aunty, is it okay if I go back to the cabin and get out of my wet dress?

I think I would like to stay in tonight and read a while, if you don't mind?"

"Yes, alright, love. I'll try not to wake you when I get in. Straight there, mind! No dawdling."

"I won't, Aunty. Good night. Night, Uncle Albert," Stella said, raising a hand in a simple farewell before rushing off through the lounge, towards the exit.

The moment she met with the outside air; she felt a rush of summer evening heat sweep across her face. The intensity of the overpowering warmth gave her the desire to take a steady stroll back and take in the serenity of the season. It wouldn't hurt to take a detour and walk back past the clock tower, would it?

Everywhere seemed so quiet and peaceful, and with hardly a soul about, Stella decided to take a seat on the bench and dally a while. Savouring the tranquillity made her forget about her wet dress, and as she sat alone, embracing her circumstances, words began to pop into her head. Words that formed a rhyme and could soon become a verse if only she had her notebook with her. Stella tried to etch the words into her mind, not wanting to lose what she thought could be the beginnings of a promising poem.

The warmth of summer fills the night, but still, the sun is full and bright.
The sultry heat will leave too soon, and in its place a sparkling moon.

She needed to get back to the cabin and write things down before they left her mind. It was beginning to get quite dark, and she really ought to be getting back before anyone missed her. Stella got up off the bench to make haste back to her cabin when she heard voices and laughter coming from behind a low wall that formed the perimeter of the camp complex. She waited to see who might appear, when a young girl stood up from behind the wall. The girl was doing her best to rearrange her clothing into some sort of respectable order. Stella darted behind a nearby bush and peered out. She could see that a young lad had also stood up now and was also readjusting his clothes. Stella watched on as the pair kissed passionately before the young lad jumped over the wall and began to make his way towards the bush. Stella stood perfectly still, thankful that the darkness would conceal her presence. As the lad passed by, Stella dared to gaze out from behind the bush... Tommy!

Wretched scoundrel, Stella thought to herself. She looked at the young girl, who was now sitting on the wall, as she had taken a compact mirror out of her handbag and was reapplying some lipstick. Eventually, once the girl had finished titivating herself, she too walked past, close enough for Stella to get a good look at her. Although she didn't know the girl, she had half a mind to let her know just what sort of creep Tommy was, and that only yesterday he had been cavorting with Carole.

After the girl had disappeared out of sight, Stella wasted no more time getting back to the cabin. She was most relieved to find that her aunt wasn't already waiting in readiness to give her a dressing down. *Slapstick Rick must be keeping them well entertained,* she thought.

Fetching her notebook and pencil out of the bedside drawer, she wrote down the lines she had composed, but nothing else came to the fore to add to them. Soon, thoughts of Will vied for the concentration of her mind. She thought about the things she had said to her aunt and uncle about him, and that spending time with him had made her realise how she wanted her life to be. The thoughts of being back at home, trying to live with her father's temper, sent shivers through her spine. She was changing, growing up, and she knew that if she was going to survive her father, her way of life needed to change along with it.

NINETEEN

Early the next morning, Stella woke suddenly to the sound of rain lashing against the wooden roof of the cabin. A sudden burst of bright light illuminated the tiny room, shortly followed by a loud clap of thunder. She looked at her clock… a quarter to five. If this storm did not pass soon, the chances of getting back to sleep would be quite slim, particularly as thoughts of meeting Will burst through to the front of her mind.

Another brief illumination, which within seconds was followed by the clap of thunder, was enough for Stella to catch a glimpse of her aunt as she slept, uninterrupted by the meteorological ruckus.

She hadn't heard her aunt arrive back last night and had managed to sleep through… until now. Another burst of light followed at once by a clap of thunder meant the storm was overhead… well at least that's what her grandpa used to say. He reckoned that if you count the number of seconds between the flash of lightning and the sound of thunder and divide it by five, you will know how far away the storm is. Stella snuggled down and pulled the covers over her head, closing her eyes tightly. Now it was her grandpa's turn to take a prime position in her thoughts. She recalled how he had always been fascinated by the weather and seemed to know a lot about it, since it was the subject of many of the poems he had written. He always kept a notebook by his side, a black leather one with the initials F.D. embossed on the bottom right-hand corner of it. She would often notice it open on a page where he had been writing something. He would nod to her in gesture as if confirming that it was all right to read what he had written. Sometimes it would just be the odd line or two, suggestive of his thoughts just at that moment. Other times, it would be a completed poem or the beginnings of a short story.

"If you want to be a writer, always keep a notebook to hand to record your thoughts and ideas," he had once said to her. And she always did.

Suddenly, another burst of light filled the room, and Stella counted in her head... *one, two, three... it must be moving away, eight, nine, ten... thunder! So, by my reckoning then, the storm has moved a couple of miles away now,* Stella thought.

Eventually, as the sound of the storm dulled, Stella managed to find sleep again, but only for a short while, as it wasn't long before a fresh new day filled the little cabin with dazzling sunlight. Stella opened her eyes, blinking a few times to reach full focus. She looked across and noticed her aunt was still fast asleep in the same position as before, with only her head visible above the covers, and wearing a pink hairnet over three rollers in her fringe. It felt a little strange looking at her fast asleep in bed, it wasn't something she had ever come up against before. Sure, she had seen her nod off a time or two in an armchair, but she had never actually seen her asleep in bed. Not wanting to disturb her, Stella gently pulled the bed covers back, slid her legs out of bed and put on her socks, shoes, and dressing gown. She picked up her washbag and towel and tip-toed across the room. Gingerly, she turned the key in the lock and opened the door to leave as quietly as possible.

Outside, the sun was shining brightly, and the wet from the storm was beginning to dry up. Stella was glad it had stopped raining, having to race across to the toilet block and washroom wasn't much fun in the rain.

By the time she had finished and left the ladies' facilities, a lot more people were out.

The smell of breakfast cooking filled the air, and some were already heading for the canteen.

Stella hoped that Will's uncle had remembered to tell him to meet her.

When she arrived back at the cabin, Sheila had awoken and was sitting up in bed reading. It didn't take Stella long to realise that what she *was* reading was *her* notebook.

"I hope you don't mind; you'd left it open on your bedside table and… Stella, I have to say, these poems are very good."

"No, I don't mind, Aunty, and thank you, I'm glad you like them."

"You certainly take after your grandpa with your ability to put words together. You must look at his poems sometime. He kept a notebook too," Sheila said, closing Stella's notebook and placing it back on the bedside table.

"I did know about that, and yes, I've read all his poems already. We spent a lot of time together discussing our writing. He helped me with it a lot."

"Really? I didn't know that." Sheila got out of bed and put her coat on over her nightdress and slipped on her shoes. "I'm going to pop over to my chalet and get ready. I do miss the luxury of having a bathroom," she whispered.

Stella smiled, "I don't mind it too much, so long as it isn't raining!"

"Oh indeed. Well, we'll see you over at the canteen for breakfast."

"Aunty, do you mind if I go over now, only I'm hoping to meet up with Will after breakfast?"

Sheila considered Stella's request for the longest moment before answering. So much so, Stella was convinced she was going to say no. Eventually, though, Sheila nodded, but in a way that made Stella wonder if her aunt wasn't completely sure of her decision.

"I think we're going to spend the day on the beach today. You'll both come along and find us," Sheila said by way of demand, rather than request and left without waiting for a reply.

Stella stood in the doorway, watching as her aunt hurried to make a shortcut across the lawn, but then upon realising that the grass was still wet, looked down at her wet shoes before quickly making for the footpath. Stella giggled, shut the door, and wasted no time getting herself dressed.

****

Making a quick scan of the dining room in search of Will was futile, as the place was full of folks enjoying their breakfast. Stella grabbed a tray and joined the queue behind a man she thought looked familiar, a tall heavy-set man whose shoulders naturally stooped forward. Stella noticed that the man had piled his plate up with more sausages than a person ought to be able to handle in one sitting. The man turned to look at Stella and grinned, and as he did, two large dimples appeared in his ruddy-coloured cheeks. He gave Stella a look that seemed to suggest he knew what she was thinking, then looked at his plate and back to Stella, winking at her as he mumbled something about saving some for later.

Stella just smiled as she picked the two remaining sausages out of the metal serving tray. As they moved further along the food counter, the man added four rounds of bread to his plate, along with several rashers of bacon. Stella was amazed at the man's shamelessness as he continued to pile food onto his plate. Finally, when the man had enough to feast on, he left the queue in search of a free table. Stella picked up two slices of toast and made her way along the counter to pick up a pot of tea.

She looked around for a free table and noticed that by now the same man was busy tucking into his banquet. She watched as he used an odd technique to fold a slice of bread around three sausages, putting all his effort into squashing it all together to keep everything in place. It was at that point that she remembered why he looked familiar… of course, it was the world champion iron bar and nail-bending strong man. *No wonder his shoulders stoop so,* Stella thought as she walked past him.

Finding herself a seat over by a window, Stella placed her tray down on the table, pulled out the chair and made herself comfortable. She lifted the lid on the one-person teapot and stirred the contents, then using a strainer, poured some tea into a cup with a small amount of milk. As she stirred the tea in her cup, Stella took a quick look around the room in search of Will but to no avail. The nail-bending man caught her eye again though, and Stella could not help but watch as he used the same technique on another round of sausages and bread. *He should go on stage as a sausage eater, I reckon he would be a world champion at that too,* she thought, grinning to herself.

Just then, Stella felt someone tap on her shoulder, she turned around and was delighted to see Will standing with a breakfast tray balanced on one arm.

"Morning," he said, setting down his tray and sitting opposite her.

"Oh Will, am I pleased to see you. I am so sorry I couldn't meet you last night I — "

Will held up his hand, "It's okay, Stella, I'm only glad you saw Uncle Jed. He said you'd gone into the entertainment lounge after the dance had finished to see if I was there, and that you'd explained there was a perfectly good reason for not meeting me." Will slid his hand across the table and covered Stella's hand with his. "I'm just relieved that you saw him, otherwise I would have carried on thinking that you had changed your mind about me," Will laughed nervously.

"Is that what you thought, after the lovely day we'd had?" Stella asked, tucking a loose tress of hair behind her ear.

Will looked down at his plate. "To be honest, that's why I was confused, *because* of the day we'd had."

"Let's finish our breakfast and take a walk, and I'll tell you about what happened." Will looked up and gazed at Stella. "Come on then, or your bacon will be cold," she giggled.

Will tucked into his breakfast, "I was rather hoping for some sausages today, but they'd all gone."

"Really?" Stella said, averting her gaze over in the direction of the champion sausage eater.

TWENTY

Will and Stella walked hand in hand along the beach, when Will stopped suddenly, looked across to his right and pointed.

"Goodness, look. It's the Big Dipper! We've been walking for so long we've arrived in Skegness."

Stella laughed. "It is only a couple of miles along the beach from the camp, not that far really."

"We seem to have been walking for ages. At least it feels like it when you're trying to trudge through dry sand...Oh hang on..." Will let go of Stella's hand to run to a stray football, kicking it back to a group of youngsters. Someone shouted their thanks over to Will as he returned to Stella's side, reaching for her hand again.

"Let's go and sit down over there for a while," Stella pointed to some steps that led up to the promenade. The pair walked across, and Stella sat down.

"I'll nip up to that little doughnut hut and fetch us some lemonade if you'd like?" Will asked.

Stella nodded and lay back to enjoy the sun on her face. Within a few minutes, Will had returned with two bottles of ice-cold lemonade and sat down beside her.

"Thank you, Will, just the ticket," Stella took the bottle from Will and wiped the ice-cold bottle across her clammy brow. Will, meanwhile, was swigging at his as though it were about to go out of fashion. Eventually, with less than half of his drink remaining, he paused to let out a refreshing sigh.

"This lemonade is just the best. Anyway, you were

telling me about Carole's father, Mr Spencer."

Stella took a few sips of her drink and nodded, "Yes, the morning after he found out that Carole had been seen on the beach with Tommy, he and his family checked out early."

"That Tommy has always been a good-for-nothing rogue," Will said.

"So it would seem. And then last night, I saw him with another girl."

Will shook his head. "What a rat. I'm sorry you were left to explain things to your aunt and uncle though."

"It's okay. To be honest, I never really thought that it might look as though I was keeping something from them. I'm glad they know about you now. Although, they have said that they'd like to meet you," Stella said dubiously.

Will tipped the bottle to get the last dregs of his lemonade. "Well, that's okay with me. I have nothing to hide, and I hope they know I would never dream of treating you the way Tommy treats girls."

Stella leaned towards Will, kissed him on the cheek, and laid her head on his shoulder.

"There's something else…"

"Oh?" Will responded uneasily.

Stella lifted her head and looked out towards the sea. "Carole's father beats her."

"Beats her?" Will burst out in disbelief. "But how… how do you know?"

"When she came back to the cabin to pack her case, she changed her clothes, and I saw the marks on her back."

"Are you certain? It could have—"

"I know the look of a beating when I see one!" Stella replied sharply.

Will was a little taken aback that Stella had cut him short. "What I meant was, are you certain it's her father and not Tommy?"

"Sorry, Will, I didn't mean to snap at you. It's just well… it's not how a father should be treating his daughter, or anyone else for that matter. And yes, it is her father, she opened up a little bit to me about it."

"Gosh, that's awful, poor Carole. She's brave for opening up about it, though. And she certainly doesn't need someone like Tommy complicating her life."

Stella nodded, painfully aware that she still had some opening up to do of her own. She really wanted to share the burden of what life was like with her father, but she just couldn't find the words, it just wasn't the right time…

Stella stood up and jumped off the step onto the sand, landing just in front of Will. "Well, I suppose we'd better be heading back then. If you're up to dragging your way back through that soft sand?" she laughed, grabbing hold of Will's hands and pulling him up.

As their eyes met, they shared a passionate kiss and a warm embrace that made Stella feel so safe, she could have stayed there forever.

As they walked toward the stretch of beach behind the miners' camp, Stella began to search for her aunt and uncle. The beach was crowded with holidaymakers enjoying the sun. She stopped and began to turn around slowly, putting her hand up to her forehead to shield her eyes from the sudden contact with the dazzling sun. Walking further on, she weaved in and out of occupied deckchairs and dodged children playing in the sand with buckets and spades.

"I can't just seem to see them anywhere," Stella said to Will as he followed behind her.

"Maybe they've not arrived yet, or left already?"

"Aunty did say they were going to spend the day on the beach, though. Maybe I ought to go to their chalet and see if they are there."

The pair made their way off the beach, back into the camp, stopping to brush the sand from their feet and put their shoes and socks back on.

"I'll nip to their chalet and see if they're there, then I'll meet you at the clock in about 15 minutes?"

Will nodded in agreement and Stella left him to make her way across camp towards the chalets. She knocked on the door and waited. Almost at once, Sheila opened the door.

"Aunty… are you alright? I thought you said you were going to spend the day on the beach?"

"Actually, no. Your uncle isn't feeling at all well, so it's best if you don't come in."

"Oh?"

"He's not been well overnight, and he was still fast asleep when I got back here this morning." Sheila leaned closer towards Stella and whispered. "He has an upset stomach. So, I don't want to leave him alone whilst he's feeling as he does."

Stella looked past her aunt and noticed a bucket on the floor at her uncle's side of the bed."

"I managed to get the bucket from one of the housekeepers. He hasn't got the strength to get up to go to the bathroom."

"Oh dear, that's not good. Have you eaten, Aunty? Is there anything I can get for you?"

"I'm alright, love. The housekeeper very kindly brought me a breakfast tray. So, we'll see how he is this evening and pop over to the canteen for a bite to eat later. I'm afraid I've missed the women's tug-of-war final though."

"Well, if you're sure you'll be alright, I'll come back and check on you both later.

And I'll see if I can find out who won the tug-of-war as well."

"Thank you," Sheila said to Stella as she turned to leave, quickly adding, "I assume I need not worry about what you might be doing whilst your uncle is confined to his bed?"

Stella stopped in her tracks and turned to look back at her aunt. "Aunty, you have no cause for any concern." Sheila merely nodded, smiled, and closed the chalet door.

Stella approached the clock tower to find Will sitting on the bench waiting for her. She walked over and sat down beside him.

"Stella, Is everything alright?"

"Well, not really, no. My uncle is unwell, some sort of sickness thing by the sounds of it. They're confining themselves to their chalet for the rest of the afternoon, at least."

"Goodness, that's a disappointment, especially when they're trying to enjoy their holiday."

"Yes, very much so. I'm going to go back later and see how they are. Shall we go back to the beach?"

"I don't think that is a good idea, given how dark those clouds look," Will said, thumbing behind him at the sky.

Stella turned to look. "Oh heavens, it looks like another storm could be on its way."

"How about we go to the games room, and see if there is a deck of cards? I could teach you how to play Rummy, if you like?"

"Okay, but first, I just want to go and check on which team won the women's tug-of-war competition."

The pair made their way into the camp reception area, where lists for the current and concluded competitions were pinned to notice boards around the foyer. Stella found the notice board marked 'Women's Competitions' and ran her finger down the list until she found the tug-of-war final. Kilburn and Denby's ladies had won against Pilsley Pit.

"Yes!" Stella shouted, fist-pumping the air. "Aunty will be pleased about that."

Will smiled. "That might just make her feel a bit better about missing it."

Just as they were about to leave the reception and go to the games room, they passed the camp photographer.

"Oh, hello, you two. Your photographs are ready

earlier than expected, you can go and collect them if you like?"

"Really? That's great, thank you," Will said to the photographer.

Will and Stella looked at each other and smiled. "Come on, let us see what they are like!"

There was still a steady queue of people waiting to have their photographs taken inside the huge wooden postcard. A long table had been placed next to the display with several boxes on it, holding envelopes arranged in alphabetical order. Before long, Will had found an envelope containing their photos. He opened it and took out a photo of himself and Stella, sitting together with big smiles on their faces. Will beamed the same big smile again at the sight of it.

"It's a lovely photograph, don't you think?" Will passed the picture to Stella.

Stella's face lit up. "It's lovely," she said with a huge grin.

Will looked inside the envelope. "There are another three other pictures in here, so we can have two each."

"Brilliant, that means I can keep one and give the other to my grandma as a souvenir. She and my grandpa had a similar one done of themselves the last time they came here," Stella said dolefully.

Will pulled Stella close and kissed her forehead. He didn't have to say anything, the embrace was enough for her to know she had his support.

Outside, the storm had announced its arrival with a sudden downpour of heavy rain, which brought people rushing in from outside to find shelter.

"Time to go and find that deck of cards, I think!" Stella said to Will with a smile.

****

Will briefly explained the rules of Rummy to Stella, and she listened intently, only interrupting him to clarify the odd instruction here and there.

"I think it's probably best if we begin a game and see how you get on, then if there's anything you're unsure of, I can explain it as we go along," Will suggested, shuffling the pack of cards quite expertly.

"Okay," Stella nodded and watched as Will began to deal out the cards.

After each of them had received seven cards, he then made a stockpile with the remaining ones, taking the top card off, and placing it face up, to form another pile beside the stock.

"So, that will be the discarded pile," he said, pointing to the face-up card. "You go first."

Stella looked at her cards, frowned and nibbled the inside of her cheek.

"If you think the face-up card will be of use to you, you can pick it up. If not, take one from the stockpile instead," he added, and waited in anticipation for her to make her move.

After contemplating it for a minute or so, Stella picked up a card from the stockpile and added it to her hand, then put one of her original cards face up on the discarded pile.

"That's the idea," Will chimed in. "Do you think you might be getting the gist of it?"

"Well, I guess time will tell," Stella said casually,

focusing on the cards in her hand.

As the pair continued to take turns to play their hands, Will asked what Stella's thoughts were, on what she might do after the few months she had left before leaving school. "My parents will be expecting me to find some sort of employment."

"Is that what you want?" Will asked, picking up a card.

Stella shook her head. "No, not really. I'd like to go to college and study English, but they won't hear of it."

Stella discarded a card, but this time, placed it face down on the pack, which as Will had already explained, showed a win. She then quickly arranged the rest of her cards across the table, in a combination form.

Will's face dropped when he realised that Stella had a perfectly workable and winning combination.

"Blimey, that was pretty good for a first go!" he said, placing his cards down to show Stella the combination he had been aiming for. Then he picked up all the cards and gave them an extra good shuffle. "Beginner's luck I should think," he said, placing the freshly shuffled deck down in front of Stella. "Your turn to deal now, but you give them a good shuffle first. I need to see if I can pull a game back," he laughed.

After Stella had dealt out the required number of cards, the second game began, and as it progressed, the two continued to chat about Stella's desire to follow her dream. She explained to Will that as she didn't know how to move forward with her writing, she had no idea how she would achieve her goal.

"If it is all just pie in the sky, why do I feel so compelled to write," Stella shrugged.

"When we get home, you must speak to my dad. I know he's been looking into getting some of his stories published. Maybe he could help you?" Will said, picking up the card that Stella had just discarded.

"That would be great. What sort of stories does he like to write?"

"Mystery and adventure, but usually set in the Golden Age of Piracy."

"That all sounds very swashbuckling," Stella said, as she once again placed her card face down and waited for Will's reaction.

However, Will was too busy fantasising about stories of pirates and smuggling gold to realise the move she had made. Eventually, when it dawned on him, he stopped mid-sentence, and as Stella laid down her second winning combination, all Will could do was stare at her cards in disbelief.

"Is it still beginner's luck, or do you think it might be that I'm quite skilled at this game?" Stella grinned.

"I'm starting to wonder! My hand was useless. It must have been the way you shuffled them," he said cheekily with a wink. "Another game?"

Stella looked outside, "I think the rain has stopped, so really I ought to go and check on my aunt and uncle. And besides, I don't want to jeopardise my winning streak just yet."

"Hmm, I still say it's beginner's luck! Can we meet

later then, in the canteen for dinner?" Will asked, collecting the cards up and placing them back in the pack.

"Yes, I'll see you over there around six o'clock. But before I go, I'd better confess.

I've played that game more times with my grandpa than I can remember."

"You little trickster!" Will cried out, as he jumped up out of his seat, grabbing Stella around her waist and tickling her until his playful torment made her squeal in delight. "I think with the crafty way you just played Rummy, you should have a go at playing poker. That's if you aren't already an expert?"

TWENTY-ONE

Stella and Will found an empty table and set their food and drinks down on it. They had both settled on the same meal - chicken and vegetable pie with mashed potato, cabbage, and broad beans.

"This all smells wonderful," Will said, tucking into his pie. "And these beans are delicious."

Stella looked over at the row of tables across from them and noticed the nail-bending champion from earlier, who once again had his plate piled so high with food, that it was spilling over the edges. He too noticed Stella, giving her one of his cheeky winks before tucking into a huge fork full of mashed potato.

"Gosh, that man can eat for England," Stella nodded in the direction of where the man was seated.

Will turned around to take a quick look. "Crikey," Will laughed. "That sure is a plateful."

"He did the same this morning with his breakfast, which is why there were no sausages left when you wanted some. Has he forgotten we're still rationing?" Stella complained.

Will laughed, "It must be hungry work bending all those iron bars and six-inch nails, though!"

"Well, I hope there's going to be enough left for me to take a tray over for Aunty," Stella said, wiping the corners of her mouth with her serviette.

"How is your uncle?"

"Still not well enough to leave his chalet, and he has no appetite whatsoever. Goodness knows where he's picked it up from."

"Gosh, I hope your aunty doesn't come down with

161

it too, or you, for that matter," Will said.

"I hope not, the last thing I want is to be spending my last few days here with my head in a bucket!" Stella grimaced.

After they had finished their dinner, Stella sought out the restaurant manager and explained her aunt's situation. He readily accepted the unfortunate situation and offered to make up a jug of cordial to take with her. He was quite happy for her to take anything else over to them that she thought might take their fancy and would also arrange for housekeeping to take some fresh towels and bedding across to their chalet. Stella was most appreciative and had soon helped herself to some ham, bread and butter and a piece of sponge cake. She also plated up some of the pie, mash and veg that she and Will had enjoyed.

Stella balanced the tray of provisions and took them across to her aunt's chalet. Although her uncle hadn't fully recovered, she was pleased to see that he felt well enough to be sitting in his chair and that he thought he'd try to manage a bite to eat. She was also pleased to see, that up to the present point, whatever unfortunate bout of sickness it was that had ailed him, had thankfully not passed to Aunty. Both her aunt and uncle were grateful to Stella for delivering the provisions, and the restaurant manager's kind offer of the extra help.

As Stella wished her uncle a continuance of his recovery, her aunt was very quick to remind Stella that she would still be staying with her in her cabin overnight.

Stella headed over towards the clock tower to meet up with Will who, she noticed, was sitting waiting patiently for her to arrive. She thought how handsome he looked, and her heart quivered a little at the sight of him. As he wasn't yet aware of her arrival, she decided to have a little bit of fun, and diverted off the path, walking around the other side of the green and towards the back of the bench. She grabbed his shoulders from behind and let out such a screech that it made him yell out in mild shock.

Upon realising that she'd managed to get one over on him again, Will jumped up out of his seat and leapt over the bench with such agility it made Stella shriek in surprise. She turned to run from him, but he was hot on her heels and soon caught up with her. He grabbed her around her waist and very gently tussled her to the ground, tickling her ribs whilst she giggled, and yelled for him to stop.

Eventually, as he relented, their eyes locked together, and after a brief and impassioned gaze, he kissed her, which evoked a strong emotional state that neither of them had ever experienced before. Their embrace was suddenly interrupted by the sharp-toned voice of a man ranting at them, it was clear that he was not at all impressed with their conduct. Will and Stella both jumped to their feet, unaware that the man was actually Mr Andrews, the camp manager.

"I'll have none of those sorts of shenanigans!" Mr Andrews wagged his finger at the two of them. "Now get yourselves off before I tell your parents what you've been up to."

Stella grabbed Will by the hand, and they both ran off before Mr Andrews could embarrass them further.

They never stopped running until they were a long way from the clock tower and had gone a reasonable distance along the promenade. Eventually, Stella drew to a halt and put her hand on her chest to catch her breath.

"That was a bit awkward," she said, still trying to collect herself.

"I wonder who he was?"

"I don't know, but he seemed quite official-looking with that clipboard under his arm.

I do hope we're not going to get into any trouble," Stella said uneasily.

"He won't know who we are, though, I'm sure he was just wanting to scare us." "Well, it worked. I hope we don't come across him again!"

Will put his arm around Stella and kissed her forehead. "We haven't done anything wrong."

"I know, but he didn't see it that way, and I don't want to get into trouble with my aunty," Stella smiled nervously.

"Come on, let's make our way back," Will said softly, taking Stella's hand.

Stella nodded in agreement and they both took a steady stroll back in the direction of the camp.

Not wanting to go back to the clock tower bench, Stella suggested that they walk on a bit further, where eventually they came across a seat under a large oak tree. The pair sat down and chatted. After their earlier conversation about Stella's plans for her future, she was curious to know what Will might like to do with his. Will seemed to go quiet and gazed into thin air.

"Surely you have plans, don't you?" she asked.

Will sighed heavily. "My father is keen for me to become an apprentice with the Royal Air Force."

"The RAF! That's wonderful, and what would you do as an apprentice?" Stella asked.

"I want to be an aircraft engineer. I would have to pass an entrance examination first, though, and I've heard it's quite difficult."

Stella looked at Will. "Why do I get the feeling that you aren't as keen as your father?"

"Oh… oh, I am. It's what I've always wanted. It's just that…"

"It's just what?"

"Well, I would be away for long periods at a time, three months initially," Will got up off the bench, and began to absent-mindedly kick at a clump of grass.

"And… you would miss your parents too much?"

Will hesitated and looked directly at Stella. "Well, yes I would miss them, of course I would, but…" Will exhaled. "It's you, Stella, I would miss *you*."

Stella genuinely felt quite staggered at Will's sudden revelation and wasn't quite sure how best to respond to it. Eventually, she got up off the bench and took hold of his hand, pulling him close to her. Looking up into his eyes, she spoke softly and gently shook her head. "You can't give up on your dream, Will, not for my sake. I wouldn't ask it of you."

"I know you wouldn't, but… would you want to try and further a relationship with me if I'm miles away?

I mean, how do we know if it would work?"

Stella reached up on her toes and kissed Will's cheek. "We don't, but I'm quite happy to give it a try."

Will beamed his usual big smile and leaned forward, giving Stella a gentle kiss. "That's exactly what I hoped you would say."

The two of them headed back towards the camp accommodation, where Will escorted Stella to her cabin.

"Good night, Stella," Will said with a smile. "I'll see you tomorrow."

Stella unlocked the cabin door and turned to wave, just as Will kissed the palm of his hand and blew in Stella's direction.

TWENTY-TWO

The following morning, Stella woke to the sound of a shuffling noise in the cabin. As her eyes adjusted, she realised it was her aunt putting her shoes and coat on over her nightdress in readiness to leave.

"Morning, Aunty," Stella yawned.

"Oh… morning, Stella love, I was doing my best to be quiet. I didn't want to wake you," Sheila said, as she expertly removed her hairnet without disturbing the rollers in her fringe. "I know it's still early, but I want to get back and see how Albert is feeling today."

"Did he manage to eat much of anything yesterday evening?" Stella asked, propping herself up against her pillow.

"Only a few mouthfuls I'm afraid. He was feeling weak by bedtime."

"Would you like me to bring a breakfast tray over for you both this morning?" Stella slid her legs out from under the covers to sit on the edge of the bed.

"Well actually, after you spoke to the restaurant manager yesterday, he informed Mr Andrews, who very kindly came across to see if he could be of any help. He's arranged for our meals to be brought over until Albert feels well enough to leave the chalet."

"That's good then. I don't think I'm familiar with Mr Andrews?"

"Mr Andrews is the camp manager. You can't miss him, a tall chap, who always carries a clipboard under his arm." Stella gulped upon realising that this must have been the same man who scolded her and Will the evening before.

"Anyway, I'll catch up with you later," Sheila checked her hair in the mirror. "I'm only sorry that we haven't yet met your beau, maybe later if Albert feels up to it," Sheila said, leaving the cabin with her usual haste.

Stella drew her legs into bed and snuggled back under the covers. An image of Mr Andrews with his clipboard under one arm, and wagging his finger, suddenly manifested itself in her mind and she shut her eyes tightly.

****

After breakfast, Stella and Will met up at their usual place and decided to take a stroll to the oak tree bench. An elderly couple were already sitting on the bench, so the pair sat down on the grass with their backs up against the huge trunk of the tree.

Stella pulled her notebook out of her bag, "I thought you might like to read some of my poems," she said, passing the book to Will.

He opened the book and read quietly, turning page after page of poems and verses, looking up every so often to smile, praise or comment.

"These are exceptionally good, Stella, and I can see by the dates on them that you've been writing from quite an early age. What do your parents say of your ability?"

Stella's stomach turned again when she remembered that Will had no idea about the circumstances surrounding her home life.

"Well, to be honest, it's always been mine and Grandpa's thing, I've never shown my parents any of my poems before."

Will seemed quite taken aback. "Really? But how can they *not* know? I mean surely your teachers must know of your talent, have they not spoken to your parents?"

"My poetry has never really been up for discussion with my teachers," Stella gently pulled her notebook from Will's hands and put it away in her bag. "And my parents only know about the one I wrote for my grandpa's funeral."

"But you have written so many poems before that one. I'm amazed that nobody, apart from your grandpa of course, has thought to…" Will searched his mind for the right words, "…nurture your skill."

Stella suddenly felt awkward, keeping up the pretence wasn't going to be practical for much longer. In the end, she managed to throw a veil over the whole thing.

"You make me sound like a seedling," she laughed.

Will sighed. "Well, I think your talent *is* a seedling, one that needs to be encouraged to grow."

Stella smiled and kissed Will's cheek, then she got up off the grass and dusted herself free of the tree and grass debris. She leaned forward and grabbed Will's hands and tried to pull him up from his seated position. Of course, she wasn't quite strong enough, and she ended up falling onto him instead, making them both laugh at her folly. The elderly couple laughed too, with the man suggesting she could do with a bit more muscle on her bones.

The two of them set off for a walk along the beach

in the opposite direction this time and soon reached the coastal village of Ingoldmells. They came across a little hut, like the one in Skegness, selling drinks, candy floss, rock, and seaside goods. Will bought two bottles of lemonade and they sat down at a nearby wooden picnic table.

"I can't believe how fast the week is going," Stella said, placing her elbow on the table to rest her chin in her hand.

"We've still got a few days left yet, and there's another teens' dance on Friday," Will said enthusiastically.

"Yes, and the competition awards will be given out that night too."

"Still lots to look forward to then!" Will said positively.

The two of them spent the rest of the morning drinking cold lemonade and chatting away under the warmth of the sun. As time passed, their inactivity, along with the heat, soon made them feel quite lethargic, and Stella felt quite sleepy.

Will yawned. "Is it just me, or are you feeling tired too?"

"I was just thinking about our balloon, and wondering where it might be by now, if it hasn't popped already, that is," she giggled.

"It'll be quite a hoot if it's waiting for us when we arrive back in Kilburn!"

"It certainly would be, considering the direction in which it floated off. It's more likely to be somewhere over Europe by now."

Kilburn… the thoughts of being back at home made Stella shudder. Even though she had only been away a brief time, it was long enough to know that in no way had she missed her father, but her mother… she wondered how her mother might be coping at home.

****

Kilburn, Derbyshire

With the extra meat coupons and one less mouth to feed, Jeanie had been able to provide meals that kept Derek sufficiently satisfied enough not to find the need for complaint.

This meant the house was exceptionally quiet, especially without Stella.

As usual, Derek spent his days either at the market, in the garden, or at his allotment and his evenings out at the pub. But the amount of time he *had* been spending at home, had been uneventful.

Jeanie had spent the whole morning tidying upstairs and had almost finished cleaning her bedroom windows. She stepped backwards to check for smears and stood on the loose floorboard where she'd hidden Stella's envelope. It creaked loudly.

She looked down and noticed that the floorboard had raised the carpet higher than when she'd first become aware of it. Crouching down, she pulled the carpet back and tried to push the floorboard back into place, but it just kept springing back up. After realising that disturbing the floorboard to hide the envelope must have displaced it, she looked around the room for something heavy to hold it down and decided a chair would do. She folded the carpet back and stamped the floorboard down with her foot, then dragged the chair across and placed it over the bump in the carpet.

"That should do it," she said to herself.

Derek's jacket cloaked the back of the chair and Jeanie decided to hang it up in the wardrobe. Placing it on a hanger, she felt at a small box in the inside pocket. Cigarettes.

There were seven cigarettes left, and Jeanie took one out of the pack. Then she placed the packet back in his pocket and hung his jacket up in the wardrobe. She made her way downstairs, grabbed the matches and stood outside by the back door.

Taking a long draw on the cigarette made Jeanie feel a little giddy at first, and she sat down on the doorstep. Eventually, though, her head adjusted, giving her mind the rush it desired. As she continued to enjoy her fix, Jeanie's mind wandered to thoughts of dinner, and she decided that baking a meat pie for Derek's tea might keep him in the good mood he had seemed to be in of late. Just as she took a final draw on the cigarette, Jeanie heard the entry gate open. Fearful that it could be Derek arriving home early, Jeanie aimed and with her usual precision, flicked the cigarette butt onto the outhouse roof, before quickly wafting the air to try and disperse the smoke, just as Mrs Hunt appeared.

"Oh, Mrs Hunt, how lovely to see you, how are you?" Jeanie said, feeling relieved.

"I'm grand, Jeanie love, except, I shan't half be glad when everyone arrives back on Saturday. It's been like a ghost town round here, and the pub… well, deathly quiet," Mrs Hunt shook her head. "Anyway, I have news. A deputy from Creswell Colliery came into the pub last night, to speak to our Roy. He's looking to take on some men, and Roy thought Derek might be interested?"

"Really? Doing what?"

Mrs Hunt shrugged her shoulders. "Rippers, I think. Anyway, its five pounds, eight shillings and tuppence a week, with an increase expected in October, and…" Mrs Hunt said, emphasising the word '*and*'.

"All he needs to do is get himself to the toll bar and transport will be provided! Roy says it's a cracking opportunity. Here, he's written all the details down," Mrs Hunt passed Jeanie a folded-up piece of paper.

"He'll be home later, so I'll let him know. Thanks, Mrs Hunt."

"Tell him our Roy will be in the pub tonight. If he wants a job, he'll have to be quick," Mrs Hunt turned to leave. "I must dash, I'll be seeing you," Mrs Hunt's voice echoed down the entry.

Jeanie unfolded the paper Mrs Hunt had given her, absorbing all the details to make certain of what the woman had said. *Rising to six pounds from October. That certainly is a cracking opportunity,* Jeanie thought to herself.

After a couple of hours' preparation and cooking, Jeanie picked up her oven gloves and lifted a metal tray from out of the stove. With the pastry baked to a perfect golden brown and a crisp crust, her minced beef pie was ready. When Jeanie lifted the pie out of its dish and placed it on a plate, a savoury aroma soon filled the kitchen. She set the plate down on the table and turned her attention to straining the potatoes, carrots, and runner beans. With a small jug of gravy already made up, all that was left to do was make sure the plates were warm and dish out the vegetables in time for Derek's arrival. Jeanie set the table and placed the folded note Mrs Hunt had given her at the side of Derek's place setting. Feeling quite confident that a delicious meal, *and* a job prospect to boot, would surely equal a contented husband, Jeanie took a step back to admire her efforts. *Ready,* she thought, and all within perfect timing of the entry gate announcing his arrival.

As usual, Derek's standard greeting remained unchanged. He took off his hat and coat and sat himself down at the table, without so much as a glance in his wife's direction. If he had bothered to look at her, he would have had an inkling that she was pleased with herself about something. Instead, he just helped himself to a portion of the pie and poured over some gravy. It was when he picked up his knife and fork in readiness to tuck into his meal, that he noticed the paper.

"What's that?" he nodded in the direction of the folded piece of paper.

"Why don't you read it?" Jeanie replied, smiling.

Derek slammed the ends of his knife and fork against the table, making Jeanie jump.

"Just answer the damn question, woman."

Jeanie swallowed hard, placed her knife and fork down on her plate, then paused for a sharp intake of breath before beginning to explain.

"Mrs Hunt brought it over this afternoon. It's details of a job that Roy Barlow thought you might be interested in…" Jeanie said cautiously, then paused again in anticipation of Derek's reaction. When there wasn't one, she continued with a little more enthusiasm.

"You just need to pop over and see Roy tonight, but I think it could be a really good opportunity for you. There's transport provided, and the pay isn't too bad, and that will increase to—"

"Enough!" Derek shouted, slamming his fists down on the table, "I'll decide whether something will be good for me. Now let me eat my tea in peace, for heaven's sake."

Jeanie just stared at her husband in disbelief, before slowly picking up her knife and fork and continuing with her meal. The rest of the time it took for them both to finish eating was spent in absolute silence, then Derek merely stood, reached for his coat, and left… without the note.

TWENTY-THREE

Roy Barlow picked up the pint of stout his sister had just freshly pulled and took it over to the corner of the room, setting it down in front of Derek. Derek nodded in appreciation.

"Right then, Felton, you think you'll be up to doing this job?"

Derek sipped on his pint, leaving a milky white froth over his top lip. "What's that supposed to mean?" he snapped, wiping away the froth with his sleeve.

"Calm down, lad. It's a ripper's job, you'll be working underground, is all I meant."

"And?"

Roy sighed. "I just want to know if you can handle it. That prisoner of war camp must have been hell —"

"What has that got to do with it?" Derek spat, slapping his glass down on the table.

"Look, all I'm asking is, can you handle the confinement?" Roy shrugged his shoulders. "You're going to be underground for long periods at a time, it can be tough for anyone, let alone someone who was held captive."

"It's not the same thing, so of course I can bloody well handle it."

Roy held up his hands in mock surrender. "Fine then. If you want the job, you start Monday morning. Be at the toll bar for 5 a.m. and someone will pick you up."

Derek just nodded, unfolded his newspaper, and continued to sup his pint.

Roy stood up. "Aye... well don't thank me, lad, eh," he said, shaking his head. He made his way back to the bar, where his sister had been busy wiping shelves down and listening in on the conversation.

"Can you believe the ignorance of the man? I don't know why I've bothered," Roy added, still shaking his head.

"Because you know he's a good worker and he won't let you down," Mrs Hunt said, placing a tot of whiskey down in front of her brother.

"Aye, well...I've done it for the sake of Jeanie and Stella, that's all," Roy said, taking a sip of his whiskey and glancing over in Derek's direction. "He'd better keep his temper as well, the Creswell lads won't take any of his shite, I can tell you."

****

The following morning, Jeanie walked into her mother's house, slammed the back door shut and plonked herself down at the table. She grabbed the teapot, topped up her mother's cup with tea and began to pour one for herself.

"And what's up with you on this wonderful Friday morning?" Elsie said nonchalantly, whilst adding some milk to her tea.

"Sorry, Mam, I'm just cross with Derek."

"What's he done now?" Elsie rolled her eyes.

"A couple of days ago, Roy Barlow sent word of a potential job opportunity for him."

"And let me guess, he's turned it down, whatever it is?"

"Well, that's just it, I don't know because he hasn't

spoken to me since. Stella will be back tomorrow, and I wanted to give her some good news."

"Can't you ask him about it? What is the job anyway?"

"It's a ripper's job, not bad pay either. But you know what he's like if I try and press him," Jeanie said, taking a sip of tea.

"Why must that man be so obnoxious? The job's probably gone anyway. I've not heard of any ripper's jobs going free around here." Elsie stood up from the table and began to put the tea things onto a tray.

"It isn't local, that's why you've not heard about it. The job is at Creswell Colliery, transport was to be provided as well," Jeanie said sullenly.

Elsie laughed. "That explains it then."

"What do you mean?" Jeanie said, frowning over her teacup.

"Nobody round here wants to work with Derek, that's why he can't get a job. Sending him off up there where nobody knows him… makes sense, I'd say."

"No…" Jeanie shook her head. "I refuse to believe that."

Elsie carried the tray to the sink. "Well, believe what you want, but I think you'll find I'm—"

Suddenly, Elsie's words were halted by a loud knock at the back door, and she just froze on the spot.

"Mam? What's wrong? Aren't you going to answer that?" Jeanie pushed her chair away from the table to get up and answer the door.

"Wait, Jeanie, check through the net curtain, see who it is first," Elsie said, not wanting to move from the spot where she stood.

Jeanie frowned at her mother, crept over to the window, and gingerly lifted one corner of the net curtain before dropping it back down again.

"It's that woman…" Jeanie searched her mind for a name, then whispered. "Norah Shaw."

Elsie just shook her head. "Leave it, Jeanie, just come away. Let's go and sit in the front room until she's gone," she said, wasting no time in heading off out of the kitchen.

As Jeanie followed, she began to get increasingly curious as to the reasons why her mother seemed to react so strangely whenever the name Norah Shaw was mentioned.

Jeanie sat down on a chair opposite her mother. "What was that all about then, why didn't you want to let her in?"

"I've told you before, I'm quite happy in my own company and that of my family. I don't need a busybody like her hanging around."

Jeanie scratched her head. "It's all just rather odd, if you ask me."

"Aye… well, I'm not asking you, so just leave it be." Elsie very quickly changed the subject, "I bet you're excited to be having Stella back tomorrow, I hope she's had a good week. You know how odd our Sheila can be with her ways," Elsie chuckled.

She's not the only one, Jeanie thought…

****

Skegness, Lincolnshire

Stella stood in front of the mirror and removed a

dozen or so plaits from her hair and unravelled each one with her fingers. When she'd finished, she had a head full of beautiful curls.

"What do you think, Aunty?" Stella asked her aunt, who was busy reading a book.

"Does it look alright?"

Sheila laid her book down in her lap. "It looks very pretty, Stella. You look very grown up."

"Are you going over for the awards presentation tonight?" Stella asked.

"I'm going to see how Albert is feeling after his afternoon nap. That sickness bug certainly drained his energy, he's hardly been able to walk more than a few yards since."

"It's such a shame that it's spoiled your holiday. I wish we could have another week here. I don't want to go home tomorrow," Stella said ruefully.

Sheila smiled. "There will be other years. Now, I think I'll go back and see if Albert is awake yet, and... I have some packing to do."

Sheila made for the door but paused short of it. "Don't forget our train leaves quite early in the morning, so we'll need to be on time for the bus to take us to the station. I'll see you later," she said, her voice echoing as she left.

Stella nodded dispiritedly, although she was looking forward to the last evening, she didn't want the holiday to end. She dragged her suitcase out from under the bed and began to fold a few things up in readiness to pack. She emptied the bedside drawer of her reading book, notebook, pencils, and a couple of handkerchiefs, and placed them in the bottom of the case. As she did so, the two photographs of herself and Will dropped onto the bed. She picked them up and smiled at how handsome he looked. She then tucked the two pictures into the back of her reading book to keep them safe and reminded herself that she must give one to her grandma.

It was at that point she realised that apart from her aunt and uncle knowing about her friendship with Will, nobody else back home knew anything about him. Nobody knew that he would be at camp the same week as her. Nor would anyone know just how close they had become. Her grandma would be happy for her, and her mother too, but no way was she going to tell her father.

Will was already waiting for Stella as she approached the clock tower, for what would be their last time meeting there. His face lit up with joy at the sight of her, and he smiled at her warmly.

"Good evening, Will," she said, with an equally warm smile.

Will leaned in and kissed her softly on her lips. "Stella… you look so beautiful, and your hair…" he shook his head gently. "It suits you curly. Shall we make our way to the dance?" he asked, offering his arm to escort her.

The entertainment lounge was the fullest it had been all week, as pretty much every camp guest was there to enjoy the last night of their holiday. As the camp musician fired up the magnificent Compton organ, the teens' dance began.

For an hour, Stella and Will enjoyed everything from an elegant waltz to navigating the quickstep, and with an energetic jive thrown in at the end for good measure, the dance floor was bustling. Eventually, when the teens' dance was over, Will and Stella were well and truly spent and took themselves off for well-deserved refreshments.

Each with a bottle of cold lemonade in hand, the pair decided that some fresh air would be most welcoming and went to sit on the wall outside.

"I'm shattered," Stella giggled. "I wish I didn't have to leave so early tomorrow. What time is your train?"

"Not till midday, I think," Will said, guzzling the last drops of his lemonade."

Stella fixed her gaze into nothingness. "I've had the best time ever."

Will put his arm around Stella and drew her close. "Me too," he said softly.

"Can we meet up on Sunday afternoon? I could come over to your house, if you like?"

"Yes, I should be back home by then, I think."

"I should hope you'd be back by Saturday night!" Stella laughed.

"What I mean is, if Uncle Jed's house move has gone according to plan, I can go straight home. If not, I may have to stay in Creswell until Dad can collect me on Sunday."

"Speaking of Jed, here comes your uncle now, with that pig-headed halfwit!" Stella fumed, standing in readiness for a verbal conflict.

As Jed and Jimmy drew level with the two of them,

Stella scowled at Jimmy. At five feet two, he was only an inch or so taller than her, which made her feel quite on par with him. With his shirt sleeves rolled up and only a waistcoat over the top, she noticed how thin his arms and frame were. He'd shaved since she last saw him, but in fact, the facial hair had at least hidden his gaunt features. She kept her gaze on him but noticed that he avoided any eye contact with her. Eventually, though, he did manage half a smile.

"Alright, Will?" Jed asked, nodding at his nephew. "Stella…you're looking very lovely this evening," he added with a smile. "We're just heading in for the presentation, so Jimmy here can collect his knobbly knees award. First, though, Jimmy has something to say… don't you, Jimmy?"

Jimmy's face suddenly altered, giving him the appearance of a startled rabbit. He took a step nearer to Stella, grabbed his flat cap from off his head and held it to his chest in remorse.

"Erm… yeah. I'm sorry, missy, sorry I wer' rude to thee, t'other night," he said, before staring down at the floor. Stella just raised her eyebrows in response.

"And?" Jed prompted. "What else are you sorry for, Jimmy?"

Jimmy looked at Stella again. "Oh, aye, and I should never have called yer grandpa an old fool, so I'm sorry for that n'all. It were all t' drink talking." Jimmy offered his hand out to Stella and Stella shook it and nodded at him in response.

"Right," Jed said. "Now that's done with, I think Jimmy would like to buy us all a drink… wouldn't you, Jimmy?"

"Aye," Jimmy agreed, placing his cap back on his head.

"We'll see you two inside then. Come on, Jimmy," Jed said, leading the way.

Stella sat back down on the wall next to Will. "I wasn't expecting that," she said. "He is an odd little fellow, though."

"He's harmless enough, just can't handle his drink, that's all. We don't have to go back in, if you prefer not to?"

"It's alright, I want to see my aunt collect her award. If my uncle feels up to it, that is."

The lounge was still bustling with people enjoying their last evening, and as the presentation started, Stella could hardly hear her voice above the whistles, cheering, shouting, and clapping, as the various competition winners took to the stage to collect their awards. When it was the turn of the ladies' tug-of-war team, Stella noticed that her aunt wasn't there to collect hers, and she assumed that her uncle Albert must still not be feeling up to it. Soon, it was Jimmy Parkin's turn to collect his knobbly knees award, and as the compère called out Jimmy's name, he raced up onto the stage and grabbed his certificate and medal. This time however, the compère's assistant, Rita, had the presence of mind to hide behind the compère, just before Jimmy had a chance to scoop her up in his arms again.

Once the awards presentation was over, the compère revealed that the final evening's entertainment would be in the form of a five-piece jazz band which he announced as "The Red Hot Five". As the band struck up, folks got to their feet, dragging partners, family, and friends up to dance. Will jumped up too, catching hold of Stella's hand to lead her to the dance floor.

The two danced the rest of the evening away, and before they knew it, 10 o'clock had soon come round, and it was time for Stella to head back to her cabin.

"I don't want to go, but I also don't want to get into any trouble with Aunty," Stella shouted over the very loud music.

Will and Stella walked back hand in hand towards the cabins and stopped to say a final goodbye before parting their ways.

"I'm sorry we won't get an opportunity to see each other in the morning," Stella said solemnly.

Will didn't respond, he just tucked a stray lock of Stella's hair behind her ear before cupping her face with his hands, then he pulled her close and kissed her softly on her mouth. A group of people walked close by, and someone gave a wolf whistle, which made the pair look up and laugh.

"I'll see you on Sunday, Stella, even if I have to walk back from Creswell!"

Stella laughed and reached up to kiss Will goodbye. She unlocked her cabin door and turned to watch Will as he walked away. When he stopped to turn and look back at her, she waved, then wiped away a solitary tear that ran down her cheek.

TWENTY-FOUR

The camp canteen opened earlier on a Saturday, to give those who had an early departure a chance to have a hearty breakfast. Stella woke to the feeling of a gentle nudge and her name being whispered.

"Stella. Albert and I are going over for breakfast, if you want some, you'd better get cracking," Sheila said quietly.

Stella rubbed her eyes and glanced at her clock. It was bad enough to know your holiday was over, but half past six in the morning made it even worse.

"Okay, Aunty, I'll see you there," she said reluctantly. "Is Uncle Albert still no better?"

"He's a lot better than he was, but we decided an early night ahead of our journey home today would be sensible."

Sheila headed for the door. "I'm just hoping he's had a restful night. I'll leave you to get organised then," she said.

Stella sat at the breakfast table with her aunt and uncle and gave them a rundown of the presentation evening. Then she told them all about how well the jazz band performed and how she'd never seen so many people get up to dance.

"I'm sorry you both missed it, Aunty. We had such a good night. You could ask at reception to see if they have your certificate and medal?"

"It doesn't matter really, I wasn't there for the final in any case," Sheila shrugged her shoulders.

"You were still part of the team though, dear," Albert said, spreading butter on his toast.

"Exactly," Stella agreed. "I've finished my breakfast, so I'll go over and ask for you," Stella said, pushing her chair back from the table.

"Very well then. Hurry, though, then you may as well go and fetch your case and meet us in reception, the bus will be here in…" Sheila checked her watch, "20 minutes." Stella nodded and made her way out of the canteen.

After Stella had picked up her aunty's certificate and medal, she walked over to collect her case. She wondered why so many of the people she passed looked so miserable until she realised that it was home time for everyone. A week at the miners' camp provided a much-needed tonic, that every man, woman, and child would look forward to thoroughly enjoying and be sad to leave. And on no other day would that be clearer, than change-over day.

By the time she arrived at the reception, the bus had already parked outside the camp and people were starting to load their luggage. A crowd had gathered in the foyer, and Stella noticed Sheila was standing at the far end, waving to get her attention. Beckoning and mouthing to her to hurry, Stella reluctantly quickened her pace over to where her aunt stood.

"Albert is outside, waiting to load our cases, love. We need to make haste."

Stella handed her aunt her medal and certificate, then took her case out to the bus where her uncle was waiting to put all their luggage on together.

Before long, the bus was full and ready to leave camp. Some of the entertainment staff stood on the steps outside, waving their goodbyes.

The journey to the train station was silent compared to the journey in; nobody spoke, let alone sang 'Roll out the Barrel'. As the bus pulled into the parking area, Stella noticed there was already a queue of holidaymakers waiting patiently for the bus she was on, almost willing it to become free of its passengers, so that they may board it and get their week at camp off to a flying start. Each person had the same air of excitement and enthusiasm that she had just a short week ago.

The train station concourse was congested with travellers, either having just arrived in Skegness or preparing to leave. As Stella walked onto the platform, the train was already waiting to take her back to Derbyshire. As the last few stages of preparation were overseen by the driver and his fireman, the guard allowed people to begin boarding. After a short while, the guard checked his pocket watch and blew his whistle. Steam hissed loudly as the train's engine fired up, the driver looked out from his cab window and gave a loud toot on the steam whistle, which echoed throughout the station. Gradually, the engine set the train in motion and within minutes the platform was empty.

Stella took a seat by the window and looked out. Before long, every sign that she'd even been to Skegness was long left behind. She rested her elbow against the narrow window ledge and sunk her chin into the palm of her hand. As she fixed her gaze on the passing landscape, the uniformity of it soon became mesmerising. What with that and the early start to her day, her eyes began to feel as heavy as her heart.

She thought about Will and the wonderful week they'd had, meeting for breakfast, sharing an evening meal and spending time together doing as they pleased. That time had brought them closer and had allowed their relationship to develop. But how well would that go once they were back to normality? How could she invite him into a home as unstable as hers? She closed her eyes to rest them, and soon the distinctive clickety-clack of the wheels rolling over the rails, along with the gentle motion of the train as it powered along its tracks, sent her off to sleep.

She had been asleep for over an hour before she woke to the feel of a slight jolt, as the train came to a halt. She sat up straight, rubbed her eyes and looked out of the window.

According to the sign, they had arrived at Grantham Station. Sheila and Albert sat opposite Stella. Albert was fast asleep and Sheila, who had been reading her book, popped a bookmark in place before closing it up.

"Ahh…miss sleepy head has woken up. You two are great company, I must say," Sheila laughed.

"Sorry, Aunty," Stella yawned. "I think I might read a while. It might keep me awake."

Stella stood up and reached her arms above her head, to lift her case down off the rack above her head. She rummaged through it, found her book, and placed her case back on the rack.

Stella pulled one of the photographs of herself and

Will out from the back of her book.

"What have you got there?" Sheila asked.

"Will and I had it taken by the camp photographer," Stella said, passing the picture to her aunt.

Sheila studied the photograph for a while and frowned. "He looks familiar."

"Who looks familiar?" Albert asked, waking with a start, and smoothing his hair back into place.

"Will, Stella's beau. Look," Sheila showed Albert the picture.

Albert pursed his lips in slight disagreement. "Young men all look the same these days."

"Well, he's a nice-looking lad, it's a shame we never got to meet him," Sheila said, passing the picture back to Stella.

Stella looked at the picture again and smiled at it warmly, then she slipped it into the back of her book and settled down to read from where she'd left off. Soon, the guard sounded his whistle, and the train left Grantham for the last leg of their journey back to Kilburn Station.

By the time the train pulled into Kilburn Station, Tom Jackson was duly waiting with his horse and cart in readiness to transport everyone's luggage back to the village.

"You had a good week of weather then, Albert?" Tom asked, taking Albert's case from him, and loading it into his cart.

"Yes, lovely, just not so good health-wise." Albert patted his stomach. "Some sort of sickness bug knocked me off my feet for most of the week."

"Really? That's a damn shame," Tom shook his head. "Here, missy, bring me your case," Tom called over to Stella.

As Stella approached the cart with her case, Tom's horse, Amos, turned his huge head towards Stella, and gently nudged her nearer to the cart, making Tom laugh out loud. "Dunna worry about him, missy, he's as soft as cart grease. He's eager to get home for his food is all."

Stella smiled and rubbed the soft, pink part of Amos's nose, making his top lip quiver a little in satisfaction.

"And he'll stand any amount of that n'all," Tom smiled.

Quite a few people had gathered at the station in readiness to greet the arrival of family and friends. A young child who had been at camp with her grandparents, suddenly spotted her mother, and rushed over to be with her. Stella felt a familiar melancholic sting upon realising her mother wasn't there to greet her.

Once the last of the luggage had been loaded onto Tom's cart, everyone followed behind to walk the mile or so back to the village. Stella began to wonder what sort of week it might have been for her mother, and on how many occasions had she found need to diffuse her husband's rage. The thoughts of it made Stella want to run back to the station and board the train back to Skegness. She shook her head. Even if by some miracle going back to Skegness had been possible, Will wouldn't be there.

Eventually as horse, cart and dispirited holidaymakers arrived back at the Traveller's Rest pub, folk began to take their luggage down off Tom's cart. Some people decided to head into the pub for a drink, others walked away jadedly in the direction of home. Either way, the reality of knowing it would be an entire year before the prospect of their next holiday, was wholly evident on their faces. Albert thanked Tom and handed him a customary tip, before he, Sheila and Stella headed in the direction of home.

When they reached the Felton house, Stella thanked her aunt and uncle for taking her away with them. "I've missed not having Grandma and Grandpa with us, but I've had the best summer ever," she said, hugging them both. "Give grandma my love and tell her I'll be round to see her soon," Stella added, before heading off up the entry.

As she got to the back door, she paused, and took a deep breath...

TWENTY-FIVE

As she walked in through the door, Stella's stomach turned. Her father was sitting at the kitchen table, his face hidden by his newspaper. Upon realising that someone had walked through the door, he gently pulled the corner of his paper down and peered over the top, then without so much as a word, allowed it to flip back up and continued to read.

Not wanting to be accused of being ignorant, Stella decided to try conversation.

"I'm home…" she said cheerfully.

No response.

"Dad… how are you?"

Still no response.

"Is Mam here?"

Derek pulled the corner of his paper down again, but this time in a certain manner that showed his disgruntlement.

"Do you see her here?" he growled.

"Okay then… where is my mother?" Stella surprised herself at the sharp retort she gave her father.

"Shopping." Derek calmly folded his paper, stood up and threw it down on the table. Then without so much as a glance in his daughter's direction, he grabbed his coat and walked out of the door.

Stella's eyes filled with tears. The way her father behaved towards her was the same as it always had been. What was she expecting? A welcome home hug? Laughter, a chat about her week away? She shook her head; there would certainly be something wrong with him if he *had* greeted her that way.

Stella took her case up to her room and unpacked it. She took the photographs of herself and Will out from the back of her book and slid one into her drawer. It would have to stay there until she had an opportunity to tell her mother about Will, and she certainly had to keep it out of sight of her father. The other, she would take over to her grandma's. At least she would be happy to know about Will and want to listen to tales of the week she'd had at camp. She put her laundry in the wash basket and everything else away where it belonged and set off.

Stella arrived at her grandma's house to find her upstairs in her bedroom, busy sorting through some of Fred's belongings. She had placed items of his clothing out in various piles on the bed, and Stella could see that her grandma had been crying. When Stella entered the room, Elsie looked up and smiled.

"I think these will fit Albert, and those should fit Robert," Elsie said, pointing at two of the five piles of clothing. "As for the rest, well... James is too portly, and your dad is too tall," Elsie shrugged her shoulders. "Now, come and give me a hug and tell me all about camp," she said, brushing away a tear.

Stella hurried over to where her grandma stood and hugged her tightly, not wanting to let her go. She nestled her head against her grandma's shoulder and spoke softly. "You don't have to be doing this now, you know, or go through it all alone. I would have gladly helped you."

Elsie gently pulled away from Stella's embrace, and

looked directly at her, "I'm sure you have better things to do than go through a load of old clothes. Now, tell me... did you have a fun week?" Elsie asked, sitting down heavily on the dressing table stool.

"I had the best time ever," Stella said in brief excitement, before remembering that in previous years, her grandparents would have been at camp too. She relaxed her shoulders and let out a sigh. "I did think about you both, and it wasn't the same without you. A lot of the old memories were still there."

"As your grandpa always said... life goes on, and you will always have those memories. I do hope you made some new ones, though?"

Stella nodded heartily and took the picture out of her bag.

"Look, we had this taken inside that wooden postcard, just like you and Grandpa did. I have two pictures, so you can have that one," Stella said, passing her grandma the photograph of herself and Will.

Elsie studied the picture for a moment before looking up at Stella with a big smile.

"And... who is this handsome young man?" "His name is Will," Stella said tenderly.

Elsie smiled warmly. "And was this a brief involvement, or shall you be seeing him again?" Elsie stood the photograph behind the picture of herself and Fred.

"Well, I haven't told Mam any of this yet, but since he only lives in Denby, yes. Although, if he passes his exams, which he thinks he will, he'll be taking an apprenticeship with the RAF."

Elsie's eyes widened. "Sounds like he's a clever lad then," she said. On trying to stand, she let out a sudden groan and bent slightly to rub her knees.

"Grandma, why don't you rest a while, and I'll go and make you a cup of tea?"

Elsie nodded in agreement, and Stella moved the piles of clothes, to make space for her grandma to rest.

"Oh, by the way, those are for you," Elsie said, pointing to Fred's flat cap and his black leather notebook. "I thought you might like them as a keepsake?"

Stella picked up the notebook and ran her fingers across her grandfather's initials. She opened it and glanced through some of the pages, smiling as she recalled the verses, poems, and his thoughts in general.

"Thank you, Grandma, I shall treasure it always. And this too." Stella picked up the flat cap and placed it on her head, doffing it in a mock greeting to Elsie, which made her grandma laugh.

"I'll go and put the kettle on, and then I'll tell you all about my week at camp," she said.

****

After Stella had spent a couple of hours with her grandma, she thought it was time to go and see if her mother had arrived home. As she walked the short distance along the street from her grandma's house to hers, she recalled the earlier conversation she'd had with her father, and how she had surprisingly managed to get away with her contemptuous response to him, which had seemed to come from nowhere. Was this, along with the fact that she'd not even given a thought of going to her den, a sign that her outlook on life had changed so much, in such a short space of time?

Signs that her mother was home were strewn about the kitchen, her handbag on the table and various groceries sitting on the worktop, waiting to be put away. Stella called out for her mother, who responded that she was upstairs. When Stella got up to her parents' room, she found her kneeling on the windowsill and leaning out of the window with the yard brush in her hand.

"Mam, what on earth are you doing?" Stella asked, rushing over to the window.

"I was about to put the shopping away, and I heard a loud bang from in here, and well, look... a pigeon has flown into the window. I think it's dead, but I can't leave it there to rot," Jeanie said, attempting again to reach the pigeon's body with the brush.

Stella looked out of the window. "Poor thing must have broken its neck. You'll never reach it, Mam... it's too far away."

With that, Jeanie gave in and tried to pull the brush back through the window, but as she did, it fell onto the outhouse roof.

"Damn it," Jeanie yelled. "Oh... I'll just have to ask your father to climb up onto the outhouse, that's all," she said grudgingly, before getting down from the windowsill.

Jeanie straightened her clothing and hugged her daughter. "Anyway, love, have you had a lovely week?"

"I've had a great time, and I've got lots to tell you, but before I do, how have *you* been, and how have things been with Dad?"

"Well, actually, I have some good news, your father has a job!" Jeanie held up her arms in delight. "Let's go and have a brew, you can tell me about camp, and I'll tell you all about the job," Jeanie put her arm around Stella's shoulder and led her out of the room.

Jeanie sat at the kitchen table and whilst Stella made the tea, she spoke a little about her week at camp. She wasn't quite ready to tell her mother about Will yet and changed the subject to that of her father's new job. Jeanie spoke optimistically about how she was certain that things would surely change now that he had something on which to focus his mind, and that she thought he would want to tell her all about it when he got home. Stella however, thought that as her father appeared just the same as he was before she went to camp, was less than convinced.

"Really? Well, I've already seen him today, and since he couldn't be civil enough to string two words together to me then… I doubt he will bother any time soon," Stella said, bringing the teapot down on the table with a thud. Jeanie just gave her daughter a look of disgruntlement and shook her head.

"He was probably in a rush to get off to the allotment, there's so much to do there at the moment, and —"

"For heaven's sake, Mam," Stella cut in. "Why must you keep defending him? I've been away for a whole week, and when I arrived home, it was quite clear that he had no intention of even asking about my holiday, let alone want to tell me about his new job! I've had it with him, he's a complete—"

Jeanie quickly put her finger to her lip. "Sshhh… I think I've just heard the entry gate go. He must be back, get him a cup and saucer out, would you."

Stella just rolled her eyes and sighed heavily with frustration. As she reached into the cupboard for another cup and saucer, the back door opened, and Derek walked in with a box of vegetables from his allotment. When Jeanie greeted him, Derek gave his usual grunt in response.

"Tea, dear?" Jeanie asked, pouring it anyway. "Erm… Derek love, there's a dead pigeon on the outhouse roof, I tried to drag it nearer with the yard brush, and silly me, I've only gone and dropped the brush," Jeanie said, laughing nervously, and tutting at her blunder.

"Would you mind getting the ladder up there?"

"I suppose I'll have to," Derek spat.

As he began to take the various vegetables out of the box, Jeanie did her best to draw him into conversation.

"I've just been telling Stella all about your new job," she said enthusiastically. "And Stella has just been telling me all about Jimmy Parkin winning the knobbly knees competition again."

Jeanie got up from the table and took Derek's tea over to him. "You're likely to be working with Jimmy. Stella says he's a ripper at Creswell Colliery too."

Derek stopped what he was doing. It was clear that his agitation was beginning to heighten, but Jeanie was oblivious and continued babbling.

"Next year, we can go to camp with Albert and Sheila. We could take Mam too! You could even give Jimmy Parkin a run for his money in the knobbly knees comp—"

"Enough! Just shut up, woman, for pity's sake," Derek yelled, slamming his fist down on the worktop. "Can't I just drink my tea in peace? Forget it. I'll take it outside," Derek said moodily, and walked off, slamming the door on his way out.

Stella looked at her mother and slowly shook her head. "And you're certain that things will change?"

TWENTY-SIX

Sunday 3rd Sept 1950

When Stella woke the following morning, she decided to leave the house early to go to her den. Since she had already decided that she no longer needed it, she would have to collect the cushions and stool that she'd left in there. As she walked down the garden, she noticed that the privet hedge had grown while she had been away, and the little gap that led through to the bush on the recreation ground had completely closed. Deciding it best not to force open a new gap, Stella walked onto the recreation ground instead, to enter the den from the other side. The foliage on the bush was also overgrown, making it quite a struggle to pass through. Eventually, once she had pushed through to the inside of the den, Stella thought how different it looked, much less inviting than it had ever seemed before.

Although it hadn't been raining, the den felt damp. Stella gave a little shudder and wrapped her cardigan tightly around her chest. She sat down on her stool and thought about all the times she'd spent in the den; times when she had needed to escape her father's wrath, or times when she just wanted to be alone. But more recently, spending time here with Will; the den had been their first meeting place and the thought of that held a certain warmth that she didn't want to part with.

Stella noticed that a spider had created the most magnificent web and was sitting in the centre of it waiting for its next meal. She thought how perfectly formed the web was, as it spanned across the side of the bush closest to the privet hedge of her garden. If she had pushed through the hedge from her garden, she would have destroyed the web for sure. She looked closely at the silken thread and how it shimmered in what dim light shone through the gaps in the bush. The colour of the spider itself was a mixture of dark chocolate brown, bright orange and yellow. Ordinarily, Stella hated spiders, especially the huge house spiders that liked to come in out of the cold and startle her with their rapid and untimely appearance, but there was something about this one, something that inspired a feeling of awe at his wanton perseverance to exist. Just then, an insect quite inadvertently became trapped upon the web, and within seconds the spider had pounced on it and began encasing it in the silken thread, weaving it round and round the insect, until nothing more could be seen of it. At that point, Stella shuddered again. She wasn't sure if she should feel sorry for the insect and its premature death or hold a feeling of awe for the spider and its fight for survival.

Stella picked up the old cushions and wooden stool and pushed her way back out through the bush for the last time. At that thought, she smiled fondly and gave a little nod of thanks to her den for all the times it had provided a sanctuary, good times… and bad.

Back at home, Stella thought she would alter her bedroom around a little. She cleared away the things on her dressing table, and dragged it nearer to the window, taking advantage of the natural light. She arranged her, albeit scarce, collection of books to sit tidily on the shelf, along with the dictionary Will had given her. She placed a pot of sharpened pencils on the dressing table, along with her notebook and her grandfather's notebook. Before long, she had created an area where she could sit to concentrate properly on her writing in the comfort of her room. It would also come in useful for revision purposes, as there would be various tests starting at school very soon. She hadn't given much thought to starting back to school, but as there were only a few more days before the new term started, Stella needed to make some decisions about the future. There wasn't long to go before she would be leaving school for good.

Looking around her bedroom, she smiled in happiness at her efforts but was even happier knowing that she no longer felt the need to hide away in a damp den ever again. Nothing pleased her more though than thoughts of seeing Will, as the time to meet him had finally come.

Down in the kitchen, her mother was busy preparing vegetables. From the kitchen window, Stella could see that her father had fetched the ladder from where he kept it hanging on brackets on the wall in the entry.

"I'm going out for a while, Mam," Stella said, heading for the door.

Jeanie turned to speak to her daughter. "Just before you go, I meant to ask yesterday, have you ever known of a lady going to visit Grandma?"

Stella frowned. "No…why? What lady?"

"An old friend from school apparently, but there's something odd about it all."

"Odd in what way?" Stella asked.

"Well, Grandma seems not to want anything to do with her, but…" Jeanie shook her head, "…I don't know. Anyway, never mind. Get the colander out for me, would you, love."

"What's for dinner? Pigeon pie?" Stella giggled.

"I wouldn't put anything past your father, but if that was his intention, I'm sure he would have climbed straight up and got it yesterday!" Jeanie laughed. "We have plenty of potatoes, so I'm going to make a meat and potato pie."

****

It didn't take Stella too long to walk over to Will's house. She only needed to follow the footpath that led from the other side of the recreation ground, then walk past Kilburn Colliery, and before long she would be in the village of Denby. Another few minutes on from there and she found herself at Will's front door. The thought that he might not have arrived home from his Uncle Jed's house was interrupted by a deep, but friendly voice.

"Good afternoon, young lady," the voice called from behind a bush.

The man's sudden presence, and the fact that he held a pair of hedge clippers in his hand, was enough to startle Stella and she stepped back in mild shock.

"Oh, I'm sorry, love, I didn't mean to scare you, I'm just doing a little seasonal pruning. Anyway, what can

I do for you?" the man asked.

"I've come to see Will. Has he arrived back home yet?"

"Ahh, you must be Stella. Will has been telling me all about you," the man said cheerfully, as he lifted his trilby sun hat slightly off his head by way of a greeting. "I'm Will's father and I'm pleased to meet you," he said, offering his arm out to shake hands with Stella.

"If you'd like to follow me, I'll show you where he is," the man led her around the back of the house and through to the garden. "Will is busy with the new arrivals, so you'll find him in there." Will's father pointed to a woodshed at the bottom of the garden.

Stella thanked him and made her way towards the shed. The door was open slightly and she could see that Will was holding something furry in his arms. As she got nearer, she realised he was stroking a rabbit. Stella smiled warmly at the affection Will showed towards the rabbit and stood to briefly watch him. Before long, Will turned, and upon realising that Stella was watching him, he beamed his usual big smile.

"Stella," he whispered, so as not to frighten the rabbit. "Come and see."

Stella walked towards the shed. "Who do we have here then?" she asked, gently ruffling the top of the rabbit's head.

"This is Misty, and these are her babies. Three boys and two girls," Will said affectionately.

At ground level, was a wooden pen with wire mesh around it. The pen held four grey and white baby rabbits and one that was completely grey like its mother. Stella crouched down to get a better view of the tiny little bundles of fur.

"Oh Will, they are adorable," Stella whispered, peering inside the pen.

"Aren't they just. Misty gave birth to them all about six weeks ago. I never said anything before, because sadly one of them died, so I wanted to see how the rest would develop first. Thankfully, these five seem to be coming along nicely. We'd better not disturb the babies, but would you like to hold Misty?"

Stella nodded and carefully took the rabbit from Will's arms and gently stroked her silvery grey fur. "She is so beautiful. I can see why you named her Misty."

The rabbit began to struggle a little in Stella's arms. "Here, I think she wants to get back to her babies," Stella said, carefully passing the rabbit back to Will.

Will carefully lowered the rabbit back into the pen, and she at once hopped over to check on her young.

"They are all so sweet. It will be lovely to watch them develop," Stella said.

Will smiled and moved closer to Stella, putting his arms around her and kissed her gently. "I know it's been less than 48 hours, but it does seem longer than that since I kissed you last," he said softly, tenderly brushing a lock of hair from her face.

Stella smiled warmly. "I miss us being at camp, we had such a fantastic week."

Will nodded. "Come on, let's go inside and I'll get us a drink." Will put his arm around Stella's shoulder and led her up to the house.

Inside, Will's mum was busy baking a pie, and the sweet smell of stewed fruit filled the kitchen, which reminded Stella that she hadn't eaten since breakfast. One slice of dried-up bread with a smattering of butter and a cup of tea was all that had amounted to. Not like camp, where one could choose from a whole manner of breakfast items, prepared and cooked ready for you to take your pick. She had eaten well that week and had felt all the better for it.

"Hello, Stella, how lovely to see you again," Will's mum said, stirring the stewed fruit as it bubbled away in the pan. "I hear you had a good week on the coast?"

"Yes, thank you, Mrs Turner, we had a wonderful time, didn't we, Will," Stella said, looking affectionately towards Will, who was busy preparing a tray of tea. Will's father came in from the garden and washed his hands at the sink.

"Looks like I've finished pruning just in time - tea and a piece of apple and blackberry pie... wonderful," Will's father said, kissing his wife on her cheek.

"Well, it won't be quite ready for a while yet, dear, this has to cool first," she said, removing the pan of fruit from the stove. "We'll take the tea tray outside, Will. It looks a perfect afternoon for it."

Will took the tray of tea things out into the garden and set it down on a little round table. They all sat together and exchanged general chatter on various subjects from gardening, growing blackberries, baby rabbits and the miners' camp.

"I hear from Uncle Jed that his friend won the knobbly knees competition again,"

Will's father laughed. "He's certainly an odd little character, that Jimmy Parkin."

"Odd, and quite curt when he's had a few beers," Will said crossly.

"Ahh yes. Uncle Jed mentioned that Jimmy had upset you, Stella, but you gave him what for, good for you!" Will's father said with a nod.

Stella laughed. "At least he apologised in the end."

"Yes, indeed. So anyway, Stella, Will tells me you like to write, and that you have a keen interest in furthering your skill. He's mentioned that I am hoping to get some short stories published, I believe?"

"Yes, I'm hoping to study English at college, but as far as getting things published is concerned, I have no idea where to start."

Will's father sat back in his chair. "Yes, that side of it would seem to be somewhat of an obstacle. I have written to three publishing houses to ask if they may be interested in my stories, but I've had no response yet."

Will's mother finished the last of her tea and got up from her seat. "Would you all excuse me, I must go and get on with baking this pie."

"I'll bring the tea tray, Mum. We'll leave Dad and Stella to discuss their ambitions."

Stella and Will's father continued to chat, each discussing their ideas and plans on how to achieve their writing goals.

"Well, Stella, it certainly sounds as though you have the determination and perseverance needed to develop your skills. The writer's mind is like an intricate painting of imagination and creation, isn't it?"

"It is, and I'm not sure whether writing is a talent that is in your blood or a skill that must be developed. Maybe both, I think."

Will's father considered what Stella had said for a while before answering. "I do often wonder about that myself, but it's certainly not something that's in my blood. Neither of my parents were creative in that way, nor any of my grandparents. Your grandfather liked to write, though?"

Stella nodded. "Yes, he did. We would spend hours together, writing poems or even just the odd line or two. He could make up a rhyme in his head and just come out with it," Stella laughed as she recalled her memories.

"It sounds as though you were both very close." Will's father said.

Stella nodded. "I must show you some of my grandpa's poems sometime, if you'd like?"

"It would be a pleasure to read them," he said with a smile. "Ahh... now what do we have here then?" he said, looking beyond Stella.

Stella turned to see Will walking towards them holding a tray, followed by his mother carrying some tea plates.

Will set the tray down on the table. "Now then," he said with a grin. "Who would like some pie?"

TWENTY-SEVEN

As the afternoon pushed on into the evening, Stella became a little mindful that she might be outstaying her welcome. She had been enjoying the company of Will and his parents so much that she hadn't quite realised how much time had passed. Although the Turners insisted she was welcome to stay, Stella gave thought to the effort her mother would have gone to in preparing dinner and decided it best to get home. She thanked Will's parents for their hospitality and Will insisted on walking her home.

As they walked, Will told Stella that a date for his apprenticeship interview had arrived and would be in just under two weeks. Until then, he would be dividing his time between odd jobs at home and helping his Uncle Jed with repairs and decorating at their new house. When they got onto the recreation ground, Stella took a seat on the bench and looked out across the openness.

"Are you alright, you seem distant suddenly," Will put his arm around Stella's shoulder.

"I'm just not looking forward to starting back to school tomorrow. I mean, I've always enjoyed school, but… I just wish I had a clearer idea of the path I want to follow, instead of thinking I'm going to be the next Enid Blyton."

Will regarded this for a moment before speaking.

"Have your teachers not offered any advice?"

Stella sighed. "If I ask any one of them, they just say secretarial college," Stella said nonchalantly. "Although… there is one teacher who I have always liked, maybe I'll speak to her."

Will pulled Stella close and kissed the top of her head. "It will all work out... you'll see."

As Stella got to the top of the entry, she noticed that her father's ladder was still propped up against the outhouse. Not thinking too much of it, she opened the kitchen door, walked in, and could hardly believe what she faced.

****

Jeanie's inertia was disturbed by noises that she couldn't make sense of. She strived to open her eyes... only the one eye, as it turned out... since the other was scrunched up by the hugely swollen cheek that now throbbed concurrently with her pulse. She tried to focus and couldn't decide if the darkness was down to the time of day or the trauma to her face. Either way, she felt as though she'd been lying in the same position for hours. She could recall, though, that there had been brief moments of semi-consciousness. Moments when the whole damned incident would flash through her mind like a bad dream. She strained to listen for a minute... all seemed quiet, but that didn't mean he wasn't still in the house. Chances were, though, he'd taken himself off to wherever he usually went, after what *he* liked to refer to as a 'misunderstanding'.

Jeanie tried to lift her head and sit up, but nothing seemed to work in coordination, and her head and shoulders met the floor with a bump that sent a shock wave of pain searing through her whole body. A second attempt, and, although it hurt like hell, she managed to drag herself to her feet. The instance she gained her balance, a rush of dizziness flooded her head, closely followed by a wave of nausea. If she didn't want to meet with the floor again, sitting down on the edge of the bed was the best choice.

As the symptoms began to ease, they were soon replaced by a loud knocking that produced a reverberating sound in her head, which Jeanie thought felt like a woodpecker drumming against her skull with its beak. Several seconds passed before her brain processed the noises… a rush of footsteps coming up the stairs. Her heart sank. Could he still be in the house?

A surge of reassurance passed through her mind, as she realised it was Stella's voice shouting in unequivocal alarm; a reassurance that relieved her such that she just burst into tears. "Stella love, I'm in…" Jeanie couldn't muster the energy to finish her sentence, and, in any case, Stella was in the room before she had a chance to.

"Mam! Oh, my goodness… what's happened? Let me see."

"Oh, Stella, I…" Jeanie shook her head and used her hand as a shield to hide her face.

Stella kneeled on the floor in front of her mother. "Why has he done this to you?"

Jeanie shook her head again. "I don't know…"

Stella gently lowered her mother's hand, which revealed the sickening sight of her father's handy work.

"Your eye…" Stella paused, deciding it was best not to go into too much detail, but rather to allow her mother to survey things in her own time.

"I'll go and fetch the iodine and some warm water to bathe your eye, and I'll make you a hot drink."

"Thanks, love," Jeanie said, easing her way to the edge of the bed to stand up.

"Mam! What are you doing, sit down put your feet up and rest."

"I need to deal with that awful mess before your father comes back."

"No! I'll sort out the kitchen; you must rest," Stella insisted.

Heading for the door, Stella stopped just short of exiting it. "Should I send for Doctor Keys?"

"Heavens, no, it'll only make things worse. I'll be fine once I get to my feet and freshen myself up. Getting that kitchen tidied is more important just now."

Stella turned and left the room to make her way downstairs, however, she couldn't stop herself from speaking her mind. "I suppose it's important if we want to keep him from getting his temper up again," she said, pausing at the top of the stairs to wait for her retort to be answered with the usual defensive response. She didn't have to wait long…

"Now then, Stella, there's no need to speak like that about your father."

And there it was. The usual bulwark of protection that her mother insisted on building around a man who was neither worthy of it, nor deserved it. Her father's behaviour infuriated Stella, but the way her mother stuck up for him… well, that was beginning to become equally as infuriating.

Stella put some milk into a saucepan and placed it over a gentle heat. She shook her head as she looked around the kitchen, wondering where to begin. Goodness only knew what could have sent her father into a rage serious enough to cause this level of devastation.

She began by picking up one of the two dining chairs that lay on their backs on the kitchen floor and pushed it back under the table. The legs of the other chair were broken, and it sickened her to think that, either he had taken his temper out on the chairs, or her mother had used them as obstacles to buy herself some time. Next, she turned her attention to a broken dish on the floor and what appeared to have once been the makings of the meat and potato pie her mother had intended to cook. The raw pastry dough and filling now hideously redecorated the kitchen wall.

Stella filled a cup with hot milk from the saucepan and stirred in a little sugar and a small tot of her father's whiskey. Then she fetched some lint padding and iodine out from the cupboard, placed everything onto a tray and took it upstairs.

As she got to the top of the landing, she noticed the door to her parents' bedroom was ajar, and that her mother was standing, just staring into the mirror that hung upon her bedroom wall. There was a huge crack across the middle of the mirror, the cause of which had been the outcome of a previous bout of her father's rage, and although it had been there as long as Stella could remember, for some reason it seemed to stand out more than she'd ever noticed before, and it distorted her mother's reflection so that it almost made her unrecognisable.

Stella watched as her mother used the pad of her middle finger to delicately pat the purple mass of bulging skin on her cheek, which was so swollen it buried her eye completely. She watched her mother's futile attempts to cover the injured side of her face with a tress of hair and then at the doleful look of dejection upon realising it had no effect.

"Here, Mam," Stella said softly. "Come and have your drink and let me bathe your eye a little."

Jeanie nodded, moved away from the mirror, and climbed into bed. Stella poured some of the iodine ointment onto the lint padding and very gently bathed her mother's cheek.

"Is everything in order downstairs?" Jeanie said, flinching at the sting from the iodine. "I'm sorry you've come home to this, love, especially when you've got to be up early for school."

Stella shook her head. "It's not you who should be apologising, Mam. I'm going back down in a moment to finish tidying up." She kissed her mother's good cheek. "I'll leave you to settle now. Try and get some sleep."

After scraping the remnants of pie and broken dish together, Stella threw the whole lot in the dustbin. She grabbed the mop bucket which had been left by the side of the ladder and shivered a little upon realising it held the dead pigeon. She frowned; apart from the pigeon, there was also a sizeable number of cigarette butts, each one was smudged with lipstick, the colour of which was unmistakably her mother's. It didn't take Stella any length of time to realise now, exactly what had been the cause for her father's rage.

Her mother had been smoking her father's cigarettes and getting rid of the evidence by flicking the butts up onto the outhouse roof. Stella could hardly believe her eyes, she had no idea that her mother still smoked, and if it hadn't been for the dead pigeon, her father would have been none the wiser either.

Eventually, by the time Stella had finished cleaning the kitchen, the clock on the mantelpiece struck a quarter to eleven, which made Stella wonder if her father might walk through the door any time soon. She had a mind to think that if he did, she would feel quite brave enough to give him a proper roasting. Instead, though, it was Jeanie who entered the kitchen.

"Mam, you startled me, why have you come back down, I thought you'd be asleep by now."

"I woke with a start, saw the time and thought I'd better come and see if you'd managed to get everything cleaned up."

"Yes, everything is in order, apart from a broken pie dish and that..." Stella said, tilting her head and nodding in the direction of the chair that lay in pieces by the kitchen door.

Jeanie sighed. "I'll see if Albert can do anything with it."

"I doubt it, the back legs have split and have broken off completely. Can't see it being any good for anything other than firewood."

"Still, I'll get him to take a look."

Stella rolled her eyes. Her mother had given no thought as to how she would explain the reasons for the broken chair to Albert, any more than she was going to explain the cigarette butts.

TWENTY-EIGHT

Stella lifted the lid on her school desk and placed her books inside. According to the chalkboard, a test in the form of a short story would be the order of the morning.

Their previous school year's history curriculum had been centred around, 'The Poor Law Act of 1834,' and the title of their story was about to be written on the chalkboard.

Mrs Cranfield stood with her back to the class, and with chalk in hand, she began to write. The whole class waited in anticipation to see what would be in store for them. Eager heads swayed from side to side, as some of the pupils tried to look past Mrs Cranfield's ample form to get a better view. She placed the chalk down, and stepped away, allowing the class to see what she had written:

'A day in the life of a workhouse child.' (In no less than 1,500 words.)

"Class, with the Poor Law Act of 1934 in mind, I want you to write a short story. You have two and a half hours, and test conditions apply," Mrs Cranfield said, patting her hands free of chalk dust.

Apart from a few sighs and groans from the odd pupil here and there, everyone just put their heads down and got on with it.

Stella copied the title down onto a fresh piece of lined paper and wrote the date neatly in the top left corner, *'Monday 4th September 1950'*.

Fortunately for Stella, she enjoyed her history lessons and retained everything she had been taught.

She dipped her nib pen into the inkwell in preparation for constructing her story; after all, writing *was* her favourite subject. However, Stella was finding it hard to concentrate properly. Her mind kept wandering to thoughts of the awful events from the evening before, and she couldn't help picturing her mother's beaten face. Before long, Mrs Cranfield was standing behind her, she leaned forward to whisper in Stella's ear.

"Miss Felton, please do share your reasons for being in cloud cuckoo land."

"I'm sorry, Mrs Cranfield, I can't seem to concentrate," Stella whispered back.

"I can see that, young lady. You haven't written anything except the title and the date.

What on earth is the matter with you?" Mrs Cranfield said, her voice no longer at a whisper.

"May I be excused a moment? I need a breath of air."

Mrs Cranfield huffed. "You have 10 minutes, and that's 10 minutes less to complete your work. Off you go!"

Stella jumped up out of her seat and hurried out of the classroom. As she stepped out into the corridor she bumped into one of her other teachers, sending a stack of exercise books into mid-air.

"Good heavens," the teacher cried in mild shock. "Where are you off to in such a hurry?"

"I'm so sorry, Miss Hutton," Stella said, crouching down to collect the books together.

"Are you unwell?" the teacher asked, bending down to help Stella.

It was all too much for Stella, and as she toppled backwards onto her bottom, her eyes filled with tears that she tried desperately to hold back.

"Hey, come now. What has upset you?" Miss Hutton asked, passing Stella a handkerchief.

Stella dabbed her eyes and stood up. "It's a long story, miss, and I really must get back to class. Mrs Cranfield has only given me 10 minutes."

Miss Hutton arranged the books into a pile and stood up. "You will find it hard to concentrate in your state. Now let's get some air, and you leave Mrs Cranfield to me."

With lessons still in progress, the schoolyard was free of pupils and eerily silent. Miss Hutton led Stella to a nearby bench and listened while Stella explained the concerns she had about her parents. Thinking it not altogether right to go into any detail, Stella kept it brief. But she did, however, explain the toll her grandfather's passing had taken on her.

Miss Hutton put her arm around Stella's shoulder. "Oh, my dear Stella, it is awful when parents don't get along, but you can't burden yourself with their troubles."

"It's just so difficult when you live under the same roof."

Miss Hutton nodded. "I know," she said softly. "And I also know that, as hard as it is to lose a loved one, time is a great healer."

"Miss Hutton, I wondered if I might speak with you, after school, I mean. There's something on which I would like your advice."

"Of course you can, Stella, I would be glad to. Now, let's get you back to class and you can crack on with that story!"

Stella sat behind her desk, inhaled deeply and began to construct her story.

Thankfully, Mrs Cranfield had accepted Miss Hutton's request that Stella be allowed an extra 20 minutes to complete her work. Eventually, when her time was up, Mrs Cranfield asked Stella to put down her pen and bring her paper to the front. All the other pupils had already been dismissed, which only left Stella and her teacher in the classroom. Mrs Cranfield put on her pince-nez spectacles and briefly scanned Stella's work. She had always been a firm, but fair teacher, who never really lost her temper, compared to some of the other teachers who wouldn't have given a second thought to using the cane. She did, however, have an annoying habit of regularly needing to clear her throat, which a lot of the pupils found distracting.

"Ahem! Well, this seems in order, so you may go," Mrs Cranfield said, placing her spectacles in her blazer pocket.

"Thank you, Mrs Cranfield, and thank you for allowing me to have the extra time."

"Yes…well, thanks are due to Miss Hutton. I trust you will be in better form tomorrow."

Stella just smiled, gathered her things, and made her way to her next lesson.

The bell, to signify the end of the school day, rang. Its usual welcoming tone, as always, created a mad scuffle of pupils desperate to leave class. Stella peered through the glass in Miss Hutton's classroom door and could see she was busy marking work in an exercise book. The teacher closed the book and added it to a pile on her desk, before reaching for another. Stella took this as her opportunity to knock. Miss Hutton looked up, and upon realising it was Stella, beckoned for her to enter.

"Thank you for seeing me, miss," Stella said, standing at the desk in front of the teacher.

"How did you get on with your story?" Miss Hutton asked.

"Perfectly well in the end, I think, owing to the extra time, which is thanks to you, miss."

"Well, we'll see, because I shall be helping Mrs Cranfield to mark everyone's tests shortly," Miss Hutton said. "Now… you take a seat, and tell me what is troubling you?"

Stella passed Miss Hutton her notebook that held the poems she had written. She explained how, from quite an early age, something inside had compelled her to write. She could never put her finger on what that something was, just that it was always there, like a strangely pleasant itch that had to be scratched. She explained how her imagination would constantly be ablaze with thoughts and ideas that just had to go down on paper regardless of the hour of day or night.

"My grandpa was the same, which is why we got along so well together. He kept a notebook too."

"I understand what you are saying to me, Stella, and I agree, your imagination and creativity certainly shine through in your work. So, what exactly is it that you want my advice about?"

"I don't know how to move forward with it. I don't know if I'm just wasting my time, chasing a dream that will never be a reality. I mean, how are you supposed to know if you are good enough?"

Miss Hutton shook her head gently. "You don't, the only way *to* know, is if you persevere with it. What do your parents think?"

Stella's chin dropped to her chest. "I think they would be quite happy for me to just find some sort of employment," she said, before looking straight at Miss Hutton. "But that's because they don't understand the *urge* that… drives me to write. I don't know where it comes from, but it's always there, waiting, needing to be released."

Miss Hutton stared briefly at Stella, as though she wasn't sure of what to say. Then suddenly, she rose from her desk with a certain swiftness that made Stella think she had said something quite frivolous.

"Stella, I need to think about everything you've said to me today, but in the meantime, may I borrow this?" Miss Hutton asked, waving Stella's notebook.

"Yes…of course, miss," Stella said, in slight bewilderment. "Jolly good, then I will see you tomorrow."

****

Miss Hutton paused at the headmaster's door and took a deep breath before knocking.

A deep voice from within the room bellowed a command to enter, to which Miss Hutton complied.

"Ahh, Miss Hutton. What can I do for you?"

"Mr Rice, if I may be so bold as to ask, would you mind reading this story? It's been written by Stella Felton, sir, and if I may say so, it is good. It would seem this young lady has an excellent mind for compiling stories and poems."

"And your point is?"

"Well forgive me, sir, but… I would like to… that is to say… if it is at all possible… I—"

"Do get to the point, Miss Hutton," Mr Rice interjected sharply, peering over his spectacles.

"Sir… I would like to tutor her and give her extra lessons in English."

"I don't understand. If you believe her to be good already, why would she need extra tuition?"

"She has a desire to become an author, and she has a talent. I also think I could help her—"

Mr Rice cut Miss Hutton short again, "I don't think that is appropriate, Miss Hutton, and I am certain that the Feltons would not be able to afford private tuition."

"No sir, they wouldn't, that is why I would offer my services on a complimentary basis—"

"Complimentary?" Mr Rice's voice boomed. "But, Miss Hutton, why on earth would you want to work for nothing?"

"Because, sir, I see something in her style of writing. She has a gift, one that could prosper, given the right guidance."

"Really…well, she must have something quite special if you're prepared to give up your time for free, Miss Hutton."

"I believe she has. If you would please look at this…" Miss Hutton handed Stella's notebook to Mr Rice.

Mr Rice read the first few poems in the notebook and tapped his index finger on his desk, a look of uncertainty appeared on his face. "Hmm… these are rather good, but how can you be sure she has written them all by herself?"

"Sir, if I may." Miss Hutton handed Mr Rice a folder holding Stella's work. "I have been teaching English to Stella for three years now, and over that time I have developed a feel for her style of writing. I have thought for some time that she does have something unique, and today I have come to learn that she also feels that way herself."

"I'm not entirely sure it's a good enough reason to—"

"Please… forgive me for butting in, sir, but after all, isn't this the reason we are working with these young people? I just feel that her talent may go to waste if I don't at least *try* to help."

Mr. Rice peered over his spectacles again. "Yes, Miss Hutton, you are correct, and I suppose… theoretically, I can't control what you do with yourself outside of school time, particularly if you're not expecting pay, but… we will need to see her parents first to gain their permission. Draft a letter to send home, and I'll have a chat with them."

"I will and thank you, Mr. Rice. Thank you very much indeed, sir," Miss Hutton beamed.

TWENTY-NINE

It was getting close to four o'clock, and Stella's chat with Miss Hutton meant she was the last pupil to leave for the day. As she made her way across the schoolyard towards the gate, she noticed that Will was sitting on the wall, waiting for her. He was sitting with his back to her and was quite unaware that she was making her way up behind him. She tiptoed quietly to where he was sitting and gave a precise poke with both of her index fingers on either side of his ribs. The mild shock made Will jump from the wall, and he turned to see Stella in fits of laughter. The smile soon left her face, however, when she realised he intended to jump the wall to retaliate.

A playful tussle ensued, one that was going in Will's favour, until she called out for him to stop. Her ribs were no longer able to tolerate the aching from her cries of laughter.

"How do you manage to get me every time?" Will joked, pulling her close.

"You're easy prey, I guess," she whispered, as her eyes met his. With nobody around to disapprove, the two of them kissed before leaving the school premises hand in hand, blissfully unaware however, that someone had been watching their antics from the classroom window.

Will's house was less than half a mile along the road from Stella's school, and before long they were standing outside.

"Mum says you can stay for your tea, if you think it will be okay?" Will asked.

Stella's immediate thoughts were of getting home to check on her mother after the horrendous events from the day before. She also wanted to pay a visit to her grandmother but quickly concluded that having tea with Will would not harm either. In any case, the chances of her mother having prepared any tea were always slim.

"If you're sure it's okay, I'd love to," Stella smiled.

Stella followed Will in through the back door, where his mum was busy preparing tea. The smell of homemade bread filled the kitchen, along with a dish of strawberry jam that she had cooked earlier. She was just putting the finishing touches to a sponge cake that smelled as equally delicious as the bread.

"Hello, you two. I hope you're both hungry?"

"Always, Mum," Will said, leaning in to kiss his mother on her cheek.

"Good. Well, the table is set. Your dad won't be home for a long while yet, so take these through for me, would you?" she requested, handing Will a tray loaded with plates, cutlery and the butter dish.

Stella and Will moved into the dining room, and Stella could hardly believe her eyes. The table had been set with a banquet of food. A freshly prepared salad with cucumber and tomatoes from the greenhouse, lettuce, spring onions and radishes from the salad garden, tinned ham and boiled eggs. Stella had to blink to believe what she was seeing.

"Goodness me, Mrs Turner. I hope you haven't gone to all this trouble just for me?"

Stella said, eyeing everything up.

"Trouble? Not at all, dear, it's lovely to have you here," she said with a smile.

"Shame Dad won't be back yet though," Will added.

"Yes, he is working over his time today, big job on apparently," Will's mother said.

From then on, apart from exchanging the odd comment here and there, they enjoyed their tea in relative silence. Afterwards, Stella insisted on helping Will's mother with the tea pots, and then Will took Stella out into the garden to check on the baby rabbits. Stella helped Will replace the bedding in their cage and put out some more food, hay and fresh water.

"Will you keep them all?" Stella asked, feeding Misty with a leftover lettuce leaf.

"No, they're all spoken for already," Will said, patting the straw bedding down inside the cage. "All except this little one here." Will pointed to the only rabbit that had its mother's silvery grey colouring.

"Why? What is happening with that one?" Stella asked.

"Well, this little girl is already reserved. She is going to be a birthday gift for someone."

"Well, whoever that someone is, they sure are lucky. She is the most beautiful of them all."

****

After a brief visit to her grandmother's, Stella arrived home. It was getting quite late. She assumed her father would be at the pub as usual, but her mother was nowhere to be seen either. Stella stood at the foot of the stairs and called up for her, but there was no response. She glanced back towards the kitchen and turned her nose up at a dried-up spam sandwich that had been left out for her on the kitchen table. Being thankful for the earlier feast at Will's house, she decided to take herself off to her room. Just as she got to the top of the stairs, her mother appeared from the bathroom.

"Ahh, Stella love, I thought I heard you come in. I was just… well, I thought I would see what make-up I had; you know… to try and disguise… oh never mind. Have you been to Grandma's house?"

"Yes, she's had quite a good day, she's managed a little walk out too," Stella said, stifling a yawn.

"Finally… she has listened then! Sheila has been trying to tell her that a short walk each day will help her knees."

"Well whatever Aunty Sheila has threatened her with, it's worked. She intends on taking a short walk each day from now on. Anyway, I'm off to bed, Mam, night."

"Just before you go… if anyone asks how I got a black eye, I tripped and bumped my face… okay?"

Stella tutted. "So, you cover up the evidence and I'll cover up the truth." Stella just sighed, shook her head, and took herself off to her room.

Stella made herself comfortable in bed and opened one of the books she'd borrowed from Will: 'A Tale of Two Cities' by Charles Dickens, which she was already halfway through. After reading a further 10 pages or so, her eyelids started to feel very heavy and kept closing involuntarily. She rubbed her eyes, yawned, and glanced across at the clock on her bedside table. It was almost a quarter past ten. She placed her bookmark in between two pages of her book and set it down next to her clock. She settled herself down under the covers, closed her eyes, and in no time, was fast asleep.

She'd only been asleep for half an hour, when her slumber was abruptly disturbed by the sound of her bedroom door being thrust open. Stella sat bolt upright in her bed to try and make sense of the sudden commotion. It was her father, and he was quite clearly livid about something…

"What the bloody hell do you call this?" he yelled, waving something he held in his hand.

Stella rubbed her eyes and tried to focus on the blurry shape of her father as he stood in the doorway. The light from the landing lit up her room, and as her vision adjusted, she could see he was holding a letter.

"This was hand-delivered this evening. Me and yer mam have been summoned into school tomorrow by your headmaster!"

"I have no idea *why* he should want to see you!" Stella said, daring to raise her voice a little to match her father's high pitch.

Derek charged over to Stella's bed and wafted the letter in front of her face. "And now you're telling me lies as well. Parents don't get hauled up in front of the headmaster for nothing."

Mindful of her position of vulnerability, Stella swung the bedclothes back and quickly got out of bed, she grabbed her dressing gown and left the room to go downstairs. Within seconds, he was behind her. He grabbed a clump of her hair, and dragged her backwards, bringing her down heavily on the top step. Still with her hair in his hand, he crouched down by the side of her, his face close enough for her to feel his unshaven skin against her cheek and whispered into her ear.

"If you've done anything to embarrass me, I swear to God I'll…"

He cut his sentence short of any intentions but shoved her head away from his own with such force, that it met with the wall with a thud. He stood up, pushed past her, and then in his usual 'post-violent' manner, quite calmly walked down the stairs and into the lounge, closing the door behind him.

Stella got to her feet, put her hand to the back of her head and grabbed a fistful of loose strands of hair that he had pulled out. She picked up her dressing gown and was about to head back into her room when her mother whispered to her from across the landing.

"Stella, are you okay, love?"

Stella looked over to her parents' room. She could see that her mother had the bedroom door slightly ajar and was peering through from behind it. Having no words of response to offer, Stella just continued into her room, shut her bedroom door, and climbed back into bed.

****

The following morning, Stella was about to leave for school, when her mother walked into the kitchen.

"Stella, love, are you alright today?"

Stella raised her hand dismissively. "I'm not discussing it, Mam. I need to get off to school. I don't want to add lateness to whatever else the headmaster wants you for."

"Are you sure you don't know why he wants to see us, love?" Jeanie asked.

"No, Mam, I don't," Stella said, shoving a slightly wizened apple into her school bag.

Jeanie sat down at the kitchen table. "I think this new job is getting to your father a bit."

Stella rolled her eyes contemptuously as Jeanie continued to make excuses for Derek's behaviour.

"After all, he's not been in full-time work since leaving the army. Try not to think too bad of him. I'm sure —"

"What are you sure of this time?" Stella scolded, leaning across the table to look directly at her mother. "That he'll change once he's settled in at Creswell?" She shook her head. "You make excuse after excuse for him, and I'm sick of it."

Stella grabbed her school bag and marched out of the house before her mother had a chance to respond.

THIRTY

Stella sat on a wooden chair in the school corridor, just along from the headmaster's office. She waited nervously to find out the reason her parents had been called into school. Her palms were sweating, and her hands were still shaking. Surely Miss Hutton hadn't felt that Stella's concerns for her parents' dysfunctional relationship really called for fetching them into school? After all, she hadn't gone into any detail about it. Jeanie, who also sat on a chair next to her daughter, pulled a tress of hair over her face. She had tried her best with the makeup, but the bruise around her eye and cheek was still visibly clear and had the colour of an over-ripe plum. Meanwhile, Derek marched up and down the corridor, and each time he drew level with Mr Rice's door, he stopped to look through the small square pane of glass. He checked his watch and huffed before pacing over to where his wife and daughter sat. He bent forward and was about to berate Stella for the umpteenth time since receiving the letter, when suddenly the door to Mr Rice's office opened and Miss Hutton appeared.

"Mr Rice will see you all now," she said and stood aside to allow the family to enter the office. As Jeanie walked past Miss Hutton, she fiddled with her hair to disguise her bruise.

"Ahh, Mr and Mrs Felton, Miss Felton, do have a seat," Mr Rice gestured to the three chairs that had been placed in front of his desk.

Mr Rice arched a brow of suspicion upon noticing Jeanie's attempt to hide the bruise on her face.

"I have called you here today to discuss your thoughts on the possibility of your daughter receiving extra English tuition with Miss Hutton," Mr Rice said with a smile on his face.

"So, what yer saying is that Stella ain't as clever as the rest and needs extra work?" Derek said firmly.

Mr Rice raised his eyebrows in response to Derek's abrupt comment. "No, Mr. Felton, I am saying the exact opposite. Miss Hutton believes… *we* believe that your daughter may have a flair, a gift, if you like, for writing stories and poetry. And if handled correctly, as in extra tuition, she may well go on to do something with it."

Jeanie turned to look for Derek's reaction, but the man just fixed his gaze upon Mr Rice. Mr Rice continued…

"Now, Miss Hutton has very kindly offered to provide the tuition in her own time, and at no cost to yourselves." Mr Rice looked over his spectacles, awaiting a reaction from the Feltons… a reaction that never came. Mr Rice removed his spectacles and sighed. "Believe me, this is an exceptional proposition. Miss Hutton is offering your daughter an opportunity to further her obvious talent. I take it you are both aware of how well she writes? I mean, her imagination and ideas are remarkable, and given the correct tuition, who knows?"

Derek and Jeanie, both at a loss for words could only stare at Mr Rice in disbelief.

"Look, if neither of you have any objections to Miss Hutton providing your daughter with extra tuition, then let's see what Miss Felton thinks of it herself."

Mr Rice waited for Stella's response. "Well, young lady? Miss Hutton thinks you have an ability for which she will give up her time. So, speak up… what do you think?"

Stella's face lit up, and she turned to Miss Hutton. "You think so?"

Miss Hutton smiled and nodded enthusiastically.

"So, what do you say, young lady?" Mr Rice asked, putting his spectacles back on.

Stella was speechless. Jeanie nudged her with her elbow, "Stella? Answer your teacher, then."

"I would be very pleased to accept Miss Hutton's kind offer, sir, thank you very much."

"Jolly good, Miss Felton. You go on back for your last lesson then, and your parents and I will discuss with Miss Hutton how best to make it work."

****

After school had ended, Will was sitting on the wall, waiting for Stella to come out from class. But this time, to avoid a prod in the ribs, he sat facing towards the schoolyard. When she appeared from amongst the other pupils, he beamed his usual big smile at her and jumped from the wall.

"I see you weren't taking any chances today," Stella giggled, as she walked towards him.

"I think I'm getting wise to your tricks now," he said, taking her school bag off her shoulder and flinging it over his own. "How has your day been?"

"Pretty good, and I have news. I'm going to be tutored!"

Will looked at Stella and raised his brows. "Tutored?"

As they walked, Stella explained to Will how the opportunity had presented itself for her to ask her teacher's advice about her vision of becoming a published writer. And that, as it turned out, the teacher had said she already recognised her potential, the result of that being the offer of extra English tuition outside of school time.

"That's wonderful, Stella. You see, it *was* worth speaking to someone after all," Will said, putting his arm around her shoulder; pulling her close, he kissed her forehead.

Eventually, when they reached Will's house, Stella asked after the baby rabbits.

"Well, I have something to show you. Come and see," he said, taking hold of her hand, and leading her around the back of the house and into the garden.

Standing by the garden shed was a little wooden rabbit hutch, with two doors and a sloping felt roof.

"I've been busy these last two days making this," Will said, crouching down by the front of the hutch.

He opened the first door that had a wire mesh front. "This bigger side is the living space, and that leads through into this concealed sleeping compartment," Will opened a second solid wood door to show Stella the sleeping area.

"Goodness, Will, it's brilliant, you are clever. But if you already have homes for the babies, why would you need to build another hutch?"

Will stood up. "Well, do you remember when I said

that one of the babies is going to be a birthday gift for someone?" Stella nodded. "Well, the hutch is too. It's all part of the birthday gift, you see."

Stella grinned. "How wonderful. I can't think of a gift any better than a beautiful baby rabbit in its own little home, especially a home you have built all by yourself."

Will took a step nearer to Stella, placed his arm around her shoulder and whispered in her ear.

"That's good then, because it's all for you."

Stella pulled away to look directly at Will. "What? What do you mean, it's all for me?"

"I know your birthday isn't until next month, but they will be ready to leave their mum soon, and I wanted to be prepared."

"Will, I don't know what to say," Stella said, putting her hand to her mouth in disbelief.

"Your parents will be okay with it, won't they? I will supply everything she'll need."

Stella's mind raced, her mother would be alright with it, but a rabbit in her father's precious garden... no way would he agree to that.

"I'm not sure what my father would say, but I think I would prefer to keep her at my grandma's. She has a secure garden and there's more space there too. I would have to ask her first, though."

"You can always keep her here if not. Either way, she's yours, so you'd better think of a name for her.

Stella threw her arms around Will's neck and kissed him. "Thank you, Will, thank you so much."

****

Later that evening, Stella took her father's habitual visit to the Traveller's Rest pub as an opportunity to speak with her mother about the recent developments in her life. She began by asking her mother what her opinion was on the unexpected offer of having extra tuition and wasn't at all surprised by the lack of enthusiasm that followed. Finding employment was still to be the priority, and if the tuition didn't hinder that, then within reason, what she did with her free time was up to her. The question of what purpose extra tuition would serve was mentioned, and the discussion was quickly changed to the suggestion that the local Co-op store would soon be taking on a shopgirl and that if she stood any chance of a position there, then now would be a suitable time to make enquiries.

Given that there was no point in trying to get her mother to understand the urge that compelled her to write, Stella gave up trying and moved on to the next subject, which was her friendship with Will. This time, however, she *was* surprised by the lack of enthusiasm.

Complete apathy would be a better way to describe her mother's disinterest in wanting to know anything further about the young man who had come into her daughter's life.

Concluding that her efforts were futile, Stella decided not to bother going into any more detail and got up out of the armchair to go up to her room. She did, however, suggest that it might be wise not to mention her friendship with Will to her father.

"Oh, don't worry, I doubt he will be interested

anyway," Jeanie said, stifling a yawn.

Well, that makes two of you then, Stella thought, before bidding her mother goodnight and taking herself off to bed.

Stella climbed into bed, settled down and closed her eyes. Immediately, the image of Misty and her babies came into her mind, and in particular, the baby that would very soon be hers. She had already cleared it with her grandma, and keeping the rabbit at her house would not be a problem. She'll have lots of garden to roam around, and plenty of dandelions to nibble on, her grandma had said.

That led her to think about names, and she soon had such a list in her head, that she just had to get up out of bed to write them all down in her notebook.

Just as she was about to get back into bed, she heard raised voices coming from outside on the street. She discreetly lifted one corner of her curtain and peered through the window. Down on the street, she could see her father bickering with a punter from the pub. The other man held up his hand dismissively and walked away. Stella was glad that the two men had parted company without coming to blows. She closed her eyes tightly, in the hopes that her mother had already come up to bed, and she too could avoid an altercation. She climbed into bed and waited anxiously. Eventually, she felt relieved to hear her father's heavy footsteps coming up the stairs and then their bedroom door shut. She gave thought to her father's new shift patterns at Creswell Colliery. He was to work a week of days, followed by a week of nights. *At least when he's at work, everyone will have some respite from his temper,* Stella thought as she snuggled down under her covers and drifted off to sleep.

THIRTY-ONE

The school day passed quickly, and as he had done for the last two days, Will was sitting on the wall, waiting for Stella. As they walked, Stella gave Will the good news that her grandma would be delighted to let her keep the rabbit in her garden. Will was most excited to tell Stella that his Uncle Jed was sure he could fit the hutch into his shooting brake and was about to ask if Saturday would be all right to transport it, when Stella stopped him midway through his sentence.

"Hold on a minute, what on earth is a shooting brake?" she said with a frown.

Will laughed. "It's a style of car, well the body of a car. It has plenty of room in the back, enough to transport the hutch, in any case," he said. "So, do you think Saturday afternoon would be alright then?

"I'll check with my grandma, but I'm sure it will be okay."

"Maybe I'll get to meet your grandma?" Will asked tactfully.

Stella nodded eagerly. "I've told her about you. I gave her one of the photographs we had taken at the miners' camp. She said you look very handsome."

Will gave half a smile, and his cheeks reddened slightly. Stella nudged him with her elbow.

"Don't be coy, she's right," she grinned.

As they arrived outside Will's house, Stella looked at her wristwatch. "I'd better be getting home, I've got my very first tutoring session with my teacher this evening, and I don't want to be late." Stella reached up to kiss Will goodbye. "I can't wait to see that beautiful little bundle of fur in her new home," she said and turned to walk away. After taking a few steps, however, she stopped to call back to Will.

"Pearl..." she said with a smile.

Will frowned.

"I'm going to call her Pearl."

****

It didn't take Stella long to eat her tea. As usual, there wasn't much on her plate. A boiled egg with a slice of toast, and a glass of milk. Her father wasn't home yet, so finishing her tea and getting out of the house before he arrived was at the forefront of her mind.

"I'm off to see Miss Hutton then, Mam," Stella said to her mother, who was so absorbed in preparing her husband's tea, that she almost didn't realise she was being spoken to.

"Oh, right yes... sorry," she eventually said, as Stella was about to walk out of the door.

Stella made her way to the address Miss Hutton had given her. It was called Rose Cottage and was at the other end of the village to where Stella lived. She arrived at a tiny brick-built cottage with leaded glass bay windows on either side of the front door. She paused at the gate to admire a pink climbing rose that wreathed its way across a high archway over the gate. Each bud was in full bloom, and the sweet smell lingered in the early evening air. She watched closely as several bees darted in and out of each bud, searching for pollen. Miss Hutton's cottage was

CHASING A DREAM

appropriately named, as rose bushes of varying colours also grew in the front garden.

Miss Hutton appeared from the house and made her way along the path to greet Stella.

"Beautiful, isn't it," she said, pulling one of the rose buds gently towards her. She positioned her nose over the large bloom to fully absorb the scent of its sweet fragrance.

"Yes, miss, very beautiful."

Miss Hutton tenderly released the bud and watched as it freely located itself back within the refuge of the shrub.

"My father bought this climbing rose as a wedding anniversary gift for my mother.

Did you know that roses are a symbol of love and romance?"

"No, miss, I didn't know that."

"And in particular the pink rose is symbolic of gratitude and admiration."

"What a lovely thought, your mother must certainly love roses," Stella said.

"She did, but unfortunately she has passed now, and my father too."

"I'm sorry about that, miss," Stella said dolefully.

"That's alright, Stella, you were not to have known, my dear. Now then, shall we go inside, and I will make us a pot of tea before we start."

Stella followed her teacher into a small hallway and through into a large sitting room. Bookshelves adorned the right-hand side of the room, holding row upon row of books. In one corner there stood a magnificent oak desk with a writing inset of green leather. The desk was arranged with a brass pen holder, a perpetual calendar, a notepad and a pot of freshly sharpened pencils.

"Now, my dear, do take a seat, and I shall be with you momentarily," Miss Hutton said, gesturing toward the desk.

Stella sat down at the desk and thought how grand it appeared before her. It was perfectly positioned in front of a sizeable window, which allowed the light to beam through. The window itself framed a flawless view of the extensive rear garden. Across the other side of the room, featured upon a plain wall, was a fireplace carved out of stone with a tiled hearth and cast-iron fire grate, the contents of which burned steadily. Dotted around the room were various photographs of whom Stella could only assume were Miss Hutton's parents. Miss Hutton walked in with a tray of tea and set it down on the desk.

"Your home is very beautiful, miss," Stella said.

"Why thank you, Stella. Do you take milk in your tea?"

"Yes, please, miss."

"Oh, I almost forgot, I have some cake if you would like some?" Miss Hutton said, making her way back towards the kitchen.

"That would be nice, miss, thank you."

"Sponge cake or tea loaf? Both are homemade," Miss Hutton's voice echoed from the kitchen.

"Oh, erm… sponge cake please, miss."

"Excellent choice. Do look at the book I've left out

on the desk," she called.

Stella picked up the book and noted the title, '*How to Write Correctly*'. She opened it up and noticed someone had penned an inscription on the inside of the front cover, it read: '*To my darling Catherine, Many happy returns. Love always, David.*'

It was dated June 25th, 1942. Stella felt a little awkward reading the inscription and quickly turned the page. But then she began to wonder if Catherine was Miss Hutton's Christian name, and if so, who was David?

"If you promise to take care of it, you may borrow it," Miss Hutton said, peering around the door from the kitchen, disturbing Stella's thoughts and making her heart jump, as though she'd just been caught doing something wrong.

"In terms of reference, it is an exceptionally informative guide to which I still refer from time to time," she added.

"Oh…thank you, miss, that would be wonderful. If you're sure you don't mind?" "Not at all, my dear," Miss Hutton replied.

Miss Hutton walked back in with another tray and set it down on the desk. It held two china tea plates, and a larger plate laden with slices of delicious-looking sponge cake.

Miss Hutton leaned over the desk and placed a fine china teacup, saucer, and matching tea plate in front of Stella.

"Now, my dear, do help yourself to cake. Do you take sugar in your tea?"

Stella nodded. "Two please, miss."

"Two!" Miss Hutton exclaimed. "Good heavens, you'll have no teeth left in your head."

Stella laughed. "We don't always have a lot of sugar left over at home. I just know that I like it in my tea when I get the chance."

Miss Hutton smiled. "Then two sugars it is," she said, spooning two good helpings of sugar into the cup. She added the milk and filled the cup with tea from a china teapot that matched the rest of the crockery.

"Now... let us take a look at this book," Miss Hutton said, and paused to run her hand across the front cover. "Yes," she said softly. "It's been a while... but I still like to refer to it from time to time."

She opened the book and ran her fingers over the inscription on the inside cover. There was a beat of awkward silence and Stella was certain she noticed a tear in Miss Hutton's eye.

"Are you alright, miss?" Stella asked in a low tone.

Miss Hutton casually looked up and met Stella's gaze. "Yes, my dear. I'm sorry, my mind drifted for a moment."

She closed the book and placed it down on the desk. "Before we go any further, I just want to say that in the three years I have been teaching English to you, I have had the pleasure of reading many of your stories and your poems. I think that with a little moulding and a lot of hard work, we can take this gift of yours and do something special with it. And if you are prepared to work hard, then I am prepared to put the time in to help you the best I can. What do you think?"

"Yes, miss, I am prepared to work hard, there's nothing I want more than to become a published writer."

"Jolly good," Miss Hutton said, picking up the book again. "Now, let us begin by looking at how efficiently you, as the writer, must 'frame' your words so that they convey the exact meaning you intend to give to your reader…"

Miss Hutton and Stella spent the rest of the evening working together until it was time for Stella to go home.

"Well, I think we will leave it there for now. Will your parents be collecting you?"

"Oh no, I shouldn't think so, my dad will be in the pub and my mam will be too busy. I will walk back on my own. I'll be alright, it's still quite light outside."

Miss Hutton frowned. "Nonetheless, I cannot let you walk on your own at this time of evening. I will see you home tonight, but you will have to arrange for one of your parents to collect you next time, or… perhaps… the young man that meets you from school each day?"

Stella darted an anxious look at Miss Hutton, but Miss Hutton just smiled and gave Stella a gentle nudge with her elbow. "It is perfectly alright, my dear, maybe you can tell me about him sometime?"

As they walked back through the village, they exchanged general chatter about everyday things, but then Stella found herself brave enough to ask questions about Miss Hutton's life.

"How long have you lived in Kilburn, miss? Only you don't speak like most folks do around here."

Miss Hutton laughed. "I came to live here in 1943 to be with my parents. We are from London originally, but Father wanted to retire to the country and of course, with the war on, London wasn't the best place to be. So, I decided to move here to be with them."

"When did they die?"

"They both passed within three months of each other, just over six years ago."

"Gosh, that must have been awful for you, I mean both of them so quickly."

"I had only been here about a year when they passed. My mother first, then my father. It was all too much for him and... well if a person can die of a broken heart, then I guess..."

Miss Hutton couldn't seem to finish her sentence. She stopped to look across at the horizon and changed the subject tactfully.

"I love to watch the sky, especially at this time of year, the way the night sweeps across and takes the sun, almost keeping it safe until morning."

Stella looked across at the sky too. "I know what you mean, miss. It reminds me of death, but in a nice way, I mean."

Miss Hutton frowned. "In what way, Stella?"

"I imagine that God is the night, and the sun is a loved one. God sweeps in and takes our loved ones and keeps them safe until it's time to see them again... in Heaven, I mean."

"What a lovely way of describing it, Stella. I had

never thought of it like that before."

THIRTY-TWO

The rest of the first week back at school soon passed, and Saturday, the day to welcome Pearl, had arrived. Stella had already arranged with Will that he and his uncle would take the rabbit hutch around to her grandma's house around one o'clock, but first, Stella reluctantly had an appointment to attend.

The Kilburn branch of the Ripley Co-operative stores was less than two minutes' walk from Stella's home, and although she couldn't be certain, she was sure her mother had only secured an interview with Mrs Bell, the store's supervisor, to deter her from wanting to be a writer. It 'is nothing but a pointless notion', were the words her mother used to dash Stella's desires, before going into detail on how lucky she was to be given such an opportunity to become a shopgirl.

Of course, to a certain extent, she knew her mother was correct. Even though Miss Hutton's tuition would help her, the likelihood of becoming an author was still a long shot. But Stella knew things within her mind were changing, and those changes had also brought about a certain determination not to give up or be hindered by obstacles or setbacks. At the very least, she had to try.

But for now, to keep her mother happy, she would do her best to secure a position at the Co-op. With any luck, it might just keep her father off her back too. There would be no point in hoping it would make him happy, though, nobody seemed to know where that key was. Working at the Co-op would mean she would have her evenings free to concentrate on her writing and to attend Miss Hutton's tutoring sessions and even put a little bit of money aside.

It was a warm day, and to allow some cool air into the store, Mrs Bell had the shop door propped open with a large wicker basket holding tins of pears, peaches, and mandarin oranges. Stella walked in to find the current shopgirl, Dorothy, standing on a two-step wooden ladder arranging boxes of Quaker Oats onto a shelf. Dorothy was four years older than Stella and had been working at the Co-op since leaving school, but she was expecting her first child, due to arrive sometime towards the end of October, and as Dorothy's husband, Bill, wasn't too keen on her having to climb up and down a ladder in her condition, she would be leaving very soon.

Dorothy stepped off the ladder, arched her spine and used both hands to rub the middle of her lower back, the curvature of which exaggerated her baby bump. She puffed up her cheeks and let out a breath, before managing a little smile, and telling Stella she would find Mrs Bell's office at the far end of the store. Stella thanked Dorothy and made her way to the back of the store, where she came to a closed door with a small wooden sign marked 'Private'. Stella knocked on the door and waited. Within a few seconds, the door opened. Mrs Bell's large form almost filled the doorway. She greeted Stella with a smile, pushing her glasses back up onto her nose.

"Morning, cherub, come in," Mrs Bell said, moving her hefty frame aside to allow Stella to pass.

A kettle whistled away to itself upon an electric two-ring hot plate situated on a wooden sideboard in the far corner of the tiny room.

"How about we start by you making me a cuppa, I'm spitting feathers!" Mrs Bell laughed, pushing her glasses back up her nose again.

Stella was completely taken aback by the instruction, but upon realising that the tea caddy, milk jug and sugar bowl were already laid out on a tray by the side of the hot plate, she merely got on with the request. After turning the hot plate off, she spooned tea leaves into a pot, and poured water from the kettle, placing a knitted tea cosy over the pot.

"Half a spoon of sugar please and make yourself one whilst you're at it. Oh, and I think you might find a tin of assorted biscuits hiding somewhere under all that paperwork. I'll have a custard cream," Mrs Bell said, nodding towards the untidy pile of papers strewn across the sideboard.

Mrs Bell sat herself down at a desk, on a chair that wasn't quite big enough to accommodate her sizeable posterior. She searched her desk for a notepad and pencil.

"Right then, cherub, I understand from your mother that you're looking to become a shopgirl?" Mrs Bell said, dabbing the lead end of the pencil on her tongue.

Stella stirred the tea in the pot. *No, I want to be a writer, I'm only here to please my parents,* she thought. "Well, yes if a position is available?" she said, searching under the papers for the biscuit tin.

"Well, that depends really. Your mother said you are due to leave school at Christmas, but Dorothy will be finishing in a few weeks." Mrs Bell tapped her pencil against her cheek as if to consider the situation, and again pushed her glasses back up her nose. "I tell you what, if you can work every Saturday and maybe run me a few errands in the week, I'm sure that between us we can manage until Christmas."

Mrs Bell looked at her watch. "Speaking of errands, where has Alfie got to? That lazy little beggar should have been here hours ago."

"Alfie?" Stella asked, taking a custard cream from the tin, and placing it on a saucer.

"Yes, Alfie Beardmore, lives at the top of High Street. He's the errand boy, or he's supposed to be. By heck, I'll give him a good scuff round his earhole when I get me hands on him!"

Stella poured tea into a cup and took it over to Mrs Bell's desk, setting it down in front of her. Mrs Bell soon picked up her cup and took a sip of her tea.

"My… you sure make a good cuppa, cherub. So, if that's anything to go by, then I'd say you've got the job," she said, pushing her glasses back up her nose for a fourth time.

Stella poured herself a cup of tea and picked up a biscuit. She wasn't quite expecting to be asked to make the tea, let alone being asked to work Saturdays, and just what did this 'run me a few errands in the week' suggestion entail? The last thing she needed was to commit herself to something that would encroach on her tutoring sessions.

Mrs Bell ate her biscuit and gulped back the rest of her tea. She got up and walked over to the door, opened it and shouted across the store.

"Dorothy! Have you seen Alfie yet this morning?"

Stella couldn't quite hear Dorothy's response but wondered why Mrs Bell didn't just go and speak to Dorothy instead of yawping across the store to her.

"That little varmint… are those orders ready?" Mrs Bell shouted again, before shutting the door. She sat back at her desk, checked her watch, and sighed deeply.

"Now then, cherub, how about you run me an errand or two?" Mrs Bell said, taking her glasses off to clean them on her apron.

"Now?" Stella questioned, aware of her arrangement with Will and Jed.

"It's not a problem, is it, cherub?" she said, holding her glasses up to the light and checking for smears.

Stella looked at her watch, ten to twelve, just over an hour before she needed to be at her grandma's. "No, Mrs Bell. What would you have me do?"

Mrs Bell led Stella back through to the store. Dorothy was busy serving a customer but pointed to a range of groceries laid out on the counter.

"Right, grab whatever you can carry from that lot, and follow me," Mrs Bell said, picking up as much as she could carry. Stella did as she was asked and followed Mrs Bell out of the store. She led her down a narrow pathway that ran along the side of the Co-op, to a bicycle that was leaning against the wall. Mrs Bell arranged the groceries into a large, square wicker basket fastened to the front of the bike.

"Is that the lot?" Mrs Bell asked.

"Erm… no, there were some other bits, but I couldn't carry any more."

"You wheel the bike round to the front of the shop then, and I'll go and fetch what's left," Mrs Bell said, and made her way back towards the front of the store.

Stella grabbed hold of the handlebars and pushed the bicycle, which felt very heavy, and she found it quite difficult to keep a balance. By the time she'd got to the front of the store, Mrs Bell was waiting with her arms full of groceries, which she positioned in the basket, rearranging some of the items to fit everything in. She then pulled some papers out of her apron pocket to show Stella. It was at that point, that Stella realised that she wasn't just wheeling the bike round to the front of the store for Alfie; no, Mrs Bell was expecting Stella to make the deliveries herself.

"There are three invoices here, one for each delivery. There are two for Highfield Road and one on Church Street, then when you've delivered them, you can pop back and collect another two orders, and they're both for the other end of the village. You can manage that, can't you, cherub?" Mrs Bell said, passing Stella the invoices. Stella took one hand off the handlebar to grab the invoices from Mrs Bell and almost lost control of the bike.

"You'll get used to it," she said with a grin, before turning on her heels and disappearing back into the store.

The only time Stella had ever ridden a bike was one

belonging to her grandpa. He had asked her to go to the Station Hotel pub and place a bet on Harry Tompkinson, a local lad who was due to fight in a boxing match that afternoon, but not to say anything to her grandma, who would never agree with wasting money on gambling. "You'll be quicker if you take my bike," he'd said, which, if it hadn't been for a rut in the Turnpike Road she would have been.

Better watch out for ruts then, she thought, lifting her leg through the bike frame. Thankfully, this bike wasn't as big as her grandpa's, and it didn't have a crossbar to contend with either. Stella positioned her feet either side of the bike. The seat felt as though it would be just at the right height for getting on and off with relative ease, so the only thing to concern herself with was steering the handlebars against the weight of the basket. Stella lifted her right foot onto the pedal and took a deep breath. She pushed forward with her foot, sat on the seat, and she was off. She swerved a little at first and thought she might lose control of the handlebars, but she soon steadied herself and felt quite confident that she had it mastered.

After she had delivered the first three orders, Stella felt she'd got it all off to a fine art and was soon heading back to the store to collect the last two orders. As she approached the store, she could see a couple of women chatting outside and thought it best to bring the bike to a halt and push it the last few yards. As she neared, a young boy of around nine or ten came rushing out of the shop, with Mrs Bell hot on his heels. She tried to take a swipe at the young boy, but he was far too quick for her. Alfie, Stella presumed.

After collecting the rest of the groceries and making the last two deliveries, Stella returned the bike to the store and leaned it back against the wall. Mrs Bell was most pleased with Stella's efforts and asked if she could start work in the shop the following Saturday, to give Dorothy a day off. She also suggested that she call in each afternoon after school to see if there were any errands to run.

"By the time you leave school, we'll have you trained up to work as a shopgirl," Mrs Bell said.

Stella looked at her watch, five to one. She rushed out of the shop and back along Chapel Street towards her grandma's, just in time to see Will and his uncle lifting the hutch out of the back of a green Morris Minor. Stella noticed Will look up, and as soon as he realised it was her running towards him, he beamed his usual smile.

"You look rather hot and bothered, what have you been doing?" he laughed, passing her his handkerchief.

"Let's get Pearl settled in, and I'll tell you all about it," she said, dabbing her brow.

THIRTY-THREE

Will sprinkled a thick layer of sawdust on both sides of the hutch and put straw bedding inside the sleeping compartment. He positioned two heavy pot dishes in the larger side of the hutch - one for water, and the other which held some rabbit food pellets. Stella picked a small handful of dandelion leaves and sprinkled them over the pellets.

"I think that's it," Will said. "We can get her out of the basket and into her new home now." Will picked up a small racing pigeon basket that he had borrowed from their next-door neighbour. He took it over to the hutch and opened the front of the basket to allow Pearl to hop in of her own accord. As soon as the tiny rabbit hopped inside, she made a point of having a good sniff around everywhere. She scuttled through to her sleeping area, where Will and Stella could hear her arranging her straw bedding. After a minute or two, she reappeared in the living quarters and hopped straight over to her food bowl to munch on a dandelion leaf.

"I think she's settled in already," Will said.

Squatting down at the front of the hutch, he poked his finger through the wire mesh and stroked her incessantly twitching nose. Stella crouched down next to Will and rested her head on his shoulder.

"Thank you so much, Will, she's the best present I have ever had."

Will explained the fundamentals of rabbit-keeping to Stella. He had brought enough dry food with him to last for at least a month and plenty of shavings and straw. "She will need her hutch cleaned out every week, but I can help you with that," he said.

"Wonderful. I'll store the food and bedding in Grandma's shed. I bet you're ready for a nice cold drink now, after all that lifting. It was kind of your Uncle Jed to help you bring everything over."

"I am thirsty, yes. And it's alright, Uncle Jed was pleased to help," Will said with a smile.

"I'll get us a drink then. I'll see if my grandma is around too, and hopefully, you can meet her!"

Stella left Will in the garden and walked up the path to the house. She opened the back door and shouted through for her grandma, but there was no reply. She shouted again, and eventually, she heard her grandma call down from upstairs. When Stella got up to her grandma's room, she found her resting on her bed.

"Are you alright, Grandma?" she asked.

Elsie nodded. "Aye, love, I'm just a bit weary today. But I have been out for a short walk.

Anything to keep Sheila happy, I suppose."

"Oh… Grandma. I do hope you aren't overdoing it?"

Elsie just gave a melodramatic sigh and closed her eyes heavily.

"Will and his uncle have brought the hutch round, and Will has just helped me to settle Pearl in. Wait till you see her, Grandma, she is beautiful! Do you feel up to coming down to meet her? And you can meet Will too!" Stella said with a smile.

"Another time, love. I feel quite done in this afternoon."

"Okay. Can I get you anything then?"

Elsie just shook her head, rested it against her pillow, and closed her eyes. Stella could see that her grandma had a few photographs laid out across the bed. She wondered if her grandma might well have been reminiscing, to the point of upsetting herself.

"I'll pop back up in a while then, and see how you are," Stella said softly, and Elsie just nodded.

Stella poured two glasses of cold lemonade from her grandma's fridge and took them outside into the garden. Will was sitting on the grass, watching Pearl as she continued to adjust to her new surroundings. "Do you think she will pine for her mother?" Stella asked.

Will shook his head. "It may take a day or two for her to settle in, but she'll be fine. So long as you give her plenty of cuddles and attention, she won't miss her mother at all."

"She will get plenty of cuddles," Stella grinned.

Will finished the last of his lemonade. "Is your grandma coming to meet her?"

Stella sat down on the grass next to Will. "I don't think she's feeling ever so good."

"Oh?" Will said, tipping his head to one side.

"She's been trying to take a short walk each day because my Aunty Sheila thinks it will help her knees. But I don't know if she's pushing herself too far. She had been looking at some photographs too, so I'm not sure if she's upset herself a bit."

"She must miss your grandpa very much," Will said.

Stella nodded and took a sip of her drink. "Do you still have your grandparents, Will?"

"Not on my mum's side, no, and my grandfather on my dad's side passed away a couple of years back. But I do still have my Granny Turner."

"Do you see her much?" Stella asked.

"Not so much since we moved to Denby. My great-aunt sees her a lot, though, that's Jed's wife. She and my Granny Turner are sisters and they've always been close," Will said, getting up off the grass. He rubbed at the back of his shorts at a damp patch and Stella laughed.

"The grass needs mowing, I suppose that's why it's still quite damp," she giggled. "I was going to mow it for her this morning before you came with the hutch, but I got waylaid at the Co-op. That's why I was flustered earlier."

"You were flustered because you'd been to the Co-op?" Will laughed.

"No... because, not only have I got myself a job, but thanks to the errand boy, I ended up starting this morning!" Stella laid back in the long grass. "Last thing I was expecting, I can tell you."

Will laughed and lay down in the grass next to Stella. "So, tell me all about it, then if you like, I'll mow the lawn for your grandma."

Will cleared grass from the blades of Elsie's push mower and emptied the clippings onto the compost heap, whilst Stella was busy weeding the border. When they had finished, the garden looked neat again.

"Thank you for helping me, Will. Grandma can't

manage to do much in the garden anymore, so she'll be pleased that you've helped me to get things looking tidy again."

Will smiled. "That's alright," he said, picking up the pigeon carrier. "I'd better be getting this back to my neighbour, though."

Stella nodded and walked with Will out of the garden and along the entry. They stopped short of the entry gate to kiss each other goodbye.

"Shall I see you tomorrow?" she asked.

"I've promised to help Uncle Jed tomorrow, but I'll see you on the recreation ground after tea?"

Stella nodded and opened the gate for Will, waving to him as he left.

As Elsie was still upstairs in her room, Stella made a cup of tea to take to her. She pushed the bedroom door open and peered through. Her grandma was lying down now, with a crocheted blanket over her, and was sleeping soundly. Stella placed the teacup down on the bedside table and picked up the photographs. Most of them were quite recent, but she realised that a few dated quite far back, especially when she recognised her mother as a child, sitting on the same lawn that Will had mown half an hour earlier. She reckoned on her mother being around three or four. Another picture was of a young couple; the woman, who had a young baby in her arms was looking up intently at a man with very curly, dark hair. Another picture, which was slightly larger than the rest, was of a young couple's wedding day. Stella thought the bride looked beautiful in her long-sleeved lace gown. Her hair had been set in high curls, and she was holding a small bouquet of roses combined with carnations. The bride stood with her arm linking that of a very dapper groom, he too looked very smart in his suit and tie. The couple stood in a vestibule that Stella recognised as being St Clement's Church. She was certain that given the man's very distinctive curly dark hair, it must be the same couple that were in the photograph with the baby.

"We never had a penny, everything we wore was either begged or borrowed," Elsie had woken up. She lifted the crocheted blanket off and tried to sit up.

Stella smiled. "I thought it must be you and Grandpa, but I wasn't sure. You both look so happy." Stella held up the earlier photo of the young couple and the baby. "Is this Mam or Aunty Sheila then?"

Elsie struggled to a seated position. "That's Sheila, she was two months old then."

Stella helped to make her grandmother more comfortable by altering her pillows a little and then passing her the tea. "I don't think I've ever seen any pictures of you or Grandpa when you were younger."

"We never had that many taken. It's not something we could afford to do very much back then."

Stella sat on the bed by her grandmother's side. "Well, I think we should get this one in a frame," she said, holding up the wedding photo. "I'll see if Mam has a spare one. Now when you've finished your tea, why don't you come down and meet Pearl? Will and I have tidied the garden up too. He mowed the lawn and I've done some weeding."

Elsie cupped Stella's hand in hers. "You're a good gal, and it certainly sounds as though you have found yourself a wonderful young man too. Hold on to him, special ones like that are hard to come by."

Stella smiled and rubbed her grandma's shoulder. "I'll leave you to drink your tea then, whilst I go down and put the gardening tools away," she said, looking at her watch. "Then I suppose I ought to get off home."

After Stella had introduced her grandmother to Pearl, she took herself off home. She was most surprised to find that her mother had prepared what looked to be quite a substantial tea. There was tinned ham, a freshly prepared salad, bread, butter, and two halves of a sponge cake cooling on a wire rack. Her father was sitting at the table reading his paper; remarkably, he managed a grunt in response to her cheerful greeting.

As they sat eating tea, Stella decided to share the good news about landing herself a job as a Saturday girl. She explained that there may also be errands to run during the week and that it would lead to her becoming a shopgirl on leaving school at Christmas. She also explained that she would still have time to attend Miss Hutton's tutoring sessions, at which her father merely tutted.

"Did you manage to mow your grandma's lawn?" Jeanie asked, offering the plate of bread and butter around.

Stella nodded. "And… I've been given a rabbit. But don't worry, Grandma said she can stay at her house."

"A rabbit? We can't afford to keep a rabbit," Jeanie

garbled over a mouthful of food.

"Where has it come from anyway?"

"A friend. They breed rabbits, so everything she needs will be provided for by them,"

Stella said, not wanting to give too much away about Will in front of her father.

Derek rolled his eyes. "What a pointless waste of time. The only thing a rabbit is good for is a pie or a stew," he said, shaking his head.

Jeanie laughed nervously, making Stella wish she hadn't bothered mentioning Pearl at all.

Later, that evening, Stella nipped around to her grandma's house to check on Pearl. She opened the cage door, and the little rabbit hopped towards her at once. She very carefully picked her up and gently stroked her soft fur, talking to her at a whisper, so as not to startle her.

"I've saved a little piece of raw carrot for her here," a voice quietly spoke from behind. Stella turned to see that her grandma had ventured out into the garden. "I was just about to come out and give it to her when I spotted you from the window," she said, as she stroked the soft bit of fur in between Pearl's ears. "Your Uncle Albert is properly taken with her. He called in earlier to see if I feel up to going to church in the morning."

"And do you?" Stella asked, carefully placing Pearl back in her hutch.

"Yes, it will do me good, I think."

"Good, I'll come with you then. I've not been for a while," Stella said, making sure the door to Pearl's hutch was shut properly. "I'll be off then. See you in the morning," she said, kissing her grandmother on her cheek.

THIRTY-FOUR

After the Reverend Bickerstaff had finished giving his morning sermon, a few parishioners began to make their way out of church, along with Sheila and Albert who had already decided that they would take a stroll down to Fred's grave, whilst Elsie stayed for a drink and a chat with one or two others. Stella fetched her grandmother a cup of tea and decided she would also pay a visit to her grandpa's grave.

"You'll be alright here, won't you? Only I think you'll find it a bit too much of a trek down to the plot," Stella said, handing her grandmother a cup and saucer.

"I'll be fine, I've just spotted Mrs Green, I'll have a chat with her," Elsie raised her hand to a woman sitting a couple of pews in front.

Stella made her way out of church, along a path through the churchyard, and down towards where her grandpa had been laid to rest. Sheila and Albert were standing at the foot of the grave and Albert had his arm around Sheila's shoulder.

"I can't believe it has been over a month already," Stella said, giving her aunt a comforting rub on her back.

The soil around the grave was beginning to sprout the odd weed here and there, and Stella crouched down to pull them out. She put her hand on a wooden cross that Albert had constructed and had since placed at the head of the grave. She traced her finger over the carving of her grandpa's name and looked up at her uncle with a fond smile.

"It will do for now," he said. "Once the ground has settled, we'll see about a proper headstone."

As the three of them headed back up towards the church, Stella noticed that a woman was waving and beckoning to them urgently. She realised that the woman who seemed most anxious to get their attention was Mrs Green.

"Something must be wrong," Stella said, running ahead of her aunt and uncle.

As she approached, Mrs Green began to explain that Elsie had 'taken a tumble', as she described it, and that a woman who said she had been a nurse was tending to her. Stella thanked Mrs Green and headed back into the church. She could see a few people standing with her grandmother, who was now sitting in the aisle on a chair next to the pew where Stella had left her.

"What on earth has happened, Grandma?" Stella asked, crouching down by the side of the chair.

"It was nothing," Elsie said, shaking her head.

Gordon, the church verger, who was busy wiping spilt tea up from the floor, along with the remnants of Elsie's cup and saucer, explained the situation. He and Mrs Green were sitting chatting with Elsie when she quite suddenly said she had to go. He said that she was in a bit of a hurry to leave, and as she stepped away from the pew, she lost her balance and stumbled backwards.

"Thankfully, the pews on that side of the aisle saved her from falling completely," Gordon said, wringing out a cloth. "The nurse checked her over, and she seems to think she will be okay."

"Sorry, what nurse?" Stella asked in confusion.

Gordon stood up to look around the church. "I don't know her name, she's new to the parish. Erm... she might have gone now. Oh no, wait a minute, she's over there, talking to Sheila and Albert."

Stella stood up and she could see the lady that Gordon was referring to, but only from the back. Elsie suddenly became agitated.

"You're alright, Grandma," Stella said, rubbing her grandma's back. "I'll go and ask Uncle Albert to come and help me and we'll get you home, eh?"

Elsie nodded. "I am alright, though, don't you go bringing that woman back over here," she said quite sternly, which made Gordon and Stella look at one another and frown.

As Stella was making her way over to her aunt and uncle, the lady said goodbye to Albert and Sheila and left the church.

"Is she alright?" Sheila's voice echoed, as it carried with the church acoustics.

Stella tipped her head from side to side with uncertainty. "I'm not sure, she's acting a little odd. Who was that lady?"

"Norah? Oh, she used to be a midwife, Mam knows of her from way back. She was just saying that Mam was suddenly in a hurry to leave church, she got as far as the aisle and then stumbled backwards a little. Norah has checked her over, she doesn't think she's done herself any injury. In what way is she acting odd?" Sheila asked.

"Well, Gordon just mentioned the same thing, that she seemed in a hurry to leave. And then she got quite irritable at the thought that I might fetch that lady… Norah, over to her again. It all seems a bit strange."

"Let's just get her home then," Albert said as he walked off.

****

After the fourth time that Sheila questioned Elsie's reasons for being in a hurry to leave church, Elsie's patience was wearing thin. She took herself off to her room on the premise that she needed a rest. Jeanie had also arrived at her mother's and sat at the kitchen table with Stella.

Albert put the kettle on the stove and fetched cups and saucers out of the cupboard. Sheila was leaning against the worktop and appeared to be deep in thought.

"I think there's something about Norah that seems to trouble Mam," she said, tapping her finger on her lip.

"What makes you say that?" Albert replied, gently moving his wife away from blocking the cutlery drawer.

"After Dad passed away and Mam found out that Doctor Keys had sent Norah across to help prepare him, she became quite… agitated. And then today, for some reason, Mam was in a hurry to leave church. She got quite snappy when she thought Stella might fetch Norah back over. It's all a bit strange," Sheila said, shrugging her shoulders.

"She's just grieving, Sheila. Grief does strange

things to people," Albert said, picking out five teaspoons from the drawer.

"No, Sheila is right," Jeanie said. "The day you all went off to camp, Mam got quite shirty with me when I suggested that she and Norah could get together for a cuppa. And then the day before you all came home, when I was round here, Norah came knocking at the door. We had to sneak into the lounge until she'd gone because Mam didn't want her to come in."

"See!" Sheila said, nodding firmly at Albert. "It would seem that every time Mam turns round, Norah is there!"

"I did ask Mam about Norah, and she said that they were best friends at school, but lost touch. Then apart from when she delivered Sheila, she never saw her again until she came to help with Dad," Jeanie added.

Albert poured the tea. "See," he said, reciprocating a firm nod back at Sheila. "Maybe they just fell out years ago, and Elsie doesn't want to reacquaint herself with Norah."

Stella stood away from the table and picked up one of the cups of tea Albert had poured. "Well, whatever it is, I'm sure she would tell us about it if she wanted to. I'll take this up to her," she said, placing the tea on a tray along with a slice of Jeanie's sponge cake.

Stella tapped lightly on her grandma's bedroom door and entered. She was sitting on a chair in the corner of the room. Stella took the tray over to her and Elsie picked up the cup and saucer and rested it in her lap.

"Mam made the sponge cake, it's not bad actually,"

Stella laughed. She sat down at the foot of her grandmother's bed.

Elsie looked at her granddaughter and gave a half smile. "I suppose Sheila sent you up to question me?"

Stella shook her head. "She and Mam are just concerned. They're wondering what it is with this Norah woman."

Elsie took a sip of her tea. "I'm sorry I chewed at you earlier," she said softly.

Stella shook her head gently and smiled. "It doesn't matter, so long as you're okay."

Elsie reached to put her cup and saucer down on her dressing table. "Me and Norah, we—"

"Grandma, you don't have to explain anything to me," Stella cut in, but Elsie continued anyway.

"We go back a long way, grew up together, we did. She had always wanted to be a midwife. Her mother was a midwife and so was her older sister. They called them handywomen back then, though, and between them, they delivered no end of babies around these parts. Anyway, when we left school, we didn't see much of each other. I was already courting your grandpa, and Norah went to work alongside her mother and sister for a couple of years, and then…" Elsie stopped mid-sentence. "And then…" she said again. But she couldn't seem to continue and just shook her head.

"Are you alright, Grandma?" Stella frowned.

"Aye… I'm alright," she said, reaching for her teacup.

"So, what happened after that then?" Stella asked.

Elsie just stared into thin air, as if she were considering what to say. "Well, in 1902, midwifery changed, and proper training came in. So, Norah and her sister went away to do three months of training, and they both became State Registered Midwives. I never saw her after that, not until Sheila was born, and that's it."

"Oh right," Stella nodded slowly, quite unconvinced that she had been told the complete story.

"I think I'll get on the bed now and have a nap," she said, finishing the rest of her tea.

Stella helped her grandmother onto the bed and covered her over with her crocheted blanket. She picked up the cup and saucer and put it on the tray along with the uneaten cake and left her grandma to rest. When she got downstairs, Albert, Sheila and Jeanie had all moved outside into the garden. Stella filled a jug with fresh water and went out to join them.

Albert had fetched Pearl out of her hutch to let her have a run around on the lawn. Stella smiled when she saw the rabbit hopping about, quite happily investigating her new surroundings. Sheila and Jeanie were busy checking on the progress of Elsie's bedding plants, deadheading here and there.

"The garden is looking nice, isn't it," Stella said to the women.

"It certainly is. Dad would be pleased with how well everything has grown. There's plenty of peas to come off too. How is Mam, Stella? Is she alright?" Sheila asked.

"Yes, she's had a cup of tea and she's going to have a nap now."

Stella walked over to Pearl's hutch and fetched her water bowl out. She topped the food bowl up with rabbit pellets and a handful of hay, emptied what was left of the water and refilled it with fresh water from the jug.

"Someone has done a good job of putting that hutch together," Albert said with a big grin.

"Ah yes, when are we going to get around to meeting this mystery young man of yours?" Sheila asked.

Jeanie, who was kneeling to deadhead some petunias stood up. "What young man?"

Stella rolled her eyes. "The one I was trying to tell you about a few days ago, Mam."

"What… and he's made that hutch?"

"Yes, and Pearl is an early birthday gift, isn't she, Stella," Sheila said.

"Oh, right. I didn't realise it was that serious, Stella. You might have said so," Jeanie crouched down to pick up the dead flower heads.

Stella rolled her eyes and sighed whilst Sheila changed the subject.

"I'll fetch a basin for those peas," Sheila said, disappearing off up the garden.

Albert picked Pearl up from behind the watering can and took her back to her hutch. He crouched down next to Stella to speak discreetly. "Sorry, lass, I assumed she knew about Will," he whispered.

"It's alright, Uncle Albert, I did try to tell her."

Albert patted Stella's back in sympathy and stood up. "Right, let's get some of these peas picked before they pass their best."

Later that afternoon, Stella went to meet Will on the recreation ground. He was playing football with his friends. He stopped when he realised that she had arrived and was sitting on the bench watching him play. He walked over to join her, and the two of them spent the next couple of hours chatting about their day. Stella told Will all about the incident with her grandma, and how well she thought that Pearl was settling in. And Will told Stella that he had spent most of the morning preparing for his upcoming RAF apprenticeship interview, and the afternoon helping Uncle Jed to do some painting in the kitchen of his new house. Eventually, as the late afternoon moved into early evening, Will said that he had to be getting home for his tea, which suddenly reminded him, that his mum had mentioned it was okay to invite Stella round for her tea after school tomorrow. Stella happily accepted, and the two of them said their goodbyes in the only way that young love would.

THIRTY-FIVE

The school bell announced the end of the first day of the second week back to school, and as it seemed quite the routine now for Will to be waiting for Stella to finish each day; today was no different. She would be quite happy for him to continue meeting her every day until the day she was due to leave. She did begin to think, though, that it may not be the case for much longer. If Will were successful with his interview, he would soon be leaving to begin his apprenticeship. With that in mind, Stella felt quite downhearted at the thought of being without him.

As they walked the short distance to Will's house, Stella explained that she wouldn't be able to stay for long once they'd had tea because she was due at Miss Hutton's house for a tutoring session at six o'clock, and also was expected to call into the Co-op to see if Mrs Bell had any errands for her to run.

"You are a busy bee, aren't you," Will smiled.

Stella sighed. "I shall feel awful for having to eat and run after your mum has so kindly asked me round again."

"It's alright, she will quite understand, honestly." Will opened the back door and gestured for Stella to enter.

Mrs Turner was busy in the kitchen. She was just turning a tin of pink salmon into a dish. She had a plate full of bread and butter and a stack of sliced cucumber prepared, ready to make sandwiches. Stella thought how well-organised she always seemed, and how everything was so effortlessly prepared. She was always made up so nicely too, her cheeks lightly brushed with a dusky pink rouge and a subtle shade of pink glossed on her lips. Her light brown hair was fashioned in a stylish bouffant, with a delicate mother-of-pearl clip placed neatly to one side. She smiled as they walked in. Stella loved her smile, it was the genuine way it drew you in, making you want to happily smile back.

"Hello, Mum," Will kissed her cheek.

"Hello, love. Hello, Stella. Your dad won't be too long, Will, so you can go straight through if you like," she said, handing him some plates.

Just as they had sat down, the back door opened and in walked Will's dad. He greeted his wife affectionately, before appearing in the dining room doorway.

"Afternoon, you two," he said to them with a smile.

He took off his jacket, removed his flat cap, and ran his fingers through the soft brown curls of his hair, making them spring back into place after being coiled up inside his hat. Will's mum stood behind him, holding a tray of tea things.

"Pop that on the table, love, and I'll fetch the sandwiches," she said.

Before long, they were all tucking into another delightful spread laid out before them and exchanged chatter on the events of their day.

"How are the renovations coming along at Uncle Jed's house, Will?" his dad asked.

"Quite well actually. We've stripped all the old wallpaper off the bedroom walls today. We're going to be busy prepping tomorrow because he wants me to help him start decorating on Wednesday and Thursday. Oh, and Aunty has about finished going through the last of the boxes."

"Well, I'm finishing work early tomorrow, and then I've got the rest of the week off, so I'll come along with you and help out," he said.

"I'm sure Uncle Jed will be grateful for that, Dad. That reminds me, he has asked me to get some wallpaper paste and a box of two-inch nails for the floorboards. He needs them for Wednesday. There's a good general store in Kilburn village… Slater's, I think he said.

You'll know it, Stella?"

"Yes, Slater's, it's on the corner of Highfield Road and Church Street," Stella confirmed.

"Well, I usually go to Belper or Ripley for anything like that, but I may as well pick them up from Slater's then. I'll nip to the store after I've finished work, then I'll go to Uncle Jed's and we can all get stuck in," Mr Turner said.

After tea, Stella made her apologies for having to leave so soon, said her goodbyes and made her way to the Co-op. When she arrived, Mrs Bell had one small delivery for her, which was easy to carry without the need for taking the push bike. Stella was relieved to find that the delivery was on the way to Miss Hutton's house. After making the delivery, she arrived at Miss Hutton's with five minutes to spare.

Miss Hutton had already prepared a tea tray which she had set down on her desk, along with a small plate on which were pieces of delicious-looking fruit cake.

"Do have a seat, my dear. Now then, how did you get along with the writing exercises and storyline idea I gave you?" Miss Hutton said, pouring tea into the cups.

Stella opened her notebook and slid it over to Miss Hutton. "I thought the exercises were helpful. They are an effective way to warm up your thought processes, which in turn helped me to be more creative with the story," Stella replied.

Miss Hutton picked up her cake slice and gestured to the plate. "May I get you a slice of fruit cake?"

"Yes please, it looks delightful," Stella said.

Miss Hutton lifted a slice of fruit cake, placed it on a tea plate and set it down in front of Stella, then picked up the notebook and began to read what Stella had written.

"Are you not having any, miss?" Stella asked.

Miss Hutton shook her head. "Unfortunately, not. I seem to be suffering a little just lately," she said, patting her stomach. "Nothing to do with my baking though, so don't worry," she added with a giggle.

Miss Hutton continued to read. She would stop every so often to either correct something or just peer over the notebook to nod and smile. Eventually, when she had finished reading, she turned the pages back to the start.

"I liked that story. I love the way you kept me wondering who the thief could be, right up to the very end. I would never have guessed at it being the old woman! Very clever indeed."

Stella grinned. "Thanks, miss."

"The only thing I would say is that on occasions you have used the same word over and over again. I have a spare thesaurus. You can have it with pleasure." Miss Hutton pushed her chair back from her desk and stood. But as she did, she let out a short, sharp cry, cupping her stomach and bending forward slightly as if to ease a pain.

"Goodness, miss, are you alright?" Stella asked, promptly standing.

Miss Hutton waved a hand dismissively, nodded her head, and sat back down in her chair heavily.

"Can I get anything for you, miss?" Stella asked, sitting back down slowly.

"I'll be fine momentarily, but thank you in any case," Miss Hutton said.

The rest of the evening passed without any further incident, and Stella managed to work through the lesson that Miss Hutton had planned for her. As their session ended, Miss Hutton handed Stella a worksheet which gave a summary of what they had discussed.

"You already have a strong and unique writing voice, Stella, so what I want is for you to push your creative boundaries. Now then, I'll get that thesaurus for you."

Miss Hutton stood up slowly, straightened herself and paused for a moment before moving as if expecting a repeat of the earlier episode. As all seemed well, she walked over to her bookshelves and sought out the thesaurus. Stella hadn't noticed it before, but she thought how pale Miss Hutton appeared and hoped she wasn't coming down with something unpleasant.

"Will someone be meeting you?" She asked, passing Stella the thesaurus.

"No, but honestly, miss, I will be fine. It's not that far to walk."

Miss Hutton nodded and walked with Stella to the door.

"I hope you feel better soon, miss, and don't worry, I'll be okay walking home," Stella said as she left, even though she got the distinct impression that Miss Hutton wasn't feeling much up to debating the issue in any case.

****

After Stella had very quickly nipped into her grandma's house to feed and check on Pearl, she arrived home to find her mother sitting on the settee, darning a hole in a pair of her father's socks. She was sitting with her sewing basket on one side, and a large mending pile on the other. Stella sat down on the chair opposite, and her mother smiled briefly before yawning twice in succession.

"I'll go and make us a cuppa, Mam, and then I'll help you with some of that mending."

"Oh, if you would, please," she said.

After tying off the darning thread, she paired the socks up and grabbed the next item in the pile, one of Derek's shirts that needed a button.

Stella placed a tray, on which were two cups of tea, down on the coffee table, and picked up the next item in the pile, a blue cardigan that also needed a button.

She threaded a needle with cotton of a similar colour to the cardigan and raked through the button tin, where she quickly managed to find a button to match the rest. Making herself comfortable in the chair opposite her mother, she checked the positioning of the button and began to sew. After a few minutes of silence passed, Stella assumed that as her mother wasn't interested enough to enquire after her tutoring session, there would be no point in offering up the information.

Instead, she enquired how the day had gone for her mother.

"Well, your father started his week of night shifts tonight. I don't think he was very keen on going, to be honest. I suppose he will have to get used to it. I popped in to see your grandma this morning too."

"Ahh… how is she today?" Stella asked, checking that the button lined up with the hole.

"She said she felt fine. Didn't know what all the fuss was all about with Norah."

"You didn't press her on the subject, did you?"

"No, no. I do think there's something she's not telling us, though."

Stella didn't think it was necessary to go into the fact that she agreed with her mother, because that would mean having to go into detail about the conversation she'd had with her grandma. Instead, she just tilted her head quizzically and shrugged her shoulders.

"Anyway, that rabbit of yours is giving her something else to think about, and I'm glad she's managing a short walk out each day," Jeanie said, tying off her sewing. She folded Derek's shirt and picked up the next item in the pile, a dress of hers that needed a section of its hem repaired. "Oh... you know what, I think I've had enough for one night," she yawned. "I think I'll get off to bed now."

Jeanie folded the dress and placed it back on the mending pile. She got up off the settee and headed for the stairs, turning round at the last second to speak. "I never thought to ask how your day has been... anyway, night love," she said, disappearing off upstairs before Stella even had a chance to answer.

Stella shook her head slowly, tutted under her breath and let out a sigh before getting up and moving to where her mother had been sitting. She picked up her mother's dress from the pile, threaded a needle with cotton and began to repair the section of hem. After a couple more hours had passed, she put all her mother's sewing things away in the box. As the clock on the mantle chimed midnight, she made her way to bed, smiling as she climbed the stairs, at the thought of knowing that the large pile of mending that had occupied one side of the settee no longer existed.

THIRTY-SIX

Even though Stella had stayed up late to work through the pile of mending, she still managed to be out early the next morning. She wanted to feed Pearl and spend a bit of time with her before school. She made her way through the entry, and into her grandma's back garden. Looking up, she could see that her bedroom curtains were still closed, so freshening up Pearl's water would have to wait for now.

She picked the rabbit up out of her hutch, taking a while to stroke her soft fur, before putting her down on the lawn to have a run round whilst she sorted out the bedding and food. Her grandma had left a container with a small carrot and a cabbage leaf in it, and Stella topped up the pellets.

She was about to pick the rabbit back up when she heard a tapping noise coming from the direction of the house. She looked round to see her grandma knocking on the kitchen window and waving. Stella waved back, she grabbed Pearl's water bowl and headed to the house.

"Morning, Grandma, I hope I haven't disturbed you?" Stella said, entering through to the kitchen.

"Not at all, love, I've been awake a while. I thought I'd come down and put the kettle on. I was quite surprised when I looked out of the kitchen window to see you here so early." "I wanted to spend a bit of time with Pearl before school," Stella said, running the tap for some fresh water. "Are you feeling better today?"

Elsie sighed deeply. "I'm fine, just as I was fine

yesterday and Sunday," she replied bitterly.

"Alright, Grandma. Don't be spiky, I was only asking," Stella replied, raising her eyebrows.

"I'm sorry, love," Elsie said, pouring water into the teapot. "Tea?"

"Oh, yes please," Stella nodded.

When Elsie had finished making the tea, the two of them sat at the kitchen table. Stella finally had a chance to tell her grandma about her tutoring sessions with Miss Hutton, in which Elsie seemed genuinely interested and was keen to know more. Stella went on to tell her all about Miss Hutton, and her quaint little cottage, and what she hoped to gain from the extra tuition.

"Well, that all sounds exciting. I do hope the sessions will be beneficial, it certainly sounds like they will," Elsie said.

"Time will tell, I guess. Speaking of time, I'd better be getting off to school," Stella downed the last of her tea.

"I think someone is waiting for you first," Elsie laughed and pointed behind Stella.

Stella looked behind her. "Pearl!" she said in surprise. "What are you doing in here!"

Elsie and Stella both laughed at the rabbit, who had decided to take it upon herself to investigate Elsie's kitchen.

****

Stella sailed through her day with the usual interest and enthusiasm she'd always had for her schoolwork. The ability to soak up knowledge and retain it had always come easy to her, which made school life all the easier to bear.

Geography, mathematics and P.E. had been the order of the morning, followed by history, with her last and most favourite lesson of the day still to come. Stella walked into her English class and greeted Miss Hutton, who was writing up the day's lesson on the chalkboard. Stella sat down at her desk and took her exercise book, fountain pen and reference book out from her bag.

When Miss Hutton had finished writing, she moved away from the chalkboard and sat down at her desk. Stella looked up and at once gained eye contact with her, smiling as she did so, and Miss Hutton gestured a nod in greeting and smiled back. Stella couldn't help but stare at Miss Hutton, and how she still looked so pale. She noticed there were dark circles around the soft areas of her eyes, which she was sure hadn't been there before.

Although the class worked through and completed the lesson that had been set, Stella thought that the energy and enthusiasm with which Miss Hutton usually conducted a lesson, just seemed to be missing. And she allowed the class to leave five minutes early, which was most unlike her. Stella dallied a while, allowing the other pupils to leave first, so she could then enquire after her teacher's well-being, but as Stella was packing away her books, Mrs Cranfield breezed in, wanting to discuss the behaviour of Harold Potter, the school delinquent. So instead, Stella bade her teachers farewell and left.

As Stella walked down the corridor, the bell rang. By the time she had made her way out, the schoolyard was bustling with pupils heading for the school gates. Stella walked across the yard and looked over towards the wall, but she couldn't see Will waiting anywhere. She exited through the gate and looked again, but she couldn't see him there either. Perhaps he had lost track of time, or maybe he was just too busy helping his uncle with the renovations. Remembering that Will had said he and Jed would be busy today, and that as his dad was finishing work early, he would collect the supplies from Slater's Store so they could all get on with it, she concluded that he must still be busy working.

As Stella had to pass Will's house to go home, she decided to call round and see if he was there. She tapped lightly on the back door, and when Mrs Turner opened it, the glorious smell of pastry wafted past, filling Stella's nostrils.

"Stella love, come in," Mrs Turner said cheerfully.

"Thank you, Mrs Turner, but I can't stay, I must be at the Co-op at four o'clock to run some errands. I just wondered if Will was about?"

"I expect that he and his dad will still be busy at Jed's house. Call in if you like, they live in that detached cottage near the toll bar.

"I know it, thank you, Mrs Turner. I'll see you soon."

Stella left Will's house and continued along the main road. The cottage where Jed and his wife lived was about half a mile further on. She looked at her watch... twenty minutes to four. There wouldn't be enough time to walk there, see Will and then continue along into the village. If she turned off past Kilburn Pit and cut through the recreation ground, she could be at the Coop in under 15 minutes. Not wanting to be late for Mrs Bell, gave Stella no choice but to forego seeing Will.

As she approached the Co-op, Alfie Beardmore, the errand boy, was sitting on the pavement with his back against the shop wall. He was writing something down in a notebook.

When Stella drew level with him, she realised that he wasn't writing, he was sketching.

"What are you drawing, Alfie?" Stella asked.

The boy looked up at Stella and frowned. "How'd you know me name?" the boy asked.

"Because I heard Mrs Bell chasing after you the other day when you were late for your errands," she said with a grin.

"Oh," Alfie responded.

"May I take a look?" Stella said, holding her hand out for Alfie's book. Alfie stood up and quite willingly passed Stella his sketchbook. Stella looked at the drawing Alfie was working on. It was of a mouse climbing an ear of wheat, and Stella thought how remarkably good it was.

"It's a harvest mouse. They like to hide in long grass, hedgerows, and crops," Alfie described keenly.

"It's very good, Alfie." Stella thumbed through the previous pages of sketch after sketch of animals, birds, and insects. She was amazed at how capable and gifted he was, especially given his age.

"And that's a sparrowhawk," he added, as Stella turned back another page. "They're me favouritist bird of prey. Real fierce n'all," Alfie exclaimed, spreading his fingers into a claw-like shape and gliding his hand through the air as if to imitate the bird.

Stella laughed at his impression and was about to correct the boy's English when Mrs Bell appeared in the shop doorway.

"Alfie! Get your idle rump on that bicycle and get going before I have your guts for garters!" Mrs Bell yelled at the top of her voice.

Alfie grabbed his sketchbook out of Stella's hand and made off down the side of the shop, appearing moments later, riding the bicycle, and doing his best to keep its balance against the heavily laden basket.

"I'm sorry, Mrs Bell, it was my fault, I kept him talking too long about his drawings.

He's talented, isn't he?"

Mrs Bell did not remark, instead she just turned and walked back into the shop, mumbling something about him being a good-for-nothing scallywag. Stella followed Mrs Bell into the store, wondering if she would still be needed if Alfie was going to be running the errands that day.

"Wait here, cherub," Mrs Bell said, as she headed off towards the back of the store towards her office. Her heavy frame would only allow her to take short steps, as her body tilted from side to side, with more of a waddle than a walk. She appeared moments later carrying a blue and white short-sleeved tabard.

"Here, this should fit," Mrs Bell offered the tabard to Stella. "Right, let's get you familiar with the art of shelf stacking, shall we? Follow me!"

****

In the hour that she worked before closing, Stella learned how to make an enticing display with tins, packets, and jars, How to stack goods with label fronts facing towards the customer and making sure the new stock was always placed behind the old.

Mrs Bell pushed her glasses up her nose. "Tinned goods have a good shelf life, but we always use up the older stock first," she said to Stella, who was perching on the two-step wooden ladder, arranging jars of pickled onions in a neat display. She nodded to Mrs Bell, as she tried to retain everything she had been told.

Eventually, on the stroke of five o'clock, Mrs Bell shouted from her office, instructing Stella to turn the shop door sign to 'closed'.

Stella headed to the back of the store, into the office, and removed her tabard.

"Oh, you can take that home with you for next time," Mrs Bell beamed. "Well, that was easy enough for you, cherub, was it not? Tomorrow, I'll show you how we go about doing a stock take." Mrs Bell tied her headscarf under the fullness of her round chin and opened the back door. "We always lock the front door from the inside, and come and go through this door, for which eventually you'll have a key."

After Mrs Bell had locked up, they both walked

from the back, and down the narrow path that ran along the side of the store. Just as they neared the top, Alfie came hurtling round the corner on the shop bike and was heading towards them at speed. As soon as he realised they were in his path, he slammed his back brakes on, bringing himself to a halt with a savvy skid right in front of the two of them.

Mrs Bell let out a loud screech and clutched her chest. "You little swine. How many times have I told you to get off that bike and walk with it down here!"

"Sorry, Mrs Bell," apologised Alfie, as he got off the bike in haste.

"I'll give you sorry," Mrs Bell scolded. "Knock your ruddy head off, I will," she threatened, clouting him round the back of his head, and sending his school cap flying, before walking away as quickly as her waddle would allow.

Stella picked Alfie's cap up and placed it back on his head. "All done?" she asked with a smile.

"Are you the new shop girl?" Alfie asked, leaning the bike against the wall.

"I'm hoping to be, why?"

"Coz if you like me drawings, I can bring some more to show yer."

"I'd like that, Alfie."

"What's yer name?" Alfie asked, fetching his sketchbook out of the bike's basket and stuffing it down the top of his jumper.

"Stella Felton," Stella held out her hand to shake with Alfie.

"I'm Alfie, Alfie Beardmore."

Stella smiled at the boy's viridity. "Well, Alfie Beardmore, I have to get off home now. I'll see you tomorrow."

Stella walked along the rest of the path.

"Do you like drawing, Stella?" Alfie asked, following on behind her.

"I'm not very good at drawing, I'm afraid. I like writing stories, though."

"Me mam won't let me draw at home, sez it's a waste of time. So, I take me sen off across the fields, there's all sorts of wildlife over there."

Stella stopped when she got to the top of the path. "I don't think it's a waste of time, Alfie, and I think you are very gifted."

Alfie smiled. "You like writing stories, you say? We should pair up, you and me. You write the stories, and I'll do the illus…illust…" Alfie scratched at his forehead.

"Illustrations?" Stella volunteered.

"Aye, that's it…illustrations. I better be off now, before me mam comes looking for me," he said. And off he sprinted.

As Stella watched Alfie run towards the high street, she took a moment to imagine his idea. *You write the stories, and I'll do the illustrations.* "That's not an altogether bad idea," she said to herself, smiling. As she turned to walk towards home, she was surprised to see her mother making her way towards her and she was in quite a hurry.

"Stella. Thank goodness I've caught up with you. It's Grandma, she's taken ill."

THIRTY-SEVEN

As Stella and her mother hurried along the street towards Elsie's house, Jeanie gave Stella a brief account of the whole story. She explained that as Elsie had used up the last of her flour, she decided to buy some more whilst she was out for her afternoon walk. She was about to go into Slater's stores when she quite suddenly felt unwell. Thankfully, a gentleman who had just come out of the store shouted for Mrs Slater. She brought a chair outside and then telephoned for Doctor Keys, but unfortunately, he was already on a house call elsewhere. Mr Slater kindly fetched his car round, and he brought Elsie home.

When Stella and Jeanie arrived at Elsie's, Sheila was in the kitchen making a pot of tea.

"Where's Mam?" Jeanie asked.

"She's being tended to upstairs," Sheila said, fetching another two teacups out of the cupboard.

"Has Doctor Keys arrived then?" Stella asked.

Sheila shook her head. "He's expected to be quite some time with the house call yet. So… anyway, he sent Norah around instead. She's up there with her now."

Jeanie and Stella looked at one another, and then they both looked to Sheila, expecting a further explanation. Sheila just shrugged her shoulders. "At least she's being checked over," she said.

"Well… her presence had better not be making Mam feel any worse," Jeanie warned.

"Look, we can't go sticking our oar in now, can we? Let's just sit and have a cup of tea, and we'll see what Norah says when she comes down."

****

Norah lifted the chair from the corner of the room, took it closer to the side of Elsie's bed and sat down. "You've had an awful shock, Elsie, but you will be fine," she reassured.

Elsie, who was resting her head against an upright pillow, couldn't bring herself to look at Norah. "It was him… wasn't it?" she said softly. There was a beat of silence before Elsie finally looked at Norah. "Wasn't it!" she repeated.

Norah nodded slowly. "Yes Elsie… it was."

Elsie put her hand to her mouth and let out a sob. Norah reached for Else's other hand, but she pulled away.

Norah sighed. "This is exactly why I've been trying to talk to you, to warn you." Norah sat forward in the chair. "He came to live here about three months ago. Just before we decided to move to my mother's cottage, as it turned out."

Norah paused, looked up to the ceiling, and sighed again as if to find the right words to continue. After a moment or two, she looked directly at Elsie. "Elsie… I wouldn't have persisted if it wasn't for the fact that… the fact that…"

Elsie reached for the drawer on her bedside table, pulled out an old photograph of Fred, and passed it to Norah. "What you're trying to say is… the fact that he has the same curly dark hair as his father. It's unmistakable."

Norah nodded. "The curly dark hair, his brown

294

eyes, his build, the way he walks. Everything, Elsie, everything is the absolute image of Fred."

Elsie rested her head back heavily against the pillow. "There hasn't been a day, not one day, where I haven't thought about him, about his childhood, his teenage years, adulthood." Elsie shook her head. "I've wondered where he might be living, if he has a wife, a family, what he does for work. Everyday, Norah, every single..." Tears spilt out onto Elsie's cheeks, and Norah gave her the time she needed to console herself.

When she had stopped crying, she dried her eyes. "If I had only been a year older, my father couldn't have stopped us from marrying then, and we could have kept our child. But instead, I was made to give him up. Give him up to your sister!" Elsie's eyes filled with tears again. "Have you got any idea what that was like? To give your child up to someone else?" There was another beat of silence before Elsie continued. "What did she call him?"

"Don't do this to yourself, Elsie."

"What did she call him?" Elsie demanded.

"Michael, but we call him Mike."

Elsie nodded slowly and closed her eyes. "Michael, I like that."

Norah looked at her watch. "Sheila will be wondering what's taking me so long."

Elsie continued. "I had no idea that was why you wanted to talk to me, you know. I thought you just wanted to be cruel and fill me in on what I've missed out on all these years."

Norah looked up swiftly at Elsie. "Why would I

want to do that? Elsie, we were best friends. I only ever wanted to try and make the best of a heartbreaking situation. I thought that the suggestion of my sister and her husband adopting him would be the best choice all around, and you agreed. It was better than him going to someone who might not have loved and cared for him like they did."

"I agreed because I had no choice, and at least if he had gone elsewhere, I wouldn't have had to suffer the shock of bumping into him!" Elsie pulled herself to the edge of the bed. "Does he know he was adopted?" she said softly.

Norah stood up and walked over to the window, she shook her head. "No. There are only three people who have ever known. Me, my sister, and her husband, and he's passed away now. Did you and Fred ever tell anyone else?"

Elsie shook her head. "What do we do now? Maybe it is time we lifted the lid on the whole thing!"

"No!" Norah cried. "That is not a good idea. My sister isn't in the best of health. The upset could finish her off."

Norah went to sit back down in the chair. She took hold of Elsie's hand, and this time

Elsie didn't pull away. "Look… you gave my sister something she could never have had, and I know she is eternally grateful. I think the best thing all around, is for us to never speak of it again, let the past stay in the past. It wouldn't be fair on either family to go raking it up now."

"But how am I going to cope with knowing that I

could bump into him at any time?

It's just too painful," Elsie said.

Norah looked to the floor before she spoke. "There's a possibility that he might be moving away again. His firm are looking to send people to work abroad, and if he decides it's for him, he could be emigrating to America."

"America?" Elsie exclaimed.

Norah nodded. "Look… Elsie, I'm going to have to get back to the surgery, Doctor Keys is a busy man. But now that you know why I needed to speak to you, I promise I will do my best to stay out of your way."

"No… Norah, please don't do that. My family are already suspicious of why I've been trying to avoid you, and if I'm not going to draw any more attention to that, we need to let them see that there's nothing hostile going on between us."

"Okay," Norah agreed. "I'll pop in and see you soon then, but remember what I said, the past needs to stay where it belongs." Norah picked up the chair, placed it back in the corner of the room and headed for the door.

"Norah… Thank you for caring all those years ago and thank you for caring now. I am grateful for what you did. Honestly."

Norah just smiled, nodded, and left the room.

****

Jeanie checked the clock on the wall. "How much longer are they going to be up there? I hope Mam is alright."

Stella sighed. "I think I'll go and feed Pearl," she

said, taking herself off outside.

A few seconds later, Sheila and Jeanie heard footsteps coming down the stairs. Both women waited in anticipation of Norah providing an update on their mother's health.

"Your mother is going to be fine. We've had a bit of a catch-up whilst I've been up there too," Norah chuckled.

"What was wrong? What made her feel ill so suddenly?" Sheila asked.

"Well, I think she's overdone things a little. She said she was in a hurry to get some flour before Slater's closed, and it's been quite a warm day. I suspect that what with the heat, the distance she's walked, and being in a hurry to boot, it's just exhausted her. I can find nothing else wrong at all," Norah explained.

"Thank goodness that's all it is," Jeanie said.

"And thank goodness that gentleman was there to help too. We should thank him. Do you know who he was?" Sheila asked.

"Erm… no, I'm afraid I don't. He was just passing through the village I think, and stopped off at Slater's," Norah replied.

"That's a shame. Can I get you a cup of tea, Norah?" Sheila asked, getting up off the chair.

"No, thank you. I really must be getting back to the surgery." Norah headed for the back door.

"Come this way, Norah, I'll see you out of the front. Thank you for everything."

After Stella had fed Pearl, she headed back into the house, hoping that by now there would be news on how her grandma was feeling. She walked into the kitchen to find it empty, and worried that her mother and aunt may have been called upstairs. Stella took the steps two at a time to reach the top and walked straight into her grandma's room.

"Has Norah gone then? How are you, Grandma?"

"She's gone, and yes… I'm perfectly fine, thank you. Norah thinks I overdid things a bit, that's all. Nothing to worry about," Elsie reassured.

"Stella love, open that window would you, it's rather stuffy in here," Sheila requested.

As Stella opened the window, a gust of fresh air blew in, sending one of the photographs on Elsie's dressing table onto the floor.

Jeanie bent down and picked it up. "Ah, I remember this. You and Dad had it taken inside that life-sized wooden postcard at the miners' camp last year. That reminds me, Stella, didn't you want a photograph frame for something?"

"Yes, for Grandma's wedding picture. You have a spare one, don't you?"

"I have a few, I think. If you come back with me now, I'll look them out," Jeanie said.

****

After Jeanie had sorted through a box of photographs, she managed to find four spare frames into which Stella could try and fit her grandma's photographs. Stella took them around and tried each one for size.

"There we are, look, the wedding photo fits perfectly in that one, and these two will do nicely for our souvenir pictures," Stella said. She set her grandma's wedding frame down on her bedside table. Then she placed one souvenir picture of herself and Will into one frame and the other of her grandma and grandpa in the other.

"These will look nice on your dressing table now," she said, positioning the two frames down. "And there is a spare frame left over, in case you find another picture you want to display."

"Thank you, love, they look nice," Elsie said.

"I'm glad you're okay, Grandma, you did have us all worried. And everything is alright between you and Norah, is it?"

"Everything is fine, we had a good chat this afternoon."

"Good. That will reassure Mam and Aunty Sheila that there's absolutely nothing to be concerned about then!"

THIRTY-EIGHT

Over the week and a half that followed, Stella's life continued as usual. She went to school, spent time with Will, and was beginning to pick up the ways of shop work. In just under two weeks, Mrs Bell had taught Stella how to build an attractive and eye-catching display, how to check the shop's inventory and reordering system and how to use the cash register. 'By the time Christmas comes, and you start working for the Co-op full-time, you'll be a dab hand at it!' Mrs Bell had said.

Her tutoring sessions were going well too, and she had written three poems as part of a compilation of works that Miss Hutton had set, simply entitled, 'Autumn'. Miss Hutton had the idea that Stella could put together a collection of poems and general thoughts, all of which pertained to her observations surrounding the various changes to the flora and fauna throughout the autumn season.

"Miss, I have an idea. How about we work on this over the next 12 months? Then, eventually, I'd have a full year's worth of poems about all four of the seasons?" Stella suggested.

Miss Hutton smiled. "That is an excellent idea, Stella, but let us not get too far ahead of ourselves. One never knows what one may face around the next corner. Now, it is high time I made a pot of tea."

Stella noticed that Miss Hutton rose from her chair in the same tentative manner that she had been doing for over a week now. And as she walked towards the kitchen, she was certain that Miss Hutton's already slender form had become dreadfully thin indeed. What with that, and her pale complexion, Stella began to wonder if there was something ominous going on.

"Do you have the reference book with you, the one I lent to you when you first came?" Miss Hutton called from the kitchen.

"How to Write Correctly? Yes, miss, I do."

Miss Hutton walked through with a tray of tea things and a plate of biscuits and set it down on the desk. "Good. Turn to page 22 and just read that section. It details the common mistakes writers make. I think you will find it most helpful," she said, sitting down in her chair with the same tentativeness.

As the evening progressed and they reached the end of the session, Stella tidied away her pencils and papers. She watched as Miss Hutton picked up the reference book and opened it to the inscription on the inside cover. She ran her fingers across the words affectionately.

"Is he your beau…the young man who usually meets you from school?" Miss Hutton asked as she closed the book and slid it across the desk towards Stella.

Stella nodded and put the book away in her bag.

Miss Hutton smiled warmly, "I don't recall him being at our school. Is he not a local lad?"

"No, miss, he only came to live here some months ago."

"Ah… I see. And what is he hoping he might do with himself? Employment-wise, I mean?"

"He went for an interview last Friday and

completed an entrance exam. If he's successful, he will become an apprentice with the Royal Air Force."

Miss Hutton's smile suddenly wavered, which made Stella feel that she had said something quite absurd, and this was followed by an awkward silence. Feeling a little uneasy, Stella stood up from her chair and made her way into the hall. She took her coat down from the peg, slipped it around her shoulders and went back to collect her bag.

"I was wondering, miss. Would you mind if I left one of my other stories with you to read?"

"I would be happy to read through any of your work."

"Thank you, miss," Stella said. Picking up her bag, she placed it on the desk and began to rummage through it.

"Stella, I think that whenever you are here at my home, I'd like you to call me Catherine. Would you feel comfortable with that?"

"Yes, miss… Catherine."

Miss Hutton smiled. "In that case, I think we can drop the prefix as well, what do you think?"

Stella nodded and put her story down on the desk in front of Catherine. She picked her bag back up from the desk and was about to say farewell when Catherine took hold of Stella's arm.

"You might be wondering about the inscription in the book, and who David is?"

"It isn't any of my business, miss… erm, sorry… Catherine," Stella said nervously.

Catherine smiled. "He was my fiancé. We were

going to have a quiet wedding. It was already planned for when he was next due for his leave. But on the 19th of August 1942, his squadron took part in the Dieppe Raid. Operation Jubilee, they called it. His plane, along with many others, was shot down by the Luftwaffe, somewhere over the English Channel." Catherine looked at Stella and gave a wistful smile. "And that was it... he was gone." There was a brief pause before Catherine continued. "The book was given to me for my birthday. It was the last thing he gave me before he was killed."

Stella desperately wanted to say something, but she couldn't find any words, let alone the right words. And so, the awkward silence returned.

Catherine slapped the palms of both of her hands on the desk. "Anyway, thankfully, the war is over now. You and your young man won't have to worry about any of that nonsense. Well, at least I hope not, anyway." Catherine looked at the clock on her mantle. "Goodness me, is that the time? Hark at me babbling on with my woes. I do apologise."

"No, please don't apologise," Stella placed her hand over Catherine's. "I... I am sorry for your loss," she said softly.

Catherine gave a nod and patted the hand that Stella had placed over hers.

"You wouldn't mind seeing yourself out, would you? Only I'd like to read your story whilst I'm comfortable," she said, holding up Stella's work.

"Not at all and thank you for having me." Stella made her way out and into the hall and opened the front door.

"I'll see you at school next week," she called back, pulling the door shut behind her.

****

The following morning, Stella woke early. She couldn't help but think about the tragic tale Catherine had told of her fiancé. To have been so happy as to have planned a wedding, and then to lose that person in such a harrowing way, must have been truly devastating. Stella wondered how one would ever get over something so dreadful. Maybe you don't get over it, maybe it is just something with which you must learn to live.

Stella was expected at the Co-op at half past eight, so she climbed out of bed, got washed and dressed, and put her tabard on over her dress. She combed her hair and tied it into a ponytail, fixing it with a blue ribbon and a hair grip on either side to keep the shorter bits off her face. When she got downstairs, her father was sitting at the kitchen table with his early morning newspaper, and a fresh pot of tea. He had just completed his third week working at Creswell Colliery and was relaxing for the weekend before starting back for a week of night shifts on Monday.

She smiled at him when he looked beyond his newspaper, looking to see who had entered the kitchen. But as expected, the gesture wasn't reciprocated.

"Morning," she said to him, sitting down at the table. He managed a grunt, but that was the extent of his response. Stella picked up the bread knife, cut herself a slice of bread, placed it on a tea plate and spread it thinly with butter, cutting it across from corner to corner.

She was about to take a bite when her father spoke from behind his newspaper.

"I'm pleased to hear you'll finally be contributing to the household income with this job of yours, instead of being a drain on it."

Stella placed the piece of bread back down on her plate. "I don't think I'll be earning that much yet. I'm only there for around an hour if I'm needed after school, and I can't expect them to pay me much on a Saturday, not whilst I'm still learning the ropes."

"Even so, nobody works for nothing," Derek remarked.

Stella sighed. She looked at the bread on her plate, suddenly it lost its appeal. She took the tea cosy and lid off the teapot and stirred the tea. She was about to pour herself some tea when he spoke again.

"Or expects to live for free," he added, wryly.

Stella slammed the teapot back down on the table and stood up forcefully. "Tell Mam I've gone to feed Pearl, and then I'll be at the Co-op," she huffed. "Or… don't tell her anything at all… I don't care anymore!" she snapped.

Grabbing her bag from the worktop, she dashed out of the back door without stopping to close it. By the time she had reached the entry gate, her father had appeared at the back door. He started shouting, his voice echoing along the passageway. "Shut the ruddy door. I'm sure you weren't born in a barn!" he yelled.

"But then who the hell would know?" he added, shrugging his shoulders. Stella stormed off up the street towards her grandma's. *Who the hell would know? What was that supposed to mean,* she thought.

****

Stella walked into her grandma's kitchen, just as she was pouring tea from the pot.

"Ooh… someone knows just when to arrive," she joked, turning to look at her granddaughter, who was noticeably upset. "Stella love, what's wrong?"

Stella brushed a tear from her cheek and shook her head. "It doesn't matter."

Elsie reached for another cup and saucer from the cupboard. "Sit down and tell me what's wrong," she insisted.

Stella sat down, rested her elbow on the kitchen table and sunk her chin in the palm of her hand. Staring at the tablecloth, she traced her finger around an embroidered flower design. Elsie hobbled over with the tea and sat down heavily opposite her granddaughter. "Stella?" she said.

Stella sighed, sat up straight and looked straight at her grandmother, pausing momentarily before she spoke. "I just feel that for some reason, Dad resents me being around," she said, her eyes welling with tears.

"Oh… I don't think so. We all know how difficult he can be, but—"

"No! You don't understand, Grandma. Sure, he's bad-tempered around everyone, but with me it's different. It's as though he just despises my actual presence. And now I think hard about it, it has always

307

been that way," Stella lamented, brushing away the tears from her cheeks.

As Elsie took a deep breath and let it out slowly, she looked down at the table as if it might suggest some word of comfort. Eventually, she stood and shuffled around the table towards Stella. She leant forward and put her arm around Stella's shoulder, pulling her close. "Come now, don't let it get to you," she said.

Stella nodded and wiped her eyes. She looked past her grandmother at the kitchen clock. "Goodness is that the time?" she said, jumping up out of her seat. "I'd better go, I don't want to be late." She headed towards the back door and stopping short of it, she looked back.

"Grandma, I haven't fed Pearl, would you mind?"

Elsie nodded and smiled. "Of course. Now get yourself off, I know what a stickler Mrs Bell can be."

THIRTY-NINE

Later that afternoon, as the last of the customers left the store, Stella turned the shop sign to read 'closed' and locked the door. She could hear Mrs Bell in her office, berating Alfie because he had buckled the front wheel of the shop bicycle after hitting a rut in the road, spilling Mrs Henshall's grocery order out of the basket in the process.

Stella made her way towards the back of the store, and as she looked towards the office, all she could see of Mrs Bell was her finger wagging furiously at Alfie. Alfie stood with his head bowed, blood running from his knee, but the lad stood there as quiet as a mouse and took his rollicking. Stella walked into the office and grabbed her bag from the coat peg, and after Mrs Bell had finished scolding Alfie, they all made their way out from the back, and round onto the street.

Without so much as a goodbye, Mrs Bell hurried towards the bus stop, moving as quickly as her frame would allow, and mumbling something about clouting Alfie if she missed the bus altogether. Thankfully for Alfie, she just managed to hold out her arm in time to flag down the half past five to Ripley.

"I don't think she likes me," Alfie weighed in, staring at the bus as it disappeared out of sight.

Stella laughed. "Now what gives you that idea, Alfie?" she said, searching through her bag. "I'll get a hanky to dab your knee." Stella took out a clean handkerchief, but as Alfie was already looking down at his knee, he noticed a tear in the leg of his shorts.

"Ahh... that's the second time this week I've

managed to rip summat, me mam'll kill me," he grumbled.

Stella knelt and dabbed at the blood on Alfie's knee. "I'm sure she won't go quite that far, Alfie."

Alfie, who very quickly forgot his woes, pulled his sketchbook out of his coat pocket.

"Here... I said I'd bring yer some more of me drawings," he thrust his book towards Stella's face. "You can keep hold of it for now, I must go before me mam comes looking for me. Ta-ra..." he called, racing off up the street.

Stella stood up and watched as Alfie disappeared out of sight; his spontaneity and playfulness made her smile. She hoped his mother wouldn't be too cross with him for tearing his shorts - after all, it was only an accident. As she strolled back towards home, she flicked through the pages of Alfie's sketchbook and was captivated by how striking his illustrations were. Page upon page of random sketches, not just of animals, but of plants and flowers too. It was obvious that the boy had talent, one that Stella hoped would not be cast aside by his parents and ignorant exemplars. She put his sketchbook in her bag and opened the entry gate. As she walked through the passage towards the back door, the delicious smell of something cooking filled the air. She walked through the house to find that her mother had dinner all prepared.

"Now that... smells good," Stella remarked. "What is it?"

"Meat pie with vegetables from your dad's

allotment. It's all ready, so sit yourself down."

As Stella sat down at the table, her father walked in from having been in the garden, and without so much as a look in her direction, went to wash his hands at the sink. With the predictability of his unpleasant manner inevitable, Stella saw no point in wasting her time on any form of greeting.

"How have you got on at the Co-op today?" Jeanie asked, cutting through the steaming hot pie she had placed in the centre of the table.

As he sat down at the table, Stella at once looked at her father; was this conversation heading in the direction of how much money she was likely to be bringing home?

"Erm... fine. I'm picking it up quite easily, I think," Stella said, spooning out some vegetables from a dish and onto her plate. As that seemed to be the only question for now, Stella quickly changed the subject.

"This pie tastes delicious, Mam, what is the meat?" Stella asked, putting a fork full of pie into her mouth.

"Your dad came home with some rabbit. Did you get it from that new butcher's shop in Ripley, Derek?" Jeanie asked.

"Can't afford to buy rabbit meat from a butcher," Derek said, chewing on a mouthful of food, pausing to swallow before continuing. "Not without a contribution to the household finances. So no, I'm afraid I was forced to find other means," he shrugged.

"What other means, Derek?" Jeanie asked, reaching for the gravy boat.

Derek continued to eat, but he kept looking at his

daughter as if trying to goad her.

Stella put her fork down and looked directly at her father, waiting for him to clarify his meaning. A clarification that wasn't coming quickly enough.

"Dad... what other means?" she said sternly.

Eventually, Derek spoke. "There's only one other place round here to get a nice lean rabbit.

Had to skin it myself, mind, but you can get a ha'penny or two for the—"

"You haven't! Please tell me you haven't. Not Pearl... please, Dad... Not my Pearl!"

Derek didn't confirm or deny, he just laughed callously, a laugh that seemed to echo through the kitchen and beyond.

"Why? Why would you do that?" Stella cried, jumping up out of her chair. "Why do you hate me so much?" she yelled, before rushing off out of the kitchen, slamming the back door behind her.

Stella ran out onto the street, her short-sleeved dress no match for the heavy shower that now descended, and by the time she had run up to her grandma's house, a mixture of tears and rain were streaming down her face. She opened the entry gate, and as she hurried along the passage, she could almost hear her heart pounding. When she got to the top, she paused for a moment, preparing herself for what she might find. As she turned the corner into her grandma's garden, she realised that a moment's pause was never going to be long enough to prepare her for what she found...

The door on Pearl's cage was wide open, Stella ran

across to the hutch in the hopes that her rabbit may still be somewhere inside. She crouched to open the door to the sleeping compartment, but the rabbit was gone. Stella dropped to her knees and sobbed. The rain came down in sheets now, the noise of which drowned out her cries, dissolving her tears before they rolled down her cheeks. A puddle of water had formed where she knelt and was soaking into her dress. Of all the times he had found ways of being cruel to her, this act was far worse than any beating or tongue-lashing she had ever received.

After a short while, Stella became aware of her name being called. She stopped crying, and upon realising it was her grandma, she turned to see her beckoning frantically and shouting to her to come on in out of the rain. Stella stumbled ungainly to her feet, ran over to her grandma, and flinging her arms around her, she sobbed again.

"Hey… hey, come now. What is wrong?" Elsie asked, gently pulling away from her granddaughter's embrace.

Stella tried to speak in between sobs. "It's Dad… he… he's taken Pearl… and he's …"

"No, no, no. Pearl is in the kitchen," Elsie said with a frown. "Look," she said, moving away from Stella to open the back door. As soon as the door opened, the little rabbit hopped towards them.

"I let her out on the lawn earlier, and the next thing I know, she's hopping around the kitchen again, just like she did the other day. I would have taken her back if it weren't raining so much, but she was happy enough to investigate the kitchen, so I saw no harm. Look, let's get inside, for heaven's sake, before we both catch our death," Elsie said, taking Stella by her hand.

Stella sat down at the kitchen table, and Elsie grabbed a towel, flinging it around Stella's shoulders.

"There, dry yourself off, eh? Now tell me, why would you think that your dad would take Pearl? What need would he have for a rabbit?" Elsie said doubtfully.

Stella used the towel to dry her hair. "Because that's what he said… well implied. And that's what he wanted me to believe. He hates me, I know he does."

"Oh, I'm sure he was just kidding you," Elsie said, giving a sideways look.

Stella flung her arms up into the air. "Why… why must everyone insist on backing him up? He manages to get away with everything, and each time he does, it makes him all the braver for the next time he feels compelled to pick on me."

Elsie shook her head. "I'm sure you're reading too much into it, love."

"Really?" Stella stood up and threw the towel down on the table. "Then ask Mam for the real reason she got that bruise on her eye. Go on, I dare you!"

Stella marched out of her grandma's house, and back off up the street towards the recreation ground. It was still raining, but she was far too upset to notice and just kept walking. Her mind began to wander, was she reading too much into it? Was it just her father's sick attempt at trying to be funny? No, she was sure that him leading her to believe that he had killed her beloved rabbit was exactly what he was hoping to achieve. But why? What had she ever done to make him always feel the need to be so unjustly cruel to her?

Stella wasn't giving much thought as to where she was going and strode angrily across the recreation ground. The rain began to come down even heavier now, and it was only with the sudden feeling of someone grabbing her arm, that she was brought to her senses. She turned sharply, and upon realising that it was Will, she broke down in tears. Will pulled her close to him, and it was only then that she realised just how wet and cold she was. She nestled her face into his neck and sobbed, unable to speak for shivering.

"Hey, come on. What is wrong?" Will said softly.

Stella tried to speak, but she couldn't form any words.

Will took off his coat and wrapped it around Stella's shoulders. "Let's get you home, eh?" he said, as he tried to scrape the wet strands of hair from her face.

Stella shook her head forcefully. "No. I don't want to go back there. I never want to go back there," she insisted.

"We'll go to my house then. We just need to get you somewhere warm."

Will grabbed hold of Stella's hand and they ran out through the other side of the recreation ground and up the main road towards Will's house. By the time they had gone the short distance along the main road, the rain had stopped, and the sun lit up the evening sky. Stella stopped short of Will's driveway and let go of his hand.

"I don't want your parents to see me in this state, Will. I'm not up for having to explain things to them yet."

Will turned to Stella and pulled her close. "It's okay. You go on down to the rabbit shed then, and I'll make you some tea."

****

Stella sipped the warm tea that Will had brought her. He had also brought one of his jumpers and a towel for her hair.

"Warmer?" Will asked.

Stella nodded. "I'm sorry Will, it wasn't my intention to bump into you like that. I wasn't thinking about where I was going."

"I was on my way to see if you were at your grandma's house because I have something to tell you. Then the rain came down and I took shelter under a tree. That's when I saw you. I shouted to you, but you just kept going. What's wrong, Stella? I've never seen you so upset."

Stella took a deep sigh. "I think it's time you knew the truth about my home life."

FORTY

Will sat with his back against Misty's cage whilst Stella relayed the story of how her father had cruelly led her to believe she was eating her pet rabbit. He listened intently as she told him everything about what life was like with her father. The wanton disregard for her very existence, the silence before the unprovoked outbursts, the beatings. She explained that as terrible as it sounded, the only time she could ever remember having felt happy at home, was whilst he was away at war. Sure enough, the war had changed many men, and it had changed her father too, but only in a way that heightened his already callous demeanour.

Jeanie didn't want to believe that, though, but she also didn't want the local gossips to know she had made the wrong marriage choice either. She needed to find something on which to pin the blame, that would account for her husband's behaviour. So, when Derek was captured by the Japanese and held captive for three years, suffering unspeakable cruelty, it provided her with what she saw as the perfect excuse on which to blame his abhorrent behaviour.

"Mam must be exhausted, hiding it as well as she has. I think it has taken its toll, though. Of course, the family, and most people you speak to around here, all know what a short fuse he has. But only Mam and I know what goes on behind closed doors." Stella dragged the towel from around her neck and rubbed at her wet hair. "But you know… the thing that gets to me, is the fact that she makes excuses for him. It doesn't matter what he's done, she'll always find a reason for it. I can't stand it anymore, Will. I must find a way to leave."

Stella got up off the floor and Will followed suit. He reached out, pulled her close and wrapped his arms around her. "I'm so sorry, Stella, I had no idea," he whispered. He brushed a clump of wet hair away from her face. "I did think a few times that something wasn't quite right at home, but I honestly thought that you were just a little shy about introducing me to your parents. However, it all makes sense now."

Stella pulled away gently and looked up at Will. "I wish that's all it was."

"Would you like me to ask my parents if you can stay in our spare room?" Will asked.

Stella shook her head. "That's kind of you, Will, but it would only make things worse. I'll just have to put up with it for now. I'm glad I have my grandma, though, and I'm glad I have you too," Stella said. Reaching up on her toes, she kissed him softly and he cupped her face in his warm hands.

"I can't stand the thought of him hurting you," he said.

Stella gave a faint smile. "The only thing I can do is try and stay out of his way as much as possible. I'd better go now, it's getting late." Stella handed the towel to Will and started to take off the jumper that he had brought for her to wear.

"No, no. Please keep it on. I'll have it back some other time," Will said, opening the door to the shed.

Stella stepped out into the garden. "Thanks, Will.

Oh… I've just remembered, you said you were coming to tell me something?"

Will looked to the floor. "Yes, although I rather wish I didn't have something to tell you now."

"What do you mean?" Stella asked confusedly, before realising that he must be referring to his RAF interview. "You got your apprenticeship, didn't you!"

Will nodded and gave a half-hearted smile. "Yes, but now I wish I hadn't."

"You must not think like that, Will. This will be a wonderful opportunity for you." Just as she said it, a mental image of Miss Hutton saying the same thing to her fiancé, forced its way into her mind. *I wonder if she said that to him,* she thought, before quickly brushing it aside. "I will miss you, though," she said softly, managing to swallow the lump that had risen in her throat. Will just looked vacantly at Stella, not knowing what to say.

"So come on then, tell me all about it," she eventually said.

Will ran his fingers through his hair, brushing his fringe away from his forehead. "I leave for RAF Halton in eight weeks, on the 18th of November. Initially, I'll be away for three months, then back home for two weeks' leave. I'm not sure yet what the schedule will be after that," Will said. "Come, I'll walk you home," he reached out for her hand.

They walked along the main road towards the Denby side of the recreation ground in relative silence. It wasn't until they got onto the ground itself, and nearer to Stella's house that Will stopped suddenly to speak.

"I'd have half a mind to tear a strip off your father if I thought it would make any difference," he snapped.

Stella swung around to meet Will's gaze. "If I thought it would make even the slightest bit of difference, I would happily let you. But the truth is... it wouldn't, and he's just not worth it!"

Will put his arm around the small of Stella's back and drew her close. With his free hand, he brushed her hair away from her face and tilted his head towards her ear.

"You're worth it, though," he whispered, gently pressing his face into hers.

He brushed his lips softly over her cheek and towards her mouth. Finding her lips, he kissed her with a passion that ignited both their souls.

****

Thinking she had some explaining to do, Stella headed straight to her grandma's house where she found her in the sitting room, snoozing in her armchair. Elsie had her elbow resting on the arm of the chair and her head proportionally weighed in the palm of her hand. Stella announced her arrival in a hushed tone, so as not to startle her, and Elsie opened her eyes slowly, grimacing at the pain she now felt in her arm after having it fixed in one position for too long. Stella sat down on the settee opposite her grandma.

"I see you've brought all of your photographs down from your room," Stella said with a smile.

"I thought they might as well be seen by everyone, rather than having them stuck up in my room. That's if you're happy to have that one of you and your young chap on show?"

Stella nodded and smiled. "Grandma... I'm sorry for my outburst earlier, I just think it's time that people knew exactly what Mam and I go through... with Dad, I mean."

Elsie sat up straight in her chair. "I think you've confirmed my suspicions. Well, your grandpa's suspicions anyway. He and your dad never got on, and I suspect that's the reason they clashed as much as they did." Elsie used the arms of the chair to push herself up and reach balance on her knees. "Oh... I rue the day she got together with him. Things could have been quite different if she had just ignored him pestering her to go out with him. Proper sweet talker he was back then n'all," she said, hobbling off in the direction of the kitchen.

Stella got up off the settee and followed her grandma into the kitchen. "Well yes, but then if they hadn't got together, I wouldn't exist," she laughed.

Stella's remark made Elsie turn and look at her granddaughter quite keenly, before quickly agreeing with her and swiftly changing the subject.

"My friend, Norah, is coming round for tea tomorrow afternoon," she said, reaching for the kettle.

"Really? That will be a pleasant change for you then. Perhaps I will get to meet her, I seem to keep missing the opportunity," Stella laughed.

"Well, you should pop in and say hello." Elsie reached into the cupboard for a cup and saucer. "Tea?" she asked.

"No… I'd better be heading off. I never know what to expect when I walk through the door. May as well get it over with."

Elsie set her cup and saucer down on the worktop and put her hand on Stella's shoulder. "I'm always here if you need me, but it's not my place to interfere with what goes on between your mam and dad. Just try and stay out of his way, and remember… you can always come here," she said.

Stella gave half a smile. "I know, Grandma," she said, heading for the door. "Thankfully, he'll be starting back on night shifts again next week, so at least he won't be around to see very much of."

Back at home and, much to Stella's surprise, the house was quiet. She breathed a sigh of relief at the thought that it probably meant that her mother would be in bed and her father would be at the pub. Stella made herself a cup of hot milk, and upon realising that the gnawing sensation in her stomach was due to it being empty, she reached for what was left of a loaf of bread and cut herself two pieces from it. She smeared a small amount of butter on each piece and topped them with some strawberry jam. She placed everything on a tray and took it up to her room, closing the bedroom door quietly behind her.

It had been an exhausting day, but she felt awake enough to work through some of the tasks Miss Hutton had set her. She wanted to be prepared for their upcoming session on Monday evening. She sat at her makeshift desk and took a bite of the bread and jam. She hadn't realised just how hungry she was until she started eating it, and after bolting it all down too quickly, it left her with an ache in her tummy. She picked up the cup of hot milk and took a sip. A skin had formed across the drink which, as it stuck to her top lip, burned a little, and Stella quickly used her handkerchief to wipe it away.

She picked up her notebook and pencil and continued with the autumn-themed project that Miss Hutton had set. She had by now created a reasonable collection of poems, together with brief notes of the general impressions she had of how the animals and plants, living and growing in their natural environment, had coped with the autumn season so far. The project was turning into a journal of sorts, and Stella thought about her idea again. If she worked on the project throughout the entire year, it would make an informative chronicle to turn into a book. But something was missing, she needed something else to add to her work that would bring it to life. Stella stood up and walked over to her window, rested her elbows on her windowsill and stared out into the street. Dusk was beginning to creep in, and the only movement outside was that of a cat running up the street with something in its mouth that resembled a mouse. Stella shuddered, and then the idea came to her... illustrations! If she could add drawings of the flowers, plants, and animals, it would add representation to the whole project. And who was the one person who would be perfect to create these illustrations? There was only one person whom Stella could think of who would fit the bill… Alfie Beardmore!

Stella hurried across to the other side of her room, picked up her bag and emptied the contents onto her bed. She grabbed Alfie's sketchbook out from among her things and sat back down at her desk. She opened the book and studied each page in turn. Goodness… the boy had a skill. This talent was not going to go unnoticed, not if Stella had anything to do with it! She put Alfie's sketchbook and her notebook into her bag. The idea of turning the project into a book was going to need a second opinion, and the only person whom she knew, interested enough to give an opinion… was Miss Hutton.

FORTY-ONE

The next morning, when Stella woke, the first thing that came to her mind was an image of how she wanted her journal to look. If Miss Hutton thought it was a promising idea, then she would speak to Alfie about the illustrations. Of course, she would have to approach his parents to gain their permission, but they surely wouldn't object. She flung the sheets back and swung her legs out of bed. Pulling the curtains back haphazardly, she sat at her desk. She had so many ideas and wanted to get them down on paper. She made notes on how she wanted the layout to appear and created a plan on what to include in each season.

Before she realised it, she had filled quite a few pages with her thoughts and ideas, and time had soon passed. Would it be too much of an imposition if she were to call on Miss Hutton on a Sunday? Stella looked at the clock on her bedside table, it read five past nine. By the time she had got dressed and called in to feed Pearl, it would be at least another 40 minutes... that's not too early for a Sunday. And if Miss Hutton wasn't a churchgoer, then she would quite likely be at home anyway.

Stella opened her bedroom door gingerly and poked her head out. The door to her parents' room had been wedged open, the curtains had been drawn back, and an open window allowed a cool breeze to blow through. She listened... all seemed quiet downstairs too. She raced across the landing to the bathroom, washed, brushed her teeth, and dashed back. After she had dressed, she brushed her hair and then straightened the curtains she had hurled back earlier. As she did so, she noticed that her father had just left the house; he was pushing his wheelbarrow and heading in the direction of his allotment. At least that meant she could leave the house without another confrontation with him.

As she entered the kitchen, her mother walked in from having been outside in the garden.

"Morning, Stella love, how are you after yesterday's misunderstanding?"

Misunderstanding? Was she for real? "Mam... If you believe that it was a misunderstanding and that there was no malice intended on his part, then I have nothing to say." Stella headed for the open door and walked out. Her mother's voice echoed out into the passage after her.

"I'm sure he was only having a bit of fun!"

Stella continued to walk on, out of the entry and onto the street. Fun? Since when did he ever know anything about having fun?

****

Stella lifted Pearl out of her hutch and placed her down on the lawn whilst she filled her feed bowl with pellets. She searched the garden and collected a handful of dandelions before freshening the water in her bowl. When everything was in place, and ready to put the rabbit back in her hutch, Stella noticed that Pearl had hopped over to her grandma's back door and was scratching at it, to get in.

"You are a cheeky little madam, aren't you," Stella laughed as she walked over to her.

She was about to pick up the rabbit when the back door opened.

"Morning, Grandma,' Stella said, as the rabbit quickly took advantage of the open door.

"Morning, love," Elsie replied. "I was just making sure my hat was on straight when I heard her scratching at the door." Elsie looked at the kitchen clock. "Albert and Sheila will be here any minute for church. Are you coming?"

"I have something I need to do this morning. I will be back here in a bit, though. I want to clean Pearl's hutch out later."

A loud tap on the front door announced the arrival of Elsie's lift to church. "That will be them now. Just lock the back door and post the key through at the front, would you?" Elsie said, heading for the front door. "Oh, and help yourself to some toast, I'll see you later!" she called back.

Stella picked up Pearl from the kitchen floor and cuddled her. "Would you like some toast?" she asked, as she smoothed the soft area of fur in between the rabbit's ears.

"No? Let's get you back in your hutch then, eh…" she said. Stella managed to pull the back door shut and lock it with one hand, before walking over to the hutch and placing the rabbit down gently inside it. She remembered to post the key through the letter box before making her way to Miss Hutton's cottage.

When she arrived, Stella was surprised to find that Miss Hutton's downstairs curtains were still shut, and yet, oddly the upstairs curtains were open. She pushed open the gate and walked partway down the garden path before stopping abruptly. She looked at her watch. It was almost half past ten. *Perhaps she has only just got up. It is Sunday, after all,* Stella thought. Thinking it best to leave and come back later, she turned and quickly headed back along the path. She was about to exit through the gate, when a man, whom Stella assumed was Miss Hutton's next-door neighbour, suddenly appeared from among a large area of tall plants and foliage in his front garden. He arched his back as he stood up, trying to straighten himself up from the bending position he'd been in for too long whilst weeding.

"Good morning young, lady. Can I help you at all?" the man asked, as he pulled a handkerchief from his pocket and dabbed at the beads of sweat that had formed across his brow.

Stella shut Miss Hutton's gate and walked along to the neighbour's front. Glad of the opportunity to take a rest, the man brought his spade down heavily into the ground and took a few steps forward, towards his side of the fence.

"I was hoping to pay Miss Hutton a visit," Stella said. "But I'm not sure that she can receive any guests yet this morning. So, I'll just come back later."

"And you are?" the man asked.

"I'm Stella Felton. Miss Hutton is my private tutor," Stella smiled proudly.

"Ah… I see. Well, I'm sorry to have to tell you this, young Stella, but I'm afraid Miss

Hutton was admitted to hospital on Friday

evening."

Stella's smile disappeared instantly, and her eyes widened. "Oh... good gracious me," she said, putting her hand to her mouth. "Do you know what is wrong with her?"

The man shrugged his shoulders. "I'm afraid I don't. To be honest, I haven't gotten to know her all that well yet. I only moved here a month ago."

Stella looked down at the floor, and then up at the man. "I wonder if this could have something to do with the mysterious complaint from which she seems to have been suffering of late," Stella said.

"I honestly don't know," the man shook his head and sighed. "I assume you know she has no family?"

Stella nodded.

The man scratched his head. "I feel quite sorry that she has nobody. I did think that I would visit her at some point, but then with not knowing her that well... I wouldn't want to impose. If you know what I mean?"

Stella nodded again.

"You could visit her, though? I know they took her to the Derbyshire Royal Infirmary, but I don't know which ward, though." The man stepped back to where he had left his spade and pulled it from the ground. "If you do go, please tell her that Don Russell sends his regards."

"Yes... yes, of course and thank you for letting me know."

The man nodded and continued with his weeding. Stella left with what felt like a cloak of sorrow that had draped itself heavily around her shoulders. As she walked back in the direction of her grandma's house, she thought about the possibility of the man's suggestion of going to see Miss Hutton in hospital. Would the ward allow someone who isn't family to visit? Would Miss Hutton want her to visit? There was only one way to find out, but how would she get to know what the visiting hours were, and how would she travel into Derby and back on a Sunday? The only person she knew who had means of transport was her Uncle Albert, and they had a telephone too! Maybe if she explained the situation, he might see fit to take her? Deciding that it was all worth a try, Stella diverted her route. By the time she arrived at her aunt and uncle's house, she didn't have to wait too long before they arrived home from church.

After explaining the situation to her aunt and uncle, Sheila suggested that Stella could telephone the exchange and ask to be put through to the hospital. She could then enquire as to the visiting hours, and which ward Miss Hutton had been taken to. Then they would happily take her there, wait while she visited, and bring her back again.

"That is so kind of you both. Thank you," Stella said.

"Here… I'll ring the exchange, and you can speak to the hospital," Albert said. Picking up the phone, he dialled the Horsley Telephone Exchange. "Ah… hello, yes. Could you connect me to the Derbyshire Royal Infirmary please?" There was a slight pause before Albert thanked the switchboard operator and handed the telephone to Stella. Stella was slightly nervous. She had never spoken to anyone on the telephone before. But after handling the conversation with ease, she placed the handset back down on the receiver and smiled.

"She's on ward 19. It's a surgical ward… whatever that is. Visiting is between two o'clock and three o'clock this afternoon."

"Surgical ward? That must mean she's either having, or already had, surgery for something then!" Sheila said before looking at her watch. "We just have time for a bite to eat first, and then we can be on our way."

****

Albert parked in the visitors' car park of the Derbyshire Royal Infirmary and pointed out the main entrance to Stella.

"You're okay with what you need to do?" Sheila asked.

Stella nodded. "Thank you both for bringing me," she said, getting out of Albert's car.

Stella walked across the car park and entered the hospital through a large set of double doors marked 'Main Entrance'. It was the first time she had been inside a hospital and thought that the likelihood of it not being the last, instantly struck her. As she approached a desk marked 'main reception', the distinct yet ambrosial smell of disinfectant entered her nostrils, giving an assured impression of freshness.

A woman, whom Stella perceived to be in her 50s, sat behind the reception desk and promptly asked whom Stella wished to visit. She then ran her finger down a list of surnames recorded in a large and heavy-looking register. Eventually, the woman nodded and confirmed that Miss Hutton was indeed on ward 19. She then pointed towards a long passageway and began to explain to Stella the route she would need to take.

"Walk along the main corridor, then eventually on your left, you will come to a set of double doors marked 'Surgical Wards'. Go through those doors and up the stairs, when you reach the top, turn left, and walk along the corridor. You will then find ward 19 on your left," the woman relayed with a smile. "You must announce your arrival with the ward sister first, and she will direct you from there," she added.

Stella thanked the receptionist and went on her way. As she walked along the endless length of the main corridor, black and white floor tiles led the way. The grey walls seemed to just appear from the floor and reach up to correspond with the ceiling, the bareness of it all broken up now and then by identical double doorways edged in white.

Before long, Stella found herself outside ward 19. Faced with another set of double doors, she peered through the glass. The room was long and narrow, with a row of a dozen or so beds on each side, each spaced with regimental precision. Stella glanced briefly at the person in each bed, noting that some were empty, and one on the right, at the far end, had a portable curtain on castors positioned around it. If that wasn't the bed Miss Hutton was in, then she just couldn't spot her.

Stella pushed open one of the doors and walked in tentatively. Situated immediately to her right was a wooden desk, with a nurse sitting behind it. A sign fastened to the front of the desk read 'All visitors must report to the nurse in charge'. As Stella approached the desk, she noticed how immaculately dressed the nurse appeared. She wore a navy-blue uniform, with a white collar, a crisp white cotton apron, and white cuffs around rolled-up sleeves. Her hair was neatly pinned back in a bun, whilst a white cotton cap edged in lace, was positioned perfectly atop her head.

The nurse was busy entering information into a thick file and whilst Stella waited patiently, she took note of a brass sign on the desk that read 'Sister Fox'. The nurse closed the file and placed it on top of a pile of others before looking up at Stella.

"May I help you… miss?"

"Felton. Stella Felton. I'm here to see Miss Catherine Hutton."

"Are you indeed, and may I ask what your relationship is to Miss Hutton?"

"She is my teacher."

Sister Fox raised an eyebrow. "I do hope I'm not going to have a horde of school pupils traipsing through my ward?"

"No, no. She is my private tutor, so there will be nobody else… she has nobody else."

A compassionate smile appeared across Sister Fox's lips as she took a moment to consider Stella's request.

"Very well," she eventually said, before turning her

gaze to the far end of the ward. "Miss Hutton is in bed 13, which is the last bed on the right. Visiting ceases at three o'clock sharp unless I say otherwise."

Stella smiled and thanked the ward sister, who merely nodded before picking up another file.

As she made her way towards bed 13, the bed that minutes earlier had the portable curtains around it, she wavered a little. What right did she have to turn up uninvited? What made her assume that her presence would be a welcome one? As she neared, Miss Hutton looked up, and as the realisation of her visitor set in, a smile appeared on her face that certainly suggested otherwise. A cheerful smile that at once quashed all of Stella's fears.

FORTY-TWO

"Let me know if you need anything else," Nurse Blake said in a soft tone, as she straightened and smoothed Miss Hutton's bed sheets.

The nurse then gestured to a stack of wooden chairs in the far-left corner of the ward. "Help yourself to a chair, my dear," she suggested to Stella with a smile, before wheeling away the portable curtain she'd folded into a concertina.

Stella fetched a chair from the stack, took it back to Miss Hutton's bedside and sat down.

"I didn't know if you might be cross at my uninvited visit," Stella said dubiously.

"Not at all, it is a delight to see you, but how did you know I was here?"

Stella tucked a stray lock of hair behind her ear. "Well… I wanted to speak to you about something, but when I arrived at your house, your neighbour, Mr Russell told me you had been brought into hospital." Stella tipped her head to one side. "How are you now? Are you feeling better?"

Miss Hutton gave half a smile. "I'm feeling much better than I was." She leaned forward to whisper. "I don't know what they've been giving me, but it certainly seems to be doing the trick for now," she said, putting her hand to her mouth to stifle a giggle.

"That is good news. So, you will be home soon?"

Miss Hutton leaned back against her pillow. "Erm… I'm afraid not. Whatever it is they've been giving me is only a temporary fix. It would appear I have to have an operation."

"Oh goodness, what kind of operation?"

A stony look appeared on Miss Hutton's face. "An investigative one. It would seem the doctors aren't entirely sure what is wrong. So, it's off to the operating theatre I go," she said, raising her eyebrows.

"I'm dreadfully sorry."

"When the ambulance brought me in, I only managed to grab my handbag, I don't have anything else with me, not even a nightdress," she said, tugging at her hospital gown.

"Is there anything I can do to help?" Stella asked.

Miss Hutton considered for a moment. "Well, I know it's an awful imposition, but if I give you my house key, would you be willing to collect a few items for me? I honestly don't know how long I'm going to be stuck in here."

"Of course, I don't mind." Stella grabbed her notebook and pencil from her bag.

"Here, you write down what you need and where I can find it, and I'll come back tomorrow."

"Stella, you are a gem. Thank you so much."

Whilst Miss Hutton was busy writing out a list, Stella watched as Nurse Blake was busy doing the rounds with the tea trolley. Momentarily, she appeared with a cup of tea and a menu card.

"Forgive me for the intrusion. Your surgery is planned for Tuesday, so you may complete your menu card for tomorrow and then you will be nil by mouth after a light meal tomorrow afternoon," she said, placing the menu card and a cup and saucer down on a side table.

"Thank you kindly, Nurse Blake," Miss Hutton nodded.

Nurse Blake continued with her trolley, pushing it across the ward to the next patient, and Stella couldn't help but overhear Nurse Blake informing another patient that as her surgery was planned for tomorrow, she would be nil by mouth from six this evening.

"There we are," Miss Hutton said, handing Stella back her notebook. "I do appreciate you doing this for me. Take my key, and… goodness, how have you managed to get here today?"

"My aunt and uncle very kindly brought me. They're waiting in the car park to take me back."

"Oh my, it would seem that I am putting a lot of people out."

Stella shook her head. "No, you aren't, they were more than happy to help."

Miss Hutton opened her purse and passed Stella some money. "Please give this to your uncle for bringing you."

Stella shook her head. "They won't accept it. I know they won't."

"Then use it if you need to get a bus here tomorrow. Please, I want to show my gratitude."

Stella nodded reluctantly. She didn't want to take money from Miss Hutton, but she couldn't ask her uncle to bring her again, and she hadn't given any thought to how else she would obtain any money to get a bus.

"Now, what was it that you wanted to speak to me about?"

Stella was still lost in her thoughts. "Sorry?"

"You said you had gone to my house because you wanted to speak to me about something?"

"Oh, yes… but it can wait. It's not important," Stella said, shaking her head.

"It must be fairly important if you wanted to see me on a Sunday?"

Stella sighed, "It was just an idea about the autumn project we've been working on, and I was excited to get your opinion on it. But honestly, it can wait."

"No, no… please, I'd love to hear about it."

Stella reached into her bag and took out the notes she had made that detailed her plan.

She was about to explain it all to Miss Hutton when a loud jingling noise filled the ward. Stella looked over in the direction of where the noise was coming from, to see the ward sister ringing a small handbell.

"Ah… that means visiting is over, I'm afraid," Miss Hutton said reluctantly.

Stella pushed the notes back into her bag, but Miss Hutton reached for Stella's arm.

"No, please… leave your plan with me and I'll happily take a look. I need something to help take my mind off things."

Stella smiled. "If you're sure, then thank you."

The ward sister rang the bell again. "I'd better be going before I get into trouble. I will see you tomorrow," Stella said.

Stella returned her chair to the stack and waved goodbye to Miss Hutton, before making her way out of the ward.

****

Out of courtesy, Stella thought it only polite to inform Miss Hutton's neighbour, Mr Russell, that she had indeed been to see her, and that she had been asked to collect some belongings. Mr Russell said that if he could be of any help, especially transport-wise, she should let him know.

Stella turned the key in the lock and pushed open Miss Hutton's front door, closing it behind her. She reached into her bag for her notebook and read from the list Miss Hutton had made. Most of the items listed… a small suitcase, a couple of nightdresses, a bed jacket, slippers and a washbag, could be found in Miss Hutton's bedroom, but also on the list was a small brown leather document wallet which could be found at the back of the wardrobe in the spare room.

Stella made her way upstairs and into the larger of the two rooms. She reached up and grabbed the suitcase from off the top of a double wardrobe, and then collected the other items listed, folding them neatly before placing them in the case. She then made her way to the spare room and found the document wallet. Briefly thinking that the need for a document wallet was a slightly odd request for someone about to undergo surgery, Stella paid no further attention, and with everything fitting nicely into the case, she closed it up and made her way back downstairs.

Also on the list was the title of the book Miss Hutton was currently reading, which could be found on the coffee table in her sitting room. After adding the book to the case, Stella locked the front door and was soon on her way. It was getting on for teatime, and a niggling in Stella's stomach gave a reminder that once again she had gone all day without eating. *You should have had some toast at Grandma's this morning!* she thought to herself. Then she suddenly remembered that her grandma had invited Norah over for tea. With the thought that there may be a sandwich or two left over, Stella decided to make her way to her grandma's house.

****

"I thoroughly enjoyed that, Elsie, you always did know how to make a delicious

Victoria sponge," Norah said, placing her napkin down on the kitchen table.

"I'm pleased you enjoyed it. Shall we take the tea tray through into the sitting room and enjoy another cup in comfort?" Elsie asked.

Norah nodded and the women made their way through to the sitting room. With Norah carrying the tray, she set it down on a side table in between the two armchairs.

Elsie pointed to a chair. "Make yourself comfy, Norah, I'll pour us another cup."

Elsie filled Norah's cup before pouring one for herself. She sat down heavily in her chair and groaned a little at the lack of flexibility in her knee joints.

"Ahh… what's the point of getting old? There's no future in it, you know!" Elsie laughed, but Norah seemed not to be listening, instead, she was staring at the row of photographs on Elsie's mantelpiece. "Norah… are you quite alright?"

Norah didn't respond, instead, she got up out of the armchair and walked across the room to the fireplace and picked up the picture of Stella and Will.

"Ahh, that is my granddaughter, Stella, and her young man. It was taken at—"

"I know where it was taken," Norah sharply chipped in.

"Well, I suppose it does say so on the front," Elsie laughed in an uneasy tone.

"No… the reason I know, is because Mike has the same picture on his mantelpiece."

"Who?"

"Michael!" Norah said raising her voice. "You know… Michael, your son, my nephew!"

Norah held up the picture of Stella and Will. "And this is Michael's son, Will. Oh goodness, gracious…" Norah walked back over to her chair, staring at the picture still in her hand, and she too sat down heavily in the chair, but out of shock rather than worn-out knees. "My husband, Jed, took Will to the miners' camp instead of taking me, because I was too busy with the house move."

Elsie had her hand to her mouth. "You mean Stella's young man is… is my grandson?"

Norah nodded slowly as the realisation of it filled her mind. "Yes, so it means that biologically… they are cousins." Norah placed the photograph face down on the side table and stood up quickly. "We're going to have to do something. They can't go on seeing each other, it's going to cause too much pain and upset for everyone."

"Stella said he might be joining the RAF. If he does, maybe the relationship will die a natural death. And… you mentioned that Michael might be offered a position in America.

Has anything come of that? What would that mean for Will, if Michael does decide to go?"

Norah sighed heavily and shook her head. "The position is his if he wants it, but there's something delaying proceedings, something to do with paperwork, I believe. But Will is joining the RAF, he starts his apprenticeship on the 18th of November. And as far as their relationship dying a natural death is concerned, from what I can gather, Will very much intends on keeping the courtship going. They are both very smitten with each other."

"Oh… I fear that this is all becoming too much for us to keep a lid on now, Norah.

First, I find out that the son, who Fred and I were forced to give up at birth is living in the next village, and now it turns out that *his* son… my grandson… is courting my granddaughter! How can we keep a cat this size in the bag? It's all too much…" Elsie covered her face with her hands and shook her head.

"We can't let the cat out of the bag, Elsie, we're just going to have to try and do our best to tactfully discourage them. And hopefully, as you say, maybe the relationship will just wither and wane of its own accord."

Elsie looked directly at Norah. "And if it doesn't…?"

Norah didn't have an answer, instead, she just

shook her head.

****

If it hadn't been for the fact that everyone was suspicious of Norah and Elsie's past, Stella would never have felt compelled to eavesdrop on their conversation. But now, on the other side of her grandmother's sitting room door, frozen to the spot in shock, Stella tried to make sense of the jaw-dropping revelation she had unwittingly stumbled on. As the harsh reality of it all whirled around in her mind like a snowstorm, something kept telling her to make a quick exit before her presence was realised.

Stella forced her feet to move, and before she knew it, she was running back in the direction of Miss Hutton's cottage...

FORTY-THREE

Stella stopped running and came to a standstill, just short of Miss Hutton's cottage. What was she thinking? She couldn't go back into her cottage without permission. But that was it... she wasn't thinking. How could she think straight after what she'd just heard?

Elm trees lined the street where Miss Hutton lived, and Stella sat with her back against one, setting Miss Hutton's suitcase down beside her. Her mind kept repeating the whole conversation until eventually it filtered out the crucial facts: Her grandparents had to give up their son at birth, and the son turned out to be Will's father, which made her and Will cousins. Stella thought back to a conversation she had with Will's father, about how he loved to write, and how he hoped, like her, to become an author. Was that a coincidence or *does* that sort of ability run in families? And her grandparents' wedding photograph... of course, she could see the significance of the curly dark-brown hair now. And the fact that biologically, this made her and Will cousins... it was all too much. Miss Hutton's illness, the discovery of the family secret and the fact that she still hadn't eaten anything, all made her feel nauseous and a little dizzy. She stood up slowly, picked up Miss Hutton's suitcase and headed back in the direction of home.

Stella walked back along Chapel Street on the opposite side of the road to her grandma's house, that way she could keep an eye on who was coming or going. As she neared, she noticed a woman appear

from her grandma's entry gate. Stella came to a halt...
Norah. Not wanting to risk the woman recognising her
from the photograph, she decided very quickly to turn
back and divert along a footpath. The footpath
bordered Windmill Farm and eventually led to fields
belonging to the farmer. After walking half a mile or
so along the footpath, Stella climbed over a stile, and
into the field recently prepared for over-wintering
barley crops. The footpath continued alongside the
field and was a popular route to take to get to the
neighbouring village of Horsley Woodhouse.
Although now, as dusk was well on its way, there
wasn't a soul in sight.

Although they weren't heavy, Stella began to feel
the burden of carrying her bag and Miss Hutton's case
and set them both down in the grass next to the high
hedge that bordered the field. She slumped down in
front of them, drew her knees up to her chest and
wrapped her arms around her legs. Because of the
events of the day, she had missed seeing Will and
thought he would be wondering why she hadn't been
around to see him. How could she continue the
courtship now, knowing they were related? Would it
matter if they were? It was only in a biological sense,
neither of them had been brought up with that
knowledge.

And of course... if Norah and her grandmother
were going to do their best to repel the relationship, as
they suggested they would, how could she not yell out
in protest at knowing the real reason for their
hindrance? Tears welled in Stella's eyes, and she lay

back to rest her head on Miss Hutton's case. As the tears left the corners of her eyes, she closed them. And once again the oppressive cloak of loneliness enshrouded her heart.

Suddenly, her lamenting was disturbed by a loud rustling noise coming from inside the hedge, which caused her to sit up with such haste, that a brief sensation of dizziness swept through her head. It was beginning to get dark, but getting to her feet, she soon realised it was the sound of someone pushing their way through a small opening in the hedge. Presently, a young boy appeared, who after getting to his feet, straightened his clothes and cap... Alfie Beardmore!

"By heck, Alfie, you scared me half to death. What are you doing here at this time of evening?"

Alfie brushed himself free of the soil and debris that clung to his clothes.

"I'm sorry, I didn't mean to. There's a badger's sett in a small copse in the next field and crawling through this gap in the hedge is the only way I can get to it. Anyway, I could ask you the same!"

"What?" Stella frowned.

"Well... why are you here at this time? It'll be dark soon," he said, looking down at Miss Hutton's case. "Have you run away from home? And why are your eyes all wet?"

"No, Alfie, I haven't run away from home. The case belongs to someone else. I'm just... well I'm going to be... Oh, never mind. Why are you hanging around a badger's sett, anyway?"

"I've been keeping watch on it these last two

evenings, and as soon as it gets dusk, they come out to find food. That's when I can sketch 'em, see…" Alfie pulled his sketchpad from his pocket and passed it to Stella and the two of them sat down on the grass. Alfie pulled a brown paper bag from the inside of his jacket pocket. "Are you hungry?" he asked, offering Stella a dried-up spam sandwich. Stella nodded.

Strangely, it was the most appealing spam sandwich she had ever set eyes on. "Thanks, Alfie, I'm starving. So, your mam does not mind you being out after dark?" she asked, speaking over a mouthful of sandwich.

"She dun't know. Sometimes, when she sends us up to bed early, I sneak out and get back without her knowing. She's always too busy with me three younger brothers to be bothering about me."

"And what about your dad? Is he busy too?"

"I haven't got a dad anymore. He got killed last year when the roof fell in at Ripley Colliery. So, it's just me, me mam and me three brothers."

"Oh goodness, that's awful. I am sorry to hear that, Alfie. It must be hard for your mam to cope with everything all by herself."

Alfie shrugged. "Well… 'tis what it is, I s'pose." He stood up and reached out for his sketchpad, and Stella gave it back to him. "Oh, here… I have your other drawings to give back to you too," she said, reaching for her bag. "Alfie… when you suggested that I could write stories, and you could illustrate them?" Alfie nodded. "Well, I might have an idea. I need to talk it over with someone first, but you may just be on to something."

Alfie beamed a big smile. "Sounds great. Anyway, we should go now, before we lose our way in the dark."

Stella slung her bag over her shoulder and picked up Miss Hutton's case. "C'mon then, you lead the way."

****

The following morning, Stella woke up with a headache, due to the upset from the evening before. She checked the clock on her bedside table. Realising she had overslept; she flung back the bed covers and raced to the bathroom.

She made it downstairs in record time, to find her mother toasting bread under the grill. One dried-up spam sandwich certainly hadn't been enough to sustain her, and she was starving. "That smells wonderful, Mam," Stella said, stopping to take in the delightful aroma of the bread as it toasted.

"Well, if you hang about a minute, you can have these two pieces, and I'll make myself some more. There's a fresh pot of tea on the table too."

"Where's Dad?" Stella asked dubiously.

"He's still in bed; he's having a lie in... he starts back on nights tonight."

Stella looked at the kitchen clock. She would be pushing it, but there might just be enough time for a quick cuppa and a couple of pieces of toast.

"You missed a lovely roast yesterday," Jeanie said, juggling hot toast from the grill onto the breadboard and blowing on her fingers to cool them. "There's some beef left. I'll make you a sandwich to take to school."

"Thanks, Mam."

"I hear Sheila and Albert took you to visit Miss Hutton in hospital yesterday?"

"Yes, she must have an operation tomorrow, I'm going to see her again today, after school. Visiting is between…" Stella looked up to the ceiling as if to recall the correct information. "Three o'clock and five o'clock on a Monday, Wednesday and Friday."

Jeanie nodded as she smeared two slices of bread with a smattering of butter and a piece of roast beef. "I guess that will be an end to your tutoring sessions then?" she said, cutting the sandwich and wrapping it in parchment paper.

Stella downed the last dregs of her tea. "I hope not, we're working on a great project at the moment, and I have plenty of ideas on what I'd like to do with it when it's finished."

Jeanie made no remark, instead, she just set the sandwich down on the table next to Stella's bag and sighed.

Realising that the 'sigh' signalled an end to the conversation, Stella sandwiched the remaining toast together, grabbed her bag and made for the door. "I'll see you later, Mam. Thank you for the sandwich."

After Stella had left, Jeanie sat down and set one elbow on the kitchen table. She sank her forehead into the palm of her hand and sighed again. She thought back to the letter and money her father had left for Stella. His wishes were that she should have it on her

16th birthday, and to use it as an aid to follow her dream of becoming a writer. As much as Jeanie thought that was all just a fanciful notion, it was her father's wishes. If Stella was serious about studying English at college, then having the money would certainly help. But then how could she get Derek to agree to that? He didn't even know about the money, and he would soon manipulate the spending of it to suit himself if he did. She must speak to her mother about it too because as far as Jeanie knew, her mother wasn't aware of it being left to Stella either. Suddenly the smell of something burning reached Jeanie's nose, alerting her to the fact that she had left her toast under the grill!

****

Mrs Cranfield stood at the front of the class and removed her pince-nez spectacles.

"Those of you who have English with Miss Hutton next... stay behind. The rest of you can leave your workbooks in a *tidy* pile on my desk and then go," Mrs Cranfield said, placing heavy emphasis on the word 'tidy'. She stayed standing until the last of the pupils who had been asked to leave had left. With the remaining pupils waiting in anticipation of the reason for their detainment, Mrs Cranfield sat down at her desk. "Unfortunately, Miss Hutton is unwell. And I am afraid that since news of her malady has come to our attention at short notice, there is nobody available to take her class."

Some of the pupils seemed genuinely concerned, whilst a brightness in the eyes of others suggested delight at an early finish to their school day.

"With this in mind, you may leave the school premises now but do bear in mind that you will be expected to catch up with your work as soon as we have a replacement. You may go…"

As Stella walked across the schoolyard with a dozen or so other pupils, the only thing she was pleased about was the fact that leaving school early meant that she could catch the five past two bus into Derby and get to the hospital in time for the start of visiting. But first, she needed to go home, collect Miss Hutton's suitcase and the money she had given her to pay for the bus. Taking the shortcut past Kilburn pit, Stella remembered her roast beef sandwich, she fetched it out of her bag and ate it as she walked along the footpath. By the time she had arrived on the recreation ground, she'd finished eating it. She paused to look over at the bush that was once her den and smiled as she recalled throwing Will's football out after it had inadvertently landed in there. That made her think about all the wonderful times they had shared since, which sent a sting of sorrow running through her soul. She continued walking, leaving the recreation ground, and onto her street. So many thoughts raced through her mind, like when they were coming back on the train from Skegness, and when she showed her Aunt Sheila the photograph of herself and Will, her aunt thought he reminded her of someone. Had she recognised something familiar in him too?

As she walked down the entry, she could hear raised voices… her parents were arguing again. Stella could see that they were in the garden, and since she wasn't expected home at this time, they were unaware of her presence. She took that as an opportunity to sneak up to her bedroom, grab Miss Hutton's case and some of the money, and get back out unnoticed. By the time she had got to the bus stop, her heart was pounding at the thought of a different outcome had she been seen.

FORTY-FOUR

The number 44 bus pulled into Derby bus station at 25 minutes to three, and as Stella stepped off the bus, she thanked the driver. It was about a 20-minute walk from the station to the infirmary, so by the time she had made her way through the hospital corridors, she should be just in time for the start of visiting. The hospital was certainly busier on a weekday, and as she arrived outside the ward, others had already congregated in readiness to visit loved ones. Moments after the stroke of 3 p.m., the double doors opened, and Nurse Blake allowed everyone to enter. Speaking quietly, she asked the visitors to form an orderly queue at sister's desk so their attendance could be recorded. Stella was last in the queue, and as she waited for her turn, she glanced across towards Miss Hutton's bed.

It was not until Stella had registered her attendance with the ward sister and was heading towards Miss Hutton's bed, that Miss Hutton became aware of her arrival. As soon as she did, however, she looked up to check the time on the clock on the wall before frowning suspiciously at Stella.

"I do hope you aren't going to be in any trouble, leaving school before you should. I wasn't expecting you until at least four o'clock."

"Oh… no, no," Stella said shaking her head. "Mrs Cranfield announced that they hadn't yet managed to find a replacement for you and that we were permitted to leave early."

Miss Hutton's face crumpled. "Ah… yes of course.

I never thought of that. Anyway, I'm pleased to see you," she said, patting Stella's hand.

Stella smiled. "I've brought everything you asked for," she said, holding up the suitcase.

"Oh... and here is your door key."

"Oh, you are an angel. Thank you so very much. And you managed to find my document wallet?"

Stella nodded. "It's in the suitcase with the rest of your things. How are you today?"

"Well, I am a little nervous at the thought of what tomorrow's surgery may entail, but aside from that, I'm keeping my chin up, as they say. I've been keeping my mind occupied by looking through your plan, and I do think it is an excellent idea. However, you have mentioned adding illustrations. Of course, you realise you would need to find an artist, and that won't come without cost."

"That's what I was hoping to speak with you about... I already have one! His name is

Alfie. We would need to speak with his mother about it though, but I'm—"

"His mother? How old is this boy... Alfie?" Miss Hutton asked, arching a brow.

"He's nearly 11. He'll be starting at your school after Christmas. You should see his drawings, they are amazing. He does have a talent."

"My... you do have this all planned out," Miss Hutton laughed.

"So... what do you think then?"

"I think that as soon as I am home and well enough, we will look into it further. In the meantime, you keep on collecting all the information you can for the rest of the autumn. Oh, that reminds me, do you mind if I keep hold of your other story, the one you left with me the last time we met?"

Stella nodded. "Of course. What did you think of it?"

"I thought it was excellent, and I did have an idea that I wanted to run past you. But all in good time."

Nurse Blake appeared at the side of Miss Hutton's bed holding a tray. "Here we are... a light meal for you and a cup of tea," she said, placing the tray down on the side table. "After that, you will be nil by mouth for the remainder of today, in preparation for your surgery tomorrow morning," she added, pinning a sign that read 'Nil by Mouth' to the end of the bed and taking away her water jug and glass.

As Nurse Blake walked away, Miss Hutton thanked her and managed a half smile. "I rather feel like the condemned woman who is being allowed her last meal," she whispered to Stella.

Stella smiled half-heartedly. "Sister Fox has already apprised me that you won't be allowed any visitors until Sunday. So, if you don't think it would be too soon after your surgery, I could visit you then?" she asked.

"Oh... I'm sure that would be perfectly fine. I'm hoping they will have put right whatever is wrong, and I will be well on the road to recovery by then," she said in an optimistic tone.

Stella smiled. "I shall be praying so."

Miss Hutton lifted the cloche from her plate and

pursed her lips… steamed fish, boiled potatoes, broad beans and parsley sauce.

"That looks nice. I'll leave and let you eat it in peace." Stella said.

Miss Hutton grabbed Stella's arm and shook her head. "No… no, please stay. Won't you go and grab yourself a chair and sit and chat with me? I'm eager to know more about this young artist of yours."

Time soon passed, and at precisely five o'clock, Sister Fox rang the handbell to announce an end to visiting, and as visitors said their goodbyes to loved ones, Stella stood and returned her chair. She walked back to the bedside, took hold of Miss Hutton's hand and wished her well. To Stella's surprise, Miss Hutton pulled her closer, and reaching up to cup the side of Stella's face with the palm of her hand, spoke softly. "Thank you for everything, Stella," she said, her eyes welling a little. "Do whatever it takes to be happy, and… take good care of yourself, won't you."

Stella gently took hold of the hand that cupped her face and gave it an endearing squeeze. "Of course. But I am coming back to see you again. I'll be back here before you know it."

Stella left Miss Hutton's bedside and walked across the room. She paused short of exiting the ward, to turn and wave a final goodbye. It was at that point that she was certain, that she had noticed Miss Hutton brush away a tear.

****

Stella arrived back at Derby bus station just in time to catch the twenty to five bus to Chesterfield, the only service that called at Kilburn Village along the way. Being woefully aware that she still had a dilemma to solve, Stella was glad that the 45-minute journey would give her time to think about her options. Visiting Miss Hutton had given her reason to avoid everyone, but she couldn't go on doing that. At some point, she would need to see her grandma *and* Will, and she had no idea what she was going to say to either of them. If she ended her relationship with Will, whatever reason she gave for it would have to be a lie, and how could she ever look her grandmother in the face again, knowing that it was her revelation that had caused their breakup? If she just continued as though nothing had come to light, how difficult would it be to keep the relationship going if the two matriarchs were hellbent on wrecking it? She could just tell Will the truth, and then he could decide for himself if he wanted to continue the relationship, but then that would mean telling him that his father had been adopted as a child, and that's not something you find out every day. It was an impossible situation, and no matter which way she went, it would have distressing consequences for someone.

Stella was so deep in her thoughts, that she hadn't realised that the bus had even arrived in the village, let alone drawn up at the stop she needed. She quickly rushed to the front of the bus and was about to get off just as Mrs Bell was getting on. Mrs Bell halted and looked up curtly to the person in her way, and then, as she realised it was Stella obstructing her entrance, spoke in a bitter tone.

"Ahh… there you are. Well, it's thanks to you that I have to get a later bus home. What happened to you calling in after school today? I've had more orders than I could point a stick at!"

"I'm sorry, Mrs Bell; I had to visit a friend in hospital. I'll make it up to you, I promise," Stella said, squeezing past Mrs Bell's bulky frame to get down from the bus.

"Hmm… a likely story," Mrs Bell replied, handing the driver her return ticket.

Thankfully for Stella, the doors closed, and the driver pulled off, putting an end to the awkward conversation.

Returning to her thoughts, Stella walked back along Chapel Street. Given that her father should already have left to get his lift to work, going home to mull things over seemed like the most appealing choice for now. However, just as she passed the entrance to the recreation ground, someone shouted her name. She looked round quickly… and saw that it was Will, and he was already running over towards her.

"I've been looking for you everywhere," he said cheerily. "I waited outside school for ages before someone told me you'd left already. I missed seeing you yesterday, and I've been worrying about you since you told me about your father. I was on my way to see if you were at your grandma's house. Are you okay?"

Stella just looked at Will, she wanted to throw her arms around him and tell him everything, but her head overruled her heart.

"I'm sorry, Stella, I don't mean to sound as though

I'm checking up on you, I was just concerned that something had happened, that's all."

Stella shook her head. "No… it's okay. Those of us in Miss Hutton's class were allowed to leave early. She has been taken ill, you see and there was nobody to take her class. I should be the one apologising, I never gave a thought about you waiting for me after school."

Will moved closer to Stella and put his arm around her waist. "So long as you're alright, that's all that matters to me," he said, kissing her softly.

"Shall we go for a walk?" he asked. "In fact, how about you show me Pearl? I bet she's grown in this last couple of –"

"I don't want to disturb my grandma," Stella said, cutting Will short. "I don't think she's feeling all that well today."

And there it was, the first lie. Stella's heart sank. Knowing that this could be the first of many lies was all too much. "Will, do you mind if we don't do anything tonight? It's been a busy couple of days and what with visiting Miss Hutton in the hospital…"

"She's in hospital? Will said, raising his eyebrows. "How do you know that?"

"It's a long story, but yes, she's got to have surgery tomorrow and, well… she has no family whatsoever."

Will rubbed Stella's shoulder. "I'm sorry to hear that. And of course, I don't mind if we don't do anything. Can I meet you from school tomorrow?"

Stella nodded and reached up to kiss Will on his cheek. As their eyes met, he pulled her close, and nothing could have prepared her for what he said next.

"I… I love you…"

And before she had a chance to reply, he'd gone…

Stella walked in through the back door and announced her presence. Having received no reply, she moved to the foot of the stairs and called out again. Still no reply. She walked back into the kitchen, looked through the window and out into the garden, but there was nobody there either. Assuming that her mother must be round at her grandma's, she did think it a little strange that, whichever of her parents were last out of the house, one of them hadn't locked the door. Stella took herself off upstairs, stopping first to check the bathroom and then her parent's bedroom. Concluding that one of them had indeed forgotten to lock the door, Stella thought no more of it. She walked into her bedroom, closed the door and lay on top of her bed.

She stared up at the ceiling. 'I love you…' Will's words echoed through her mind as she pictured his face close to hers. If he hadn't taken off so quickly, she would most definitely have said the same thing back to him. It was at that point that she made her decision, that no way was she going to end her relationship with him. There was only one thing for it. She would just have to negotiate every hurdle that Norah and her grandmother placed in their way. If anyone was going to be responsible for causing pain and misery, it would have to be them! This was their doing, they should be the ones forced into a corner, not her!

Miss Hutton's words ran through Stella's mind… 'Do whatever it takes to be happy', she had said. And

Stella had every intention of doing just that.

FORTY-FIVE

Stella woke with a start, still in the same position, lying on top of her bed. She grabbed her clock - a quarter past nine. Wondering if her mother had come home, she left her room and went downstairs to check, finding her fast asleep on the settee.

"Mam," Stella said softly. "Is everything okay?"

Jeanie opened her eyes slowly. "I must have dozed off," she said with a yawn. "I didn't realise you were back yet. Was your father still here when you came home?"

"Ah… so he was the last to leave then," Stella said cynically.

"I don't follow?" Jeanie said with a puzzled look.

"When I got home, the door was unlocked. I assumed you'd be at Grandma's and Dad had gone to work, but I didn't know which one of you had left the door unlocked."

Jeanie hung her head. "We had a row earlier. I said I was going round to my mam's and that I didn't care if I never saw him again. I suppose he just forgot to lock the door when he left for work."

Stella shook her head and sighed. "Well, I'm not going to ask what the argument was about this time," she said, heading for the stairs. "I do wonder if there has ever been a point when you did love each other!"

****

Tuesday 26th Sept 1950

The following morning, Stella woke at half past five, to the sound of someone banging quite furiously on the back door. She got out of bed and almost bumped into her mother on the landing.

"Someone is determined to get our attention," Stella said, being the first to head down the stairs.

"Well, it can't be your father, he won't have finished his shift yet," Jeanie replied, following on behind.

Stella walked through the kitchen and opened the door. "Aunt Sheila, what is wrong? It's not Grandma, is it?"

Sheila rushed into the kitchen, quite out of breath and patting her chest. "No... no, it isn't Mam..." She paused, trying to catch her breath. "Albert had a..." She sat down at the table and took a deep breath.

"Is Albert unwell?" Jeanie asked.

Sheila shook her head. "Albert had a call from Ilkeston Mines rescue just after half past four this morning, asking him to report for duty as soon as possible. Something major has happened at Creswell, Jeanie and..." Sheila paused to catch her breath again.

"And what, Sheila?" Jeanie worried.

"And it involves the men on the night shift... I think you'd better get dressed and we'll try and find a way of getting up to Creswell."

Jeanie sat down steadily in the chair opposite Sheila, bringing her elbows down heavily on the table and sinking her head into her hands. Stella took a step towards her mother and put an arm on her shoulder.

"Come on, Mam, let's go and get dressed, and we'll see what we can find out," she said, gently encouraging her mother to move. "Aunty Sheila, would you mind putting the kettle on? I think we could all do with a cup of tea."

Once they were both dressed, Jeanie and Stella returned to the kitchen where Sheila was pouring tea. Just as she handed Jeanie a cup and saucer, a knock came at the door.

"Come in," Stella called. The door opened and Roy Barlow walked in.

Jeanie placed her teacup down clumsily on the table. "Roy… what's happening, do you have any further news?"

Roy bowed his head. "You've heard from Albert then? I suspected he would have been called in to help. I've just got off the telephone with one of the deputies up at Creswell and, Jeanie… it's not good news…"

Jeanie sat down heavily on the kitchen chair, and put her hand to her mouth, almost looking through Roy as he continued to speak.

"A faulty trunk-belt conveyor inside the pit caused a fire to break out just after half past three this morning. There are over 90 men still unaccounted for, Jeanie, and given the location where Derek works, we can only assume that it's likely he is one of them. I've come across to see if you want me to drive you up there. Families are already gathering at the pithead… desperate for news."

"Come on, Mam, I'll come with you," Stella offered, and Jeanie merely nodded.

****

At just after 7 a.m. Jeanie, Stella and Roy arrived in Creswell. The hour's journey they had made in silence, was now broken by the sound of the emergency siren as it blew from the colliery, echoing into every home in the village, and carrying with it a cold, deathly chill. Stella held on to her mother's hand, as they both stared vacantly out of the car windows at the volume of people heading for the colliery, a place that had now become a nerve centre of distressing activity.

The three of them got out of the car and Roy led them to the pithead, where a crowd of people, most of whom were women, waited in desperation outside the manager's office.

"Wait here," Roy said, walking off in the direction of the office. "I'll see what I can find out." Stella watched as scores of men dashed here and there with purpose. Some had breathing apparatus attached to their backs, others carried sandbags on their shoulders, whilst many just aided casualties to ambulances. She looked around for Albert, but, with dirty faces and clothes, all the men looked the same.

Stella's attention was suddenly diverted as a commotion amongst the crowd ensued when two official-looking gentlemen appeared from the manager's office, one of whom pinned a list of names onto a wooden board. Moments later, a loud wailing noise could be heard, that of a woman who fell to her knees in despair upon learning of the tragic news that her husband had perished. This was shortly followed by others, as so many of the women became aware of the fate of their loved ones. Jeanie and Stella stared at one another, not knowing what to say or do.

Stella looked over her mother's shoulder. "Mam,

Roy is beckoning us over... c'mon quickly," she said. Grabbing her mother's hand, she led her over to where Roy stood in the office doorway.

"I think you had better have a word with this gentleman," Roy gestured to a man sitting behind one of the two desks in the office. Jeanie frowned. She understood very quickly that something wasn't quite right, as nobody else in the crowd had been asked into the office as they had. The man behind the desk stood courteously as Stella and Jeanie walked in, then gestured to them to take a seat before sitting himself back down.

"Mrs Felton, my name is Joseph Wood, and I am one of the night shift managers here at the colliery."

Jeanie did not comment, she just fixed her gaze on the man, waiting for him to continue.

"Your husband isn't on my list of men having been injured or killed."

Jeanie put her hand to her chest and let out a sigh of relief.

"Actually, Mrs Felton, your husband isn't on my list of men who were working the night shift at all."

"So... what *are* you saying?" Jeanie said sternly.

"What I am saying, Mrs Felton, is that your husband never arrived for his shift last night."

"What? That's not possible. Are you sure? Check the list again, his name must be on it."

"Mrs Felton, we have a very foolproof clocking in and out process, and I can assure you that he never turned up."

"Well, if he never turned up, then where is he?"

Jeanie shrugged her shoulders.

"I was hoping that you may be able to tell me. We assumed that he must be unwell and unable to send word."

"He's not unwell! He was perfectly fine yesterday, and he most certainly left to get his lift as usual," Jeanie said sharply.

Stella reached across to take her mother's hand. "Mam, we don't know that for sure, do we?"

"Of course we do! Check the list again," Jeanie said, raising her voice to the man.

"Mam, calm down."

"I want him to check it again!" she repeated.

The man, who was losing patience, sighed heavily and looked beyond Jeanie and Stella, to Roy, who was still standing in the doorway. Roy made his way to where Jeanie and Stella were sitting and took hold of Jeanie's arm. "Come on, Jeanie love, let's get you back home. I'm sure there's a perfectly good reason for all of this."

Stella stood up. "Thank you for your time, Mr Wood," she said, and between them, Stella and Roy led Jeanie out of the manager's office and back to the car.

The journey back was made in just the same silence as when they came. When they arrived back at Kilburn village, Jeanie got out of the car and walked away without saying a word. It was left to Stella to thank Roy for his kindness.

"Mr Barlow, I would appreciate it if we could keep this between us for now. The last thing my mother needs is for village gossips drawing their conclusions."

Roy nodded. "Of course, lass. Will you be alright? Is there anything else I can do to help?"

"Thank you, but we'll be fine. I'm sure he will turn up soon."

"Aye… well if that's the case, he's certainly had a lucky escape. Those poor, poor souls."

Stella nodded in agreement. "The thought of all those men and their families… it sends a chill to your very core. Thank you again, Mr Barlow."

Stella got out of the car, walked along the entry and in through the open back door, into the kitchen. Although it was a school day, there was no way Stella could expect her mother to cope alone in trying to establish her father's whereabouts. She made a pot of tea and took it upstairs on a tray. Walking into her parents' bedroom, she found her mother sobbing and curled up on the floor in the corner of the room. The carpet had been pulled back and one of the floorboards had been removed. Stella quickly set the tea tray down, rushed over and knelt by the side of where her mother lay coiled up.

"Mam, what is wrong? What on earth are you doing?"

Jeanie tried in vain to sit, she reached for Stella's arm. "He's gone… he's gone, Stella."

Stella took hold of her mother's hand and helped her to sit. "Come on now… what do you mean, he's gone? How can you know that for certain?"

"Because he's taken all of your money," she wailed.

"Mam, you're not making any sense. What money? Look, come sit on this chair, and try to calm yourself down."

Stella helped her mother to her feet and steered her over to the chair, guiding her down onto the seat. "Now, take a deep breath and let it out slowly."

Jeanie did as her daughter suggested before continuing to explain. "Your grandpa left you a considerable amount of money. He gave it to me the day he passed away, along with a letter explaining that it wasn't to be given to you until your 16th birthday and that he hoped you would use it to help further your writing ambition. At the time, it was only going to be a couple of months before your 16th, so I hid it under the floorboard. I hid it because I didn't want your father to use it to his advantage. Now he's gone and he's taken all the money with him."

Stella sat down on the edge of the bed opposite her mother. There was a long pause before she spoke.

"How would he have known it was there?"

Jeanie sighed. "Oh... I don't know... but this floorboard kept springing up, so I put the chair over it to try and keep it down. He must have used the chair to stand on to reach that top cupboard and get his suitcase. I wondered why the chair had moved when I came up to bed last night, but I was too tired to give it any further thought."

Stella tipped her head to one side. "It sounds like he was intending to go before he found the money then."

"What?" Jeanie said, confusedly.

"If all this happened after you had gone to Grandma's house, then he must have come up here intending to leave, grabbed the chair to get his suitcase and wondered why the floorboard had sprung up. He must have found the money and left. It's just a thought."

"Does it matter which way round it happened? The point is he's gone and so has —"

"Sshhh…" Stella held her finger to her lip. "Listen… I think someone is knocking on the front door."

"Well go and tell whoever it is to go away. I'm in no mood for visitors," Jeanie said sternly.

Stella purposely took her time getting to the front door, hoping that whoever it was might get fed up with waiting. But as she neared the door, the sound of someone now banging on it suggested otherwise.

FORTY-SIX

Stella placed a cup of tea down on the kitchen table in front of Police Constable Lewis and sat down next to her mother. Constable Lewis lived in the police house across the road and had been the local village bobby for over 20 years. Everyone knew him, and if he wasn't on official police business, then most people would just call him by his first name - Henry. Today, however, Henry was on official business, the business of delivering dreadful news. News that a body had been found, and that the deceased had been murdered. As the tears streamed down Jeanie's face, Constable Lewis turned the pages of his notebook and continued to give further facts, in as tactful a way as was possible.

"After the dog walker had made the discovery, Ripley police arrived at the scene.

They found a letter in a brown envelope, in the inside pocket of the deceased man's jacket. Since the envelope had Stella's name and address on it, Ripley Police telephoned and asked me to attend, in the hopes that I could identify the victim."

Jeanie sat up straight in her chair, waiting for the confirmation she knew to be inevitable.

"Jeanie, I am so very sorry to inform you that I was able to make an identification, and I am afraid the body discovered this morning is that of your husband, Derek."

Jeanie took a deep breath and let it out before nodding slowly. "I understand," she said, taking a handkerchief out of her pocket and wiping away her tears.

"Jeanie, the letter mentions a…" Constable Lewis turned a couple of pages back in his notebook before continuing, "… a *vast* sum of money being left to Stella by your father. Since Ripley Police also found a suitcase close to the body, would I be correct in assuming that Derek took that money and left, intending to never return?"

Once again, Jeanie nodded, and the steady flow of tears resumed.

"It may help us to piece things together if we know roughly how much these men may have taken from him."

"A hundred and fifty pounds," Jeanie declared. "So, they'll be able to get as far away as they please with that," she added, sternly.

There was a beat of silence as Constable Lewis and Stella both darted a look of utter surprise at the figure revealed by Jeanie.

"Constable Lewis, how do you think these… thieves knew that my father had this money about his person?"

Constable Lewis looked to Stella. "Once I confirmed the name of the deceased to Ripley Police, they informed me that there had been a complaint made yesterday evening, at…" the constable checked his notebook again, "half past nine, by the landlord of The Red Lion Public House in Ripley. The complaint was that two men, who were unknown to the landlord, had arrived at the pub and were causing trouble with his regular customers, goading one man in particular, a customer whom he knew only by the name of Derek. The landlord said that he thought Derek seemed to be acting a little out of character, because not only had he walked in carrying a suitcase, he'd also been flashing money around. He said that eventually, Derek lost patience with the two men, and he gave them a mouthful before finishing his drink and leaving. Moments later, the two men also left. We think the two men then followed your father, hit him over the head and proceeded to rob him of the money."

"Do you think they intended to kill him?" Stella asked.

Constable Lewis shrugged his shoulders. "One of the men delivered a very hefty blow to the back of your father's head, but at this stage, I'm afraid we can't possibly know whether or not they intended to kill him."

Stella nodded, "Thank you, Constable Lewis."

The policeman closed his notebook and stood up. He placed a hand on Jeanie's shoulder. "Ripley will be dealing with the case, Jeanie, but I have asked them to liaise with me. Also, I am afraid they will need you to formally identify your husband's body. I can drive you over there this afternoon, if you'd like."

Jeanie nodded. "Thank you, I would appreciate you doing that."

Stella also thanked the constable and led him to the front door. Out on the street, several people going about their normal business passed by, one or two of whom turned their heads at the sight of Constable

Lewis leaving the home of, probably, the most disliked man in the village.

****

In the five days that followed, many of the mining families in the village of Kilburn were doing their best to come to terms with the disaster at Creswell Colliery. Various events across the mining communities were being arranged, from coffee mornings to jumble sales, dances, and fetes, all to try and raise funds for the families of the men who perished. Meanwhile, others were making their assumptions about the events that surrounded Derek's death. Whilst most people felt sorry for Jeanie and Stella, some had said that they would most certainly be better off without him.

Whilst the family were beginning to come to terms with Derek's death, it was still very raw for Jeanie, and little had been spoken about other than organising his funeral. This also meant that Stella had felt free enough to see Will without the worry of any interference from her grandmother. However, although Stella had decided to keep seeing Will, the awkwardness of keeping a lid on the truth was starting to become a hindrance, as Will had already twice mentioned that he would very much like to meet her mother and grandmother. As the two of them sat in the garden enjoying the early autumn sun, she wondered for how much longer she would be able to keep putting him off.

"Would you like me to come with you to see Miss Hutton this afternoon?" Will asked, topping up their glasses with the homemade lemonade his mother

374

had made for them.

Stella shook her head. "It's kind of you to offer, but I think it best if I go alone."

Will nodded reluctantly. "And what time do you have to be at your grandma's house for lunch?"

Stella looked at her watch. "She wants us all to be there for half past twelve, then my Uncle Albert is going to drive me to the hospital after. He's going to wait for me though, because visiting is only for an hour on a Sunday, and in any case, she may not be feeling up to my being there for too long. I just hope the doctors have managed to find out what is wrong and put it right."

Will nodded again.

"I'm not looking forward to it, to be honest," Stella said.

"Visiting Miss Hutton?" Will frowned.

"No, the family lunch."

"Really? Why so?"

"Well… understandably, Mam still isn't feeling particularly sociable, and I think that

Albert is struggling to come to terms with the rescue teams being unable to save those men."

"It has been so devastating, Uncle Jed is thanking his lucky stars that he retired when he did, else he would have been working that night too. It's a shame we can't say the same for Jimmy Parkin though. God rest his soul," Will said.

Stella smiled. "He certainly was a character," she said, getting to her feet. "I guess I'd better go then. Shall we meet up when I get back from the hospital?"

Will stood up too. "Well, maybe this evening. We're going to visit Granny Turner later this afternoon." Will moved closer towards Stella and whispered. "Between you and me, I think Dad has been offered a position somewhere else, and he may very well be announcing it this afternoon whilst we are at Granny's house."

As she began to think about the significance of Will's parents moving abroad, Stella felt a little relief. If they were to move away, maybe the distance might be enough to stop Norah and her grandmother from worrying about the truth getting out. The concern of what it may do to Will's granny seemed to be greater than the fact that she and Will were cousins. It wasn't illegal for cousins to court each other, so what harm would it do? But then, her stomach sank, what she hadn't thought about was the likelihood of his parents trying to persuade Will to go with them! Suddenly, her thoughts were interrupted, as she realised that Will was trying to get her attention.

"Stella… Stella! Are you okay? If you're worried about me moving away, you needn't be. I've already thought that if I am right, and he has been offered a position elsewhere, I shall still join the RAF as planned and just stay here with Uncle Jed and Aunty Norah when I'm on leave. That way I can still spend all my time with you. RAF Halton is only half a day's journey by train."

Stella laughed. "You must have been reading my mind, I was just thinking of what might happen if they want you to go with them. America isn't just a train ride away, is it!" she giggled.

"America? I don't even know if I'm right in thinking that he has been offered anything yet. And if he has, I can't imagine that it would be something overseas. What would make you come up with America?"

Suddenly Stella felt as though every fluid ounce of blood had been drained from her body. How could she be so stupid as to go and mention America? Thankfully, her quick thinking got her out of a very sticky situation.

"Well, I'm only surmising. I just assumed it would be America because I've known of kids whose fathers work at Rolls-Royce go to live there before."

Will raised his eyebrows. "Ahh, I see. I thought you knew something I didn't then!" he laughed.

****

Lunch at her grandmother's house proved to be just as wearing as expected. Jeanie hardly ate a thing and seemed to be in a world of her own, while Albert felt it helped him to talk about some of the men who the rescue teams had been unable to save.

"He'd only been married a fortnight. They were due to go on their honeymoon this weekend. Then there's poor old Rodney, he only had four days left before his retirement and Philip only swapped shifts with someone as a favour."

"Tragic, all so very tragic," Elsie said, reaching for the gravy.

"Forty-seven men, Elsie... forty-seven," he repeated. "There's still another thirty-three bodies yet to be recovered and we won't be able to get to them until conditions have improved sufficiently to—"

Jeanie interrupted Albert, by slamming her knife and fork down abruptly on the table.

"Whilst I feel sorry for every single person that has been affected by the Creswell disaster, you all seem to be forgetting the fact that I too have lost my husband under just as tragic circumstances." Jeanie turned her focus on Stella. "And you, do you care that your father has been murdered?" she burst out before standing up to walk out of the room.

"Mam... of course I... Mam, come back," Stella called after her mother.

Stella rose to her feet and was about to follow her mother, when Sheila grabbed her arm. "Leave her be, Stella love, your mam's grieving, she doesn't mean it."

Stella sat back down. "That's just it, Aunty Sheila, I think she does mean it. She's hardly spoken to me since we learned of his death. She said he'd left a note under the floorboard where Mam hid the money."

"A note?" Elsie said, puzzled. "Well, what did it say?"

"I don't know. When I asked her, she got all defensive and insisted it didn't matter."

"Well maybe it doesn't matter," Albert said. "Maybe it's best to just give everything time to settle." Albert looked at his watch. "Come on, lass, we'd better be going, else you'll miss the visiting hour."

****

Albert parked his car in the visitors' car park and switched off the engine.

"Take as much time as you want to, Stella lass, I'm quite happy sitting here amongst my thoughts."

"Thank you, Uncle Albert, there's only about 50 minutes left anyway."

"And, Stella, try not to read too much into what your mam said. Shock and grief can play some terrible tricks on us."

Stella nodded and gave a half smile before getting out of Albert's car. Walking along the long corridor, she gave further thought to what her mother had said earlier. Of course she cared, she would never have wished for her father's demise to have been so gruesome, but the fact remained that there had never been any love lost between them. The upshot of all of this was that if he hadn't decided to steal his daughter's money and leave his wife, then he would most definitely have perished along with the other men in the disaster at Creswell. And if that had been the case, then at least Jeanie could have held her head up high, knowing that her husband died a hero instead of a thief.

Stella was about to push open one of the double doors, when someone on the other side beat her to it, almost bumping into her in the process.

"Oh, good heavens, I do beg your pardon, young lady," a gentleman said. "I was simply not paying enough attention. I am sorry." Stella thought the gentleman appeared to be quite official-looking. He wore a navy-blue suit and a trilby hat. He was carrying a briefcase and had a black coat draped over his other arm, in which he also held a brown leather document wallet that Stella thought looked familiar. The man tried to hold the door open for Stella but struggled with what he carried.

"Oh no... please, allow me. You do seem to have your hands full," Stella said, holding the door open.

"You are most kind, young lady, and a good day to you," the gentleman said, as he walked through the door and out into the corridor. Stella stood for a moment, watching the gentleman as he walked away. She was certain that the document wallet was the one she had brought in for Miss Hutton. Concluding that it could just be the sort of thing that any official person might carry, Stella paid it no further mind.

When she arrived on the ward, Stella glanced over in the direction of Miss Hutton's bed and could see that the portable curtains had been placed around her. As before, she walked up to the sister's desk to announce her arrival and Sister Fox looked up with a smile. However, upon recognising who stood before her, her smile was soon replaced with an uneasy stare.

FORTY-SEVEN

Sister Fox led Stella into an empty room and gestured for her to take a seat. The room was quite small and lit only by a lamp standing alongside a vase of white carnations, both of which were set upon a wooden console table that seemed too big for the room. Sister Fox picked up a chair and placed it down opposite Stella, and as she sat down, she clasped her hands together before laying them gently in her lap. There was a beat of silence and just at that moment, Stella knew that whatever sister had to say, it was not going to be good.

"You've brought me in here to tell me she's dying... haven't you?" Stella said suddenly.

Sister Fox reached forward and placed her hands over Stella's. "I am afraid that the investigative surgery revealed a disease of the stomach, which had already spread to surrounding organs."

"Meaning...?"

"Meaning that, sadly, you are correct in your assumption. There is nothing further we can do for her, I am afraid."

A single tear fell onto Stella's cheek, which she quickly brushed away.

"She was incredibly determined to fight it for a day or two, but I think that was because she wanted to get her affairs in order. There has been a steady decline since then, especially in this last hour. A man came to visit, and although he said he was a friend of her late father's, I know he was here in an official capacity," Sister Fox said, nodding slowly.

'*The man on the corridor…*' Stella thought. "May I sit with her a while?"

"Yes… it would be comforting to her if she had someone there with her. And feel free to speak to her - likely, she will still be able to hear you."

Stella sat down and shuffled her chair as near to Miss Hutton's bedside as she could. She reached for her hand, it felt cold and clammy, and her fingertips were tinged with the same dark blue colour that was evident around her nose and mouth. At first, Stella could only sit in silence, whilst the harsh familiarity of death acquainted itself with her again. But then she quickly recalled her grandfather's passing and the fact that she never had the opportunity to say goodbye. Sitting there now in that moment, was her opportunity to do just that.

"Hello, Catherine…" Stella whispered. "It's Stella. I've come to see you… just like I promised I would." Stella's voice quavered a moment and then she regained control. "I was going to tell you so much today… but… none of that matters now. All that matters is that you know I am here and that you aren't alone."

Rapid eye movements and an intake of breath prompted Stella to continue. "Do you remember saying that you loved to watch the sky, as the night sweeps in and keeps the sun safe till morning? And I said I imagined God to be the night, and the sun to be a loved one, and when he sweeps in to take our loved ones, he keeps them safe until it is time to see them again in heaven?" Stella lifted Miss Hutton's cold hand

and tried to warm it against her cheek. "I think that your fiancé and your parents must be waiting in Heaven now for *their* sun."

Stella thought she felt Miss Hutton's hand try to squeeze hers, and although she couldn't be certain, she was sure she saw a faint smile appear on her face. But then a strange crackling sound formed, which accompanied each breath that Miss Hutton took thereafter. As the tears ran freely down Stella's cheeks, Miss Hutton took her final breath.

"Goodbye, Catherine," Stella whispered. "We will meet again one day... but until then... I will miss you."

Stella wasn't sure for how long she had been sitting there before she felt a hand on her shoulder. As she turned to look, Sister Fox gave a wistful smile and a gentle nod, almost as though she was confirming to Stella that Miss Hutton had passed.

"Take whatever time you need," she said. "I'll see you before you go." When Stella eventually felt ready to leave, she made her way over to Sister Fox's desk.

"You wanted to see me, Sister?" Stella asked.

"Ahh yes..." Sister Fox handed Stella's project to her. "Miss Hutton asked if I would make sure that this is returned to you," she said.

Stella's heart sank, as she tucked her project under her arm, she wondered what use it would be to her now.

"Sister... what will happen now? To Miss Hutton, I mean."

"Her body will be prepared and then taken to our mortuary. Once her wishes have been established, further arrangements will be made."

Stella nodded and thanked Sister Fox before leaving the ward. As she made her way back along the corridor, she came across a little wooden sign that read, 'Chapel open. All welcome.' Needing a moment to herself before she went back to Uncle Albert, Stella walked in and sat down on one of the four pews. Although the room was small, it had been tastefully decorated to resemble a place of worship, with sculptures and paintings, prayer books and hassocks. At the back of the room, a console table had been laid out with a candelabra large enough to hold at least 30 candles. Some had yet to be lit, some burned steadily, whilst others had already melted away to nothing more than a stump. Under the table, Stella noticed a rubbish bin, she took her project from under her arm and stared vacantly at it. Deciding that it was pointless now to continue with it any further, she stood, walked over to the bin, and threw her project away.

Seconds later, someone walked into the room, and Stella averted her gaze. It was a man whom Stella thought looked to be in his 40s, with short dark hair and glasses. He wore a black suit and black shirt, with a white clerical collar that instantly identified him as being a clergyman.

"Good afternoon, young lady. I do hope I am not disturbing you?"

Stella shook her head. "No, not at all."

"Were you about to light a candle?" The clergyman asked as he moved nearer to Stella. She looked down at the table and then back at the clergyman.

"Oh… erm… yes, if that is alright?"

"Of course. May I ask if it is in memory of someone who has already passed, or is it for someone you are visiting?"

Stella bowed her head. "Someone I was visiting who has just passed."

The clergyman paused and gave a wistful smile. "I am sorry for your loss," he said. Picking up a wax taper, he lit it from another candle and passed it to Stella. "The lighting of a memorial candle is a comforting way to pay tribute to the life of the deceased and is a way to honour them. It is also a symbol that serves as a reminder that the memory of the loved one will live on," he added.

Stella found it a struggle to hold back her emotions and swallowed hard, and as she lit one of the spare candles, the tears fell relentlessly. Tears, not only for Miss Hutton but for her grandfather too, and for the sadness of being unable to feel that same grief for her father. She blew the taper out and handed it back to the clergyman.

Realising just how upset she was, the clergyman put his hand on her shoulder and spoke softly. "When someone passes, it can be difficult to cope with the emotions you may feel, and you may find it hard to accept that the person has gone. You may think that life will never be quite the same again and that all hope is lost. But in time, your sorrow will ease, and you will start to look to the future with new hope. The memories you have of your loved one will be an aid to that recovery, and they will always be there to help you move forward with your life. I will leave you in peace with your thoughts now."

Before she had a chance to thank him for his comforting words, the clergyman had gone. Stella sat back down on the pew and stared at the candle she had just lit. The clergyman was right, she did feel that her life would never be quite the same again, and what hope did she have now that the only two people who recognised her ability to write were gone?

But just as the candle burned, so did her desire to write, and she knew in her heart that while ever she had a breath in her body and a pencil in her hand, that would always be so. Stella stood up, and although she was not sure how she was going to do it, she knew that if she was going to honour the memory of her grandfather and Miss Hutton, she had to keep that flame inside her from extinguishing. She walked over to the table, lit another candle, and grabbed her project from out of the bin.

****

Elsie had made herself a cup of cocoa and had just sat down in her armchair when someone knocked on the back door. By the time her ailing knees had allowed her to get to her feet, the knocking became a loud banging. As Elsie made her way towards the kitchen, the loud banging became louder still. "Alright, alright… I am coming as quickly as I can…"

Elsie opened the back door to find Norah standing there, out of breath and clearly in all a fluster. "Norah… what on earth is —"

"Elsie, we need to talk…"

"But it's almost half past nine?"

"Never mind what time it is. I've come to warn you."

"Warn me? Warn me of what?"

"Well, if you let me in, I'll tell you!" Norah said with a deep sigh, as she tried to regulate her breathing.

"Go on through to the sitting room and I'll get you a glass of water."

Elsie ran the tap until the water was cold and filled a glass. She took it through to the sitting room and placed it down on the side table between the two armchairs.

"What has happened, Norah?" Elsie asked as she sat down in her armchair.

"Oh Elsie… the lid we were hoping to keep on the secret hasn't just been lifted, it has exploded into a million pieces," Norah rubbed at her forehead in agitation. "I've had Mike round to see me this evening. He's been over to his mother's this afternoon."

Elsie put her hand to her mouth. "She hasn't told him, has she?"

"She didn't need to. He's found out for himself!"

Elsie frowned. "But how?"

"When I said there was some delay with the paperwork for Mike's job transfer to America, well it turned out that he needed his birth certificate. He couldn't find it at home, so he went over to see if it was at his mother's," Norah said, taking a sip of water.

"But my name was never registered on the birth certificate, nor Fred's," Elsie responded.

Norah waved her hand dismissively. "The

certificate isn't the problem. Elsie... Mike found a letter hidden amongst his parent's things. A letter that was written in your father's hand."

Elsie frowned again. "Letter? What letter."

"A gentleman's agreement of sorts. There was no such thing as legal adoption back then, so it was an informal agreement between your father and my sister's husband. It was signed and dated by both of them the day before Mike was born. It said that all the rights and responsibilities relating to *your* unborn child would be transferred to my sister immediately after the child is born."

"Oh, good grief," Elsie said. "And I assume he hasn't taken the news well?"

"No, he's distraught."

"Does Will know?"

Norah shook her head. "Not yet, no. But that is what I've come to warn you about, Elsie. Mike says he plans on telling Will all about it tomorrow. He says that Will is to finish his relationship with Stella, *and* he's insisting on taking him to America."

"Oh, good heavens. What are we going to do now? Stella is going to be devastated when she finds out. And then there's Jeanie and Sheila, how are they going to react when they find out they have a brother? Poor Jeanie is already in turmoil as it is, losing Derek under such tragic circumstances."

Norah arched a brow at Elsie's remark surrounding the nature of Derek's demise, and she shuffled uncomfortably in her seat. "I don't know, Elsie. But perhaps Mike might feel differently about it all when he's had a chance to calm down and think about it," she said, shrugging her shoulders.

"What I don't understand is… if your sister and her husband had never planned to tell Michael the truth about his adoption, why did they not just destroy the agreement after the birth had been registered in their name? Surely no one would have disputed a legal document."

Norah sighed deeply. "My brother-in-law was uneasy about the adoption from the day I suggested it. He could never seem to shake off this… worry that you and Fred might one day try and take your son back. I can only assume that is why he asked your father to draw up the agreement in the first place. Mike said that when he confronted his mother with the letter, she was shocked because she thought it *had* been destroyed. What I think is… that my brother-in-law had secretly kept the agreement in case there *were* ever any discrepancies."

Elsie shuffled to the edge of her chair. "There's only one thing left for it, I'm going to have to tell Jeanie and Sheila the truth before they hear it from someone else."

"Maybe telling the truth is what we should all have done right from the start!" Norah exclaimed.

Elsie looked towards Norah. "You are right, and with that in mind… there is something else you should know. But before you say anything to Michael, I will need to speak to Jeanie first."

Norah frowned. "I don't think I can cope with any more revelations, Elsie."

"Well, as tough as it's going to be to hear it, this just

may help."

FORTY-EIGHT

Having an early night had certainly helped Stella to wake up feeling quite positive. After giving some thought to one or two of her quandaries, the solid night's sleep provided a fresh perspective on how she might move forward with her writing. She left the house early before her mother had woken, nipped into her grandma's house to feed Pearl, and was out again, even before her grandma had risen. Although she had been off school for a few days following her father's death, Stella thought she would be better off keeping busy, and as she walked to school, she gave further thought to the decisions she had come to, and now that her father wasn't there to control her, the choices would be hers to make.

She decided that instead of leaving school at Christmas, she would leave on her 16th birthday in three weeks, which coincided with the end of the school term. She could start working full-time at the Co-op straight away. Mrs Bell would be grateful because it would mean that Dorothy could leave to have her baby. Contributing to the household bills would also keep her mother happy. Then in the meantime, she would look into going to college to study English. She would keep working on her season-themed project, and maybe once she had collated a year's worth of poems and stories to put into it, perhaps one of the college tutors might be able to advise her on how to work towards getting it published. She could still think about including Alfie's drawings too. As she walked across the schoolyard she smiled, as the reassuring feeling that *just* maybe everything might be okay, passed through her.

Stella thought how quiet it was as she walked towards her classroom. Normally at this time of morning, there was always one pupil or another around to cause a ruckus. She pulled the door handle down to find that it was locked. After checking her watch for time, she realised a note had been pinned to the door informing pupils that all English classes had been cancelled until further notice. *'Word has reached school about the death of Miss Hutton then,'* Stella thought.

Stella looked at her watch again, since she was supposed to be taking English until lunchtime, she may as well go back home for now. She walked back up the corridor towards the exit, just as Mr Rice, the headmaster was coming out of his office.

"Ah… Miss Felton, I'm glad I have caught you. Could you spare a moment please?" he gestured for her to follow him into his office. "Take a seat, would you." Knowing exactly what he was about to say, Stella sat down.

"To be honest, Miss Felton, I was quite surprised to see you back in school today, but given that you are, I have some distressing news. It grieves me to inform you that sadly, our lovely Miss Hutton passed away yesterday. Although my staff and I have decided to announce it to all our pupils in a special assembly tomorrow morning, I thought it only fair to inform you personally. Given that you and she had your… private arrangement, as it were."

"I do appreciate you taking the time to inform me personally, sir, but in fact, I did know yesterday that she had passed."

Mr Rice removed his spectacles and frowned. "Really? How could you possibly know that when I only found out myself this morning?"

"Because I was with her when she died, sir," Stella said quite casually.

"Oh, my dear Stella, I had no idea you were both so close."

Stella nodded. "We had a lot in common as it turned out, and I would like to think that I was of significant help and comfort to her in her final days. But Mr Rice… if you don't mind my asking, sir, if you had no idea that I already knew, why would you be surprised to see me in school today?"

Mr Rice paused briefly before speaking. "I read about your father's death in the Daily Telegraph… terrible business indeed. And under the circumstances, I am quite happy to allow you to take as much time off school as you need. I am sure your mother would prefer to have you home at the moment."

Stella nodded. "Thank you, sir. I was hoping to attend Miss Hutton's funeral?"

Mr Rice nodded. "Of course, my dear. I will be sure to let you know of the arrangements as soon as I know myself. Now, you go on home and please pass on my condolences to your mother."

Stella walked back across the schoolyard and along the main road. Thinking that Will might well want to meet her from school, she decided to call round to his house. Just as she neared the house, she noticed him walk down his driveway and turn to walk along the main road towards his Aunt Norah and Uncle Jed's cottage. Stella called his name twice before he finally turned round, but as soon as he realised it was her, he turned back to walk and meet her.

Will arched a brow. "You aren't playing truant, are you?" he said, pulling her close and kissing her softly, before frowning suspiciously. "And... you aren't unwell, are you?" he asked, checking her forehead.

Stella moved Will's hand from her forehead and laughed. "I am perfectly well, thank you, but

I *was* on my way to see you. Have you got time to talk?"

Will looked at his watch, "I'm expected at my uncle's cottage in 10 minutes, but yes, of course. Walk with me?"

As they walked, Stella explained to Will the real reason she had been allowed to go home. She told him about Miss Hutton's passing, and what it had been like to be with her in her final moments. Then she told him that if it had not been for meeting the clergyman, she would have given up on her project and thrown it away for sure. She was about to tell him about the decisions she had come to on leaving school at the end of term, when she realised they had got to Jed and Norah's cottage.

"Hark at me babbling on. I had better let you go," she said.

"Goodness, Stella, I am sorry to hear about Miss

Hutton, but I am glad that you have decided to keep on with your project. It would be a shame to give up on your idea now." Stella agreed. "Shall we meet up later on this afternoon and I'll tell you all about the rest of my decisions then?"

Will nodded. "You certainly have been doing a lot of thinking, haven't you," he said with a smile. "Can we meet up on the recreation ground at about six o'clock? Only my mum says that Dad wants to speak to me when he gets home from work. I am certain he's going to tell me that he has been offered a job somewhere else."

Stella frowned. "He never announced it when you were at your granny's yesterday then?"

Will shook his head. "No, he never mentioned anything about it. He did tell Granny that he'd come to fetch some paperwork and that it was something to do with his job though. To be honest, after I had said hello to Granny, I went off to catch up with Trevor, my old school friend, whose father died in the disaster at Creswell. But... you know, now I come to think of it, he did seem incredibly quiet on the drive home from Granny's house, so he might have mentioned something to her."

"Ah right, I see," Stella said. "Well, maybe that is what he wants to talk to you about.

I will see you later then," she reached to kiss Will goodbye.

Stella turned back the way she had come, took the shortcut past Kilburn pit and onto the recreation ground. Taking a seat on the bench, she began to wonder just what Will's father might have to say to him. Would he try and persuade his son to go to America? And what if, once Will learns that the job offer *is* in America, he decides that he does want to go with his parents after all? It had been eight days since she had eavesdropped on the conversation between her grandmother and Norah, and strangely, up to now, her grandmother had not done anything to try and put a stop to her relationship with Will.

Stella's thoughts continued to run away with her. Perhaps they'd both decided it is better to let sleeping dogs lie, as it were. And if Norah thought there was a chance that Will might go to America with his parents, that would be the 'natural death' of the relationship that the two of them were hoping for.

"Ahh… it's all ifs buts and maybes," Stella said to herself, as she got up from the bench to make her way to the Co-op to see if Mrs Bell had any errands for her to run.

Mrs Bell was not the only person to be surprised at seeing Stella, not only because it was mid-morning on a school day, but also because she assumed that if Stella wasn't at school, then she would be at home, still grieving the death of her father. She was, however, most pleased to hear that Stella would likely be able to begin full-time work sooner than planned, pending her mother's permission, of course.

"Well, that is welcoming news, cherub. Dorothy will be pleased too, she's fit to burst," Mrs Bell laughed. "Anyway, I don't have any errands that I need you to run today, but if you're sure you feel up to it, I could do with some help tomorrow," she said.

With nothing much else to do, Stella decided that she would put her time to effective use and shut herself away in her bedroom to work on a story she had in mind. This reminded her that she had left one of her short stories at Miss Hutton's cottage for her to read. It was one that she had written before she started her autumn-themed project and was all about a young woman who had inherited a lighthouse from a Scottish grandmother she didn't know she had, only to find out there were sinister connections to its past.

'I guess I won't be able to get that back now,' she thought. *'I'll never know what Miss Hutton's idea was either.'*

Stella arrived home and was quite surprised to find her mother, grandmother and Aunt Sheila all sitting around the kitchen table drinking tea. As she walked in, they each stared at her as though she were some sort of stranger from another realm.

"Before you say anything... Mr Rice permitted me to come home," Stella said, holding up her arms in mock defence.

None of the women spoke a word, they just continued to stare at Stella and then at each other. Stella stood facing the women and frowned. "You all look as miserable as sin. What is the matter?"

Finally, Jeanie and Sheila both looked to their mother. Elsie nodded to them, and Jeanie and Sheila both stood up.

Stella looked at her mother. "Mam, what's up? Has something come to light about Dad?"

Jeanie shook her head. "Aunty Sheila and I are going to leave you with Grandma. She needs to have a little chat with you," Jeanie said, before following her sister out of the back door.

Stella had a reasonably good idea of what was about to come and began to get quite defensive. "What's the matter? Why have Mam and Sheila left?"

"Sit down, love," Elsie pulled out a chair.

Stella shook her head. "No. I won't sit down, Grandma. I know exactly what you are about to tell me, and I don't want to hear it!" she protested.

Elsie frowned. "How can you possibly know what I am about to say... just sit down, gal... please."

Stella remained standing. "No... because you're going to tell me that Will's father is your son. And because of that, you want me to stop seeing him! Well, I won't, it isn't against the law!"

Elsie raised her eyebrows. "Have you been speaking to Norah?"

Stella shook her head. "No, Grandma... I overheard you when you were both talking about it."

Elsie frowned again. "You mean last night?"

"No... last week when Norah realised that the young man in the picture on your mantelpiece was Will. I won't give him up, Grandma. You don't understand... we love each other!" Stella wailed.

Elsie closed her eyes and sighed heavily.

Stella grabbed her handkerchief from her pocket. "Is that why Norah was here again last night then? So, you both could cook up your plan on how to split us up."

There was a brief pause before Elsie spoke. "No… it wasn't, love. Norah came to warn me that Will's father stumbled across a letter yesterday. A letter that has revealed the adoption about which he knew nothing."

Stella calmed slightly. "Is he going to tell Will?"

Elsie nodded and pursed her lips. "Norah says Michael was intending to take Will to America. But then, Michael was upset when he found out, so he might change his mind when he's had a chance to think about it."

"He can't force Will to go to America *or* stop us from seeing each other. Any more than you or Norah can."

Elsie shook her head. "But, Stella, we don't want to stop you."

"What? Well, I certainly overheard you both planning to!"

"Then you didn't stick around long enough to hear us change our minds about that." Elsie reached out and took her granddaughter's hand. "Stella… please sit down, love, there's something you need to know. Something that, as difficult as it will be to hear, will be for the best in the long run."

Stella sat down slowly…

FORTY-NINE

It is not every day that you are told you were adopted. And as surprised as she was to hear it, she wasn't shocked or upset. Strangely, as she sat and thought about it for that brief moment, it explained a heck of a lot. It was that long pause leading up to all the details that was the nerve-wracking bit, the long pause where she was supposed to let the… '*you were adopted as a baby*,' part sink in before the full extent of her grandma's latest revelation was thrust upon her. Stella shuffled impatiently in her seat, and eventually, it was she who broke the silence.

"So, it doesn't necessarily run in families then," Stella said nonchalantly.

Elsie frowned. "What doesn't?"

"The ability to write… Will's dad and I had a conversation about it. I mean, as it turns out for Will's dad, that ability *was* passed to him from Grandpa. But I wonder where my writing ability comes from then? I always assumed it was from Grandpa, but clearly not."

Stella paused. "I can still call him Grandpa, can I?"

Elsie dropped her shoulders and sighed. "Oh, Stella love… of course you can. Look, let me try and explain it all to you." Elsie took a deep breath. "Your mam was almost 30 weeks pregnant when she took an awful tumble down the stairs. The fall brought on an early and difficult labour and sadly the baby… a girl, was pronounced dead at birth. Because the birth was so traumatic, your mam was told that it would be too dangerous for her to ever carry another child." Elsie reached to tuck a lock of hair behind Stella's ear. "That's when I suggested that she and your father adopt, and not long after that, you came into our lives."

"It was your idea?" Stella asked.

Elsie nodded slowly. "It probably sounds silly now, but at the time, my suggestion that they adopt a baby somehow made up for me having to give up mine."

"Now I know why Dad hated me so much then," Stella said bitterly.

"Ahh… Stella… Hate is such a strong word. I think that if anything, he never forgave your mam for losing the baby. He wasn't struck by the idea of adopting, and then with all that awful business of him being held prisoner in Japan… it all seemed to… *alter* him. But what you didn't hear that day, when Norah and I spoke, was me deciding that it is not her *or* my place to interfere in your and Will's relationship. You see, if it were not for my father's interference in my relationship with your grandpa, we would have just kept our baby and got married."

Stella looked down at the tablecloth and used her finger to trace the embroidered pattern on it. "If it wasn't for Will's father finding out, would anyone have bothered to tell me?"

Elsie paused briefly, tipping her head slightly in an attempt to find the right words. "I had been thinking of suggesting to your mam that we tell you, largely because of the way things were going between you and your dad. But it was only when Norah came to tell me that Will's father had found the letter proving his adoption, that I realised that we *had* to tell you the truth too. Keeping secrets hidden such as this, is only ever going to cause hurt, anger and upset, usually when you least expect it."

"So, who are my real parents then? Are they likely to come crawling out of the woodwork any time soon?"

Elsie shook her head. "The only information we were told about your father is that he died a few months before you were born, in a mining accident somewhere up north. Then sadly, through complications during labour, your mother died shortly after giving birth to you. When you feel up to it, I will tell you more about it. I do have a few more details about them, but nothing much."

Stella nodded quite reluctantly, and Elsie reached out and cupped Stella's hands in hers. "Sweetheart, none of this changes anything about the love your mam and I have for you, and you know your grandpa thought the world of you."

"And what do Mam and Aunty Sheila think about the fact that they have an older brother?"

Elsie looked up towards the ceiling. "Oh… it's going to take time, of course it is, but at least they both understand the reasons behind it all, and I am hoping that given time, Michael will too. There is no reason you and Will can't continue to see each other, if that's what you both want."

"That's going to be somewhat difficult if his father does insist that he goes with them to America."

"Once Michael has had a chance to calm down and

absorb everything, he might feel differently about it all.

"And does Michael know that I am adopted? Does Norah know? Just who does know? Stella said standing up abruptly.

Elsie looked up at her granddaughter and trying to keep the conversation calm, spoke softly.

"Norah knows… but I asked her not to say anything to Michael about it because I—"

Stella cut her grandmother short and shook her head angrily. "Oh… this is all such a mess." Elsie struggled to her feet and continued with her sentence but in a slightly firmer tone. "Because I wanted to speak to your mam about telling you first. And in any case, it has got to be *your* choice whether you tell Will."

"Of course I'm going to tell him! You know why… because I'm never going to keep secrets from him, or anybody else for that matter, it's just not fair!" Stella headed towards the stairs before turning to speak. "If you have nothing else you want to say, then I am going up to my room. I just need to be alone for a while to think things through."

****

Stella spent what was left of the morning and all afternoon in her room, reflecting on everything that had happened in the last week. Her adoption, Michael's adoption, Miss Hutton's death, her father's murder. But mostly, she thought about the relationship she had with her father, and how clear it was to her now, that so many of the remarks he made towards her were his way of jibing at her for not being his, and without her even realising it at the time. Like the very last time they had argued, and she had stormed out of the house, leaving the door open, and he followed her out, asking if she had been born in a barn... and who was likely to know if she had. He had wanted her to work it out for herself, and the taunts were his twisted way of doing it. Stella looked at her watch, she had wasted enough thinking time on the man she called Dad... now it was time to go and explain things to Will.

She half expected to see her grandma still sitting at the kitchen table, but with the house empty, she just took herself off to the recreation ground. Arriving at exactly the time they had arranged, Stella expected that Will might already be waiting for her, but there was nobody around at all. She sat down on the bench to wait and began to wonder just what Michael may have decided to tell his son. If the job offer is the only thing he revealed for now, then Will could arrive all keen to tell her that he is correct in his assumption. But then Michael may decide to reveal everything and insist that Will is to stop seeing Stella and go with his parents to America.

What is Will going to make of the news, that he and I share the same grandmother? Stella thought. All the assumptions and theories rolled around in Stella's head, making her feel quite uneasy. She stood up and began to take a stroll around the recreation ground, looking over every few seconds in the direction from which Will should come. Time passed... nothing... no sign of Will. She could not possibly go to his house, not when she had no idea what reception she may receive. She sat back down on the bench. Half an hour passed, three quarters of an hour… still no sign. If he had been pushed into ending their relationship, surely, he would at least come and say so? A sudden feeling of dread rushed through Stella's stomach, and she stood up. The uncertainty of it all seemed to temporarily glue her to where she stood, and then with a sense of despair and one last look across the rec, Stella turned to leave.

Just as she neared the exit, a familiar voice called her name. Stella turned to look… Will. Once again, her feet virtually bonded irresolutely to the spot. He wasn't rushing towards her as he normally might, especially given his lateness. The absence of his pleasing smile, his fingers rubbing contemplatively across his forehead… Stella knew this wasn't going to be a joyful moment. She forced her feet to move, heading slowly towards him.

Neither of them spoke for a moment or two, and then it was she who broke the silence.

"I guess your dad had a lot to say then…?"

Will nodded slowly, and they both seemed to drift back towards the bench. Stella sat down and Will sat opposite on the grass, not next to her as he usually would. He ran his fingers slowly through his hair and sighed, keeping his focus on picking at blades of grass instead of looking at her.

"I don't know what I'm surprised at more, the fact that biologically we share the same grandma, or that she gave my father up at birth."

"She wasn't given a choice," Stella said softly. There was a pause, then eventually he looked straight at her. "What do you make of it all?"

"There is a lot they need to talk about. If your dad can bring himself to hear it, that is."

Will shook his head. "It's too raw for him at the moment." Stella got up from the bench and knelt at Will's side. "And what about us? Has it spoiled everything between us?"

Will took hold of Stella's hand. "The other day when I said that I love you... I meant it, Stella, and I still do, but..." Will pinched the soft part of his nose, in between his eyes. "I was right about my dad being offered another job, and now all this has come to light, he's insisting I go with them."

Stella's heart sank. "I see, well... RAF Halton might be only half a day by train, but America certainly isn't."

Will rubbed Stella's back. "Hey... c'mon... I've not said I'm going yet. I just have to... hang on a minute, there you go with the America thing again." Will got up suddenly and stood with his hands on his hips. "You already knew about all this, didn't you? That's why you mentioned America the other day when we spoke!"

Stella stood up too. "Yes, but I could hardly have said anything. It wasn't my —"

"How long have you known?" Will interrupted

"Just over a week ago. I just happened to overhear —"

"You knew over a week ago that my father was

adopted and that he'd been asked to go to America, and you never said anything?"

"Well… yes, but…"

Will turned away from Stella, leaving her rooted to the spot.

"Will… please…" Stella said. "It wasn't my place to tell you…" Will held up his hands and started to walk away.

"Will, please don't go," Stella begged, but he kept walking.

"I know how your father feels…" she added in desperation. But still, he kept on walking. "I know because I was adopted too…"

Will stopped in his tracks.

"And I only found out myself today," she added solemnly. "So, you see… we don't share the same grandma after all."

Will turned to look at Stella and shook his head in disbelief. Slowly, he walked the short distance back towards Stella. "You know what, Stella… It's not our biological status that troubles me, even if we were cousins, it's not against the law."

"Then what is it?"

"It's all the secrets, lies and deceit. And now I find out that you have been part of it too. I'm sorry, Stella, it's all a bit too much. I don't think we can see each other anymore." Will turned and walked away again quicker this time. All that Stella could do was watch him go.

It was dark by the time she had made her way to St Clement's churchyard, but having never been phased by the dark, Stella continued to make her way along the closely connected footpaths between the graves. The only darkness that bothered her now was the one that clung to her like a heavy weight across her shoulders. She kneeled at the foot of her grandfather's grave and wept. There was nothing left to hope for now, nothing left to believe in. Eventually, Stella grabbed her handkerchief from her pocket and dabbed at her tears.

"Why couldn't *you* have told me, Grandpa? I would not have loved you any less," Stella stood up. "It's easier to manage the truth than it is to cope with the discovery of a lie," she said, and made her way back along the footpath, out of the churchyard to take a lonely walk home.

FIFTY

Monday 9th October.

In the week that had passed since learning of her adoption, Stella hadn't returned to school. Her mother agreed that there was no point now, and what with needing the income more than ever, she was pleased that Stella would be working full-time at the Co-op. They had also endured Derek's funeral, a meagre affair with only a handful of people attending, and with the police having no further leads on the perpetrators responsible for his death, Jeanie was still desperate for closure. Stella noticed that she had become withdrawn, isolating herself within the home and doing nothing to keep it in order.

Having no desire to write, Stella had already turned her makeshift desk back into a dressing table. She had dumped all her books, papers and writing implements in one corner of her room, along with the autumn-themed project. She picked up her hairbrush and stared into the mirror. Without taking notice of the reflection staring back at her, she brushed her hair and pinned it back away from her face. Mrs Bell had asked Stella to work alongside Dorothy for the week leading up to her leaving to have her baby, and as such, was due to begin her shift in less than an hour. She stood up, pulled her work tabard over her head, and smoothed it down before fastening the press-studs at either side. Finally taking notice of herself in the mirror, she stared at her reflection. Was this the best she could expect from her life now? Stacking shelves at the local Co-op, with little hope of studying English or becoming a writer, along with the prospect of coping with her mother's apparent disconsolation. The crux of it all was that she was missing Will, and for the umpteenth time that morning, she wondered if he was missing her too.

Stella walked into the kitchen to find unwashed pots, a basket full of laundry, and her mother sitting at the table with her head in her hands, staring into a large tot of what was left of her father's whiskey. Stella sighed heavily. "For heaven's sake, Mam, what are you drinking that for?" she said, swiping the glass from under her mother's nose. Jeanie did not respond, she just lifted her head, looked at her daughter and then resumed her position.

"You needn't bother starting that game, you know. I'm not going to work to pay for that!"

Jeanie sighed and sat back in her chair. "I know, love… I know. I haven't drunk any of it anyway."

"Well see as you don't. Nobody ever found the answer to anything at the bottom of a glass," Stella said sharply.

Jeanie stood up and walked over to her daughter. "You are so wise, Stella, wise beyond your years." Jeanie hung her head. "I may not have given birth to you, but I am so proud to call you my daughter. I am so sorry for everything you have been through, love, and I promise I will make it up to you." Jeanie held out her arms to embrace her daughter, a gesture that Stella welcomed, even if it had come a little too late.

****

It had been a busy Monday at the Co-op, but Stella's shift was almost over. She was perched on the two-step ladder, stacking a shelf with boxes of wash powder when she heard the bell chime above the shop door.

"I'll go," Dorothy said, before waddling her way over to the counter to greet whoever had entered the shop. Moments later, Dorothy reappeared.

"It's a gentleman, and he is asking for you. Proper well-to-do he looks n'all," she said. Stella frowned and peered discreetly between two boxes of wash powder on the shelf to take a furtive look… It was the official-looking gentleman she had passed on the hospital corridor the day Miss Hutton passed away. What could he want with her? Stella stepped off the ladder and made her way towards the counter. "Can I help you, sir?" she asked.

The gentleman, who was dressed exactly as he was the first time she saw him, smiled. "Miss Felton?" he said, holding out his hand. "Mr Flanders, Sheldon Flanders, I am Miss Hutton's appointee. Your mother told me I would find you here. Is there somewhere we can talk privately?"

Having been alerted by Dorothy to the presence of the mysterious gentleman, Mrs Bell stood in the doorway of her office. "You can use my room if you wish, Stella," she said, standing aside.

Stella thanked Mrs Bell and led Mr Flanders into the office. After gesturing for him to take a seat in Mrs Bell's chair, she closed the door and stood somewhat restlessly, whilst Mr Flanders took off his trilby and began to take official-looking documents out of his leather briefcase. "Do take a seat, my dear, you are not in trouble."

Stella cleared a pile of papers from another chair and sat down. Mr Flanders took a pair of spectacles from his top pocket and put them on, before clearing his throat in readiness to speak. "I am sure you are aware Miss Hutton passed away last week," Mr Flanders said, looking up from his paperwork.

"Yes, sir… I was with her when she passed."

"Ahh yes… I thought I recognised you. You were kind enough to hold the door open for me on the hospital corridor that day, were you not?" Stella nodded.

Mr Flanders continued. "When Miss Hutton learned that her illness was terminal, she appointed my firm of solicitors to take care of her legal matters, and having been a close friend of her father's, I was more than willing to do so." Mr Flanders looked closely at one of the documents. "Miss Felton, I have here, a copy of Miss Hutton's last will and testament. And although it was drawn up rather hastily, I have no reason to question the legitimacy of its content."

Being unsure of what this had to do with her, Stella sat in silence, waiting for clarification.

Mr Flanders continued. "With having no living relatives, Miss Hutton's specific instructions were that her cottage and its contents be sold at auction. Whatever profit is raised, alongside any other assets, will be left to you. She has stipulated that a donation of 35 pounds is to be given to the school at which she worked, then there are funeral expenses, legal fees, et cetera... et cetera."

Stella looked at Mr Flanders, expecting a punch line of some sort. He in turn stared at her, awaiting her response. Eventually, Stella spoke. "I... I don't understand. Why would she want to leave me money?"

Mr Flanders passed Stella an envelope. "She dictated this letter to..." Mr Flanders checked his paperwork. "Ah yes, Sister Fox, which I think will explain everything. However, with you being under 18 |, certain stipulations will go with the inheritance."

Stella struggled to make sense of everything and swallowed hard.

"I realise this is an awful lot to take in, my dear, but rest assured, I will guide you through the entire process. Now... I understand from Miss Hutton that you had hoped to study English with a view to becoming a writer. Is that correct?" Stella nodded again.

Mr Flanders continued. "When we come to know the final value of her estate, your half will be placed into a trust fund and managed by my firm. Miss Hutton's wishes were very concise... You may withdraw money from the fund for use in whatever way necessary to aid with your studies and writing ambitions, and you will also be provided with a small personal allowance each month. Any withdrawals will be managed by myself, but once you turn 18, you will have sole access to the fund yourself. Do you understand?" Stella had no words. All she could do was nod for a third time.

"Very good then. I will write to you in due course, but in the meantime, if you have any questions, feel free to contact my office." Mr Flanders handed Stella a small card showing details of his office in London.

"London? You have come from London to see me?"

Mr Flanders nodded. "Yes, Miss Hutton and her family originated from Ealing in west London. She will be buried privately in Hanwell Cemetery, in the family plot which is alongside her fiancé I believe."

"Privately?" Stella frowned. "I was rather hoping to attend her funeral."

"I am afraid those were her wishes, my dear." Mr Flanders stood up and returned the documents to his briefcase before offering to shake Stella's hand again. "It has been a pleasure to meet you Miss Felton, and I wish you every success."

Stella stood up and shook hands with Mr Flanders. "Thank you, sir," she said.

Mr Flanders paused to put his trilby on before opening the door. "You know, when this is finalised, you will be a very wealthy young lady. And from what I knew of Catherine, she would not have done this if she had not thought you worthy. I hope you make the most of it, my dear."

Stella watched Mr Flanders head out of the office and through the shop, stopping briefly to raise his trilby at Dorothy and Mrs Bell. As soon as he left the shop, the two women rushed into the office where Stella was rooted to the spot, still in clear disbelief.

"Come on then, spill the beans!" Mrs Bell giggled.

Stella sat down heavily on the chair. "I honestly don't know where to begin!" she said, as a big smile appeared slowly on her face.

****

After swearing Mrs Bell and Dorothy to secrecy, Stella left the Co-op with the envelope Mr Flanders had given her. She wanted to go somewhere to be alone to read it without being disturbed and headed out to a quieter part of the village. Stella sat down on a bench and slid her finger under the seal of the envelope, took a deep breath and unfolded the letter. It read:

Wednesday 27th September 1950

Dearest Stella,

Please accept my apologies for not writing to you in my own hand. Since I now find myself unable to perform such a task, Sister Fox has very kindly offered to be my scribe. I regret that I must pass on the dreary news that this wretched illness with which I have been suffering, is irrecoverable, and sadly, the circumstances in which I now find myself are terminal.

The purpose of my letter to you is twofold. Firstly, by the time you read this, you will already have been informed by my father's good friend, Sheldon Flanders, of my wish to nominate you as sole beneficiary of my estate. Secondly, I do not doubt that you are expecting an explanation as to why, and that, my dear, is the easy part. The spirit in your heart has not gone unnoticed, I can see how it drives you in your desire to succeed. You remind me so much of myself when I was your age. I too wanted to be a writer, and although my father had my best interests at heart, he desired that I should become a teacher. I know that you are often faced with similar difficulties at home, and I cannot bear to think of that being a hindrance to you.

You have an opportunity now, to make something special of the life that lies ahead of you, and it gives me great pleasure in my final few days to think that I have helped to make that possible. Be happy with your beau and live the life of which my fiancé and I were only ever able to dream.

Yours sincerely, Catherine.

Stella could hardly see for the tears that welled in her eyes. She placed the letter back in the envelope and reached for her handkerchief. How one person's misfortune could be a fortuity to someone else was unfathomable to her. At that point, she knew she had to try and talk to Will… To try and make him understand that it was never her intention to deceive him or anyone else. To try and make him understand how uncertain life can be, and that they should grab every chance of happiness that came along. Disregarding the reception she may receive; Stella wasted no time in making her way to Will's house. From her location in the village, it was quicker to walk down to the toll bar and along the main road.

She arrived at Will's house and hesitated. She hadn't given a thought as to what she would do if Will refused to see her. Deciding that there was only one way to find out, she continued up the drive, made her way around the back and knocked loudly on the door.

It was Will's mother who opened the door, and she was most surprised to see Stella.

"Stella, I—"

Stella held up her hand. "I'm sorry to interrupt you, Mrs Turner, and I know I am no longer welcome, but please may I just speak to Will for a few minutes?"

"Oh Stella… as far as I am concerned you *are* welcome," Mrs Turner said softly. "And I do not doubt that once the dust has settled, Mike will be just as welcoming too. And I think you will find that Will has had a change of heart. I'm surprised you haven't bumped into him; he left here not five minutes ago. He said he couldn't leave it any longer, and that he must see you."

Having quite expected a rebuff, Stella was amazed at Mrs Turner's compassion, and a large smile appeared on her face. "Really?" she said in disbelief.

"Really," Mrs Turner reaffirmed. "Well, what are you waiting for? Go and find him!" she added with a smile.

Stella turned on her heels and rushed back down the drive, shouting her thanks back to Mrs Turner. She ran towards the colliery footpath, past the pit and towards the rec as fast as her legs would allow. Just as she arrived at the rec, she saw him walking towards the exit and stopped to call out his name. Will stalled in his tracks and turned. The moment he realised it was her; he began to run towards her. Her heart pounded as she ran to meet him, and it felt like a lifetime before she finally reached him and fell headlong into his open arms.

"I'm so sorry, I've been such a fool," he said, kissing her eagerly. "Can you ever forgive me?"

Stella looked up at Will. "There's nothing to forgive you for," she said. Nestling her face against his, she whispered into his ear. "I love you, Will Turner."

Epilogue

Friday 9th February 1951

A winter chill greets a young couple who have just stepped out of London's St Pancras Station. He looks so handsome in his Royal Air Force uniform, and she is dressed smartly, but modestly. They walk hand-in-hand along Euston Road before hailing a cab. The cab arrives outside a prestigious-looking building, the name of which reads Sheldon Flanders and Associates, Solicitors. The couple enter the building and re-emerge about half an hour or so later. She looks so happy, and they laugh as she waves a letter about in front of them. The letter has been passed to her by a solicitor, who has been appointed to act on her behalf. It is from a top London publishing firm and provides details of a prize for a short story competition in which the winner has received the opportunity to pitch a book idea to an agent. The winning story was simply entitled, 'The Lighthouse,' and had been unknowingly entered into the competition by the author's tutor, some months earlier.

He hails another cab. This time, their destination is Uxbridge Road, Ealing. The pair exit the cab and walk a short distance to a stand selling flowers. He buys a red rose before offering it to her with a kiss. She picks out a beautiful bouquet of pink roses, knowing that they are a symbol of gratitude and admiration. The two walk towards the entrance of a nearby cemetery. Once inside, they make their way through the cemetery to a distinctive family plot. The name on the plot bears the name Hutton. She crouches to arrange the bouquet neatly in a vase at the foot of the plot, before standing back to admire its grandeur. With tears in her eyes, she looks at him, and he pulls her close, kissing her tenderly.

Before they leave, she points to the grave next to the family plot. It is that of an RAF pilot killed in the line of duty. The young man turns and salutes toward the grave, in a mark of respect to a fallen comrade. Afterwards, he reaches for the young woman's hand and the two of them head back out of the cemetery to the cab waiting for them.

They arrive back at St Pancras Station, and she buys a ticket for the next train to Derby. They make their way to the platform and hold each other in a loving embrace before kissing passionately. She boards the train and reaches out to him from an open window. As the train pulls away, his hand slips from hers and he blows her a kiss, she waves to him until he is out of sight. Finding a seat, she takes a novel out of her bag for the long journey home.

She smiles to herself because, although she is travelling alone, she knows she will never feel alone again, for she will see him again very soon.

ABOUT THE AUTHOR

Alison has lived in Derbyshire all her life, spending the last 30 years in the village of Kilburn. She has always harboured a passion for writing, and has a deep-rooted interest in history, particularly local history. Her research into the rich past of Kilburn inspired her to begin drafting this novel, often scribbling down ideas between work and everyday life.

Although this novel has been in the making for several years, much of that time has been spent building and running Alison's own successful business as a registered podiatrist - a career she has dedicated herself to for over 25 years. Now, with slightly more time to explore her creative side, Alison is delighted to bring this long-awaited story to readers.

If you have enjoyed reading the book, Alison would be grateful if you would consider leaving a review, as it means a great deal to first-time authors.

For more information about our books and services, please visit

www.greencatbooks.com

9 781918 028034